THE FOUR FACES

A MYSTERY

WILLIAM LE QUEUX

The Four Faces

William le Queux

PO Box 2211
Fairfield, IA 52556
www.1stworldlibrary.org
First Edition

LCCN: 2005901395

Softcover ISBN: 1-4218-1197-9
Hardcover ISBN: 1-4218-1097-2
eBook ISBN: 1-4218-1297-5

The Four Faces

contributed by Tim, Ed & Rodney
in support of
1st World Library Literary Society

CONTENTS

I. CURIOSITY IS AROUSED 9

II. THE ANGEL FACES 19

III. A HAMPSTEAD MYSTERY 32

IV. IN FULL CRY 45

V. HUGESSON GASTRELL AT HOME 58

VI. THE HOUSE IN GRAFTON STREET 71

VII. OSBORNE'S STORY 83

VIII. MORE SUSPICIONS 92

IX. THE SNARE 103

X. NARRATES A CONFESSION 115

XI. CONCERNS MRS. STAPLETON 123

XII. THE BROAD HIGHWAY 132

XIII. THE BARON 145

XIV. IN THE MISTS 154

XV. THE MODERN VICE 162

XVI. SECRETS OF DUSKY FOWL 172

XVII. IS SUSPICIOUS 186

XVIII. CONTAINS ANOTHER SURPRISE 195

XIX. "IN THE PAPERS" 205

XX. PRESTON AGAIN 216

XXI. A CHANNEL MYSTERY 227

XXII. THE THIN-FACED STRANGER 237

XXIII. RELATES A QUEER ADVENTURE 248

XXIV. IN STRANGE COMPANY 257

XXV. THE GLITTERING UNDERWORLD 269
XXVI. "THAT WOMAN!" 279
XXVII. THE FOUR FACES 291
XXVIII. THE FACES UNMASKED 306
CONCLUSION 316

CHAPTER I

CURIOSITY IS AROUSED

"I confess I'd like to know somethin' more about him."

"Where did you run across him first?"

"I didn't run across him; he ran across me, and in rather a curious way. We live in Linden Gardens now, you know. Several of the houses there are almost exactly alike, and about a month ago, at a dinner party we were givin', a young man was shown in. His name was unknown to me, so I supposed that he must be some friend of my wife's. Then I saw that he was a stranger to her too, and then all at once he became very confused, inquired if he were in Sir Harry Dawson's house - Sir Harry lives in the house next to ours - and, findin' he was not, apologized profusely for his mistake, and left hurriedly."

"Anyone might make a mistake of that kind in some London houses," the second speaker said. "What is he like? Is he a gentleman?"

"Oh, quite."

"And for how long have you leased him your house in Cumberland Place?"

"Seven years, with option of renewal."

"And you mean to say you know nothing about him?"

"I won't say 'nothin',' but I know comparatively little about him. Houston and Prince, the house agents, assure me they've made inquiries, and that he is a rich young man whose uncle amassed a large fortune in Tasmania - I didn't know fortunes were to be made in Tasmania, did you? The uncle died six months ago, Houston and Prince tell me, and Hugesson Gastrell has inherited everything he left. They say that they have ascertained that Gastrell's parents died when he was quite a child, and that this uncle who has died has been his guardian ever since."

"That sounds right enough. What more do you want to know?"

"It somehow seems to me very strange that I should have come to know this man, Gastrell, without introduction of any kind - even have become intimate with him. On the day after he had come to my house by accident, he called to fetch a pair of gloves which, in his confusion on the previous evenin', he had left in the hall. He asked if he might see me, and then he again apologized for the mistake he had made the night before. We stayed talkin' for, I suppose, fully half an hour - he's an excellent talker, and exceedingly well-informed - and incidentally he mentioned that he was lookin' for a house. From his description of what he wanted it at once struck me that my Cumberland Place house would be the very thing for him - I simply can't afford to live there now, as you know, and for months I have been tryin' to let it. I told him about it, and he asked if he might see it, and - well, the thing's done; he has it now, as I say, on a seven years' lease."

"Then why worry?"

"I am not worryin' - I never worry - the most foolish thing any man can do is to worry. All I say is - I should like to know somethin' more about the feller. He may be quite all right - I have not the least reason for supposin' he isn't - but my wife has taken a strong dislike to him. She says she mistrusts him. She has said so from the beginnin'. After he had asked to see me that mornin', the mornin' he called for his gloves, and we had talked about the house, I invited him to lunch and introduced him to my wife. Since then he has dined with us several times, and - well, my wife is most insistent about it - she declares she is sure he isn't what he seems to be, and she wanted me not to let him the house."

"Women have wonderful intuition in reading characters."

"I know they have, and that's why I feel - well, why I feel just the least bit uneasy. What has made me feel so to-day is that I have just heard from Sir Harry Dawson, who is on the Riviera, and he says that he doesn't know Hugesson Gastrell, has never heard of him. There, read his letter."

Seated in my club on a dull December afternoon, that was part of a conversation I overheard, which greatly interested me. It interested me because only a short time before I had, while staying in Geneva, become acquainted at the hotel with a man named Gastrell, and I wondered if he could be the same. From the remarks I had just heard I suspected that he must be, for the young man in Geneva had also been an individual of considerable personality, and a good conversationalist.

If I had been personally acquainted with either of the two speakers, who still stood with their backs to the fire and their hands under their coat-tails, talking now about some wonderful run with the Pytchley, I should have told him I believed I had met the individual they had just been discussing; but at Brooks's it is not usual for members to talk to other members unintroduced. Therefore I remained sprawling in the big arm-chair, where I had been pretending to read a newspaper, hoping that something more would be said about Gastrell. Presently my patience was rewarded.

"By the way, this feller Gastrell who's taken my house tells me he's fond of huntin'," the first speaker - whom I knew to be Lord Easterton, a man said to have spent three small fortunes in trying to make a big one - remarked. "Said somethin' about huntin' with the Belvoir or the Quorn. Shouldn't be surprised if he got put up for this club later."

"Should you propose him if he asked you?"

"Certainly, provided I found out all about him. He's a gentleman although he is an Australian - he told Houston and Prince he was born and educated in Melbourne, and went to his uncle in Tasmania immediately he left school; but he hasn't a scrap of that ugly Australian accent; in fact, he talks just like you or me or anybody else, and would pass for an Englishman anywhere."

Without a doubt that must be the man I had met, I reflected as the two speakers presently sauntered out of the room, talking again of hunting, one of the principal topics of conversation in Brooks's. I, Michael Berrington, am a man of leisure, an idler I am ashamed to say, my parents having brought me up to be what is commonly and often so erroneously termed "a gentleman," and left me, when they died, heir to a cosy little property in Northamptonshire, and with some L80,000 safely invested. As a result I spend many months of the year in travel, for I am a bachelor with no ties of any kind, and the more I travel and the more my mind expands, the more cosmopolitan I become and the more inclined I feel to kick against silly conventions such as this one at Brooks's which prevented my addressing Lord Easterton or his friend - men I see in the club every day I am there, and who know me quite well by sight, though we only stare stonily at each other - and asking more about Gastrell.

So Lady Easterton had taken an instinctive dislike to this young man, Hugesson Gastrell, and openly told her husband that she mistrusted him. Now, that was curious, I reflected, for I had spoken to him several times while in Geneva, and though his personality had appealed to me, yet -

Well, there was something about him that puzzled me, something - I cannot define what it was, for it was more like a feeling or sensation which came over me while I was with him - a feeling that he was not what he appeared to be, and that I saw, so to speak, only his outer surface.

"Hullo, Michael!"

The greeting cut my train of thought, and, screwing myself round in the big arm-chair, I looked up.

"Why, Jack!" I exclaimed, "I had no idea you were in England. I thought you were bagging rhinoceroses and things in Nigeria or somewhere."

"So I have been. Got back yesterday. Sorry I am back, to tell you the truth," and he glanced significantly towards the window. A fine, wetting drizzle was falling; dozens of umbrellas passed to and fro outside; the street lamps were lit, though it was barely three o'clock, and in the room that we were in the electric lights were switched on. The sky was the colour of street mud, through which the sun, a huge, blood-red disc, strove to pierce the depressing murk of London's winter atmosphere, thereby creating a lurid and dismal effect.

Jack Osborne is a man I rather like, in spite of the fact that his sole aim in life is to kill things. When he isn't shooting "hippos" and "rhinos" and bears and lions in out-of-the-way parts of the world, he is usually plastering pheasants in the home covers, or tramping the fields and moors where partridges and grouse abound.

"Had a good time?" I asked some moments later.

"Ripping," he answered, "quite ripping," and he went on to tell me the number of beasts he had slain, particulars about them and the way he had outwitted them. I managed to listen for ten minutes or so without yawning, and then suddenly he remarked:

"I met a man on board ship, on the way home, who said he

knew you - feller named Gastrell. Said he met you in Geneva, and liked you like anything. Struck me as rather a rum sort - what? Couldn't quite make him out. Who is he and what is he? What's he do?"

"I know as little about him as you do," I answered. "I know him only slightly - we were staying at the same hotel in Geneva. I heard Lord Easterton, who was in here half an hour ago, saying he had let his house in Cumberland Place to a man named Gastrell - Hugesson Gastrell. I wonder if it is the man I met in Geneva and that you say you met on board ship. When did you land?"

"Yesterday, at Southampton. Came by the *Masonic* from Capetown."

"And where did Gastrell come from?"

"Capetown too. I didn't notice him until we were near the end of the voyage. He must have remained below a good deal, I think."

I paused, thinking.

"In that case," I said, "the Gastrell who has leased Easterton's house can't be the man you and I have met, because, from what Easterton said, he saw his man quite recently. Ah, here is Lord Easterton," I added, as the door opened and he re-entered. "You know him, don't you?"

"Quite well," Jack Osborne answered, "Don't you? Come, I'll introduce you, and then we'll clear this thing up."

It was not until Osborne and Lord Easterton had talked for some time about shooting in general, and about "hippo" and "rhino" and "'gator" killing in particular, and I had been forced to listen to a repetition of incidents to do with the sport that Jack Osborne had obtained in Nigeria and elsewhere, that Jack presently said:

"Berrington tells me, Easterton, he heard you say that you have let your house to a man named Gastrell, and we were wondering if he is the Gastrell we both know - a tall man of twenty-eight or so, with dark hair and very good-looking, queer kind of eyes - what?"

"Oh, so you know him?" Easterton exclaimed. "That's good. I want to find out who he is, where he comes from, in fact all about him. I have a reason for wanting to know."

"He came from Capetown with me - landed at Southampton yesterday," Osborne said quickly.

"Capetown? Arrived yesterday? Oh, then yours must be a different man. Tell me what he is like."

Osborne gave a detailed description.

"And at the side of his chin," he ended, "he's got a little scar, sort of scar you see on German students' faces, only quite small - doesn't disfigure him a bit."

"But this is extraordinary," Lord Easterton exclaimed. "You have described my man to the letter - even to the scar. Can they be twins? Even twins, though, wouldn't have the same scar, the result probably of some accident. You say your man landed only yesterday?"

"Yes, we came off the ship together."

"Then he was on board on - let me think - ten days or so ago?"

"Oh, yes."

"It's most singular, this apparent likeness between the two men."

"It is - if they really are alike. When shall you see your man again?"

Osborne inquired.

"I have this moment had a letter from him," Easterton answered. "He asks me to lunch with him at the Cafe Royal to-morrow. Look here, I'll tell you what I'll do - I'll say I'm engaged or somethin', and ask him to dine here one evenin'. Then if you will both give me the pleasure of your company, we shall at once find out if your Gastrell and mine are the same - they can't be the same, of course, as your man was in the middle of the ocean on the day mine was here in London; I mean we'll find out if he has a twin brother."

"Have you met his wife?" Jack Osborne inquired carelessly, as he lit a long cigar.

"Phew! Yes. I should say so. One of the most gloriously beautiful women I have ever seen in my life. She was on board with him, and I believe everybody on the ship was head over ears in love with her. I know I was."

"Ah, that settles it," Easterton said. "My man is a bachelor."

Osborne smiled in a curious way, and blew a cloud of smoke towards the ceiling without saying anything.

"Why, what is it?" Easterton asked, noticing the smile.

"Oh, nothing. A little thought that crept into my brain, that's all."

"Tell us what your Gastrell's wife is like," Easterton pursued.

"Like? What is she not like! Think of all the most lovely girls and women you have ever set eyes on, and roll them into one, and still you won't get the equal of Jasmine Gastrell. What is she like? By heaven, you might as well ask me to describe the taste of nectar!"

"Dark or fair?"

"Both."

"Oh, nonsense."

"It isn't nonsense, Easterton. She has the strangest eyes - they are really green, I suppose, but they look quite blue in some lights, and in other lights deep purple. They are the most extraordinary eyes I have ever seen; a woman with eyes like that must have tremendous intelligence and quite exceptional personality. It's useless for me to try to describe the rest of her face; it's too lovely for anything."

"And her hair?" Easterton asked. "Has she dark hair or fair?"

"Both."

"Ah, Jack, stop rottin'," Easterton exclaimed, laughing. "What is the colour of the hair of this woman who has so set your heart on end?"

"It may be auburn; it may be chestnut-brown; it may be red for all I know, but I am hanged if I can say for certain which it is, or if it's only one colour or all three shades. But whatever it is it's perfectly lovely hair, and she has any amount of it. I wouldn't mind betting that when she lets it down it falls quite to her feet and hangs all round her like a cloak."

"I should like to meet this goddess, Jack," Easterton said, his curiosity aroused. "Though you are so wedded to hippos, and rhinos, and 'gators and things, you don't seem entirely to have lost your sense of appreciation of 'woman beautiful.' Where are she and her husband staying?"

"I've not the least idea."

"Didn't they tell you their plans?"

"They said nothing whatever about themselves, though I tried once or twice to draw them out. In that respect they were extraordinarily reserved. In every other way they were delightful - especially Mrs. Gastrell, though I was greatly attracted by Gastrell too, when I came to know him towards the end of the voyage."

CHAPTER II

THE ANGEL FACES

Hugesson Gastrell had accepted Lord Easterton's invitation to dine at the club, and the three men were seated near the fire as I entered, Easterton and Jack Osborne on one of the large settees, their visitor facing them in an arm-chair, with his back to me. I went towards them across the big room, apologizing for my unpunctuality, for I was nearly ten minutes late. To my surprise they remained silent; even Easterton did not rise, or greet me in any way. He looked strangely serious, and so did Jack, as a rule the cheeriest of mortals.

"I am dreadfully sorry for being so late," I exclaimed, thinking that my unpunctuality must have given them offence. I was about to invent some elaborate excuse to account for my "delay," when the man seated with his back to me suddenly rose, and, turning abruptly, faced me.

I recognized him at once. It was Gastrell, whom I had met at the Hotel Metropol in Geneva. As he stood there before me, with his back half turned to the light of the big bay window, there could be no mistaking him. Again I was struck by his remarkable appearance - the determined, clean-cut features, the straight, short nose, the broad forehead, the square-shaped chin denoting rigid strength of purpose. Once more I noticed the cleft in his chin - it was quite deep. His thick hair was dark, with a slight kink in it behind the ears. But perhaps the strangest, most arresting thing about Gastrell's face was his eyes - daring eyes of a bright, light blue, such as one sees in some Canadians, the bold, almost hard eyes of a man who is accustomed to gazing across far distances of sunlit snow, who habitually looks up into vast, pale blue skies - one might have imagined that his eyes had caught their shade. He wore upon his watch-chain a small gold medallion, a trinket which had attracted my attention before. It was about the size of a sovereign, and embossed upon it were several heads of chubby cupids - four sweet little faces.

At first glance at him a woman might have said mentally, "What nice eyes!" At the second, she would probably have noticed a strange thing - the eyes were quite opaque; they seemed to stare rather than look at you, there was no depth whatever in them. Certainly there was no guessing at Gastrell's character from his eyes - you could take it or leave it, as you pleased, for the eyes gave you no help. The glance was perfectly direct, bright and piercing, but there could be absolutely no telling if the man when speaking were lying to you or not. The hard, blue eyes never changed, never deepened, nor was there any emotion in them.

To sum up, the effect the man's personality produced was that of an extraordinarily strong character carving its way undaunted through every obstacle to its purpose; but whether the trend of that character were likely to lean to the side of truth and goodness, or to that of lying and villainy, there was no guessing.

All these points I observed again - I say "again," for they had struck me forcibly the first time I had met him in Geneva - as he stood there facing me, his gaze riveted on mine. We must have stayed thus staring at each other for several moments before anybody spoke. Then it was Lord Easterton who broke the silence.

"Well?" he asked.

I glanced at him quickly, uncertain which of us he had addressed. After some instants' pause he repeated:

"Well?"

"Are you speaking to me?" I asked quickly.

"Of course," he replied, almost sharply. "You don't seem to know each other after all."

"Oh, but yes," I exclaimed, and I turned quickly to Gastrell, instinctively extending my hand to him as I did so. "We met in Geneva."

He still stood looking at me, motionless. Then gradually an expression, partly of surprise, partly of amusement, crept into his eyes.

"You mistake me for someone else, I am afraid," he said, and his voice was the voice of the man I had met in Geneva - that I would have sworn to in any court of law, "It is rather remarkable," he went on, his eyes still set on mine, "that Mr. Osborne, to whom Lord Easterton has just introduced me, also thought he and I had met before."

"But I am certain I did meet you," Osborne exclaimed in a curious tone, from where he sat. "I am quite positive we were together on board the *Masonic*, unless you have a twin brother, and even then - "

He stopped, gazing literally open-mouthed at Hugesson Gastrell, while I, standing staring at the man, wondered if this were some curious dream from which I should presently awaken, for there could be no two questions about it - the man before me was the Gastrell I had met in Geneva and conversed with on one or two occasions for quite a long time. Beside, he wore the little medallion of the Four Faces.

Easterton looked ill at ease; so did Osborne; and certainly I felt considerably perturbed. It was unnatural, uncanny, this resemblance. And the resemblance as well as the name must, it would seem, be shared by three men at least. For here was

Lord Easterton's friend, Hugesson Gastrell, whom Easterton had told us he had met frequently in London during the past month; here was Jack Osborne claiming to be acquainted with a man named Gastrell, whom he had met on his way home from Africa, and who, as he put it to us afterwards, was "the dead facsimile" of Easterton's guest; and here was I with a distinct recollection of a man called Gastrell who - well, the more I stared at Easterton's guest the more mystified I felt at this Hugesson Gastrell's declaring that he was not my Geneva companion; indeed that we had never met before, and that he had never been in Geneva.

The dinner was not a great success. Gastrell talked at considerable length on all sorts of subjects, talked, too, in a most interesting and sometimes very amusing way; yet all the time the thought that was in Osborne's mind was in my mind also - it was impossible, he was thinking, that this man seated at dinner with us could be other than the individual he had met on board ship; it was impossible, I was thinking, that this man seated at dinner with us could be other than the individual I had met in Geneva.

Easterton, a great talker in the club, was particularly silent. He too was puzzled; worse than that - he felt, I could see, anxious and uncomfortable. He had let his house to this man - the lease was already signed - and now his tenant seemed to be, in some sense, a man of mystery.

We sat in the big room with the bay window, after dinner, until about half-past ten, when Gastrell said he must be going. During the whole time he had been with us he had kept us entertained by his interesting conversation, full of quaint reminiscences, and touched with flashes of humour.

"I hope we shall see a great deal of each other when I am settled in Cumberland Place," he said, as he prepared to leave. The remark, though spoken to Easterton, had been addressed to us all, and we made some conventional reply in acknowledgment.

"And if, later, I decide to join this club," he said presently, "you won't mind proposing me, will you, Easterton?"

"I? Er - oh, of course, not in the least!" Easterton answered awkwardly, taken off his guard. "But it will take you a good time to get in, you know," he added as an afterthought, hopeful that the prospect of delay might cause Gastrell to change his mind. "Two, even three years, some men have to wait."

"That won't matter," Gastrell said carelessly, as the hall porter helped him on with his coat. "I can join some other club meanwhile, though I draw the line at pot-houses. Well, good night to you all, and you must all come to my house-warming - a sort of reception I'm going to give. I ought to be settled into the house in a month. And I hope," he added lightly, addressing Jack Osborne and myself, "you won't run across any more of my 'doubles.' I don't like the thought of being mistaken for other men!"

The door of the taxi shut with a bang. In the hall, where the tape machines were busy, Osborne and I stood looking at each other thoughtfully. Presently Osborne spoke.

"What do you make of it?" he asked abruptly. "I am as certain that is the fellow who was with me on board ship as I am that I am standing here."

"And I am equally positive," I answered, "he's the man I met in Geneva. It's impossible there could be two individuals so absolutely identical - I tell you it's not possible."

Osborne paused for some moments, thinking.

"Berrington," he said suddenly.

"Yes? What?" I asked, taken aback at his change of tone.

He took a step forward and laid his hand upon my shoulder.

"Berrington," he repeated - and in his eyes there was a singular expression - "I have an idea."

He turned to a page who was standing near.

"Boy," he said sharply, "what address did that gentleman who has just gone tell you to give to his driver?"

"He told the driver himself, sir," the boy answered, "but I heard the address he gave, sir."

"What was it?"

"Three forty, Maresfield Gardens, sir. It's near Swiss Cottage - up Fitzjohn's Avenue on the right."

Osborne turned to me quickly.

"Come into this room," he said. "There is something I want to ask you. The place is empty, and we shall not be disturbed."

When he had closed the door, and glanced about him to make sure that we were alone, he said in a low voice:

"Look here, Mike, I tell you again, I have an idea: I wonder if you will fall in with it. I have watched that fellow Gastrell pretty closely all the evening; I am rather a good judge of men, you know, and I believe him to be an impostor of some kind - I can't say just yet of what kind. Anyway, he is the man I met on the *Masonic*; he can deny it as much as he likes - he is. Either he is impersonating some other man, or some other man is impersonating him. Now listen. I am going to that address in Maresfield Gardens that he gave to his taxi-driver. I am going to find out if he lives there, or what he is doing there. What I want to know is - Will you come with me?"

"Good heavens, Jack!" I exclaimed, "what an extraordinary thing to do. But what will you say when you get there? Supposing he does live there - or, for that matter, supposing he doesn't - what reason will you give for calling at the house?"

"Oh, I'll invent some reason quick enough, but I want someone to be with me. Will you come? Will you or won't you?"

I glanced up at the clock. It wanted twenty minutes to eleven.

"Do you mean now? Do you intend to go at this time of the night?"

"I intend to go at once - as fast as a taxi will take me there," he answered.

I paused, undecided. It seemed such a strange thing to do, under the circumstances; but then, as I knew, Jack Osborne had always been fond of doing strange things. Though a member of Brooks's, he was unconventional in the extreme.

"Yes, I will," I said, the originality of the idea suddenly appealing to me. In point of fact I, too, mistrusted this man Gastrell. Though he had looked me so straight in the eyes when, two hours before, he had calmly assured me that I was mistaken in believing him to be "his namesake in Geneva," as he put it; still, as I say, I felt convinced he was the same man.

"Good," Osborne answered in a tone of satisfaction. "Come, we will start at once."

A strange feeling of repressed excitement obsessed me as our taxi passed up Bond Street, turned into Oxford Street, then to the right into Orchard Street, and sped thence by way of Baker Street past Lord's cricket ground and up the Finchley Road. What would happen when we reached Maresfield Gardens? Would the door be opened by a stolid footman or by some frigid maidservant who would coldly inform us that "Mr. Gastrell was not at home"; or should we be shown in, and, if we were shown in, what excuse would Jack Osborne make for calling so late at night? I cannot say that I felt in the least anxious, however, for Osborne is a man who has knocked about the world and seen many queer sides of life, and who never, under any circumstances, is at a loss how to act.

I glanced at my watch as our taxi turned into Maresfield Gardens. It was ten minutes past eleven. At the house indicated half-way up the hill the taxi suddenly pulled up.

Osborne got out and pressed the electric bell-push. As I looked up at the windows, I noticed that nowhere was any light visible. Nor was there a light in the ground-floor windows.

"I believe everybody is in bed," I said to him, when the bell remained unanswered. Without replying, he pressed the push again, and kept his finger on it.

Still no one came.

"We'd better call to-morrow," I suggested, when he had rung a third time with the same result.

The words had hardly left my lips, when we heard the door-chain rattle. Then the bolts were pulled back, and a moment later the door was carefully drawn open to the length of its chain.

Inside all was darkness, nor was anybody visible.

"What do you want?" a woman's voice inquired.

The voice had a most pleasant *timbre*; also the speaker was obviously a lady. She did not sound in the least alarmed, but there was a note of surprise in the tone.

"Has Mr. Gastrell come home yet?" Osborne asked.

"Not yet. Do you want to see him?"

"Yes. He dined at Brooks's Club this evening with Lord

Easterton. Soon after he had left, a purse was found, and, as nobody in the club claimed it, I concluded that it must be his, so I have brought it back."

"That is really very good of you, Mr. Osborne," the hidden speaker answered. "If you will wait a moment I will let you in. Are you alone?"

"No, I have a friend with me. But who are you? How do you know my name?"

There was no answer. The door was shut quietly. Then we heard the sound of the chain being removed.

By the time Jack Osborne had paid our driver, and dismissed the taxi, the door had been opened sufficiently wide to admit us. We entered, and at once the door was shut.

We were now in inky blackness.

"Won't you switch on the light?" Osborne asked, when a minute or so had elapsed, and we remained in total darkness.

Nobody answered, and we waited, wondering. Fully another minute passed, and still we stood there.

I felt Osborne touch me. Then, coming close to me, he whispered in my ear:

"Strike a match, Mike; I haven't one."

I felt in my pockets. I had not one either. I was about to tell him so when something clicked behind us, and the hall was flooded with light.

Never before had I beheld, and I doubt if I shall ever behold again, a woman as lovely as the tall, graceful being upon whom our eyes rested at that instant. In height quite five foot nine, as she stood there beneath the glow of the electrolier in the luxurious hall, in her dinner dress, the snowy slope of the shoulders and the deep, curved breast, strong, yet all so softly, delicately rounded, gleamed like rosy alabaster in the reflection from the red-shaded light above her.

Our eyes wandered from exquisite figure to exquisite face - and there was no sense of disappointment. For the face was as nearly perfect as a woman's may be upon this earth of imperfections. The uplift of the brow, the curve of the cheek to the rounded chin, the noble sweep of delicate, dark eyebrows were extraordinarily beautiful. Her hair was "a net for the sunlight," its colour that of a new chestnut in the spring when the sun shines hotly upon it, making it glow and shimmer and glisten with red and yellow and deepest browns. Now it was drawn about her head in shining twists, and across the front and rather low down on the brow was a slim and delicate wreath of roses and foliage in very small diamonds beautifully set in platinum. The gleam of the diamonds against the red-brown of the wonderful hair was an effect impossible to describe - yet one felt that the hair would have been the same miracle without it.

"Mrs. Gastrell! Why, I didn't recognize your voice," I had heard Osborne exclaim in a tone of amazement just after the light had been turned on. but my attention had been so centred upon the Vision standing there before us that I had hardly noticed the remark, or the emphasis with which it was uttered. I suppose half a minute must have passed before anybody spoke again, and then it was the woman who broke the silence.

"Will you show me the purse?" she asked, holding out her hand for it and addressing Osborne.

On the instant he produced his own and gave it to her. She glanced at it, then handed it back.

"It is not his," she said quietly. Her gaze rested steadily upon Osborne's face for some moments, then she said:

"How exceedingly kind of you to come all this way, and in the middle of the night, just to find out if a purse picked up at your club happens to belong to the guest of a friend of yours."

In her low, soft voice there was a touch of irony, almost of mockery. Looking at her now, I felt puzzled. Was she what she appeared to be, or was this amazing beauty of hers a cloak, a weapon if you will, perhaps the most dangerous weapon of a clever, scheming woman? Easterton had told us that Gastrell was a bachelor. Gastrell had declared that he had never before met either Jack Osborne or myself. Yet here at the address that Gastrell had given to the taxi-driver was the very woman the man calling himself Gastrell, with whom Osborne had returned from Africa, had passed off as his wife.

"My husband isn't in at present," she said calmly, a moment later, "but I expect him back at any minute. Won't you come in and wait for him?"

Before either of us could answer she had walked across the hall, unlocked and opened a door, and switched on the light in the room.

Mechanically we followed her. As we entered, a strange, heavy perfume of some subtle Eastern scent struck my nostrils - I had noticed it in the hall, but in this room it was pungent, oppressive, even overpowering. The apartment, I noticed, was luxuriously furnished. What chiefly attracted my attention, however, were the pictures on the walls. Beautifully executed, the subjects were, to say the least, peculiar. The fire in the grate still burned brightly. Upon a table were two syphons in silver stands, also decanters containing spirits, and several tumblers. Some of the tumblers had been used. As I sank, some moments later, into an easy chair, I felt that its leather-covered arms were warm, as if someone had just vacated it.

And yet the door of this room had been locked. Also, when we had arrived, no light had been visible in any of the windows of the house, and the front door had been chained and bolted.

"Make yourselves quite at home," our beautiful hostess said, and, as she spoke, she placed a box of cigars, newly opened, upon the table at my elbow. "I am sorry," she added, "that I must leave you now."

There was a curious expression in her eyes as she smiled down at us, an expression that later I came to know too well. Then, turning, she swept gracefully out of the room, closing the door behind her.

I looked across at Osborne. For some moments neither of us spoke. The mysterious house was still as death.

"Well, Jack," I said lightly, though somehow I felt uneasy, "what do you make of it, old man?"

"It is just as I thought," he answered, taking a cigar out of the box and beginning to trim it.

"How do you mean - 'just as you thought'?" I asked, puzzled.

"Gastrell is an impostor, and - and that isn't his wife."

He did not speak again for some moments, being busily occupied in lighting his long cigar. Presently he leaned back, then blew a great cloud of smoke towards the ceiling.

Suddenly we heard a click, like the wooden lid of a box suddenly shut.

"Hullo!" he exclaimed suddenly, "what's that?"

"What's what?"

"Why! Look!" he gasped.

His gaze was set upon something in the shadow of a small table in a corner of the room - something on the floor. In silence, now, we both stood staring at it, for Osborne had risen suddenly. Slowly it moved. It was gradually gliding along the floor, with a sound like paper being pushed along a carpet. Whence it came, where it began and where it ended, we could not see, for the shadow it was in was very deep. Nor was its colour in the least discernible.

All we could make out was that some long, sinuous, apparently endless Thing was passing along the room, close to the wall farthest from us, coming from under the sofa and disappearing beneath the table.

All at once Osborne sprang towards me with an exclamation of alarm, and I felt his grip tighten upon my arm.

"Good God!" he cried.

An instant later a broad, flat head slowly reared itself from beneath the red table-cover which hung down almost to the floor, rose higher and higher until the black, beady, merciless eyes were set upon mine, and in that brief instant of supreme suspense my attention became riveted on the strange, slate-grey mark between and just behind the reptile's cruel eyes. Then, as its head suddenly shot back, Osborne dashed towards the door.

Once, twice, three times he pulled frantically at the handle with all his force.

"Good God! Berrington," he cried, his face blanched to the lips, "we're locked in!"

Almost as he spoke, the serpent with head extended swept forward towards us, along the floor.

I held my breath. Escape from its venomous fangs was impossible.

We had been trapped!

CHAPTER III

A HAMPSTEAD MYSTERY

With a shriek of alarm I leapt to the further side of the table which stood in the middle of the room, and at that moment hurried footsteps became audible.

Our wild shouts for help had evidently been heard, for someone was hurrying down the bare oak stairs into the hall.

"Hang this confounded lock - it catches!" we heard a voice exclaim as the handle turned. Then an instant later the door was flung open, and Gastrell stood before us.

"I am dreadfully sorry, you fellows," he said apologetically, "that you should have been alarmed in this way, because I can assure you that my tame cobra, 'Maharaja,' is quite harmless - look at him now," and we saw that the horrid reptile had swung round the instant its master had entered, and was sliding towards his feet. "He's a pet of mine - I brought him home with me, and he follows me like a dog - no, you needn't be in the least nervous," he added quickly, seeing that I instinctively edged away as the reptile passed. "I'm awfully sorry to have kept you waiting. I must apologize, too, for that confounded door - I myself got locked in here the other day. My wife told you I was out, but I was not. I came in by the side door, and she didn't know I was back, because I went straight upstairs. If you'll wait a moment I'll take our friend 'Maharaja' out."

He left the room, and the snake slid rapidly along the floor after him, almost, as he had said, like a dog following his steps.

"A nice cheerful pet to keep," I remarked, annoyed at my experience; but at that moment the mysterious Gastrell bustled in alone.

"So sorry," he said, and, after thanking us for coming out so far to ascertain if he had lost his purse, he pulled up a chair, seated himself between us, lit a big cigar, and helped us to whiskey from a silver tantalus.

"You had better add the soda yourselves," he said. "And now there is something I want to say to you both. You must have been surprised at my declaring so emphatically this evening that I had not met either of you before - eh?"

"I can answer for myself," Osborne exclaimed quickly. "Are you going to admit, after all, that you were on the *Masonic*?"

"Of course! Who else could it have been? Any more," he added, addressing me, than it could have been someone other than me whom you met in Geneva?"

"Then why did you deny it?" Osborne said rather irritably, looking hard at him with an expression of disapproval and mistrust, while my eyes wandered to that little gold medallion upon his chain.

"Because I had to, - that is, it was expedient that I should," was his reply. "I have a reason for not wanting it to be generally known that I am married, - least of all did I want Easterton, whose house I have just leased, to know me to be a married man; indeed, I told him some weeks ago that I was a bachelor - I had to, for reasons which I can't reveal at present."

He stopped speaking, and we watched him narrowly.

"Still," I remarked, "I don't see how you could have been on board ship in the middle of the ocean, and at the same time in London."

"I didn't say I was. I wasn't. I was in London a fortnight ago, and spent some hours with Lord Easterton. On the same day I sailed for Madeira, where I joined my wife on the homeward-bound *Masonic*. Think, Mr. Osborne," he ended, his curious gaze set on my companion's face, "think when we first met on board. It was not before the ship reached Madeira, surely."

Jack Osborne reflected.

"By Jove, no!" he suddenly exclaimed. "How odd I should all along have thought you had embarked at Capetown with the rest of us. But Mrs. Gastrell came from the Cape, surely?"

"She did, and the name 'Mr. Gastrell' was also in the passenger list, because a cousin of mine should have been on board. At the eleventh hour he was prevented from sailing, and it was upon receipt of a cable from him that I decided to catch the next boat to the Canaries and there meet my wife."

I admit that, as he paused, I felt rather "small"; and I believe Osborne felt the same. We had driven from the club right out here to Swiss Cottage, and on the way we had conjured up in our imaginations all sorts of mysterious happenings, even possible intrigues; and now the whole affair proved to have been "quite ordinary," with a few commonplace incidents to relieve its monotony - notably the incident of the giant cobra.

True, there was the mystery of the locked door. But then, had it really been locked? I had not myself tried to open it, and now as I thought about it, it seemed to me quite possible that Jack Osborne might, in the excitement of the moment, have failed to turn the handle sufficiently, and so have believed that the door was locked when it was not. Again we had Gastrell's assurance that he had found himself locked in one day. As for his declaration to Easterton that he was not the Gastrell whom Osborne had met on the *Masonic*, it was clear now that he had some secret reason for wishing to pass in London as a bachelor, and as Osborne had told Easterton that the Gastrell on the *Masonic* had told him that he had met me in Geneva, naturally Gastrell had been driven - in order to conceal his identity - to maintain that he had never before met me either.

Our host insisted upon our taking another of his very excellent cigars before we left, - it was close upon one o'clock when we rose to go. He rang up a taxi for us, helped us on with our coats, accompanied us to the door, and shook hands with each of us most cordially.

"What do you make of it, Michael?" Osborne asked, when we had remained silent in the swift-travelling taxi for five minutes or more, and were approaching Marlboro' Road Station."

"Nothing," I answered bluntly. "I don't know what to make of it."

"Suspect anything?"

"Yes - and no."

"That's just how I feel, and yet - "

"Well?"

"I mistrust him. I don't know why, but I do. I mistrust them both. There's something queer happening in that house. I am certain there is."

"You can't be certain, as you don't know."

"My suspicions are so strong that they amount to convictions."

"So I think, too. And those dirty tumblers on the tray, and the hot arm-chair I sat down in - Jack, I believe there were a lot of people in that house, hidden away somewhere, all the time we were there. I believe Gastrell admitted his identity only because he was obliged to. Our calling like that, so unexpectedly, and being admitted by his wife - if she is his wife - disconcerted him and took him unawares. I can't think why she admitted us - especially I can't think why she kept us so long in the dark in the hall before she switched on the light. By Jove! What a stunning woman!"

"She is - but crafty. I thought that when I met her on board ship. And those eyes of hers. Phew! They seem to read right into one's soul, and discover one's secret thoughts." He stopped for an instant, then added, meditatively, "I wonder what makes Gastrell keep that horrible cobra as a pet."

I yawned, and we relapsed into silence. Then gradually my thoughts drifted - drifted away from London, far from crowds and hustle, the rumble of motor 'buses and the hootings and squawkings of ears, to a peaceful, rural solitude.

I was in Berkshire. Down in the picturesque valley into which I gazed from the summit of a wooded slope stood a Manor house, ivy-grown, old, very beautiful Facing it an enormous plateau, hewn out of the Down, had been converted to various uses - there were gardens, shrubberies, tennis lawns. Lower came terrace after terrace of smoothly mown grass, each with its little path and borders of shrubs, interspersed with the finest Wellingtonias in the county, tapering gracefully to heaven, copper-beeches and grand oaks.

The house itself was very long and low, its frontage white, mellowed with age, and broken up by old-fashioned, latticed windows which gleamed blue and grey in the translucent, frosted air. The roof of the Manor boasted a mass of beautiful red-brown gables, many half hidden from sight by the wealth of ivy; last summer also by a veritable tangle of Virginia creeper and crimson rambler, now sleeping their winter sleep.

My thoughts wandered on. They travelled with extraordinary rapidity, as thought does, picture after picture rising into the vision of my imagination like the scenes in a kaleidoscopic cinema.

Now I was seated in the old Manor. I could see the room distinctly. It was a small boudoir or ante-room opening into the large drawing-room - a cosy, homely place, its low, latticed windows, divided into four, opening outwards on to garden and terraces, its broad, inviting window-seat comfortably cushioned. Nearly all the furniture was quite old, dark oak, elaborately carved - writing-table, high-backed chairs, an old French "armoury" in the corner; but near the hearth there were two or three deep, modern armchairs of peculiarly restful character, covered with exquisite flowered chintzes.

This vision deepened. I started. The door of the quiet room had suddenly opened, and, humming a gay little French air, a young girl had entered - fresh, exquisite, like a breath of early Springtime itself in the midst of Winter. With her deep eyes, so soft and brown, her skin of a healthy olive pallor, the cheeks just flushed with crimson, and her nimbus of light brown hair through which the golden threads strayed so charmingly, she made a perfect picture standing there in her long gown of sapphire-blue velvet.

The soft contours of her young face were outlined against a tall screen embroidered gorgeously with silken peacocks, before which she stopped to lay down upon a small table the sheaf of red and brown and golden chrysanthemums which she carried in her arms.

My pulses throbbed as they always did in her presence, or when, indeed, she so much as crossed my daydreams, as at this moment. For this girl was Dulcie Challoner - the woman who was fast becoming the one woman in the world to me, and thus had I seen her enter that very room when last I had spent a week-end at Holt Manor, four miles from the little village of Holt Stacey - and that happened to have been only three weeks from the present moment.

The taxi stopped abruptly, shattering my dreams. We had reached the club. Some letters were awaiting me. My spirits rose as I recognized the handwriting on one of them.

Dulcie wrote to say that her father hoped, if I were not "already booked," I would spend Christmas with them.

I was "already booked." I had accepted an invitation a month before to dine on Christmas Day with an hysterical aunt from whom I had expectations. Well, the expectations must take their chance. Then and there I sat down and wrote a long letter to Dulcie saying what joy the contents of her letter had given me, and a brief line to my aunt explaining that "unavoidable circumstances had arisen" which necessitated my cancelling my promise to come to her, much as I regretted doing so.

Snow was falling slowly and persistently, as it had done all the afternoon, when, about ten days later, I arrived at the little station of Holt Stacey, the nearest to Holt Manor. The motor brougham awaited my rather late train, and I was quickly installed among the fur rugs in its cosy interior and being whirled along the silent whiteness of the narrow lanes between the station and my destination. The weather was very cold, and I saw through the windows of the car that every branch and twig had its thick covering of pure white snow, while the thatched roofs of the tiny cottages we passed were heavily laden. By four o'clock in the afternoon most of the cottage windows were lit up, and the glow of the oil lamps shining through tiny panes on to the gleaming carpet of snow without, produced a most picturesque effect.

Now we were purring up the hilly drive; then rounding the sweep to the hall door. The man did not have to ring. Before he could get off the box I heard heavy footsteps leaping down the stairs three at a time and flying across the hall. The door was flung open, and a wild war-whoop from Dick announced my arrival to whoever cared to know of it.

"Good old sport!" shouted Dick, snatching the travelling-rug from my arm, after telling the footman behind him to "take Mr. Berrington's things to the green room in the west wing," and almost pushing me into the hall. "Good old sport! You're awfully late. We've all done tea."

I told him we had been quite half an hour after the scheduled time in starting from Paddington, and that the crowds had been enormous.

"Just what I told Dulcie," he exclaimed. "You don't want to see her, I suppose? What a beastly long time it seems since you were here! Three weeks, isn't it, since I was home, ill?"

In vain I endeavoured to quiet Dick's ringing voice as a girlish, lithe figure appeared between the curtains which divided the stairs from the hall, a figure clad in soft rosy silk with a little lacy tea-jacket over it, and with golden-brown hair waving naturally about a broad, white forehead, with starry brown eyes full of welcome. Taking my hand in hers quietly for an instant, Dulcie asked me what sort of journey I had had, and presently led me across the hall to the drawing-room.

"You will like to see father," she said. "He and Aunt Hannah are in the drawing-room; they've looked forward so much to your coming."

With a heart beating faster than usual I followed Dulcie. Her father I was always glad to see, and we were exceedingly good friends, having much in common. Of a good old county family, Sir Roland Challoner had succeeded late in life to the title on the sudden death in the hunting field of his father, Sir Nelson Challoner.

Dulcie's mother had died just after the birth of Dick, and Sir Roland had tried to make up the loss to Dulcie by getting his only and elderly sister Hannah - "Aunt Hannah" as she was inevitably called by all who stayed at Holt Manor, and in fact by everybody who had seen her more than twice - to come and live with him. And there at Holt she had, in her eccentric way, ever since superintended domestic arrangements and mothered his beautiful little girl and her only brother, by this time an obstreperous boy of fourteen, at Eton and on his way to Oxford.

Aunt Hannah was, as Dulcie expressed it, "rather a dear, quaint thing." But she was more than that, I thought. She had such a pungent wit, her sayings were at times so downright - not to say acrid - that many stood in terror of her and positively dreaded her quick tongue. I rather liked Aunt Hannah myself, perhaps because, by the greatest of good luck, I happened not to have done anything so far to incur her displeasure, which she was never backward in expressing forcibly, or, as Dick the schoolboy brother put it, "in no measured terms." Still, as it is the unexpected that always happens, I knew there might yet come a day when I should be called upon to break a lance with Aunt Hannah, and I must say I devoutly hoped that in the event of so deplorable an occurrence, heaven would vouchsafe me the victory. Steeped in intrigue up to her old ears, Aunt Hannah had, I believed, several times laid deep plans touching her niece's future - plans mysterious to the last degree, which seemed to afford her the liveliest satisfaction. None of these schemes, however, had succeeded up to the present, for Dulcie seemed with delightful inconsistence consistently to "turn down" the admirable suitors whom Aunt Hannah metaphorically dangled before her eyes. Yet so cleverly did she do this that, in some wondrous way known only to herself, she continued to retain them all in the capacity of firm friends, and apparently no hearts were ever permanently bruised.

As I say, I quite liked Aunt Hannah, and she had afforded me a good deal of innocent amusement during my not infrequent visits at Holt Manor. Certainly on these occasions I had managed to adopt, if not actually a brotherly, at any rate an almost brotherly demeanour towards Dulcie whenever the sharp-eyed old lady chanced to be in the vicinity. As a result, after much careful chaperonage, and even astute watching, of my manner towards her niece, Aunt Hannah had "slacked off" delightfully, evidently regarding me as one of those stolid and casual nonentities who, from lack of much interest in anything can safely be trusted anywhere and under the most trying circumstances.

"Here is a telegram for you, Mike," Dulcie said to me one morning, when I had been several days at Holt and the slow routine of life was beginning to reassert itself in the sleepy village after the excitement created by Christmas. The sight of the envelope she handed to me sent my thoughts back to London, the very existence of which I seemed to have entirely forgotten during the past delightful days in this happy, peaceful spot. My gaze was riveted upon Dulcie, standing there before me, straight and slim in her dark violet breakfast gown, with its ruffles of old lace at neck and wrists, the warm light from the fire turning her fluffy brown hair to gold, as I mechanically tore open the envelope, then pulled the telegram out.

"You don't seem in a hurry to read it," she exclaimed lightly, as I sat there looking at her still, the telegram open in my hands.

I glanced down. It was from Osborne, and ran:

"Read report to-day's papers about Maresfield Gardens fire. Write me what you think about it.

"JACK OSBORNE."

I read it through again, then looked up at Dulcie, who still stood there before me.

"Have the papers come?" I asked.

She glanced up at the clock.

"They won't be here just yet," she answered. "We don't get them before midday, you know, and during these days they haven't arrived until lunch time, owing to Christmas."

"You can read it if you like," I said, handing her the telegram, for I had seen her glance at it inquisitively. "It will interest you enormously."

She made a little grimace when she had read it.

"'Interest me enormously,'" she said contemptuously, crumpling up the paper and tossing it into the grate. For some moments she did not speak.

"What fire was there at Maresfield Gardens?" she inquired suddenly, "and why does he ask you what you think about it?"

"Ah, so it does interest you a little," I exclaimed, taking hold of her hand and drawing her towards me, for as she stood there looking down at me she seemed somehow to magnetize me. "Sit by me, here, and I'll tell you."

I told her of the conversation at the club, of Lord Easterton's dinner, of Osborne's queer suggestion, of our visit to the house at Maresfield Gardens in the middle of the night, of our being admitted by the strange woman, including, of course, the incident of the serpent.

When I had finished, she looked at me seriously for some moments without speaking.

"I don't think I like that adventure," she said at last.

For a moment she paused.

"Don't go to that house again, Mike," she suddenly exclaimed. "Promise me you won't."

I was deliberating what reply I should make to this request, though I did not think it likely I should want to go to the house again, when our attention was distracted by the footman entering with the morning papers - we were sitting in the big hall, before the fire of blazing logs.

Dulcie sprang up and snatched the papers from the man, and Dick, bouncing in at that instant, exclaimed with mock solemnity:

"Oh fie! 'Thou shalt not snatch,' Dulcie, you are 'no lady.'"

"Thank heaven for that," she retorted quickly, then began to tantalize me by holding the papers just beyond my reach.

At last she gave me two, and Dick one, opened one herself, and sat upon the rest. They made quite a pile, for Sir Roland was one of those broad-minded men who like to read both sides on questions of any importance.

I soon found the report I sought. It occupied a prominent position, and was headed:

HAMPSTEAD FIRE MYSTERY
BODY FOUND STABBED
POLICE PUZZLED

The disastrous fire at Number 340 Maresfield Gardens, on Christmas Eve, has given rise to an interesting sequel.

I had not been aware that a fire had occurred there, and I read on:

It was confidently hoped that no lives had been lost, but about midday yesterday the charred body of a woman was discovered among the *debris*.

Upon careful examination it was ascertained beyond doubt that the body had been several times stabbed, apparently with some sharp weapon or instrument. All the wounds were in the breast, and it is stated that any one of them might have caused death.

The police are instituting searching inquiries, and a sensational announcement will most likely be made shortly. The origin of the conflagration remains a mystery. Apparently nobody occupied the house when the fire broke out, the sub-tenants, whose identity is veiled in obscurity, having left some days previously.

"Have you read the account in your paper?" I asked, turning to Dulcie as I put mine down.

"Yes," she answered, "I have just finished it. Isn't it terrible?"

"I have a theory," a boy's voice exclaimed suddenly. Dick, seated on the floor, tossed aside the newspaper I had thrown to him.

"That woman whose body has been found may have been stabbed, but I believe that big cobra had something to do with her death. I don't know why I think that, but I do. It's instinct, I suppose. Michael, I believe you were spoofed by that man Gastrell, whoever he is - absolutely spoofed."

"Good heavens, Dick!" I exclaimed in dismay, "how do you come to know what I have just told to Dulcie in confidence?"

"Oh, ask me another, old sport!" he cried out, and burst into laughter. "If you will 'exchange confidences' - isn't that the phrase? - with Dulcie, and be so engrossed that you don't notice me in the room - well, what can you expect?"

CHAPTER IV

IN FULL CRY

Riding to hounds is one of the few forms of sport which appeal to me, and I should like it better still if no fox or other creature were tortured.

On that point Dulcie and I had long been agreed; it was one of many questions upon which we saw eye to eye, for on some subjects our views differed.

"It seems to me grotesque," I remember her saying to me once, "that we English should hold up our hands in horror at the thought of bull-fights, while so many of us take pleasure in the hateful business of the kill in fox-hunting."

In reply I had explained to her that the art of diplomacy lies in seeing the beam in the other man's eye and drawing attention to it, while blinding oneself to the mote in one's own, and if possible convincing the other man that the mote does not exist. Dulcie, however, had her full share of intelligence, with the result that, in modern slang, she "wasn't taking any."

"In that case," she had retorted, "you should feel thankful that you are not a diplomat, Mike. You have your points, but tact and logic are not among them, you know!"

Sir Roland always mounted me when I stayed at Holt Manor in the hunting season, and already I had enjoyed two capital days' sport. Pressed to do so - and it had not needed great persuasion - instead of returning to town on the second

Saturday after Christmas, I had stayed over the Sunday, for on the Monday hounds were to meet at the Manor House. All the other guests, with the exception of two cousins of Sir Roland's, had left on the Saturday, so that we were a family party to all intents; in secret I was determined that before the dawn of spring I should be a member of the family in reality.

Mounted on a well-shaped chestnut three parts thoroughbred, Dulcie had never, I thought, looked so wholly captivating as she did on that Monday morning; I overtook her, I remember, while the chattering cavalcade trotted from the meet at Holt Manor to the first cover to be drawn.

The first cover proved to be tenantless. So did a small, thickly underwooded copse. So did a stretch of bracken. So did a large pine wood some miles from Holt Manor, which was usually a sure find.

"You may say what you like," Dulcie exclaimed as the notes of the huntsman's horn warned us that the pack was once more being blown out of cover, "I maintain still that a drag hunt has advantages over a fox hunt - your red herring or your sack of aniseed rags never disappoint you, and you are bound to get a run."

As we turned out of the lane into a broad meadow, then broke into a hand canter across the soft, springy turf, to take up our position at a point where we could easily slip forward if hounds should find, I told Dulcie jokingly that if her father preserved foxes as carefully as he always said he did, these covers on his estate would not have been drawn blank.

She turned her head sharply.

"Father always says," she exclaimed, "that - "

But what he always said I never heard, for at that instant a piercing "Tally-ho!" rent the air, and, looking up, we saw a long, yellow, lean-bodied fox which apparently had jumped up within a hundred yards of the pack, lolloping unconcernedly towards a hedge near by. He reached the fence, paused, cast a single glance behind him at the fifteen or so couple of relentless four-footed pursuers, then popped calmly through a gap in the fence, and disappeared.

A few moments later hounds had settled to the line, and were streaming out across the broad, undulating pasture which spread away before us in the distance, cut here and there by thorn fences, a winding stream marked by pollards, and several post-and-rails. From all directions came the field, galloping at top speed for the only gate in the thick hedge, fifty yards ahead of us, crowding and jostling one another in their anxiety to get through. Six or eight horsemen had cleared the fence at the few places where it was jumpable. Others were preparing to follow them. The music of the flying pack grew less distinct.

"Come along, Mike!" Dulcie called to me, turning her horse abruptly in the direction of the hedge, "we shall get left if we hang about here."

She was thirty yards from the hedge now - twenty - ten. Timing his stroke to a nicety her horse rose. An instant later he had cleared the fence, with a foot or more to spare. I followed, and almost as my mare landed I saw Dulcie lower her head and cast a backward glance.

Now we were sailing side by side over the broad, undulating pastures which form a feature of that part of Berkshire. A hundred yards ahead of us the pack tore ever onward, their sterns and noses mostly to the ground, their music rising at intervals - a confused medley of sound in various cadences, above which a single, deep, bell-like note seemed ever prominent, insistent.

"That's Merry Boy," Dulcie exclaimed as she began to steady her mount - a stiff post-and-rails was fifty yards in front of us. "I know his voice well. Dan always declares that Merry Boy couldn't blunder if he tried" - I knew Dan to be the huntsman.

On and on the pack swept, now heading apparently for a cover of dark pines visible upon a hill to the left of us, away against the skyline. In front of us and to right and left horses were clearing fences, which here were very numerous, some jumping well and freely, some blundering, some pecking on landing, a few falling. Yet, considering the size of the field, there was very little grief.

"Who is the girl in the brown habit?" I asked Dulcie, soon after we had negotiated a rather high-banked brook. I had noticed this girl in the brown habit almost from the beginning of the run - tall, graceful, a finished horsewoman, mounted on a black thoroughbred, and apparently unaccompanied, even by a groom.

"That?" Dulcie exclaimed, bringing her horse a little nearer, so that she need not speak too loud. "Oh, she is something of a mystery. She is a widow, though she can't be more than twenty-four or five. She lives at the Rook Hotel, in Newbury, and has three horses stabled there. She must have been there a couple of months, now. A few people have called upon her, including my father and Aunt Hannah, but nobody seems to know anything about her, who she is or was, or where she comes from. Doesn't she ride well? I like her, though as yet I hardly know her. She's so pretty, too, and has such a nice voice. I'll introduce you, if you like, if I get a chance later."

I remembered that this widow in the brown habit had been one of the first to arrive at the meet, but she had not dismounted. Dulcie also told me that she had dined at Holt once, and evinced great interest in the house. She had brought with her an old volume containing pictures of the place as it was in some early century, a book Sir Roland had never seen before, and that he had read with avidity, for everything to do with the past history of his house appealed to him. Mrs. Stapleton had ended by making him a present of the book, and before she had left, that night Sir Roland had shown her over the whole house, pointing out the priests' hiding-hole - a curious chamber which fifty years before had come to light while repairs were being made in the great hall chimney - also a secret door which led apparently nowhere.

"I think my father was greatly attracted by her," Dulcie said, "and I am not surprised. I think she is quite lovely, though in such a curious, irregular way; but besides that there is something awfully 'taking' about her. She doesn't, however, seem to 'go down' very well with the people about here; but then you know what county society is. She seems to have hardly any friends, and to live an almost solitary life."

Though I had spared her as much as I could, and though I ride barely ten stone seven, my mare was beginning to sob. Unbuttoning my coat and pulling out my watch as we still galloped along, I found that hounds had been running close on forty minutes without a moment's check.

"Dulcie," I said, coming up alongside her again, "my mare is nearly beat. Have you a second horse out?"

She told me she had not - that my mount would have been her second horse had she been out alone.

"Look," she exclaimed suddenly, "they have turned sharp to the right. Oh, I hope they won't kill! I feel miserable when they kill, especially when the fox has shown us such good sport."

I answered something about hounds deserving blood: about the way the farmers grumbled when foxes were not killed, and so on; but, woman-like, she stuck to her point and would listen to no argument.

"I hope they'll lose him in that cover just ahead," she exclaimed. "Hounds may deserve blood, but such a good fox as this deserves to get away, while as for the farmers - well, let them grumble!"

Half a minute later the pack disappeared into the dense pine wood. Then suddenly there was silence, all but the sound of horses galloping still; of horses blowing, panting, sobbing. From all directions they seemed to come.

"Whoo-whoop!"

The scream, issuing from the depths of the wood, rent the air. An instant later it came again:

"Whoo-whoo-*whoop*!"

There was a sound of cracking twigs, of a heavy body forcing its way through undergrowth, and the first whip crashed out of the cover, his horse stumbling as he landed, but recovering himself cleverly.

"Have they killed?" several voices called.

"No, worse luck - gone to ground," the hunt servant answered, and Dulcie, close beside me, exclaimed in a tone of exultation:

"Oh, good!"

I had dismounted, loosened my mare's girths, and turned her nose to the light breeze. Sweat was pouring off her, and she was still blowing hard.

"Shall I unmount you, Dulcie?" I asked.

She nodded, and presently she stood beside me while I attended to her horse.

"Ah, Mrs. Stapleton!" I heard her exclaim suddenly.

I had loosened the girths of Dulcie's horse, and now I looked up.

Seated upon a black thoroughbred, an exceedingly beautiful young woman gazed down with flushed face and shining eyes.

It was a rather strange face, all things considered. The features were irregular, yet small and refined. The eyes were bright and brown - at least not exactly brown; rather they were the colour of a brilliant red-brown wallflower, and large and full of expression. Her skin, though extremely clear, was slightly freckled.

Dulcie had exchanged a few remarks with her. Now she turned to me.

"Mike," she said, "I want to introduce you to Mrs. Stapleton. Mrs. Stapleton, do you know Mr. Berrington?"

The beautiful young widow, gazing down at me as I looked up at her and raised my hat, presently made some complimentary remark about my mount and the way she jumped, then added:

"I noticed her all through the run - she's just the stamp of animal I have been looking for. Is she for sale, by any chance, Mr. Berrington?"

I replied that the mare was not mine, that she must ask Miss Challoner or Sir Roland. For the instant it struck me as odd that, hunting regularly with this pack, she should not have recognized the animal, for I knew that Dulcie rode it frequently. Then I remembered that some people can no more recognize horses than they can recognize their casual friends when they meet them in the street, and the thought faded.

There was talk of digging out the fox - an operation which Dulcie and I equally detested - and that, added to the knowledge that we were many miles from Holt, also that our horses had had enough, made us decide to set out for home.

Looking back, for some reason, as we walked our horses away from the cover-side towards the nearest lane, I noticed the young widow seated erect upon her black horse, staring after us. I turned to shut the gate, after we had passed into the lane; she was still sitting there, outlined against the wood and apparently still staring in our direction.

Why, I don't know, but as I trotted quietly along the lane, to overtake Dulcie, whose horse was an exceptionally fast walker, I felt uneasy.

Presently my thoughts drifted into quite a different channel. All recollection of the day's sport, of the pretty widow I had just talked to, and of the impression she had left upon my mind, faded completely. I was thinking of someone else, someone close beside me, almost touching me, and yet -

Neither of us spoke. It was nearly four o'clock. The afternoon was quickly closing in. Away beyond the woods which sloped upward in the western distance until they touched the sky, the sun's blood-red beam pierced the slowly-rising mist rolling down into the valley where the pollards marked the winding course of the narrow, sluggish stream. Over brown woods and furrowed fields it cast a curious glow.

Now the light of the winter's sun, sinking still, fell full on my companion's face, I caught the outline of her profile, and my pulses seemed to quicken. Her hair was burnished gold. Her eyes shone strangely. Her expression, to my eyes, seemed to be entirely transformed. How young she looked at that instant, how absolutely, how indescribably attractive! Would she, I wondered, ever come to understand how deeply she had stolen into my heart? Until this instant I myself seemed not fully to have realized it.

Presently she turned her head. Her gaze rested on mine. Gravely, steadily, her wonderful brown eyes read - I firmly believe - what was in my soul: how madly I had come to love her. Without meaning to, I started. A sensation of thrilling expectancy took possession of me. I was approaching, I felt, the crisis of my life, the outcome of which must mean everything to both of us.

"You are very silent , Mike," she said in a low, and, as I

thought, rather strained voice. "Is anything the matter?"

I swallowed before answering.

"Yes - something is the matter," I said limply.

"What?"

I caught my breath. How could she look into my eyes like that, ask that question - such a foolish question it seemed - as though I were naught to her but a stranger, or, at most, some merely casual acquaintance? Was it possible she realized nothing, suspected nothing, had no faint idea of the feeling I entertained for her?

"What is the matter?" she asked again, as I had not answered.

"Oh, it's something - well, something I can't well explain to you under the circumstances," I replied awkwardly, an anxious, hot feeling coming over me.

"Under what circumstances?"

"What circumstances!"

"Yes."

"This is our gap," I exclaimed hurriedly, as we came to a broken bank by the lane-side - I was glad of the excuse for not answering. I turned my mare's nose towards the bank, touched her with the spur, and at once she scrambled over.

Dulcie followed.

Around us a forest of pines, dark, motionless, forbidding, towered into the sky. To right and left moss-grown rides wound their way into the undulating cover, becoming tunnels in the distance as they vanished into blackness, for the day was almost spent.

Slowly we turned into the broader of the two rides. We still rode side by side. Still neither of us spoke. Now the moss beneath our horses' hoofs grew so thick and soft that their very footfalls became muffled.

Ten minutes must have passed. In the heart of the dense wood all was still as death, save for a pheasant's evening crow, and the sudden rush of a rabbit signalling danger to its companions.

"What circumstances, Mike?" Dulcie repeated. She spoke in a strange tone. Her voice was very low, as though she feared to break the silence which surrounded us.

Taken aback, I hesitated. We were very close together now - my leg touched her horse. Already, overhead in a moonless sky, the stars shone brightly. In the growing gloom her face was visible, though partly blurred.

"Why not stop here a moment?" I said, hardly knowing that I spoke, or why I spoke. My mouth had grown suddenly dry. The *timbre* of my voice somehow founded different. Without answering she shortened her reins, and her horse was still.

Why had we stopped? Why had I suggested our stopping? I saw her, in the darkness, turn her face to mine, but she said nothing.

"Dulcie!" I exclaimed suddenly, no longer able to control myself. Without knowing it I leant forward in my saddle. I could see her eyes, now. Her gaze was set on mine. Her lips were slightly parted. Her breast rose and fell.

Some strange, irresistible force seemed all at once to master me, deadening my will, my brain, my power of self-restraint. My arm was about her; I was drawing her towards me. I felt surprise that she should offer no resistance. My lips were pressed on hers....

* * * * *

She was kissing me feverishly, passionately. Her whole soul seemed to have become suddenly transformed. Her arms were about my neck - I could not draw away.

"Oh, Mike! Mike!" she gasped, "tell me you really mean it - that you are not just playing with me - flirting with me - tell me you ... oh, I love you so, dearest. Ah, yes. I love you so, I love you so!"

It was very dark by the time we had made our way through the extensive wood - a short cut to Holt Manor - and were once more in the lanes, I felt strangely happy, and yet a curious feeling which I could neither explain nor account for obsessed me.

Our joy was so great - would it last? That was the purport of my sensation, if I may express it so. I longed at that moment to be able to look into the future. What had the Fates in store for me - for us both?

Perhaps it was as well I didn't know.

We had entered the park gates, and were half-way up the long avenue of tall elms and stately oaks, when I saw a light approaching through the darkness. It came nearer, and we guessed it must be a man on foot, carrying a lantern.

Now he was quite close.

"Is that Miss Dulcie? a voice inquired out of the blackness, as the light became stationary.

"Yes. That you, Churchill?" Dulcie called back.

Churchill was the head gardener. Born and bred on the estate, there were few things he loved better than to recall to mind, and relate to anybody sufficiently patient to listen to him, stories and anecdotes of the family. Of "Miss Dulcie" he would talk for an hour if you let him, telling you how he remembered her when she was "not so high," and of the things she had done and said as a child.

"What do you want, Churchill?" she called to him, as he remained silent.

Still for some moments he did not speak. At last he apparently plucked up courage.

"There's been sad doings at the house," he said, and his voice was strained.

"Sad doings!" Dulcie exclaimed in alarm. "Why, what do you mean?"

"There's been a shocking robbery, Miss Dulcie - shocking. You'll hear all about it when you go in. I thought it best to warn you about it. And Master Dick - "

He stopped abruptly.

"Good heavens, Churchill!" she cried out in great alarm, "quick, tell me what has happened, tell me everything. What about Master Dick?"

"He's been served shocking, Miss. Oh, it's a terrible affair. The whole house looted during the hunt breakfast this, morning, and Master Dick - "

"Yes! Yes!"

"Treated something crool."

"Dick! They haven't hurt Dick. Oh, don't say they have done him some injury!"

The tone of agony in her voice was piteous.

"He's come round now, Miss Dulcie, but he's been

unconscious for hours. They put chloroform or something on him - Sir Roland himself found him in one of the upstairs rooms, lying on the floor just like dead."

"Oh, heavens, how awful! How is he now?"

"The two doctors are with him still, Miss, and as I come away, not ten minutes ago, they telled me he was goin' on as well as could be expected. It was at lunch time Sir Roland found him, and then the robbery was discovered. Every bit of jewellery's been stolen, 'tis said, and a whole chest-full of plate - the plate chests were open all the morning as some of the old silver had been used at the breakfast. The robbery must have took place during the meet, when the hall and rooms downstairs was full of people and all the servants as busy as could be. There was lots of cars there as you know, Miss, and the police think the thieves must have come in a car and gone into the house as if they were hunting-folk. But nobody don't seem to have seen any stranger going upstairs - the police say there must have been several thieves on the job. Master Dick may be able to tell something when he's hisself again, pore young gentleman."

We didn't wait to hear more, but set our horses into a smart trot up the avenue to the house.

CHAPTER V

HUGESSON GASTRELL AT HOME

A week had passed since Dulcie had promised to become my wife, and since the amazing robbery in broad daylight at Holt Manor.

I had been five days back in town, where I had some estate business to attend to. It was the evening of Hugesson Gastrell's house - warming reception in his newly furnished mansion in Cumberland Place, and the muster of well-known people was extraordinary.

Peers and peeresses, prosperous City financiers, celebrities of the drama and of the operatic stage, luminaries of the law, diplomats, and rich retired traders who had shed the "tradesman" and blossomed into "gentleman," jostled one another in the rooms and on the stairs. It is surprising how people will rush to the house of a wealthy man. At least one Duke was present, a Cabinet Minister too, also a distinguished Judge and two Archbishops, for I noticed them as I fought my way up into the room where music was being performed, music the quality of which the majority of the listeners gauged by the fees known to be paid to the artists engaged, and by the amount of newspaper publicity those artists' Press agents had succeeded in securing for them.

Nor were journalists lacking at this "interesting social function," as some of them afterwards termed it in their papers. In London I move a good deal in many kinds of society, and now I noticed, mingling in the crowd, several men and women I was in the habit of meeting frequently, though I did not know them to speak to - Press representatives whose exclusive duty I knew it to be to attend social gatherings of this description. As I edged my way through the dense throng I could hear my favourite composition, Dvorak's "Humoresque," being played on the violin by Beatrice Langley, who I had been told was to appear, and for a few brief minutes the crowd was hushed. To my chagrin the music ended almost as I succeeded in forcing my way into the room, so that I was in time only for the applause.

Now the hall and the large rooms where the guests were, were filled with the buzz of conversation. In two of these rooms supper was in progress, a supper in keeping with the sumptuousness, the luxury and the general extravagance noticeable everywhere.

For this house in Cumberland Place which he had rented from Lord Easterton lent itself admirably to Hugesson Gastrell's distorted ideas as to plenishing, at which some people laughed, calling them almost Oriental in their splendour and their lavishness. Upon entering, the idea conveyed was that here was a man who had suddenly found himself possessed of a great deal more money than he had ever expected to come by, and who, not being accustomed to wide means, had at once set to work to fling his fortune broadcast, purchasing, wherever he went, everything costly that took his fancy.

For after mounting some steps and entering under a wide portico, one found oneself in a spacious, lofty vestibule where two flights of warmly tinted marble steps, shallow and heavily carpeted, ran up to right and left to a wide gallery on three sides of the hall. The marble was so beautiful, the steps were so impressive to look upon, that one was forcibly reminded of the staircase in the Opera House in Paris, of course in miniature. On the lowest step on either side were carved marble pillars supporting nude figures of great size and bearing each an electric lamp gold-shaded to set off the yellow-tinted marble and the Turkey carpets of gold and of richest blue. In one corner stood a Mongolian monster, a green and gold dragon of porcelain resting on a valuable faience pedestal - a bit of ancient Cathay set down in the heart of London.

In their magnificence the reception rooms excelled even this hall, boasting, as they did, a heterogeneous collection of rare antiques, of valuable relics, and of *articles de virtu* from practically the world over. Everywhere they lay in strange confusion - on the mantelpieces, tops of cupboards, on shelves, angle brackets, and on almost every table. Here was a delicate lute of jade, used by Chinese lovers of a thousand years ago. There stood silver lamps, carved most marvellously and once trimmed by vestal virgins, lamps from the temples of Herculaneum, of Rome and of Pompeii. Shadowy gods and goddesses, dragons, fetishes of more or less hideous mien, glared everywhere at one another in a manner most unpleasant. Porcelains; wonderful blue-patterned plates from Pekin; willow-patterned dishes from Japan; ancient hammered beer tankards from Bavaria and the Rhine; long-stemmed Venetian glasses of iridescent hues, were scattered everywhere in bewildering profusion. In an ante-room was a priceless crucifix in three different woods, from Ober-Ammergau; on the mantelpieces of three of the reception rooms were old French gilt clocks - the kind found nowadays only in secluded and old inns of the Bohemian Quartier Latin, inns which the tourist never sees, and where "collectors" are to all intents unknown. Set upon this landing of polished oak upon the first floor was a very ancient sundial, taken from some French chateau, a truly beautiful *objet d'art* in azure and faded gold, with foliated crest above, borne long ago, no doubt, by some highly pompous dignitary. Here and there, too, were suits of armour of beaten steel - glittering figures, rigid and erect and marvellously inlaid with several different metals. Two rooms of the building, I was told by a guest with whom I had entered into conversation, were set aside entirely as an armoury.

Hardly had I finished observing all this, and a great deal more besides, when a voice at my elbow exclaimed:

"Good evening, Mr. Berrington. I wonder, now, if you'll remember me - eh?"

As I turned, I instantly recognized the speaker.

"Of course I recollect you - Mrs. Stapleton," I exclaimed, looking into her eyes with, I am afraid, rather unconcealed admiration, for I don't pretend that I am not of a very susceptible nature. "I have met many people I know, this evening," I continued, "but this is an unlooked-for pleasure. I was told in Berkshire that you never came to town."

"Were you really?" she exclaimed with a ripple of merry laughter. "They seem, down there, to know more about one's movements than one knows oneself."

For an instant she paused.

"And how is your lovely and delightful friend - Dulcie Challoner?" she
inquired presently. "Is she here to-night?"

"No," I said, wondering for the moment if she knew or suspected my secret, for our engagement had not yet been announced. "The Challoners don't know our host, though, judging by the people here to-night, he seems to know nearly everybody."

"Do you know him well? Have you known him long?" she inquired carelessly, letting her gaze rest on mine.

I told her that our acquaintanceship was very slight, that I had made his acquaintance in Geneva, and met him once afterwards in London.

"I don't know him well, either," she observed, then added with some emphasis, "Hc strikes me as being a most charming young man."

Naturally I agreed with her, though I had been unable to make up my mind whether, upon the whole, I liked him or not. I thought that upon the whole I didn't, seeing what strange things had happened.

"By the by," I said suddenly, "have you had supper?"

She answered that she had not, and added that she was "starving." Several people were emerging from one of the supper rooms, and thus it came that I presently found myself seated *tete-a-tete* with the beautiful widow, and at last beginning to enjoy an evening which until now I had found rather dull.

It was natural that we should presently speak of Berkshire and of Holt Manor, and soon we were discussing at length the subject of the robbery.

"And have the police as yet no clues?" Mrs. Stapleton suddenly asked.

"None, apparently. I suppose you have heard all about what happened, and the statements made by Sir Roland's little son, Dick Challoner."

"I know nothing beyond what I read in the newspapers," she replied. "The papers mentioned that Sir Roland's boy had been chloroformed by the thief or thieves - that was all so far as I remember."

"Yes," I answered, "he was chloroformed, but he need not have been according to his own account - and as he is extremely truthful and never boasts, I think we may believe his story. He had his head and shoulders in a big oak chest in his father's bedroom, where his father had sent him to find a hunting apron to lend to somebody, and when he stood upright again he heard two men talking, upon the opposite side of the screen which hid the oak chest.

"The voices were those of strangers, and the boy naturally supposed that the speakers were some friends of Sir Roland's. He was about to show himself, when he heard one of the men say:

"'She says this drawer has money in it: give me your key.'

"He heard a key being pushed into a drawer lock, the drawer pulled out, the chink of coin and the crackle of bank-notes. Then he heard the other man suddenly say:

"'Hurry up. They'll have got the plate by this time and be waiting for us.'

"The boy was awfully frightened, of course, but he didn't lose his head. Knowing that his presence must be discovered in a moment, he sprang out from behind the screen, intending to dash past the men and downstairs and give the alarm. Unfortunately he rushed right up against one of them, who instantly gripped him and clapped his hand over his mouth while the other man pressed his hand over his eyes - presumably to prevent Dick's being afterwards able to identify them. Dick says that one of the men twisted his arm until he couldn't stir without extreme pain, then told him that he must show them where the key of Sir Roland's safe was - a little safe in the wall in his bedroom. Dick knew where the key was - Sir Roland keeps it, it seems, in a drawer of his dressing-table - but he refused to tell, though the man screwed his arm until he nearly broke it - he strained it badly, and the poor little chap has it still in a sling. Then, finding that they could do nothing with him, and that nothing would make him 'peach,' as he says - though he says they threatened to hit him on the head - one of them pressed something over his mouth and nose, which seemed to suffocate him. What happened after that he doesn't know, as he lost consciousness."

"What a brave little boy," my beautiful companion exclaimed in a tone of admiration. "Did he say at all what the men were like?"

"He didn't catch even a glimpse of their faces, they pounced on him so quickly. But he says that both wore hunting kit, and he thinks both were tall. One wore pink."

"It was a carefully planned affair, anyway," Mrs. Stapleton said thoughtfully, as I refilled her glass with Pol Roger. "What was the actual value of the things stolen?"

"Sir Roland puts it at twelve or fourteen thousand pounds, roughly. You see, he had a lot of jewellery that had belonged to Lady Challoner and that would have been Miss Challoner's; most of that was stolen. It should have been in the safe, of course, but Sir Roland had taken it out the week before, intending to send it all to London to be thoroughly overhauled and cleaned - he was going to give it to Dulcie - to Miss Challoner on her twenty-first birthday; she comes of age next month, you know. It was in one of the drawers that the thieves unlocked, and they took most of it. They would have taken the lot, only some of it was in a back partition of the drawer, and they apparently overlooked it."

"But how did they manage to steal the plate? I read in some paper that a lot of plate was stolen."

"Heaven knows - but they got it somehow. The police think that other men, disguised probably as gentlemen's servants, must have made their way into the pantry during the hunt breakfast, while Sir Roland's servants were up to their eyes in work, attending to everybody, and have slipped it into bags and taken it out to a waiting motor. Strangers could easily have gone into the back premises like that, unnoticed, in the middle of the bustle and confusion. If Dick had told the men who bullied him what they wanted to know, Sir Roland's safe would have been ransacked too, and several thousands of pounds more worth of stuff stolen, most likely. He is a little brick, that boy."

"He is, indeed. How long did he remain unconscious?"

"Until Sir Roland himself found him, just before lunch. The ruffians had pushed him under the bed, and if Sir Roland had not happened to catch sight of his foot, which protruded a little, the boy might have been left there until night, or even until next day, and the whole household have been hunting for him."

Mrs. Stapleton sipped some champagne, then asked:

"Is anybody suspected?"

"That's difficult to say," I answered. "Naturally the police think that one or other of the servants at Holt must know something of the affair, even have been an actual accomplice - but which? None of the servants has been there less than four years, it seems, and several have been in Sir Roland's service ten and fifteen years - the old butler was born on the estate. Sir Roland scouts the idea that any of his servants had a hand in the affair, and he told the police so at once. Even the fact that one of the thieves had, according to Dick, referred to some woman - he had said, '*She* says this drawer has money in it' - wouldn't make Sir Roland suspect any of the maids.

"The police then asked him in a roundabout way if he thought any of his guests could have had anything to say to it. Phew! How furious Sir Roland became with them! You should have seen him - I was with him at the time. Then suddenly he grew quite calm, realizing that they were, after all, only trying to do their duty and to help him to trace the thieves.

"'Up to the present I have not, so far as I am aware,' he said in that cold, dignified way of his, 'entertained criminals at Holt Manor or elsewhere. No, my man,' he ended, turning to the sergeant, or the inspector, or whatever he was, 'the men who have stolen my property were not any of my guests. You may set your minds at rest on that point.'"

Conversation drifted to other topics. Several times during supper I endeavoured to lead my beautiful companion on to talk about herself, but on each occasion she cleverly diverted conversation to some other subject. I confess that when she casually questioned me concerning my own affairs I was less successful in evading her inquiries; or it may have been that I, in common with most of my sex, like to talk freely about "self" and "self's" affairs, especially when the listener is a beautiful woman who appears to be sympathetic and deeply interested in all one has to say about oneself.

During that brief half-hour our intimacy grew apace. There are people with whom one seems to have been on terms of friendship, almost as though one had known them for years, within ten minutes after being introduced to them; others who, when one has known them quite a long time, seem still to remain comparatively strangers. Mrs. Stapleton belonged to the first group, although she spoke so little about herself. Yet I was not in the least attracted by her in the way Dulcie Challoner attracted me. I found her capital company; I could imagine our becoming great friends; I could think of her in the light of a *bonne camarade*. But that was all. As for feeling tempted to fall in love with her - but the bare thought was grotesque.

"What a charming, delightful girl that is - I mean Miss Challoner," Mrs. Stapleton exclaimed suddenly, when, after talking a great deal, we had been silent for a few moments. "And how exquisitely pretty," she added after an instant's pause.

I hardly knew what to say. I know enough of women to be aware that no woman is particularly anxious, save in exceptional cases, to listen to a panegyric on the charms and the physical attractions of some other woman. Therefore, after a moment's reflection, I answered with affected indifference:

"I think I agree with you. I have known her a number of years. Her father was a great friend of my father's."

"Indeed?" she replied, raising her eyebrows a little, then letting her gaze rest full on mine. "That is interesting. I am a believer in platonic friendships. I wonder if you are."

"Oh, of course," I said quickly. "It is ridiculous to suppose that a man and woman can't be friends without - without - "

"Yes?" she said encouragingly.

"Oh, well - I suppose I mean without falling in love with each other."

She smiled in a way that puzzled me a little, but said nothing.

"Do you mean in all cases?" she suddenly inquired.

"In most cases, anyway."

"And when would you make an exception?"

This was a problem I felt I could not solve. However, I made a dash atit.

"In the case of people of abnormally susceptible temperament," I said, "I suppose such people couldn't be friends without soon becoming - well, lovers."

"Ah, I see," she observed thoughtfully.

She was toying with a strawberry ice, and her lowered eyelids displayed the extraordinary length of their lashes. Certainly I was talking to an interesting and very lovely woman - though again here, as before in the hunting field in Berkshire, I found myself wondering in what her beauty consisted. Not a feature was regular; the freckles on nose and forehead seemed to show more plainly under the glare of the electric lights; the eyes were red-brown. But how large they were, and how they seemed to sparkle with intelligence!

She looked up suddenly. Her expression was serious now. Up

to the present her eyes, while she talked, had been singularly animated, often full of laughter.

"Mr. Berrington, have you ever been in love?"

I was so surprised at this question, from a woman to whom I was practically a stranger, that I thought it best to treat it as a jest.

"Yes, a dozen times," I answered. "I am in love at this moment," I added lightly, as if joking.

"You need not have told me that," she said, serious still. "I knew it the moment I saw you both together. I asked - but only to hear what you would say."

"But - but - " I stammered, "I - you - that is I don't quite catch your meaning. When did you see 'us' both together - and who is the other person you are thinking of?"

She had finished her ice.

"Please give me some more champagne," she said.

I picked up the half-empty bottle, refilled her glass, then my own. She held out her glass until it clinked against mine.

"Here is health and long life to your friend on the chestnut," she exclaimed, smiling again, "and to you too. I only hope that your married life will be happier than - "

She checked herself. Her tongue had run away with her, and, as our lips touched our glasses, I mentally finished her sentence.

But who, I wondered, had her husband been?

People were still flocking into the room. Others were moving out. From a distance there came to us above the noise and the buzz of conversation the words of a song I love:

> "Mon coeur s'ouvre a ta voix
> Comme s'ouvre les fleurs
> Aux baisers de l'aurore,
> Mais O! Mon bien aime
> Pour mieux secher mes pleurs
> Que ta voix parle encore,
> Dis moi qu'a Dalila
> Tu reviens pour jamais.
> Redis a ma tendresse
> Les serments d'autrefois
> Les serments que j'aimais.
> Ah, reponds a ma tendresse,
> Ah, verse-moi l'ivresse!"

"How gorgeous!" I exclaimed, straining my ears in a vain attempt to hear better. "Who is it?"

"Kirkby-Lunn," my companion answered quickly. "Are you fond - "

She stopped. Her face was partly turned. I saw a glance of recognition flash into her eyes and vanish instantly. Following the direction of her glance, my gaze rested upon the strange, striking woman I had seen but once but could not possibly forget. Mrs. Gastrell had just entered, and with her, to my astonishment, Jack Osborne. It was Jasmine Gastrell with whom my companion had exchanged that momentary glance of recognition.

"Are you fond of music?" Mrs. Stapleton asked, looking at me again.

"Very," I answered absently, "of music that is music."

For my attention had become suddenly distracted. How came this woman to be here, this woman who called herself Gastrell's wife? Lord Easterton was somewhere about, for I had seen him in the crowd. Such a striking woman would be sure to attract his attention, he would inquire who she was, he might even ask Gastrell, and then what would happen? What would Gastrell say? Was the woman actually his wife, or was she -

Mechanically I conversed with my companion for a minute or two longer, then suddenly she suggested that we should go.

"And let some of these starving people take our table," she added, as she prepared to rise.

Osborne and his singularly lovely companion were now seated at a table only a few yards off. His back was turned to us, and I had not caught Mrs. Gastrell's glance.

"D'you know who that is, that woman who has just come in?" I inquired carelessly, indicating her as I rose.

"That?" Mrs. Stapleton answered, looking full at her, and this time their eyes met in a cold stare. "No, I have no idea."

I confess that this flat untruth, spoken with such absolute *sang-froid,* somewhat disconcerted me. For I could not be in the least doubt that I had distinctly seen the two women greet each other with that brief glance of mutual recognition.

CHAPTER VI

THE HOUSE IN GRAFTON STREET

One afternoon, some days later, I was sitting in my flat in South Molton Street, smoking a pipe and carelessly skimming an evening paper, when my man brought me some letters which had just arrived.

Several I tossed aside unopened - I recognized the handwritings and was in no haste to absorb the contents of epistles from acquaintances whose company, at the best of times, "bored me stiff," as some Americans say. But the letter was there that I had expected in the morning, and at once I tore it open.

Dulcie wrote chiefly about herself - which was all I wanted to hear - about her father and "Aunt Hannah," while two pages she devoted to her little brother Dick, of whom she was inordinately fond.

Dick, she said, had shown the utmost pluck and endurance throughout his painful convalescence after his rough-and-tumble with the burglars. She told me how he had from the first sat up in bed with his "honourable wounds" upon him, bandaged and swathed, joking and making light of the occurrence now, as perhaps only the best breed of English schoolboy knows how. One thing still puzzled both little Dick and herself, and for that matter the whole family, she said - who could the woman be to whom the thieves had alluded? No word, added Dulcie, had as yet been forthcoming as to the whereabouts of any of the valuables stolen on that memorable day, either family jewels or plate, and the detectives at Scotland Yard acknowledged that so far matters were at a deadlock.

Further on in her newsy letter Dulcie made mention of the fascinating widow staying at the Rook Hotel in Newbury, and of her wish to know her better. She added incidentally that Mrs. Stapleton had been away since the day after the meet at Holt Manor, and that no one knew where she was staying. She hoped she would soon be back, she said, as she wished so much to renew her acquaintance, and to strengthen it. Dulcie then spoke of her Aunt Hannah, who had been particularly amusing and crochety of late, but added that she was really such a "dear" at heart that people all loved her when they came to know her well. "My dear," she wrote, "Aunt Hannah has surpassed herself lately. You know what vigorous likes and dislikes she takes, all of a sudden? Well, now Auntie has conceived an inordinate aversion for poor Mrs. Stapleton, and seems inclined not only to give her the cold shoulder, but to hound her down by saying the nastiest things about her, just as the other people in the county did when she first came to live among us. I rather believe that she had this feeling all along, more or less, but now she seems positively to hate her - though she confesses that she doesn't know why she does! Isn't that like Auntie? And now she has been asking me never to notice Mrs. Stapleton, and not to speak to her again when she returns, in fact to drop the acquaintance entirely - and that just as we have called, and I've tried to be nice to her out hunting, and we've had her to dine; I told you how taken father was with her, and how he took her all over the house and showed her simply everything. I really don't see why I should draw back now. Nor does father. As a matter of fact, I don't see how we can - it has gone too far - and just to satisfy one of dear old Auntie's whims! She has a good many, as you know, Mike. There is just this one thing, however, that sometimes one of her unaccountable whims or dislikes turns out to have been well grounded."

My darling then went on to speak of her father and of the happiness our engagement afforded him, happiness tempered, as she could not help knowing, by the sorrow her leaving him would bring to him, for the most wonderful confidence and companionship existed between father and daughter. This sadness, Dulcie went on, came out almost pathetically in her father's even added tenderness to her - he whose tenderness and affection had always been such a wonderful thing to her since her earliest childhood. But now, she said, her father sometimes followed her about the house and grounds when she had been absent from him for a short time, seeking occasion for talks with her, giving her his confidence, and consulting her wishes on matters about the gardens and stables in a way that was quite touching. It was as though, now that the parting was so soon to take place, he could not get enough of his only daughter's company, as if the old man clung to her more than ever before.

The closely-written sheets dropped from my hand on to my knee. "Ah, my own little girl," I thought, "who wouldn't miss you - sadly, yes, terribly? Your delightful presence, the truth and honour that seem to be manifest in your smallest gesture, in every glance from your clear eyes; the companionship of your fearless intellect cutting through conventionalities like a knife, arriving at the right point with the unerring instinct of a woman, yet with the *naivete* of a child."

Memories crowded in upon me, memories of all my happy days with Dulcie in the country - in the hunting field, in the gardens about her home, of afternoons spent among the books and prints and pictures in her father's quiet, book-lined library at Holt, of the evenings in the drawing-room at the piano, of hours of pleasant talk in the beautiful conservatories and on the grassy terraces, and by the lake-side below the tennis lawn. What, I thought, would life be like when at last I had her always with me, brightening my life, filling my own home - our home - with laughter and with the music of her voice! Again and again she rose to my enthralled vision, and ever she was Youth and Love, the vision crowned with the wonder of her nebulous, brown-gold hair as she gazed at me out of her sweet, clear eyes in which I seemed still to read unfathomable purity and truth.

It is a terrible thing to be in love. Some savage races there are which hold to the belief that the spirits of lovers changing places, give rise to the feverish mental upheaval which we prosaically term "falling in love," the spirits being restless at their enforced imprisonment and unsatisfied until they have returned each to its appointed sphere. Now that I have recovered from the affliction I sometimes wonder if it might not with advantage be treated as ordinary maladies and some passions are - with the aid of drugs. Perhaps some day it will be. Certainly it soon will be if the eugenists get their way.

And, thinking of the letter I had just read, which now lay folded in my pocket, my memory drifted backward. For since the day I had met Jack Osborne at Brooks's on his return from Nigeria, many incidents had occurred which puzzled me. Trifling incidents individually, no doubt, yet significant when considered in the concrete. There was the incident, for instance, of Sir Harry Dawson's declaring in a letter written to Lord Easterton from the Riviera that he had never met Gastrell, never heard of him even, though Lord Easterton had Gastrell's assurance that he knew Sir Harry Dawson and had intended to call upon him on the evening he had unwittingly entered Lord Easterton's house, which was next door.

Then there was something not quite normal in Gastrell's posing one day as a married man, the next as a bachelor; also in his pretending at one moment that he had never seen Osborne and myself before, yet admitting at the next that he had met us. True, he had advanced an apparently sound reason for this *volte-face* of his, but still -

The affair, too, in Maresfield Gardens. That surely was an "incident" which bordered on a mystery. I felt I should never forget our extraordinary reception that night - the "black out" house, as stage managers say; our repeated ringing the door bell; the slow unlocking and unbolting the door; the cautious inquiry; our wait in the darkness after our admission; the discovery of that horrible serpent with its chilling eyes; the locked door; the sudden entry of Gastrell, and his odd conversation.

Then the conflagration which had occurred a few days later, and the subsequent discovery among the *debris* of a body, charred and stabbed; the apparent ignorance of everybody as to whose body it was; the statement made by the police that none knew the names of the sub-tenants who had occupied that house when the fire had broken out, or what had since become of them - the actual tenant was in America. Without a doubt, I reflected as I knocked the ashes out of my pipe into the grate, something "queer" was going on, and I had inadvertently got myself mixed up in it.

The last "incident" to puzzle me had been that momentary glance of mutual recognition exchanged between the woman I knew only as "Mrs. Gastrell" - or "Jasmine Gastrell," as Osborne always spoke of her - and Mrs. Stapleton, and their subsequent apparent entire lack of recognition. That, certainly, had been most odd. What could have been the cause of it? Why, knowing each other, did they all at once feign to be strangers? And the extraordinarily calm way Mrs. Stapleton had, looking me full in the eyes, assured me that she had never before even seen the woman she had just smiled at. Lastly - though this was of less consequence - how came Jack Osborne to be dancing attendance upon the woman I knew as "Mrs. Gastrell," when he had assured me as we drove away in the taxi from Maresfield Gardens that night that though he admired her he mistrusted her?

I had filled my pipe again, and, as I puffed at it to set it going, one more thought occurred to me. And this thought, I must say, perplexed me as much as any.

Hugesson Gastrell was said to have spent the whole of his life, until six months previously, in Australia and Tasmania. If that were so, then how did he come to have so large a circle of friends, or at any rate of acquaintances - acquaintances, too, of such distinction and high position? Was it possible he could in a few months have come to know all these peers and peeresses and baronets and knights, distinguished musicians and actors and actresses, leading members of the learned professions, and all the rest of the Society crowd who had thronged his house that evening?

Suddenly something I had been told at the club an hour or so before flashed back into my mind. Another club member besides Easterton had, it seemed, become acquainted with Gastrell through Gastrell's calling at the wrong house - by mistake.

A coincidence? Possibly. And yet -

I sucked meditatively at my pipe.

Suddenly the telephone rang. Easterton was speaking.

"What!" I exclaimed, in answer to the startling information he gave me. "When did he disappear?"

"Where was he last seen?"

"No, he has not been here. I haven't seen him since Gastrell's reception."

"Oh, yes, I saw you there."

"Yes, very extraordinary."

"No."

"Oh, no."

"Good. I'll come to you at once. Are you at Linden Gardens?"

"Very well, I'll come straight to the club."

Mechanically I hung up the receiver. Curious thoughts,

strange conjectures, wonderings, arguments, crowded my brain in confusion. Five days had passed since the date of Gastrell's reception, when I had seen Jack Osborne at supper with the woman he had said he mistrusted. Since that evening, according to what Easterton had just told me, nobody had seen or heard of him. He had not been to his chambers; he had not left any message there or elsewhere; he had not written; he had neither telegraphed nor telephoned.

Where was he? What was he doing? Could some misfortune have befallen him? Had he -

I did not end the sentence my mind had formed. Instead I went out, hailed a taxi, and in a few minutes was on my way to Brooks's.

Outside a house in Grafton Street a group of people stood clustered about the door. Others, on the pavement opposite, stared up at the windows. Two policemen upon the doorstep prevented anyone from entering.

Leaning forward as my taxi sped by, I peered in through the open door of the house, then up at the windows, but there was nothing out of the ordinary to be seen. Further down the street we passed three policemen walking briskly along the pavement in the direction of the house.

"What's the commotion in Grafton Street?" I inquired of my driver as I paid him off at Brooks's.

"I've no idea, sir," he answered. "Looks as though there was trouble of some sort." Another fare hailed him, so our conversation ended.

I found Easterton awaiting me in a deserted card-room.

"This may be a serious affair, Berrington," he said in a tone of anxiety as I seated myself in the opposite corner of the big, leather-covered settee. "Here five days have gone by, and there isn't a sign of Jack Osborne, though he had not told anybody that he intended to absent himself, had not even hinted to anybody that he had any idea of doing so."

"You say he has not been seen since Gastrell's reception?"

"Not since then - five days ago. The fellows here at the club are getting quite alarmed about him - they want to advertise in the newspapers for news of his whereabouts."

"That means publicity, a shoal of inquiries, and maybe a scandal," I answered thoughtfully. "If Jack has intentionally disappeared for a day or two and all at once finds himself notorious he will be furious."

"Just what I tell them," Easterton exclaimed; "I wish you would back me up. You see, Jack hasn't any relatives to speak of, and those he has live abroad. Consequently the fellows here consider it is what the Americans call 'up to them' to institute inquiries, even if such inquiries should necessitate publicity."

I pondered for a moment or two.

"You know," I said, "Jack is a curious fellow in some ways - some call him a crank, but he isn't that. Still, he is something of a 'character,' and absolutely unconventional. I remember his making a bet, once, that he would punch out a boastful pugilist at the National Sporting Club - no, it wasn't at the N.S.C., it was at a place down East - 'Wonderland,' they call it."

"And did he do it?" Easterton asked.

"Did he? By heaven, the poor chap he tackled was carried out unconscious at the end of the second round - Jack's bet was with Teddy Forsyth, and he pocketed a couple of ponies then and there."

"Did he really? Capital! And Teddy's such a mean chap; he

didn't like partin', did he?"

"Like it? He went about for the rest of the night with a face like a funeral mute's."

"Capital!" Lord Easterton repeated. "But to return to the point, Jack's eccentricities and vagaries can have nothin' to do with his disappearance."

"Why not? How do you know?"

"Well, why should they? I only hope he hasn't gone and made a fool of himself in any way that'll make a scandal or get him into trouble. In a way, you know, we are connections. His mother and mine were second cousins. That's really why I feel that I ought to do somethin' to find out what has happened to him. Do you - do you think he can have got mixed up with some woman?"

"I won't say that I actually think so, but I think it's more than possible."

"No! Why? What woman?"

At that instant I remembered that the woman I had in my mind was the woman who on board the *Masonic* had, so Jack had told me, called herself Hugesson Gastrell's wife, and called herself his wife again at the house in Maresfield Gardens. But Gastrell had told Easterton, or at any rate led him to suppose, he was unmarried. How, then, could I refer to this woman by name without causing possible friction between Easterton and his tenant, Gastrell?

"I am afraid I can't tell you, Easterton," I said after an instant's hesitation. "I don't want to make mischief, and if what I think is possible is not the case, and I tell you about it, I shall have made mischief."

Easterton was silent. For some moments he remained seated in his corner of the settee, looking at me rather strangely.

"I quite understand what you mean, Berrington," he said at last. "Still, under the circumstances I should have thought - and yet no, I dare say you are right. I may tell you candidly, though, that I can't help thinkin' you must be mistaken in your supposition. Jack doesn't care about women in that way. He never has cared about them. The only thing he cares about is sport, though, of course, he admires a pretty woman, as we all do."

To that observation I deemed it prudent to make no reply, and at that moment a waiter entered and came across the room to us.

"Your lordship is wanted on the telephone," he said solemnly.

"Who is it?" Easterton asked, looking up.

"Scotland Yard, my lord."

"Oh, say, hold the line, and I'll come down."

"Have you informed the police, then?" I asked quickly, when the servant had left the room.

"Yes. I went to Scotland Yard this mornin', but I told them not to let a word about the disappearance get into the newspapers, if they could help it, until they heard further from me, and they promised they would respect my wish. You had better come down with me. They may have found out something."

I waited outside the glass hutch, which effectually shut in all sound, watching Lord Easterton's face below the electric light. His lips moved rapidly, and by the way his expression suddenly changed I judged that he was hearing news of importance. After talking for a minute or two he hung up the receiver, pushed open the door and came out. His face betrayed his emotion.

"Come over here," he said in a curious tone. "I have something to tell you."

I followed him a little way down the passage which led to the card-rooms. When we were out of sight and earshot of the club servants he stopped abruptly and turned to me.

"Jack has been found," he said quickly. "He was found gagged and bound in a house in Grafton Street half an hour ago. He is there now, and the police are with him."

"Good God!" I exclaimed. "How did they identify him?"

"He was not unconscious. The police want me to go there at once. Come."

We walked up to Grafton Street, as it was such a little way, also Easterton wanted to tell me more. The Inspector who had just spoken to him had not told him what had led to the police entering the house in Grafton Street, or if anybody else had been found upon the premises. He had only told him that Scotland Yard had for some weeks had the house under surveillance - they had suspected that something irregular was going on there, but they did not know what.

"I expect they have a pretty shrewd idea," Easterton added, as we crossed Piccadilly, "but they won't say what it is. Hello! Just look at the crowd!"

Up at the end of Dover Street, where Grafton Street begins, the roadway was blocked with people. When we reached the crowd we had some difficulty in forcing our way through it. A dozen policemen were keeping people back.

"Are you Lord Easterton?" the officer at the entrance asked, as Easterton handed him his card. "Ah, then come this way, please, m'lord. This gentleman a friend of yours? Follow the constable, please."

We were shown into a room on the ground floor, to the right of the hall. It was large, high-ceilinged, with a billiard table in the middle. Half a dozen men were standing about, two in police uniform; the remainder I guessed to be constables in plain clothes.

Suddenly I started, and uttered an exclamation.

Seated in a big arm-chair was Dulcie Challoner, looking pale, frightened. Beside her, with her back to me, stood Aunt Hannah!

CHAPTER VII

OSBORNE'S STORY

"Good heavens, Dulcie!" I exclaimed, hurrying across to her, "whatever are you doing here? And you, Aunt Hannah?"

At the sound of my voice Dulcie started up in her chair, and Aunt Hannah turned quickly. To my amazement they both looked at me without uttering. Dulcie's eyes were troubled. She seemed inclined to speak, yet afraid to. The expression with which Aunt Hannah peered at me chilled me.

"What is the meaning of this, Mr. Berrington?" she asked coldly, after a brief pause. Even in that moment of tense anxiety it struck me that Aunt Hannah looked and spoke as though reproving a naughty schoolboy.

"Meaning of what?" I said stupidly, astonishment for the moment deadening my intelligence.

"Of your bringing us up to London to find - this."

"Bringing you up? What do you mean, Miss Challoner?" I exclaimed, mystified.

In spite of my deep anxiety, a feeling of annoyance, of resentment, had come over me. No man likes to be made to look ridiculous, and here was I standing before a lot of constables, all of them staring in inquisitive astonishment at my being thus addressed by the old lady.

"Is this Mr. Berrington, madam?" an immensely tall, bull-necked, plain-clothes policeman, of pompous, forbidding mien, suddenly asked.

"Yes, officer, it is," she snapped. During all the time I had known her I had never seen her quite like this.

"See here," he said, turning to me, "I want your address, and for the present you will stay here."

I am considered good-tempered. Usually, too, I can control my feelings. There is a limit, however, to the amount of incivility I can stand, and this fellow was deliberately insulting me.

"How dare you speak like that to me!" I burst out. "What has this affair to do with me? Do you know who I am?"

"Aren't you Mr. Michael Berrington?" he inquired more guardedly, apparently taken aback at my outburst of indignation.

"I am."

"Then read that," he said, producing a telegram and holding it out before me.

It was addressed to:

"Miss Dulcie Challoner, Holt Manor, Holt Stacey," and ran:

"The police have recovered property which they believe to have been stolen from Holt Manor. Please come at once to 430 Grafton Street, Bond Street, to identify it. Shall expect you by train due Paddington 12:17. Please don't fail to come as matter very urgent.

"MICHAEL BERRINGTON."

It had been handed in at the office in Regent Street at 9:30

that morning, and received at Holt Stacey village at 9:43.

"How absurd! How ridiculous!" I exclaimed. "My name has been forged, of course. I never sent that telegram; this is the first I have seen or heard of it."

"That you will have to prove," the detective answered, with official stolidity.

"Surely, Aunt Hannah," I almost shouted - so excited did I feel - as I again turned to her, "you can't think I sent that telegram?"

"I certainly think nothing else," she replied, and her eyes were like shining beads. "Who would send a telegram signed with your name but you, or someone instructed by you?"

I saw that to argue with her in the frame of mind she was then in would be futile - my presentiment at Holt that some day I should fall foul of her had come true! I turned to the officer.

"I must see the original of that telegram," I said quickly, "and shall then quickly prove that it was not sent by me. How soon can I get hold of it?"

"Oh, we can see about it at once, sir," he answered much more civilly, for, pretending to look for something in my pocket, I had intentionally pulled out my leather wallet, containing two hundred pounds or more in notes, and opened it for an instant. There is nothing like the sight of paper money to ensure civility from a policeman disposed to be impertinent - I should like, in justice, to add that most policemen are not.

Also Easterton had come over and spoken to me, and of course pooh-poohed the idea of my having sent the telegram, which had just been shown to him. Dulcie stared at me with large, pathetic eyes, and I knew that, but for Aunt Hannah's so-to-speak mounting guard, she would have asked me endless questions instead of sitting there mute.

"You had better come with me and hear Jack Osborne's story," Easterton said some moments later. "The Inspector tells me he is upstairs, and still rather weak from the effect of the treatment he has received."

I had seen a puzzled look come into Aunt Hannah's eyes while Easterton was speaking, but she remained sour and unbending.

Osborne was sitting up in a chair, partly undressed - he still wore his evening clothes - cotton wool bound round his ankles and one wrist. He smiled weakly as we entered, and the policeman who sat at his bedside immediately rose. It was easy to see that Jack had suffered a good deal; he looked, for him, quite pale, and there were dark marks beneath his eyes. Nor was his appearance improved by several days' growth of beard - he was usually clean-shaven.

His story was quickly told, and points in it gave food for thought, also for conjecture.

It seemed that, while he was at supper with the woman I knew as "Mrs. Gastrell," at Gastrell's reception, two men, unable to find a vacant table, had asked if they might sit at his table, where there were two vacant seats. Both were strangers to him, and apparently to "Mrs. Gastrell" too. They seemed, however, pleasant fellows, and presently he had drifted into conversation with them, or they with him, and with his fair companion - Jack, as I have said, is extremely cosmopolitan, and picks up all sorts of acquaintances. I could well believe that at a reception such as Gastrell's he would waive all formality of introduction if he found himself with companionable strangers.

Supper over, the four had remained together, and later, when Jack had seen his fair friend safely into a cab, he had rejoined the two strangers, becoming gradually more and more friendly with them. The reception had not ended until past one in the morning, and he and his two acquaintances had been among the last to leave. Having all to go in the same direction, they had shared a taxi, and on arriving at the chambers which the strangers had told him they shared - these chambers were in Bloomsbury, but Jack had not noticed in what street - one of the strangers had suggested his coming in for a few minutes before returning to the Russell Hotel, where he had his rooms, which was close by.

At first disinclined to do this, he had finally yielded to their persuasion. He had a whiskey-and-soda with them, he said - he mentioned that the chambers were comfortable and well furnished - and one of them had then suggested a game of cards. They had all sat down to play, and -

Well, he remembered, he said, seeing cards being dealt - but that was all he did remember. He supposed that after that he must have fainted, or been made unconscious; he now suspected that the drink he had taken had been drugged.

When he recovered consciousness he had no idea where he was, or how long he had been insensible. The room was unfamiliar to him, and everything about him strange. He was stretched upon a bed, in an apartment much larger than the one he was now in, with hands and feet tightly tied. The two windows faced a blank wall, the wall apparently of the next house; later he came to know, by the sound of Big Ben booming in the night, that he was still in London.

The door of the room was at the back of the bed; he could not see it from where he lay, and, bound as he was, could not even turn, but was forced to lie flat upon his back.

He had not long been conscious, when the light of day began to fade. Soon the room was in pitch darkness. Then it was he became aware that someone was in the room. He listened attentively, but could hear nothing; nevertheless the presence of a man or woman made itself "felt" beyond a doubt. He judged the time of day to be about six o'clock in the evening, when suddenly somebody touched him - a hand in the darkness. He started, and called out; but there was no answer. Some minutes later a man spoke.

The voice was not that of either of the men he had met at Gastrell's reception; he could swear to that, he said. Yet he seemed to recognize the voice, indeed, to have heard it recently. He racked his brains to remember where, but to no purpose.

The man spoke in a low tone, and its *timbre* and inflection betrayed what is called the voice of a gentleman, he said.

"You have been brought here," the man said, "to give certain information, and to reveal certain secrets. If you do this, you will be released at once - you will be taken away from here in an unconscious state, just as you were brought here, and set down in the night not far from your hotel. If you refuse, you will be taken out during the night, and dropped into the Thames."

The man had then gone on to question him. The questions he had asked had been numerous, and one and all had had to do with persons of high station with whom Jack was on terms of intimacy - all of them rich people. What most astonished him, he said, was that his unseen interlocutor should know so much about him - his questions and remarks showed how much he knew - and that he should apparently know who all his friends were.

Jack could not remember all the questions he had been asked, but he repeated some of them. Whereabouts did the Duchesse de Montparnasse keep her jewels in her chateau on the Meuse? The questioner said he knew that Osborne could tell him, because he knew that Osborne, just before going to Nigeria, had, while staying at that chateau, been shown by the Duchesse herself her priceless jewellery - one of the finest collections in the world, chiefly valuable owing to its interesting historic associations.

Then, in which apartment in Eldon Hall, in Northumberland, the seat of the Earl of Cranmere, was the large safe that Lord Cranmere had bought ten months before from an American firm, the name of which was given? He said that he, Osborne, must know, because he was a guest at Lord Cranmere's when the safe arrived - which was the truth. He also wanted to know if there were a priests' hiding-hole in Eldon Hall, as was the case in so many of the large country mansions built about the same period, and, if so, its exact whereabouts in the house.

As Jack Osborne said this, my thoughts flashed away to Berkshire, to Holt Manor, to the dark, depressing hiding-hole there that I had peered down into more than once. Who had spoken to me of that hiding-hole only recently? Why, Dulcie, of course. She had mentioned it whilst telling me about Mrs. Stapleton, and about Sir Roland's showing the young widow over the house. Dulcie had mentioned it specially, because Mrs. Stapleton had evinced such evident interest in it.

I checked my train of thought, focussing my mind upon that single incident.

Mrs. Stapleton, the "mysterious widow" of whom nobody appeared to know anything, had been strangely interested in that hiding-hole and in all that Sir Roland had said about it - Dulcie had told me that. The hiding-hole was in close proximity to Sir Roland's bedroom, and to one other room from which valuable jewellery had been stolen. Mrs. Stapleton had left the neighbourhood on the day after the robbery, had been absent ever since - that of course might be, and probably was, merely a coincidence. At supper at Gastrell's reception in Cumberland Place Mrs. Stapleton had acknowledged "Mrs. Gastrell's" smile of recognition, and an instant later the two women had stared at each other stonily, and Mrs. Stapleton had assured me that she did not know the other woman, that she had "never seen her before." Then those two men, of whom Osborne had just spoken, had of their own accord joined him and "Mrs. Gastrell" at supper, and eventually he had gone with the men to their flat in Bloomsbury. And now here was an unseen man, evidently a scoundrel, inquiring the whereabouts of a safe in a country house belonging to a nobleman known to be extremely rich, and asking in particular if the house possessed a priests' hiding-hole, and if so, exactly where it was located - a man who threatened evil if the information were withheld. Could all this, I could not help wondering, be mere coincidence? Then on the top of it came that extraordinary telegram sent to Dulcie from London, with my name attached to it.

Jack, however, had not done relating his adventures, so I turned again to listen to him.

"A third thing the fellow asked," he said, "was the name of Hugo Salmonsteiner's bankers - Salmonsteiner the millionaire timber-merchant whose son was out big-game shooting with me a year ago. It seemed an absurd question, for surely it must be easy to find out who any man's bankers are, but still he asked me, and appeared to be most anxious that I should tell him. Oh, but there were scores of other questions, all much on the same lines, and tending to extract from me information of a peculiar kind."

"Did you answer any of them?" Easterton asked.

"Answer them? Why, of course - all of 'em. I didn't want to remain here in durance vile an hour longer than I could help, I can assure you. But naturally my answers were - well, 'inaccurate,' to say the least. I had to word them very carefully, though, or the fellow would have caught me out. He suspected that I might be misleading him, I think, for once or twice he put questions which might have unmasked me if I had not been on my guard when answering them. Really we pitted our brains and cunning against each other's all the time, and, if I may say so without boasting, I think my cunning won."

"Then why were you not released?" I said.

"I was to have been, to-night - *so he said.* Do you think, though, he would, whoever he was, have let me go after questioning me like that? He said not a word about my not giving information to the police, or warning the people he had questioned me about. Do you think he would have let me go? I don't.

"Every day food and drink were left by me - set on a table within reach of me, while the room was in inky blackness, for the man who had touched me in the dark had also released my right arm and left it so. Several times I tried to free my other arm, and my feet, but I couldn't manage it. I have been lying here with both feet and one arm bound for four nights and three days, to my knowledge, without seeing anybody, and, of course, without shaving or washing. I can't tell you what these days and nights have been like - they have been like a long, awful nightmare; even the house has all the time been as still as death. My God, what a relief it was to hear the door bell ringing this afternoon, and the knocker going as though the place was on fire!

"And when the police did force an entrance it seems they found nobody but me!"

CHAPTER VIII

MORE SUSPICIONS

Women are extraordinary - a platitude, of course, for everybody who has mixed with women and who possesses a gleam of intelligence knows that they are extraordinary, just as he knows, or ought to know, that if they were not *bizarre* and mystifying, complex and erratic, they would be less insidiously captivating than they are.

There are, however, exceptions to most rules - some misguided *savant* of a bygone epoch formulated a maxim which says that "the exception proves the rule," obviously an absurd statement, for if one man has no nose on his face it is no proof that all other men have noses on theirs. Aunt Hannah constituted an exception to the rule that women are rendered additionally attractive through being extraordinary. Had she been less extraordinary she would have been more lovable. As it was she came near, at this time, to being the reverse of lovable, or so it struck me when, upon my endeavour to talk calmly and rationally to her after hearing all that Jack Osborne had just told us, and striving to induce her to listen to reason, she remained prejudiced, illogical.

I should not have cared a button, naturally, had it not been for Dulcie and the estrangement between us that the foolish old lady's behaviour created. Dulcie thought no end of her aunt, respected her views and sentiments - she had been brought up to do so, poor child - and, I knew, really loved her. "Well," I said to myself tartly, "she will now have to choose between Aunt Hannah and me," and feeling cock-sure, after all that had occurred between us, that I should be the favoured one and that Aunt Hannah would be metaphorically relegated to the scrap-heap, I decided to approach Dulcie at once.

No, first I must see the original of that telegram, I reflected. Accompanied, therefore, by the police officer, I made my way to the post office in Regent Street. Having explained that I wanted to see the original of the telegram "because," as I said, "I think a mistake has been made in transcribing it," I was presently confronted by the postmaster, a most courteous, obliging person.

"Why, certainly," he said, when I had repeated my untruth. "You shall see it at once."

I waited in anxious expectancy, chatting lightly with the policeman, while the postmaster looked through the file of the day's messages.

"This is it, I think," he said presently - we were in his private room. "But," he went on, glancing from the message that had been sent to the original, "your original message is unsigned. Is that the alleged mistake of which you complain?"

"Unsigned!" I exclaimed, taking both papers from him. "Why yes, so it is! Then how does that message that was sent off come to be signed?"

The original message was type-written. The wording was exactly the same as that in the telegram received, with this exception - the telegram received was signed "Michael Berrington," the typed message had no signature.

"How do you account for this discrepancy?" I asked quickly.

"If you will kindly wait a moment," he answered, "I will inquire into this."

He left the room. The policeman, to whom I had handed both

messages, was still contemplating them with a look of perplexity in his round eyes, when the postmaster returned, bringing with him an intelligent-looking girl.

"This," he said, "is the young lady who transmitted the message."

I am afraid I smiled. How long, I wonder, will post-office assistants, and shop girls, bar tenders, and others continue to be "young ladies," while ladies in the correct sense of the word never think, when talking of one another, of using terms more distinctive and dignified than "girl" and "woman"?

"Do you remember my sending this telegram this morning?" I asked, looking her full in the eyes.

"I remember taking in the message, but I'm afraid I don't remember your face, sir," she answered nervously, evidently afraid that I was about to get her into trouble. "You see, we see so many people, and most of them only for a few moments. I recall rather clearly taking in that message, because it was typed, which most telegrams are not. And - and I thought it was handed in by a lady, and not by a gentleman. In fact I feel sure it was. Was it really you who gave it to me to send off?"

"No, it was not," I answered quickly. "A lady? Can you remember what she was like?"

"I can. She was, I think, really the most beautiful lady I have ever seen. She was quite tall, as tall as a man, and she had a lovely figure. It did seem to set off her beautiful clothes so well. Then her face was lovely too - long, dark eyebrows she had, if I remember rightly, and her eyes were large. Oh, and she had a lot of auburn hair - red you might almost call it - I don't know which it was really, but I never saw such hair."

"Good!" I exclaimed.

I turned to the policeman.

"She has described beyond doubt a woman I know; a woman you will probably soon know something about too."

"Indeed, sir?" he said, interested.

"But about this signature," I went on, again addressing the operator. "How does this telegram you sent off come to be signed if the original was not signed?"

"It was signed, sir. It must have been. Otherwise the name wouldn't have been telegraphed. Ah - I remember!"

"Remember what?"

"The signature was in pencil. Just after the telegram had been despatched, the lady came in again and asked if she might see the message again just for a moment - she was not sure if she had said something she had meant to say, she said. I got it and gave it to her, and a moment or two afterwards she gave it back to me, thanking me very much for having let her see it. She must have rubbed off the signature then. She could do it easy with a damp finger. Of course, I ought to have looked, but I didn't think to."

"I think we have now solved the mystery - in part," I exclaimed triumphantly. "This is some abominable conspiracy, and I am going to get to the bottom of it. My name was evidently signed, telegraphed, and then purposely obliterated."

After thanking the postmaster for his extreme courtesy and for the trouble he had taken, and impressing upon him that under no circumstances was the bright-eyed little operator to be censured, or allowed to get into any trouble, I returned with the policeman, who was now quite apologetic, to the house in Grafton Street. The door was locked. A constable standing by, however, told us that Osborne and Easterton had driven away together in a car - "his lordship's car, which his lordship had telephoned for," he said, and that "the two ladies had gone to the Ritz for tea" - he had heard them say, as they walked away, that they were going there.

Alone I followed them. I know my way about the Ritz as though I lived there, being there so often with friends, and I soon found Aunt Hannah and Dulcie. They were alone in a cosy private tea-room leading out of one of the large rooms which is but seldom used, having tea.

I saw Aunt Hannah stiffen as I approached. I saw too - and this disturbed me far more - that Dulcie had been weeping. Her eyes were still quite moist.

"What do you wish, Mr. Berrington?" Aunt Hannah inquired starchily, sitting bolt upright in her chair as I approached.

I detest the use of the word "wish" in place of "want"; I don't know why, but I always associate it with prim, prudish, highly-conventional old ladies.

"I have come to explain everything, and to set your mind at rest," I said, trying to speak lightly, and intentionally saying "mind" instead of "minds," for I did not want Dulcie to suppose that I thought she shared her aunt's grotesque belief in this matter - the belief that I actually had sent that hateful telegram.

"I hope you will succeed," Aunt Hannah observed, then shut her lips tightly.

She did not offer me a cup of tea, but I feigned not to notice this paltry affront, and proceeded briefly to relate what had just taken place at the post office. At last, when I had, as I thought, completely cleared my character, I stopped speaking. To my surprise the old lady remained as unbending as ever.

"I don't know why I've gone to the trouble of telling you all this," I said, hiding the mortification I felt, "but you see, at any rate, that I *had* an explanation to offer, though I grant you that at present it can only be a partial one. That is no fault of mine, however."

"'Partial' - yes, it certainly is that," muttered the old lady.

Aunt Hannah has small green eyes, and they seemed to snap. She still sat up stiffly, her entire aspect rigid.

"This," I thought, "is the limit. Decidedly the moment of battle has arrived" - indeed, the initial encounter had already taken place. I don't mind confessing that my spirit quailed - for an instant. Then, realizing that I was "up against it," my courage returned. My engagement to Dulcie hung in the balance. I must face the music.

Perhaps at first I overdid it, but something is to be conceded to nervousness. Aunt Hannah kept tapping her teaspoon against her saucer with nervous little taps. The constant "small noise" was very irritating. Determined to stop it, I leant suddenly forward across the little table, till my face was close to Aunt Hannah's. Anger boiled in my heart. Sympathy for Dulcie rose up and flooded my mind. Though I allowed my most charming "boudoir" smile to overspread my face, it was all I could do not to seize hold of that old lady and shake her. Inwardly I craved to grasp her lean wrists in a firm grip, and force her to listen to reason. "A dear" Dulcie had sometimes called her. "A dear" she might be when in a nice mood, but in the peevish vein she was now in, her obstinacy held a particularly maddening quality.

"You know," I said, still smiling hypocritically, "you are really *trying* to disbelieve me now. You are trying to make mischief between Dulcie and me - and you enjoy it," and I glanced in the direction of my darling, whose eyes were shining strangely. "Why don't you answer?" I went on, as Aunt Hannah remained silent; I could hear her gulping with rage. At last she spoke:

"What impudence - what unwarrantable impudence!" The

words were shot from between her teeth. "You - you dare to speak to me like this - you - you - "

"After all, Miss Challoner," I cut in, "it's true. I no more sent that, or any telegram, to Dulcie than I am flying over the moon at this moment. And if you still disbelieve me, at least tell me why. Yes, I must know. Don't evade an answer. You have something else in your mind, I can see that, and I am not going to rest until I know what that something is."

"Oh, you very rude young man," she burst out. "Yes, you shall know what it is! If, as you say, the telegram was not sent by you - and I suppose I must believe you - why was it not sent to Sir Roland? Such a telegram should have been sent to him, and not to his daughter - if the stolen property had been found, it was for him to come to Town, or even for me to, but certainly it was not Dulcie's place to go gallivanting about in London. Now, I maintain it was sent to Dulcie because the sender knew Sir Roland to be away from home - and who, but you, knew him to be away? He left only yesterday, and he should return to-night. You knew because, so my niece tells me, she told you in a letter that he was to leave home for a day."

"My niece!" Really, Aunt Hannah was qualifying for *opera bouffe!* Just then she knocked her spoon so loudly against her cup that it startled me.

"Don't worry, Dulcie," I said, seeing how distressed she looked. "You believe I didn't send it, anyway - I don't mind what anybody else thinks," I added spitefully. "The mystery will be cleared up sooner or later, and 'he laughs longest ...' you know the rest. Only one thing I wonder," I ended, again facing Aunt Hannah, "if you thought that, why did you bring Dulcie up to town? Why didn't you leave her at Holt, and come up alone?"

"I will tell you why," she snapped back. "Because, wilful and disobedient as she has always been, she refused to stay at Holt and let me come up alone."

Dulcie looked at me without answering, and I read love and confidence in her eyes. That was all I really cared to know, and the look afforded me immense relief.

I felt there was no good purpose to be served by remaining there longer, so after shaking hands warmly with Dulcie - to the manifold disapproval of Aunt Hannah, who stared at me frigidly and barely even bowed as I took my leave - I sauntered out into Piccadilly.

My thoughts wandered. They were not, I must say, of the happiest. Obviously there was an enemy somewhere - it might be enemies. But who could it be? Why should I have, we have - for Dulcie suffered equally - an enemy? What reason could anyone have for wishing to make Dulcie, or me, or any of the Challoners, unhappy? Everybody I knew who knew them seemed to love them, particularly the tenantry. Sir Roland was looked up to and respected by both county people and villagers for miles around Holt Stacey, while Dulcie was literally adored by men and women alike, or so I believed. True, old Aunt Hannah sometimes put people out owing to her eccentricities and her irascible temper, but then they mostly looked upon her as a rather queer old lady, and made allowances for her, and she had not, I felt sure, an enemy in the country-side.

As for myself, well, I could not recollect ever doing any particularly bad turn - I had my likes and dislikes among the people I knew, naturally. Then suddenly a thought struck me - my engagement to Dulcie. Could that be -

I smiled as I dismissed the thought - it seemed too grotesque. No; once and for all I decided that the whole affair could have nothing to do with any kind of personal animosity. Criminals were at work, desperate criminals, perhaps, and Osborne and Dulcie and I had chanced to prove very useful as pawns in some scheme of theirs for securing plunder. I glanced at my watch. It was just five o'clock. Concluding that Jack Osborne must now be at his rooms, I drove to the Russell Hotel. Yes, he particularly wanted to see me; would I please go up at once, the clerk said when he had telephoned up my name and my inquiry if Mr. Osborne were at home to anybody.

Easterton was with him still; a doctor was on the point of leaving as I entered the room where Jack sat in his dressing-gown in a big chair, drinking a cup of soup. Already he looked better, I thought, than when I had seen him at the house in Grafton Street, barely two hours before.

After exchanging a few remarks with him, and being assured by Easterton that the doctor had said that Jack might now see anyone he pleased, I came straight to the question of the telegram, repeating to him almost word for word what I had told Aunt Hannah.

For nearly a minute after I had stopped speaking he did not utter. He appeared to be thinking deeply, judging by the way his brows were knit. Then, suddenly looking straight at me, he said:

"Mike, I don't like this business - I don't like it at all. There's something radically wrong about the whole thing. Now, look here, you know that when I say a thing I mean it. Therefore I tell you this - I am going to set to work, as soon as I have quite recovered from the nightmare I have been through, to discover what is happening. I am going to solve every detail of this mystery, and if there is some gang of scoundrels at work committing burglaries and what not - because I feel quite sure this affair is in some way connected with the robbery at Holt - I am going to get them convicted. The doctor tells me I shall be perfectly all right in a couple of days. I have nothing to do. You have nothing to do. Will you join me in this attempt I am going to make to track these men down? I hear it said that you are engaged to be married to Dulcie Challoner. If that's so, then you should be even more anxious than I am to get this gang arrested - the police say it must be a gang. They have looted some thousands of pounds' worth of jewellery which practically belonged to Dulcie Challoner. Think what it will mean to her if through your efforts all that is restored to her.

Besides, she will think you a hero - I mean an even greater hero than she already considers you, most likely; I confess I don't agree with her, old man. You are a very good chap - but a hero? No. Say, then, will you help me in this search? It may prove exciting too; on the other hand, it may not."

Jack's breezy manner and almost boyish enthusiasm appealed to me. After all, I had, as he said, nothing on earth to do - I often wished I had - and I was rather keen on anything that might lead to or savour of adventure. Though I was engaged to Dulcie, there were family reasons why the marriage could not take place at once, and then I thought again of what Jack had just said about the stolen jewels - Dulcie was still greatly upset at their loss, and there was even the possibility, I thought with a smile, that if I were directly or indirectly responsible for their recovery Aunt Hannah might eventually deign again to smile upon me - which would, of course, give me great joy!

"Yes, old chap," I said, "I'll do anything you jolly well like. I'm sick of doing nothing."

"First rate!" he answered. "Then that's settled. I've all sorts of ideas and theories about the Holt Manor robbery and this affair of mine, and that telegram to-day, and other things that have happened - some you know about, some you don't. I have a friend who was for twenty years at Scotland Yard - George Preston, wonderful chap, knows London upside-down and inside-out, and now he's kicking his heels with nothing to do he'll be only too glad to earn a bit. You might ring him up for me now, and ask him to come here to-morrow."

Somebody knocked, and I went to the door, Jack having told me that he did not want to see anybody likely to bore him.

It was only an hotel messenger. The clerk in the office had tried to ring up the room, he said, but could get no answer. Turning, I saw that Jack had forgotten to replace the receiver the last time he had spoken.

"What do you want?" I asked.

The messenger said that a "young gentleman" had just called. He wanted to see "a Mr. Berrington" who was probably with Mr. Osborne.

"What about?" I said. "And didn't he give his name?"

"He wouldn't say what about, sir, though he was asked. He said it was 'most important.' He said to say 'Mr. Richard Challoner.'"

"Dick!" I exclaimed. "Good heavens, what is Dick doing up in London? Oh, go down," I said to the messenger, "and send him up at once."

"It's Dick Challoner," I said, turning to Osborne and Easterton, "Sir Roland's boy, the little chap I told you about who behaved so pluckily when the thieves at Holt got hold of him. I wonder what *he's* doing in town, and why he wants to see me."

Then I sat down, lit a cigarette, and waited. I little suspected what an amazing story I was about to hear.

CHAPTER IX

THE SNARE

Dick's face bore a broad grin as he entered the room. He looked dreadfully mischievous. Assuming as serious an expression as I could conjure, I said to him:

"Why, what's the meaning of this, Dick? How do you come to be in town? Are you with Aunt Hannah?"

"It's all right - brother-in-law," he answered lightly. "No, I am not with Aunt Hannah, nor is Aunt Hannah with me. I have come up on my own."

"'On your own'? What do you mean?"

"I'll tell you, but - won't you introduce me, Mike?"

"Easterton," I said, "this is Roland Challoner's boy, Dick. Jack, this is the boy I told you about who was chloroformed by the thieves at Holt."

Jack's eyes rested on Dick. Then he put out his hand.

"Come here, old chap," he said in his deep voice. For several moments he held Dick's hand in his while he sat looking at him.

"Yes," he said at last, "I have heard about you - Dick. I heard about what you did that day those men caught you. Keep that spirit up, my boy - your family has never lacked pluck, if history is to be trusted - and you'll become one of the kind of men England so badly needs. What are you doing in London? Is your father with you?"

"No, I have come up on my own," Dick repeated. "I am going to tell Mike why, in a moment. Are you Mr. Jack Osborne that Mike is always talking to my sister about, who took Mike to that house - the house where the fire was?"

"Yes, I am," Jack answered, laughing. "Why?"

"Oh, because my sister didn't like your taking Mike there, you know - she didn't like it a bit. She and Mike are going to be married, you know, and Mike is going to be my brother-in-law."

I pounced upon him to make him be quiet, though Easterton and Osborne clamoured that he should be left alone and allowed to say anything he liked, Jack declaring that he wanted to hear "more of this romance."

At last we all became serious, and then Dick said:

"I made a discovery this morning at Holt. There is someone hidden in the old hiding-hole close to father's bedroom."

"Hidden in it!" I exclaimed. "Oh, nonsense!"

"Your telegram to Dulcie arrived at about half-past ten this morning," he went on, not heeding my remark, "and she and Aunt Hannah at once got ready to go to town - I know what was in the telegram, because Dulcie told me. About an hour after they were gone, I happened to go up to father's bedroom to fetch something, and when I came out again I noticed an odd sound - at first I couldn't think where it came from. It was like someone breathing very heavily, someone asleep. I stood quite still, and soon I found that it came from the priests' hiding-hole - you know it, you have seen it. I went over on tip-toe, got into the angle where the opening to the hole is, and pressed my ear down on the sliding board. I could hear the sound quite well then - somebody breathing awfully heavily. First I thought of sliding back the board and peeping in. Then I decided I wouldn't do that until I'd got somebody else with me. I noticed that the sliding board was unbolted - there is a little bolt on the side of it, you know - so I very quietly pushed forward the bolt and then went downstairs to look for James or Charles - that's the butler and the footman, you know," he said to Jack. "Cook told me they had both gone into Newbury for the day, and of course father's chauffeur was out with the car - he had taken Aunt Hannah and Dulcie to Holt Stacey to catch the train to London, and I knew that he would take a day off too, because he always does when he gets the chance - father isn't expected back until to-night. So then I went to try to find Churchill, or one of the other gardeners - goodness knows where they were hiding themselves. Anyway, I couldn't find them, nor could I find either of the keepers; in fact, I seemed to be the only man on the place."

"Well, go on," I said, as he paused. "You were the only man on the place. What did the only 'man' do then?"

"I'll tell you if you'll wait a moment - my brother-in-law is always so beastly impatient," he said, turning again to Jack. "Don't you find him like that, Mr. Osborne?"

"I do - always. But go on, old boy, I'm very interested."

"And so am I," Easterton laughed.

"Of course, it was no use telling cook or the maids; they'd have got what cook calls 'styricks' or something, so then it suddenly struck me the best thing for me to do would be to come right up to town and find Aunt Hannah and tell her. I knew where she'd be, because you'd said in your telegram - four hundred and thirty Grafton Street. I didn't know where Grafton Street was, but I thought I could find out - I borrowed money from cook for the railway ticket, though I didn't tell her what I wanted it for, or she wouldn't have given it to me, and directly after lunch I bicycled to Holt Stacey station and caught the train.

"I got to Grafton Street all right by a 'bus down Bond Street. There was a policeman standing near the house in Grafton Street, and when I rang the bell he came up and asked me what I wanted. I told him, and he said he thought I'd find 'the two ladies I wanted' at the Ritz Hotel. I knew where that was, and he showed me the way to get to it, down Dover Street - of course, if I'd had money enough I'd have taken taxis and got about much quicker. A giant in livery at the Ritz Hotel told me that 'two ladies answering to the description of the ladies I sought' had left the hotel about a quarter of an hour before I got there, and he didn't know where they had gone. Then I went to Brooks's to see if you were there, but you weren't, though they said you'd been there. That put the lid on it. I didn't know what to do, and I'd only got tenpence ha'penny left. I was awfully hungry, so I went and had tea and buns at the A.B.C. shop at Piccadilly Circus. While I was having tea I remembered hearing you tell Dulcie that Mr. Osborne lived at the Russell Hotel. I'd have telephoned to Mr. Osborne and explained who I was and asked him if he could tell me where I could find you, and I'd have telephoned too to your flat in South Molton Street to ask if you were there, but I'd got only fivepence ha'penny left after tea, and you might both have been out and then I'd have had only a penny-ha'penny and Paddington seemed an awfully long way to walk to, and I wasn't quite sure of the way, so I'd have had to keep asking, and that's such a bore, isn't it?

"So after tea I got on to the tube and came here and asked for Mr. Osborne. The man downstairs told me 'two gentlemen were with him,' and I asked him what they were like. He told me as well as he could, and I guessed from the description one of them must be you, and then just after the messenger had come up to ask if it was you and to tell you I was there, another hotel man turned up downstairs, and I talked to him, and he said he knew a Mr. Berrington was with Mr. Osborne because he, the man, had telephoned up your name a little while before, and Mr. Osborne had said to show you up. And so here I am, and that's all."

He stopped abruptly, breathless after his long talk, which had been delivered without an instant's pause.

"For your age you seem fairly intelligent," Jack said, with a look of amusement.

"Yes, fairly," Dick retorted. "But my brother-in-law says that 'when he was my age' the world was a much better and finer place, that the boys did wonderful things - 'when he was my age.' He says, for instance, that he talked Latin and Greek and German and French and one or two other languages just as you talk English, Mr. Osborne, 'when he was my age' - funny how he has forgotten them all, isn't it? My sister told me only yesterday that Mike talks French fluently, but that his German 'leaves much to be desired.' Those were her words. Were all the boys wonderful when you were my age too, Mr. Osborne, can you remember? Another thing Mike says is that 'when he was my age' all boys were taught to swim by being taken to the ends of piers and flung into the sea - Mike says he was taught like that just as the rest were, and that he jolly well had to swim or he'd have been drowned, which seems pretty obvious, doesn't it, when you come to think of it? When did the fashion of teaching boys to swim like that go out, Mr. Osborne? I'm jolly glad it has gone out."

When I had succeeded in checking Dick's flow of talk and quelling his high spirits, and had questioned him further with regard to the man he declared to be in hiding at Holt - though without my being able to obtain from him any further information - I turned to Jack.

"What do you make of it?" I said. "What do you suggest ought to be done?"

"I think," he answered after a moment's pause, "that it affords an excellent excuse for you to run down to Holt to-night."

"Oh, good!" Dick exclaimed, jumping with excitement. "And there's a train at a quarter to seven that we can catch; it gets to Holt Stacey at five minutes to eight."

Jack glanced up at the clock.

"In three quarters of an hour's time," he said. "That will suit you, Mike, and you'll be glad, I know, of the excuse to go down to Holt to see the flowers and - and things. Don't think I suppose for a moment that you want to see either Dulcie Challoner or the old lady you call 'Aunt Hannah,' but still if you should see them, and of course you will - "

"Oh, he'll see them right enough," Dick burst out, "especially my sister. There aren't any flies on my brother-in-law, you bet!"

I boxed Dick's ears, but he didn't seem to mind. Perhaps I didn't box them very hard, for instead of howling as he ought to have done, he looked up at me sharply and exclaimed:

"Then you're coming down to Holt now! Hooray! We'll go down together - how ripping! I'll telephone to say you're coming, and say to get your room ready," and he sprang across to the instrument by the bedside.

I stopped him, gripping him by the shoulder, though not before he had pulled off the receiver and called through to the operator - "Trunks, please!"

"You'll do nothing of the sort," I said, "and look here, Dick, you are in Mr. Osborne's rooms, and not in your own playroom, so don't forget it."

I felt greatly preoccupied as the train sped down to Berkshire - anxious, too, about many things, not the least of these being how I should be received. Would Sir Roland have returned? Would Aunt Hannah have told him everything? If so would he have adopted her view with regard to the sending of that telegram, and with regard to other matters? And Dulcie, would she at last have come to think as Aunt Hannah thought? I could not believe she would have, but still -

As I have said, women are so extraordinary, that there is no knowing what they may not do, no accounting for what they may do.

Knowing there would be no conveyance obtainable at Holt Stacey, I had decided to go on to Newbury. On our alighting at Newbury I suddenly heard Dick's shrill voice calling:

"Why, Mike, there's father!"

Sir Roland had just got out of a compartment further up the train, and soon we were in conversation. He too had come from London, but whereas Dick and I had only just caught the train, Sir Roland had, he said, entered it as soon as it came into the station, which accounted for our not having seen him at Paddington. As we walked along the Newbury platform I explained to him very briefly the reason I had come down, and how it was I had Dick with me, inwardly congratulating myself upon my good fortune in thus meeting Sir Roland and so being able to explain everything to him concerning what had happened that day, before he should meet his sister and hear what she would tell him.

"It was only at the last moment I decided to come by this train," Sir Roland said as he entered the taxi that a porter had hailed, and I followed him, while Dick hopped in after us. "How tiresome it is one can't get a conveyance at Holt Stacey; people are for ever complaining to me about it. As I have not telegraphed for the car to meet me I had to come on to Newbury."

"I came to Newbury for the same reason," I said; and then, as the taxi rolled swiftly along the dark lanes, for we had a twelve miles' run before us, I gave Sir Roland a detailed account of all that had happened that day, from the time Easterton had rung me up at my flat to tell me of Jack Osborne's disappearance and to ask me to come to him at once, down to the sudden and unexpected arrival of Dick at Jack's rooms at the Russell Hotel.

Sir Roland was astounded, and a good deal perturbed. Several times during the course of my narrative he had interrupted in order to put some question or other to Dick. At first he had reproved him for going to London on what Dick called "his own"; but when I told him more he admitted that what the boy had done he had done probably for the best.

"Oh, I haven't told you one thing," Dick suddenly interrupted.

"Well, what?" Sir Roland asked.

"While I was on my way to Holt Stacey this morning, Mrs. Stapleton passed me in her car. I was on that part of the road, about a mile from the lodge, where if you look round you can see a long bit of the avenue. I wondered if Mrs. Stapleton were going to Holt by any chance, so I bicycled rather slowly for a minute or two, and looked round once or twice. I had guessed right, because all at once I saw her car going up the avenue."

"Are you sure it was Mrs. Stapleton?" I asked, suddenly interested.

"Oh, quite. But I don't think she saw me, her car went by so fast."

"Was anybody with her?"

"No, she was alone - the chauffeur was driving."

"And the car that went up the drive, are you sure it was the same?"

"Positive - that long grey car of hers, I'd know it anywhere;

you can recognize it ever so far away."

We were half a mile from the lodge, now. Soon we had shot through the open gates, and were sliding up the splendid avenue. I felt intensely excited, also happier than when in the train, for I knew I now possessed Sir Roland's entire confidence. Delicious was it to think that in a few minutes I should see Dulcie again, but what excited me - and I knew it must be exciting Sir Roland too - was the thought of that man - or would it prove to be a woman? - lying concealed in the hiding-hole. Who could he be? How long had he been there? How had he got there and what could he be doing?

I had told Sir Roland of the false conclusion Aunt Hannah had come to with regard to the sending of that typed telegram, and how bitterly she had spoken to me about it - I had thought it best to prepare him for the absurd story that I felt sure Aunt Hannah would proceed to pour into his ear directly she met him. To my relief he had laughed, appearing to treat the matter of her annoyance and suspicion as a joke, though the sending of the telegram he looked upon, naturally, as a very grave matter. Consequently, upon our arrival at Holt, instead of inquiring for his sister, and at once consulting her upon the subject of the day's events, as he would, I knew, have done under ordinary circumstances, he told Charles, the footman, to send the butler to him at once, and to return with him.

We were now in the little library - Sir Roland and myself, Dick, the butler and the footman, and the door was shut. Without any preliminaries Sir Roland came straight to the point. He told the two servants of Dick's discovery that morning, told them that presumably the man was still in hiding where Dick had bolted him down, and that the four of us were at once going, as he put it, "to unearth the scoundrel."

"And you will stay here, Dick," Sir Roland added. "We shall not need your services at this juncture."

Dick was, I could see, deeply disappointed at, as he put it to me in an undertone, "being side-tracked like this by the guv'nor when it was I who marked the beggar to ground "; but his father's word was law, and he knew it.

"Never mind, my dear old chap," I said, as I noticed a slight quiver of the under lip, "directly we've unearthed him and got him safely bagged I'll come and tell you what he looks like and all about him. You see, your father doesn't want to run unnecessary risk - you're the only boy he's got, and this man may be armed. You would be annoyed if the fellow were to make holes in you, and I should be vexed too; greatly vexed."

Dick laughed at that, and when, a minute later, we left him, he was happier in his mind.

No sound was audible as we stood above the priests' hole, listening intently. This hiding-place was oddly situated, and ingeniously constructed. In an angle formed by two walls with old oak wainscoting was a sliding floor - in reality it was a single board, but it was made to resemble so exactly several boards set parallel and horizontally that none could believe it to be a single board unless they were shown. Immediately beneath was a room, or closet, not much bigger than a very large cupboard, which could accommodate three men standing, or two seated. In olden days this sliding board was covered with tapestry, and being made in such a way that, when stamped upon or struck, no hollow sound was emitted, it formed a safe place of concealment for any outlawed person for whom the emissaries of the law might be in search. To this day the board slides away into the wall as "sweetly" as it did in the days of the Reformation; but Sir Roland, owing to an accident having once occurred through someone leaving the hole uncovered, had affixed a small bolt to the board and given orders that this bolt should always be kept pushed into its socket.

When we had all stood listening for fully a minute, Sir Roland said suddenly:

"Charles, draw the bolt and slide back the board - get back, James!" he exclaimed sharply to the butler, who in his anxiety to see what would be revealed was bending forward.

"D'you want to be shot? Whoever the man may be he is pretty sure to be armed."

An instant later the board had vanished into the wall, and Sir Roland stood peering down exactly as he had warned his butler not to do.

"By Jove!" he exclaimed.

Casting prudence aside, we all pressed forward and looked down into the hole. Huddled in a heap at the bottom was a man in hunting kit - white breeches, top boots and "pink" coat. Sitting along the floor, he was bent almost double, so that we could not see his face.

"Hello!" Sir Roland called out, "who are you? What are you doing there?"

But the figure didn't move.

At one end of the hiding-hole a ladder was nailed vertically. The feet of the man touched its lowest rung. Turning, Sir Roland began carefully to descend.

"Let me, sir!" the butler exclaimed excitedly, "let me - it's not safe - he may attack you, sir!"

Without answering Sir Roland continued to clamber down. Now he stood upon the floor of the hiding-hole, at the foot of the figure. We saw him stoop, raise the man's head, and bend the body upward until the back rested against the other end of the hole.

An exclamation escaped us simultaneously. The face was that of a man of twenty-seven or so, though the stubbly beard and moustache, apparently a week's growth or more, at first gave the idea that he was much older. The eyes were closed and sunken. The mouth gaped. The face was deathly pale and terribly emaciated.

"By Gad!" gasped Sir Roland, as he took hold of the wrist and felt for the pulse. "My Gad, I think he's dead!"

CHAPTER X

NARRATES A CONFESSION

Half an hour later the man found in the hiding-hole lay upon a bed in one of the spare rooms.

Though not dead, he had, when discovered, been in the last stage of exhaustion. The doctor telephoned for had at once discovered that what we already suspected was true - the man's left ankle was very badly sprained. It must, he said, have been sprained ten or twelve days previously. In addition, the man was almost like a skeleton.

"You found him not an hour too soon," the doctor said when, after completing his diagnosis, and giving instructions concerning the treatment of his patient to the nurse who had just arrived, he rejoined us in the smoking-room downstairs. "He is in a state of complete collapse. For days he has evidently not touched food."

He looked at us in turn with an odd expression as he said this. He was clearly mystified at finding a man at Holt Manor dying of starvation - a starving man dressed for the chase, a man obviously of refinement, and undoubtedly to be described as a gentleman.

Sir Roland decided under the circumstances to tell the doctor everything: how the man's presence had been discovered by Dick, how we had afterwards found him lying upon the floor of the hiding-hole, apparently dead, and how, with the help of ropes, we had finally pulled him out. The doctor had, of course, heard of the robbery at Holt nearly a fortnight before, and he at once put two and two together.

For two days the stranger quivered between life and death. Two nurses were in constant attendance, and the doctor called frequently. It was on the afternoon of the third day that he expressed a desire to talk to Sir Roland; he had, until then, been allowed to speak only a word or two.

He wanted, he said, "to speak with Sir Roland alone"; but to this Sir Roland would not agree.

"If you want to speak to me, you can speak quite freely before this gentleman," he said; I was in the room at the time.

At first the man seemed distressed, but at last, finding that Sir Roland would make no concession, he said in a weak voice:

"I'm dying, Sir Roland, I feel it, and before I go there are things I should like to say to you - things that it may be to your advantage to hear."

His voice, I noticed, had in it the *timbre* peculiar to the voices of men of education.

"Say anything you like," Sir Roland answered coldly.

"You have been exceedingly kind to me: there are men who, finding me in concealment as you found me, and after what has happened in this house, would at once have called in the police. You may believe me or not, but I am extremely grateful to you. And I want to show my gratitude in the only way I can."

He paused for nearly a minute, then continued:

"Sir Roland, I will tell you as much as I am justified in telling about the robbery; but first, has anybody concerned in it been arrested?"

Sir Roland shook his head.

"Nobody - as yet," he answered. "The police have not discovered even the smallest clue."

"I and another were in your bedroom when your son suddenly sprang from behind the screen," the stranger went on. "Again you may believe me or not, but I tried to prevent my companion from doing him any injury. It was I who put the chloroform on the boy, but I did him no other harm, I swear, sir."

I saw Sir Roland's eyes blaze. Then, as his glance rested upon the stranger's starved, almost ashen face - it seemed to be gradually growing livid - the sternness of his expression relaxed.

"How came you to be in hiding here?" he asked abruptly. "How many accomplices had you?"

"Seven," the stranger replied, without an instant's hesitation. "The robbery was carefully planned; it was planned so carefully that it seemed without the bounds of possibility that it could fail to succeed. I and others were at your hunt breakfast - "

"Were your accomplices all men?" I interrupted sharply.

The man's stare met mine. He looked at me with, I thought, singular malevolence.

"They were not," he answered quietly. He turned again to Sir Roland. "Just after your son had been rendered unconscious, I had the misfortune to slip up on the polished floor and sprain my ankle badly. No sooner did my companion realize what had happened, than he snatched from me all the stolen property I held, in spite of my endeavour to prevent him, then emptied my pockets, and left me. Dismayed at being thus deserted - for unless I could hide at once I must, I knew, quickly be discovered - I crawled out of the room on all fours, and along the landing as far as the angle where the hiding-place is. The hole was open - we had opened it before entering your room, lest we might be surprised and suddenly forced to hide. Almost as I reached it I heard somebody coming. Instantly I scrambled down and slid the board over my head."

"How came you to know of the existence and the whereabouts of the hiding-hole at all?" Sir Roland inquired, eyeing the stranger suspiciously.

"That I do not wish to tell. I hoped ultimately to be rescued by my accomplices, and for that reason I made no sound which might have revealed my presence. My ankle had swollen considerably, and, confined in my riding-boot, which I couldn't pull off, it gave me intense pain. To clamber out unaided was consequently an impossibility; so there I lay, slowly starving, hoping, night after night, that my accomplices would force an entrance into the house and rescue me, for my companion who left me must have guessed where I was in hiding - we had agreed, as I have said, to seek concealment in that hole should either of us be driven to hide in order to escape detection."

"Was the man who deserted you the man who deliberately strained my boy's arm by twisting it?" Sir Roland asked.

"Yes."

"What is his name?"

"Gastrell - Hugesson Gastrell, that's the name the brute is known by. He always was a blackguard - a perisher! I shall refuse to betray any of the others; they are my friends. But Hugesson Gastrell - don't forget that name, Sir Roland. You may some day be very glad I told it to you - the man of The Four Faces!"

He paused. He seemed suddenly to be growing weaker. As we sat there, watching him, I could not help in a sense feeling pity for the fellow, and I knew that Sir Roland felt the same. It seemed terrible to find a man like this, quite young - he was certainly under thirty - a man with the unmistakable *cachet* of public school and university, engaged in a career of infamy. What was his life's story I wondered as I looked at him, noting how refined his features were, what well-shaped hands he had. Why had he sunk so low? Above all, who was he? for certainly he was no ordinary malefactor.

Suddenly he turned on to his back, wincing with pain as he did so; he had been lying partly on his side.

"I can't betray my friends, Sir Roland," he murmured, "but believe me when I say I am deeply grateful for your kindness to me. I was not always what I am now, you know," his voice grew weaker still; "not always an adventurer - a criminal if you will. Yes, I am a criminal, and have been for many years; unconvicted as yet, but none the less a criminal. I was once what you are, Sir Roland; I took pride in being a gentleman and in calling myself one. Educated at Marlborough and at Trinity - but why should I bore you with my story - eh, Sir Roland? Why should I bore you with, with - ah! The Four Faces! The Four Faces!" he repeated.

His eyes rolled strangely, then looked dully up at the ceiling. What did he mean by "The Four Faces"? Did he refer to the medallion worn by Gastrell? His mind was beginning to wander. He muttered and murmured for a minute, then again his words became articulate.

"Jasmine - oh, Jasmine my darling, I love you so!"

I started.

"Jasmine, if only you would ... oh, yes, that is all I ask, all I want, my darling woman, all I ... you remember it all, don't you? ... yes ... oh, it was her fault ... he wouldn't otherwise have killed her ... oh, no, discovery is impossible, the ... it was quite unrecognizable.... The Four Faces - ha! ha! ... I myself saw it, black, charred beyond all hope of recognition ... he did right to ... dear, I should have done the same...."

Between these scraps of sentences were words impossible to catch the meaning of, so indistinctly were they uttered, some being said beneath his breath, some muttered and inarticulate, some little more than murmurings.

He moved restlessly on the bed. Then his eyes slowly closed, and for a minute he lay still. And then, all at once, he seemed to spring back into life.

"Mother!" he shouted suddenly in quite a strong voice.

He started up in bed, and now sat erect and still, his wide-stretched eyes staring straight before him.

The nurse had, at Sir Roland's request, left the room before the stranger had begun to speak to him. Now, opening the door quickly, Sir Roland called to her to return.

The stranger's eyes were fixed. Motionless he sat there glaring, as it seemed to us, at some figure facing him. Instinctively we followed the direction of his gaze, but naught was visible to us save the artistic

pattern upon the pink-tinted wall-paper opposite the foot of the bed.

His lips were slightly parted, now. We saw them move as though he spoke rapidly, but no words came. And then, all at once, he smiled.

"The Four Faces!" he repeated, almost inaudibly.

It was not a vacant smile, not the smile of a man mentally deficient, but a smile charged with meaning, with intelligent expression; a smile of delight, of greeting - a smile full of love. It was the first time we had seen a smile, or anything approaching one, upon his face, and in an instant it revealed how handsome the man had been.

"Mother!"

This time the word was only murmured, a murmur so low as to be barely audible. The fellow's pyjama jacket, one Sir Roland Challoner had lent to him, had become unfastened at the throat, and now I noticed that a thin gold chain was round his neck, and that from it there depended a flat, circular locket.

Sir Roland was seated close beside the bed. Almost as I noticed this locket, he saw it too. I saw him bend forward a little, and take it in his fingers, and turn it over. I could see it distinctly from where I sat. Upon the reverse side was a miniature - the portrait of a woman - a woman of forty-five or so, very beautiful still, a striking face of singular refinement. Yes, there could be no doubt whatever - the eyes of the miniature bore a striking likeness to the stranger's, which now gazed at nothing with that fixed, unmeaning stare.

I had noticed Sir Roland raised his eyebrows. Now he sat staring intently at the miniature which lay flat upon the palm on his hand. At last he let it drop and turned to me, while the stranger still sat upright in the bed, gazing still at something he seemed to see before him.

"I believe I have discovered his identity," Sir Roland whispered. "I recognize the portrait in that locket; I couldn't possibly mistake it seeing that years ago I knew the original well. It's a miniature of Lady Logan, who died some years ago. Her husband, Lord Logan, was a gambler, a spendthrift, and a drunkard, and he treated her with abominable cruelty. They had one child, a son. I remember the son sitting on my knee when he was quite a little chap - he couldn't at that time have been more than five or six. He went to Marlborough, I know; then crammed for the army, but failed to pass; and yet he was undoubtedly clever. His father became infuriated upon hearing that he had not qualified, and, in a fit of drunkenness, turned him with curses out of the house, forbidding him ever to return, in spite of Lady Logan's pleading on the lad's behalf. The lad had from infancy been passionately devoted to his mother, though he couldn't bear his father. The mother died soon afterwards - of a broken heart it was said - and Lord Logan survived her only a few months, dying eventually of *delirium tremens*. Upon his death the little money he left was swallowed up in paying his debts. The son, whose name was Harold, didn't show up even at the funerals - none knew where he was or what had become of him. It was generally believed that he had gone abroad, and Logan's executors thought it probable that the son had not had news of either his mother's or his father's death. Altogether it was a very sad story and - "

He checked himself, for the stranger had turned his head and was looking at us - never shall I forget the infinite pathos of his expression at that moment. There was something in the face which betrayed misery and dejection so abject that for days afterwards the look haunted me. Again I saw the lips move, but no sound came.

He had sunk back upon his pillows. Once more his eyes gazed fixedly at the ceiling. Some moments later the mouth gaped, the lips turned slowly blue, a dull, leaden hue spread over the pale features.

The nurse hurried forward, but there was nothing to be done. Harold Logan, Lord Logan's wastrel son, was dead.

CHAPTER XI

CONCERNS MRS. STAPLETON

Ten days had passed since the events I have set down in the previous chapter, and still no clue of any kind had been obtained to the robbers at Holt, or the perpetrators of the outrage at the house in Grafton Street. Nor, indeed, had any light been thrown upon the mystery of the forged telegram, while the incident of the discovery of the charred body of a murdered woman among the *debris* of the house in Maresfield Gardens destroyed by fire on Christmas Eve had, to all intents, been entirely forgotten.

In the firelight in a small room leading out of the large library, Dulcie and I sat and talked. Perched on the broad arm of a giant padded chair, swinging her small, grey-spatted feet to and fro, she glanced at me moodily, replying in monosyllables to most of my remarks. Presently I rose with a gesture of annoyance, and began to pace the floor.

It was not a comfortable atmosphere by any means - metaphorically. In point of fact, Dulcie and I quarrelled.

We had quarrelled during our afternoon walk over the hard-frozen snow to a neighbouring hamlet to take a deserving widow a can of soup, and old "Captain" Barnacle in Wheat-sheaf Lane a promising Christmas pudding.

The cause of our quarrel was a curious one. Though Aunt Hannah appeared to have overcome her belief concerning the telegram she had felt so certain I had sent, I felt that she was now prejudiced against me - why, heaven only knew. Her manner towards me, as well as her expression, and the way she spoke to me, all betrayed this. Women dislike being proved to be in the wrong even more than men do, and the conclusion I had come to was that Aunt Hannah would never forgive my having, in a sense, made her eat her words and look ridiculous. It was on the subject of Aunt Hannah, then, that Dulcie and I had begun our quarrel, for Dulcie had stood up for her when I condemned her - that I condemned her rather bitterly, I admit. From that we had presently come to talk of Mrs. Stapleton, for whom Dulcie had suddenly developed a most extraordinary infatuation.

On the morning that Dick, on his way to the station, had passed Mrs. Stapleton in her car, Mrs. Stapleton had called at Holt and asked to see Dulcie. At that moment Dulcie was in the train with Aunt Hannah, on her way to London in response to the telegram. The widow had then asked to see Aunt Hannah Challoner, and then Sir Roland.

Upon hearing that all three were absent from home, she had asked if she might come into the house to write a note to Dulcie, and the maid who had opened the door to her - the butler and footman having, as we know, gone into Newbury - had politely but firmly refused to admit her, declaring that she had orders to admit nobody whomsoever.

This refusal had apparently annoyed Mrs. Stapleton a good deal, and on the same evening she had called again, and again asked to see Dulcie, who by that time had returned. It was while she was alone with Dulcie in her boudoir that Sir Roland and Dick and I had returned to Holt, and that the stranger - whom we now knew to have been Lord Logan's son - had been discovered in the hiding-hole. Mrs. Stapleton had remained with Dulcie over an hour, and during that hour it was that she had apparently cast the spell of her personality over Dulcie. It was on the subject of this infatuation of Dulcie's that Dulcie and I had ended by quarrelling rather seriously.

"I won't hear a word said against her," Dulcie suddenly declared impetuously, kicking her heel viciously against the chair. "I think she is the most fascinating woman I have ever met, and the more you abuse her the more I shall stand up for her - so there."

"Abuse her!" I answered irritably. "When did I abuse her? Repeat one word of abuse that I have uttered against her. You know quite well that I haven't said a syllable that you can twist into abuse. All I have said is that I mistrust her, and that I think it a pity you should for ever be metaphorically sitting on her skirts, as you have been during the past few days."

"And you don't call that abuse?" Dulcie retorted. "Then tell me what you do call it."

"I myself like Mrs. Stapleton up to a point," I answered, evading the question. "She is capital company and all that, but - "

"But what?" Dulcie asked quickly, as I hesitated.

"But who is she? And where does she come from? How is it that nobody about here, and apparently nobody in town either, knows anything at all about her? Such an attractive-looking woman, young, apparently well off, and a widow - surely somebody ought to know something or other about her if she is quite - well, quite all right. It's most singular that she shouldn't have any friends at all among our rather large circle of acquaintance."

"I shall tell her just what you have said about her," Dulcie exclaimed quite hotly. "I never thought you were that kind, Michael - never. You pride yourself upon being broadminded - you have often told me so - and yet because Tom, Dick and Harry don't know all about poor Mrs. Stapleton - who her husband was, who her parents were, and where she comes from - you immediately become suspicious, and begin to wonder all sorts of horrid things about her."

"My dear Dulcie," I said, becoming suddenly quite calm, so anxious was I to soothe her at any cost, for I hated our falling out like this, "you put words into my mouth I never spoke, and thoughts into my mind which never occurred to me. I have said only one thing, and I shall say it again. I mistrust Mrs. Stapleton, and I advise you to be on your guard against her."

The door opened at that moment, and Charles, entering, announced:

"Mrs. Stapleton."

"Oh, Connie, how glad I am you've come!" Dulcie burst out, jumping off the arm of the big chair impetuously, and hurrying forward to meet the widow, who at once embraced her affectionately. "We were just this instant talking about you. Isn't that strange?"

"And I hope not saying nasty things, as I have reason to believe some of my 'friends' do," Mrs. Stapleton answered, with a charming smile, casting a careless glance at me. "But, of course, I couldn't imagine you or Mr. Berrington saying anything unpleasant about anybody," she added quickly; "you are both much - much too nice."

This was heaping coals of fire upon me, and I believe I winced as Dulcie's eyes met mine for a brief instant and I noticed the look of scorn that was in them. She did not, however, repeat to Mrs. Stapleton what I had just said about her, as she had threatened to do. Instead, she slipped her arm affectionately through the young widow's, led her over to the big arm-chair, made her sit down in it, and once more perched herself upon its arm.

"Ring for tea, Mike, like a dear," she said to me. Her tone had completely changed. Once more she had become her own, delightful self. This sudden *volte-face* did not, I must admit, in the least surprise me, for I knew what a child of moods she was, how impulsive and impetuous, and I think I loved her the more because she was like that.

We now formed, indeed, quite a merry trio. By the time tea was finished Connie Stapleton's magnetic personality must, I think, have begun to affect me to some extent, for I found myself wondering whether, after all, I had not been mistaken in the opinion I had formed that she was a woman one would be well-advised not to trust too implicitly - become too intimate with.

"And your jewels, dear!" she suddenly asked, as though the recollection of the robbery had but at that instant occurred to her. "Have you recovered any of them? Have the police found any clue?"

"Yes," Dulcie answered at once, "the police have a clue, though, as yet, none of the stolen things have been recovered."

"Indeed?" I exclaimed. "Why, Dulcie, you never told me. What is it? What is the clue?"

"I forgot to tell you; at least, I should have told you, but you've been so snappy all the afternoon that I thought there was no need," Dulcie answered equivocally. "Well, the clue is merely this. When Churchill - that's the head gardener, you know," she said to Mrs. Stapleton - "was sweeping away the snow in the drive at the back of the house, that narrow drive which leads down to the lane that joins the main road to Newbury, just by Stag's Leap, he saw something shining on the ground. He picked it up and found it was a buckle, set in diamonds, as he thought, so when he brought it to me of course he was tremendously excited - he made sure it was one of the stolen bits of jewellery. As a matter of fact, it was one of a set of very old paste buckles which belonged to my mother, and those buckles were among the stolen things."

"When did he find it?" Mrs. Stapleton asked, interested.

"Why, only a few hours ago - it was just after lunch when he came to me, and he had then only just found it. You see, the ground has been covered with snow ever since the day of the robbery; that was the last day we hunted."

"Did the gardener say anything else? Has he any theory to account for the buckle being there?"

Again it was Mrs. Stapleton who put the question.

"None, Connie," Dulcie answered. "At least, yes," she corrected, "he has a sort of theory, but I don't think much of it. That narrow drive is rarely used, you know; the gate into the lane is nearly always locked - it was unlocked and the gate set open the day the hounds met here in order to save people coming from the direction of Stag's Leap the trouble of going round by the lodge. I don't think, all the same, that many people came in that way."

"I don't see much 'theory' in that," I observed drily. Somehow I could not shake off the feeling of irritability that my quarrel with Dulcie during the afternoon had created.

"Naturally, because I haven't yet come to the theory part," Dulcie answered sharply, noticing the tone in which I spoke. "I am coming to it now. Churchill says he happened to come along that drive between about eleven o'clock and half-past on the morning of the meet - that would be just about the time when everybody was at the breakfast - and he distinctly remembers seeing a car drawn up close to the shrubbery. There was nobody in it, he says, but as far as he can recollect it was drawn up at the exact spot where he found the buckle this afternoon. Of course, there was no snow on the ground then."

"Has he any idea what the car was like?"

As Connie Stapleton made this inquiry I happened to glance at her. I could only see her profile, but there was, I thought, something unusual in her expression, something I did not seem to recollect having ever seen in it before. It was not exactly a look of anxiety; rather it was a look of extreme interest, of singular curiosity.

"Churchill is most mysterious and secretive on that point," Dulcie answered. "I asked him to tell me what the car was like, if he had any idea whose it was. He said it was a grey car, but he wouldn't tell me more than that. He said he believed he had 'hit the line,' and would soon be on a 'hot scent.' Try as I would, I couldn't get him to say another word. He asked if he might have this afternoon off, and gave me to understand he wanted to go into Newbury. I believe he is going to try to do a little detective work," she ended, with a laugh; "but, as I say, I don't put much faith in any theory Churchill may have formed."

"Well, my dear Dulcie, if you succeed in recovering your jewellery you know I shall be the first to congratulate you," Mrs. Stapleton said, taking Dulcie's hand and patting it affectionately. "It is too dreadful to think all those lovely things should have been stolen from you, things of such exceptional value to you because of their long association with your family. Oh, how stupid of me," she suddenly said, interrupting herself, "I have forgotten to tell you what I have come to see you for. I have some friends from town dining with me to-night - some of them are going to stay the night at 'The Rook,' the others will return to town in their cars - and I want you and Mr. Berrington to join us. It's quite an informal little dinner party, so I hope you will forgive my asking you in this offhanded way and at such short notice. The fact is, two people telegraphed at lunch time that they wouldn't be able to come, so I thought that if I motored over here I might be able to persuade you to come instead. Will you come, dear? And you, Mr. Berrington? Do say 'yes.' Don't disappoint me when I have come all this way out to try to persuade you - if I were not really anxious that you should join us I should have telephoned or telegraphed!"

"Of course - why, I shall love to come!" Dulcie exclaimed,

without a moment's hesitation. "And, Mike will come - I know he will."

"You mean he won't be able to let you be away from him so long," Connie Stapleton said mischievously, and there was something very peculiar in her laugh. It flashed across me at that moment that for an instant or two she looked a singularly wicked woman.

Dulcie smiled self-consciously, but said nothing. I knew that she rather disliked any joking allusion being made to our engagement.

"May I use your telephone, darling Dulcie?" Connie Stapleton asked suddenly. "I want to tell the hotel people that we shall be the original number. I told them after lunch that we might be two short."

Dulcie had a telephone extension in the little room which adjoined her boudoir, and some moments later Mrs. Stapleton was talking rapidly into the transmitter in her smooth, soft voice. She spoke in a tongue that neither of us understood, and when, after she had conversed for over five minutes, she hung up the receiver, Dulcie called out to her gaily:

"Why, Connie, what language was that?"

'Polish,' she answered. "Didn't you recognize it? Of course, you know that I am Russian."

"Russian! Why, no, I hadn't the least idea. I always thought you were not English, although you speak English perfectly. I remember wondering, the first time I met you, to what nationality you belonged, and I came to the conclusion that possibly you were Austrian."

"No, Russian," Mrs. Stapleton repeated. "I have a Polish maid who speaks hardly any English, and I was talking to her. And now, my dear, I really must be going. What is the exact time?"

It was five minutes past six. Dulcie pressed the electric button.

"Mrs. Stapleton's car at once," she said, when the footman entered.

A few minutes later Mrs. Stapleton's long grey Rolls-Royce was gliding noiselessly down the avenue, over the snow, its tail lights fast disappearing into the darkness.

CHAPTER XII

THE BROAD HIGHWAY

Had Dulcie consulted me before accepting Mrs. Stapleton's invitation to dinner I should have improvised some plausible excuse for declining. She had not, however, given me the chance of refusing, for she had then and there accepted for both of us unconditionally, so that I could not, without being rude, make any excuse for staying away.

"Dulcie," I said, when we were again alone, "I wish you hadn't accepted that invitation without first of all consulting me. I really am not keen to go."

"Oh, don't be silly!" she exclaimed joyously, and, putting her arms about my neck, she gave me three delicious kisses. "We have quarrelled all the afternoon - you were perfectly horrid to me, you know you were - and if we mope here together all the evening we shall most likely fall out again, and that will be absurd. Besides, I feel just in the humour for a jolly dinner party, and I'm sure any party given by Connie is bound to be jolly, just as jolly as she is. I *do* think she is such a fascinating person, don't you, Mike? Oh, I am sorry; I quite forget you don't like her."

"I have not said I don't like her - I do like her, Dulcie, in a sense, and up to a point. But I still hold to the opinion I formed of her when I met her first - I wouldn't trust her implicitly."

"Never mind, Mike," she cried in high spirits. "We'll set all your prejudices aside to-night, and try to enjoy ourselves. I wonder who'll be there. I quite forgot to ask her."

"Probably nobody you know, or she would have told you. She said 'friends from town,' so there are not likely to be any of our friends from about here. We ought to start soon after seven, as she said dinner would be at eight; with the snow as thick as it is it may take us quite an hour to get to Newbury - twelve miles, remember."

We were the last to arrive, and I confess that the moment we were shown into the room and I realized who Mrs. Stapleton's other guests were I mentally upbraided myself for having come, or rather, for having let Dulcie come. The first to whom our hostess introduced Dulcie was "Mrs. Gastrell," and directly afterwards she presented to Dulcie "Mrs. Gastrell's cousin," as she called him - none other than Hugesson Gastrell, who was standing by. To my surprise Easterton and Jack Osborne were there, and the widow seemed pleased at finding that I knew them - I guessed it was owing to Easterton's being there that Jasmine Gastrell was made to pass as Gastrell's cousin.

With singular formality she made Dulcie and me acquainted with everybody, which struck me as odd in these days when introductions at dinner parties, receptions and balls have gone quite out of fashion.

"Mr. Berrington," Mrs. Stapleton said, taking me across the room to two men engaged apparently in earnest conversation, "I want to make you and Lord Cranmere and Mr. Wollaston known to one another," and, interrupting them, she introduced us.

There was nothing striking about the Earl of Cranmere. A man past middle age, he had, I thought a rather weak face. A small, fair beard, neatly trimmed and pointed, concealed his chin: as I looked at him I wondered whether, were that beard removed, I should see any chin at all. The short upper lip was hidden by a fair moustache; he had also whiskers. The fair hair, which was rather thin on the top, was carefully parted in the middle, and plastered down on both sides. His complexion was clear, the complexion of a man who lives a good deal in the open, and his eyes were pale blue, with almost golden lashes and eyebrows. He inclined to stoutness, and spoke with a slight lisp. This then was the man, or rather one of the men, I thought, as I noted these points about him while we exchanged remarks, concerning whom Jack Osborne had been so mysteriously questioned while he lay bound upon the bed in that dark room in Grafton Street. I knew Lord Cranmere to be a particular friend of Jack's, though in appearance no two men could have presented a greater contrast.

What mostly kept my thoughts busy, however, was the presence of Hugesson Gastrell.

Since his name had been mentioned by Harold Logan on his dying bed, I had carefully debated whether or not to tell Easterton, who had let him his house, what I now knew about him; also whether to tell Sir Roland Challoner that Osborne and I had actually met Gastrell. Unable to decide, I had put the case to Osborne, and eventually we had decided to say nothing, at any rate for the moment, to anybody at all.

"What would be the good?" Jack had argued. "You have the word of a dying man, and that's all; and what is there that you can prove against this man Gastrell - at present? Besides, if you say anything, you may find yourself forced to reveal that you know who the dead man was, that you know him to have been Lord Logan's son, and you told me that Sir Roland wants particularly to avoid doing that. No, keep silent and await developments, that's my advice, as you have asked for it. He'll probably end by hanging himself if you give him rope enough. I wouldn't tell even Dulcie, if I were you."

I was thinking of all this again, when my train of thought was suddenly cut by a voice at my elbow:

"Mr. Berrington, I want to introduce you to Mrs. Gastrell.

Come with me, will you?"

I turned abruptly. Connie Stapleton was at my elbow, and she spoke in soft, purring tones.

"She's the woman you asked me if I knew, the other night at Mr. Gastrell's reception," she went on in an undertone, as we walked towards the woman. "I was introduced to her a couple of nights later. She is a cousin of Mr. Gastrell's."

Almost before I had time to collect my thoughts, she had introduced me, adding, a moment later, with one of her charming smiles:

"And will you take Mrs. Gastrell in to dinner?"

I was debating whether or not to refer to our previous meeting, at Maresfield Gardens, when Mrs. Gastrell herself solved the difficulty.

"I wonder," she said, her great eyes very wide open, her gaze resting full on mine, "if you remember that we have met before. It was just before Christmas. You and Mr. Osborne called in the middle of the night to ask if Hugesson had lost his purse: we both thought it so kind of you."

I remembered a good deal more than that, but I did not tell her so. I remembered too that she had seemed to speak sarcastically, almost mockingly, that night when she had said she thought it kind of Jack to have come out "all that way" just to inquire if Gastrell had accidentally left his purse at the club. She appeared now, however, to mean what she said, and so I only answered:

"How, having met you once, Mrs. Gastrell, could I forget our meeting? What rather astonishes me is that you should remember me by sight, seeing that we spoke for a few minutes only."

She smiled in acknowledgment of the compliment, and I found myself wondering how many men that terribly alluring smile of hers had enslaved from first to last.

"Would you believe it," she went on almost without a pause, "we were very nearly burnt in a dreadful fire that broke out in that house on Christmas Eve. We only just managed to escape with a few of our belongings; we had not, I am thankful to say, anything very valuable there, because the house had been sub-let to us, so that the furniture was not ours."

"You certainly were fortunate, in a sense," I answered, marvelling at her self-possession, and mentally asking myself if she spoke with conviction and whether I had, after all, formed a wrong opinion about her as well as about our hostess. Then I heard Gastrell's voice behind me, and that brought me to my senses. If such a man were a guest of Mrs. Stapleton's it seemed quite on the cards that men and women of equally bad character might also be included among her friends. I had several reasons for suspecting Mrs. Gastrell of duplicity, and I determined to remain on my guard.

The dinner, I confess, was excellent. I was glad to see that Dulcie sat between Jack Osborne and Lord Easterton, and was thus out of harm's way. We dined at a round table, and almost facing me were two unintelligent-looking women - I had heard their names, but the names conveyed nothing to me. These women, both past middle age, somehow had the appearance of being extremely rich. They sat on either side of Hugesson Gastrell, whose conversation appeared to be amusing them immensely. One other woman made up the party of twelve - a dark, demure, very quiet little person, with large, dreamy eyes, a singularly pale complexion, and very red lips. She was dressed almost simply, which the other two women certainly were not, and altogether she struck me as looking somewhat out of place in that *galere*.

Champagne flowed freely, and gradually we all became exceedingly vivacious. Once, when I glanced across at Dulcie, after conversing animatedly for ten minutes or so with the beautiful woman at my side, I thought I noticed a troubled look in her eyes, but instantly it disappeared, and she smiled quite happily. Then, turning to her neighbour, Jack Osborne, she said something to him in an undertone which made him laugh, and he too looked across at me. It had struck me all the evening that Jack was in exceptionally high spirits, and more than once I had wondered if he had some special reason for being so.

It was an extraordinary dinner party. The more I looked about me, the more astonishing it seemed. A stranger entering the room would have noticed nothing unusual; he would have seen a number of apparently quite ordinary men and women dining, and enjoying themselves, people rather more sociable, perhaps, than the guests at dinner parties often are. And yet I had reason to believe that among these ostensibly respectable people three at least there were whose lives were veiled in a mystery of some sort - I hoped it might be nothing worse. The opinion I had formed of our hostess is already known. In addition there was that strange young man, Hugesson Gastrell, who, knowing everyone in London, was, in a sense, known by no one. For what did anybody know about him? Questioned, people invariably answered that he came from Australia or Tasmania and had inherited a large fortune from an uncle. That was all. They knew naught of his parents or his antecedents; his private life was a closed book.

My glance rested on my neighbour's white, well-manicured hands. Several times already, during dinner, I had observed how graceful they were, and had noticed the long, slender fingers, the well-shaped, polished nails - fingers on which precious stones shone and sparkled as the rays cast down from beneath the shades of the subdued electric lamps touched them at frequent intervals. Suddenly a thought flashed in upon me, and involuntarily I caught my breath. The voice of a dying man was calling to me, was crying a name in my ears as it had done that day I had sat with Sir Roland Challoner by Harold Logan's bed and watched the fearful eyes gazing into vacancy.

"Jasmine ... it is all I ask, all I want, my darling woman ... wouldn't otherwise have killed her ... it was her fault ... oh, no, discovery is impossible ... black, charred beyond all hope of recognition ... did right to kill her, dear, I ..."

The sound of the voice - I seemed to hear it distinctly in spite of the conversation and laughter all around - and the picture which rose simultaneously into the vision of my imagination, made me recoil. Mygaze was set again upon those pale, graceful hands with their blue veins, their scintillating gems. As in a dream I heard Jasmine Gastrell in conversation with Cranmere, seated upon her other side; heard, too, his silly talk, his empty laughter. Her hands seemed now completely to hold my gaze. I could not look away. And, as I watched them, the feeling of revulsion rose.

Conjectures, suspicions, hideous thoughts filled my brain as my eyes remained riveted. Now the fingers looked like snakes - strange, flesh-tinted reptiles with eyes emerald green and ruby red, cruel, sinuous. Now great knots of muscle stood out upon her bare arms. Her hands were clutching something - what it was I could not see. The fingers grew twisted and distorted ... they had crimson stains upon them ... the very nails were shot with blood and I thought I saw -

My train of thought was cut by my neighbour on my right. What she said I hardly knew, and did not care. Still, I was glad that she had spoken. The interruption had diverted my attention, and brought my thoughts from dreamland back into actual life.

Then the thought came to me, What was the object of this dinner party? Why had Connie Stapleton invited these people down to Newbury? Why, if she wished to give a dinner party, had she not given it in town? From the conversation during dinner I had gathered that the guests, one and all, lived in London. It seemed strange therefore to the verge of eccentricity to ask them to come fifty miles to dine. True, the *cuisine* at "The Rook" was above reproach, the hotel itself excellently appointed, but none the less -

"Don't you agree, Mr. Berrington?" Mrs. Gastrell exclaimed, laughing as she turned from Cranmere to me.

"I didn't catch the question," I said with a start, again brought suddenly to earth.

"Lord Cranmere is of opinion that the man you found in hiding at Holt must, from the descriptions which have been given of him, at some time or other have been a gentleman. I say, 'No; that no gentleman could sink so low as to become a common criminal of that kind.' One can understand a gentleman, by which I mean a man of education and careful upbringing, being driven, through force of circumstances, to rob a bank, or even to forge a signature to a cheque; but for such a man to sink to the level of a common housebreaker is unthinkable - don't you agree with me?"

Her eyes shone strangely as they rested upon mine. Not until now had the wonderful intelligence in their purple-green depths struck me so forcibly. From the orange-tinted lamps before her on the table the light which shone up in her face seemed to increase their brilliance, accentuate their expression and their power. It imparted, too, to her extraordinary complexion a peculiar, livid tint, while the masses of her burnished, red-brown hair, coiled about her head in great ropes and dressed low in her neck, was shot with a chestnut shade which greatly enhanced its beauty.

I paused before answering. For fully ten minutes she had not addressed me, so deeply engaged had she been in conversation with Lord Cranmere. Why should she all at once interrupt her talk and put this question to me? None but Sir Roland Challoner and I were aware of the dead man's identity; even we had no actual proof that he had been Lord Logan's son, though our discovery of the locket, considered in relation to certain facts known to Sir Roland, left no room for doubt. That locket Sir Roland had appropriated in order that the dead man's identity might not be traced and the family name tarnished. Jasmine Gastrell must of course be aware of his identity? Did she suspect that I knew his name, and could this be an attempt to entrap me into revealing that I knew it?

"That is a question difficult to answer," I said guardedly. "I believe there are instances on record of men of education, of men even of good birth, sinking to the lowest depth of degradation when once they had begun to tread the downward path. It would be interesting to know who that man really was. He wouldn't tell his name, wouldn't even hint at it."

"So that of course you don't know it."

"Naturally."

Again that keen, searching expression in the large, luminous eyes. They seemed to look right through me. They seemed to read my thoughts and wrest my secrets from me.

"And you found nothing upon him that might have given you a clue, I suppose; nothing in his pockets, no marks upon the body, there was nothing he was wearing that might have put you on the track?"

"Absolutely nothing," I answered, thinking of the locket as I looked straight into her eyes. Never before had I realized how cleverly I could lie.

It was close on midnight when we all assembled in the hall preparatory to leaving - those of us who were leaving. Hugesson Gastrell had left long before, in fact immediately after dinner, as he had, he said, an important appointment in London. Somebody nudged me lightly as he brushed past, and glancing round I caught Osborne's eye. He made no sign whatever, yet there was something in his look which made me think he wanted me, and a minute later I sauntered after him into the room where the hats and coats had been.

But for us, the room was now deserted. Glancing quickly to right and left, Jack walked over to a corner where a tall screen stood. There was nobody behind it.

He beckoned to me, and I approached.

"We are among a set of scoundrels," he said rapidly, under his breath. "I am glad to see that you too didn't recognize him."

"Recognize whom?" I asked in astonishment, also speaking in a whisper.

"Preston, the ex-detective. I introduced him to you the last time we met in town."

"I remember the man perfectly, but surely he isn't here."

Jack's lips stretched into a grin.

"'Lord Cranmere,'" he said. "That's Preston!"

He chuckled.

"Cranmere's own brother was actually deceived when we brought the two together, as a test," he went on. "Preston is a genius. He doesn't merely 'make up' to look like someone else; he doesn't, when he is made up, just impersonate the character; for the time he *is* the man, he 'feels like him,' he says, he shares his views, he becomes his other ego. He has the advantage in this case of knowing Cranmere well, and he has, in consequence, excelled himself to-night. The way he has hit off Cranmere's lisp is marvellous. Easterton, who meets Cranmere frequently, is at this moment in the hall arguing with Preston about land taxation and small holdings, under the impression that he is talking to Cranmere. It really is rather amusing."

When I had expressed my astonishment, and we had talked for a minute or two, he suddenly grew serious.

"But remember, Mike," he said, laying his hand upon my shoulder, "nobody knows this - nobody but you and I. Preston has assured me that the success of our efforts to run the leaders of this gang to ground - he tells me he is sure there is a gang working together and playing into one another's hands very cleverly - will largely depend upon our discreetness and our secretiveness, also upon our tact and our knowledge of when to act. So not a word, mind; not a syllable even to Dulcie Challoner - have I your promise?"

Dulcie and I talked but little as we sped homeward through the darkness. She seemed depressed, I thought, though she assured me that she had thoroughly enjoyed herself and was feeling quite well. I must say that the "mental atmosphere" of that party had affected me unpleasantly, though I could not have said precisely why.

On and on the car travelled, smoothly, almost noiselessly. Snow was falling - it had been falling for two hours, the chauffeur had told us before we started - though not very heavily. The night was quite still. We had long passed the tiny hamlets a mile or two from Newbury and were now on the five miles' stretch of winding road between there and Holt Stacey. Soon we passed the sign-post close to Holt Stacey railway station. As we sped through the village some moments later the houses and cottages all wrapped in darkness seemed to spring forward into the light one after another as though to peer at us as we shot by.

Now Holt Stacey lay behind us, and only four miles remained. From the time we had left Newbury no vehicle of any kind had passed us, nor any human being, nor had we overtaken any. Dulcie, nestling close to me in the warm, comfortable brougham, was more than half asleep. I too felt drowsy, and I fear that more than once my chin had dropped forward with a jerk. Suddenly the car swerved abruptly to the right. So tightly were the brakes applied at the same instant that we were both thrown forward almost on to the floor. The car lurched, rose up on one side, then as I instinctively threw my arms about

Dulcie to protect her if possible from what seemed about to be a very serious accident, the car righted itself and stopped dead.

"Good heavens! What has happened?" I exclaimed, as the chauffeur, who had sprung off his seat, opened the door. Dulcie still lay in my arms, trembling with fear, though from the first she had not uttered a sound, or in the least lost her head.

"Someone lying in the road, sir," he answered, "drunk, I shouldn't wonder. He was half covered with snow, and I all but ran over him."

"Lying in the snow! Why, he'll die if he's left there," I exclaimed. "Go and have a look at him, and then come back to me."

Several minutes passed, and the chauffeur did not return. Becoming impatient, I opened the door of the brougham, and called out. A moment later the man appeared. The electric torch he carried - one he used when occasion arose to examine the car in the dark - was still switched on. The hand that held it trembled a little, and in the light which shone down inside the brougham I noticed that the chauffeur looked singularly pale.

"Could you kindly step out for a moment, please, sir?" he said in a curious tone.

Guessing that something serious must be amiss to prompt him to ask me to step out into the deep snow in my evening shoes, I got out at once, in spite of Dulcie's entreating me not to do so and get my feet soaked.

When I had shut the car door, and we had walked a few paces, the chauffeur stopped abruptly.

"Sir," he said in a hoarse voice.

"Well, what?" I asked, also stopping.

"Sir - it's Churchill, the gardener. Poor fellow! It's awful! He's dead, sir, quite cold. He - he's been killed - *murdered*!"

CHAPTER XIII

THE BARON

Coming so soon after the robbery at Holt, the brutal murder of Sir Roland's head gardener created an immense sensation throughout both Berkshire and Hampshire - for the Holt Manor estate, though actually in Berkshire, is also upon the border of Hampshire. The London papers, too, devoted much space to the matter, the problem they set their readers to solve being: whether the murder could have any bearing upon the robbery. Some of the leading journals declared that both crimes must have been in some way related; others urged that this was most unlikely, and then proceeded to "prove" the accuracy of their own individual reasoning.

The man had been done to death in a peculiarly horrible manner. He had been hit upon the back of the head with some heavy implement - probably a "jemmy" the police said when the wound, with the wounds upon the forehead, had been examined beneath a microscope. The theory they held was that some person had crept up unheard behind the victim - as this could easily have been done with snow so thick upon the ground - stunned him with a blow upon the back of the head, and then despatched him outright by blows upon the forehead. No footsteps were anywhere visible, the falling snow having hidden them.

Churchill's movements during that afternoon had in part been traced. Directly after taking to Dulcie the buckle he had found and obtaining her permission to absent himself for the afternoon, he had walked to Holt Stacey, and there caught the

4:05 train to Newbury. He had exchanged the time of day with the ticket-collector at Newbury, who had taken the half of his ticket. The return half had afterwards been found in the dead man's pocket. Where he had been, or what he had done, between 4:20 - from the time he left Newbury station, on foot - and 6:10, when he had looked in at the "Dog and Clown" and had a drink and a chat with the landlord, was unknown. He had not told the landlord why he was in Newbury, or said anything concerning his movements in that town.

The fact of his having bought a return ticket showed that he had intended to return to Holt Stacey by train. But he had not gone back by train. The last train for Holt Stacey left Newbury at 9:11, and at 9:30 he had been seen by a seedsman who kept a shop in the town, and who knew Churchill well, standing in the High Street talking to an unknown man he had never seen before. After that, nobody appeared to have seen Churchill until - just before 10:30, at which time the inn at Holt Stacey closed - he had come into the inn and ordered a hot drink. Nobody was with him then. He appeared, so the innkeeper said, to already have drunk to excess, and this had surprised the innkeeper, who knew him to be a temperate man, adding that that was the first time he had ever seen him even partially intoxicated. Incidentally Churchill had mentioned that "a gentleman had given him a lift from Newbury in his car." He had not said who the gentleman was - if a stranger or somebody he knew, or where he was going. Presumably the man in the car had branched off at Holt Stacey - for he had not put up there for the night. Had he been going on past Holt Manor he would, it was reasonable to suppose, have taken Churchill all the way, and dropped him at the gate.

Soon after 10:30 Churchill had left the inn, saying that he was about to walk home to Holt Manor, a distance of four miles. That was the last time he was known to have been seen alive. It was snowing when he set out.

Poor Dulcie was terribly cut up. I had always known her to be very partial to the old gardener, who remembered her as a baby, but until after his death I had not realized how deeply attached to him she really had been. What most distressed me was that she blamed herself, indirectly, for what had happened. Again and again did she declare to me that, had she not given him leave to take the afternoon off the tragedy would not have happened. In vain I tried to make her see the fallacy of her argument - she would not listen to reason.

A fortnight went by, and nothing was discovered. The secret of the murder remained even a greater mystery than the secret of the robbery. True, I had my suspicions, but until I had some slight shreds of evidence to go upon it would, I knew, be futile to make known those suspicions. And it was because I suspected somebody of indirect, if not direct, connivance at Churchill's murder, that I became more and more distressed, indeed alarmed, at Dulcie's daily increasing affection for the woman Stapleton. Their friendship was now firmly established - at any rate, Dulcie's feeling of friendship for the widow. Whether the widow's feeling of friendship for Dulcie was actual or only apparent was, I thought, quite another matter.

"*Come at once. Urgent: - Jack.*"

That telegram reached me on this afternoon, exactly two weeks after the murder, two weeks that I had spent at Holt Manor with Dulcie, during which time, I am bound to say, Aunt Hannah had revealed herself in quite a new light, being friendly, even affectionate in the extreme.

"Don't go - oh! don't go, Mike!" Dulcie cried out, suddenly clutching my arm, after reading the telegram which I had handed to her.

"But I must, darling," I exclaimed. "Jack wouldn't send me that wire if the matter were not really urgent. It has most likely to do with the robbery - I have told you that he is determined to find out who committed it, with the help of that detective friend of his, George Preston. It may even have to do with the other affair - or possibly with Jack being kept confined in the house in Grafton Street."

"I don't care what it has to do with - don't go, dearest - please don't, I ask you as a favour," and, bending over, she kissed me on the lips.

It was horribly hard to resist such an appeal, and yet I felt I should be a cur if Jack really needed me - and obviously he did - and I failed to go to him. And what would Dulcie think of me later if, through my giving way to her entreaty, some serious harm should befall my friend? Much as I loved her, I could not let her influence me in such a case; even if I did, it might in the end make her despise me.

"I would do anything in the world for you, sweetheart," I said, kissing her fondly. "You know that, as well as I do. I would grant you any favour provided - "

"Provided what?" she asked quickly as I paused.

"Provided that my doing so could have no harmful result. Prevent my going to Jack in such a crisis, and - "

I stopped abruptly. My tongue had, alas, outrun my discretion.

"Crisis? What crisis?" Dulcie burst forth, startled at my tone. "Oh, Mike, you are keeping something from me, you are deceiving me - don't say that you aren't, for I know you are!"

"Darling," I exclaimed, taking her in my arms, "I am not deceiving you - indeed, indeed I am not. I may have been wrong in using the word 'crisis.' What I meant was that, knowing that Jack and a friend of his are striving tooth and nail to track down the thieves who robbed this house, and seeing that I have promised to help Jack to the best of my ability, I feel that this urgent telegram of his means that something has come to light, that he has heard something or discovered some clue which makes it imperative that I should go to him at once. And I am going - now."

Quickly I released her. Then, fearing that further delay - added, possibly, to further persuasion on her part - might end by weakening my determination, I gave her a final kiss, and hurried out of the room.

Again I glanced at the telegram -

"*Come at once. Urgent. - Jack.*"

Then I crumpled the paper and tossed it into the fire.

Having arrived at Paddington I went straight to Jack Osborne's hotel. He had left word that, upon my arrival, I should be told to go to a house in Warwick Street, Regent Street, and there inquire for him.

It was George Preston's address. I hastened there in a taxi, and, as I rang the bell, I heard a clock strike six. Preston himself admitted me.

"Mr. Osborne has not yet arrived," he said as, after a word of explanation, we shook hands, "but I expect him any minute, and he is expecting you. Will you come in and wait?"

As I had not previously been to Preston's house its appearance surprised me. One does not associate a police detective, even an ex-detective, with a taste in things artistic, but here on all sides was evidence of refinement and a cultured mind - shelves loaded with carefully selected books, volumes by classic authors; treatises on art; standard works by deep thinkers of world-wide repute, while on the walls hung mezzotints I knew to be extremely rare. In addition there were several beautiful statues, cloisonne vases from Tokio and Osaka, antique furniture from Naples and from Florence, also treasures from Burma, the West Indies, and New Guinea.

The door opened, and the maid announced: "Baron Poppenheimer."

"Ah, my dear Baron," Preston exclaimed as he advanced to meet him, "this is a real pleasure; I didn't expect you so soon, but, as you are here, come and sit down," and he drew forward a chair. "But first let me present to you Mr. Michael Berrington, a friend of our mutual friend Jack Osborne's."

"Delighted to meet you - delighted, I am sure," Baron Poppenheimer said, with a slight accent, extending two fingers - a form of handshake which I particularly dislike. "Dreadfully cold again, is it not? - hein? Dreadfully cold, I am sure."

His appearance rather amused me. His was a queer figure. He wore a thick, dark blue box-cloth overcoat, double-breasted, with large pearl buttons, and a wide collar of yellow fur, which came well down on the shoulders; the fur cuffs matched it. His gloves were woolly ones, lavender-coloured, and the black silk hat which he carried in his right hand was burnished until it rivalled the shine of his patent boots - the "uppers" being hidden by spats. He had curly, black hair; black, rather bushy eyebrows; and a small imperial. While he carried a stout malacca cane with a large gold head to it, and in his left eye was a gold-rimmed monocle secured round his neck by a broad black ribbon.

We conversed for a little time, and from his talk I could see that he was something of a character. He knew many of my friends, and, upon my repeating my name to him, he seemed to know a good deal about me. I expressed surprise at this, whereupon he looked up at Preston, who stood immediately behind me, and observed drily:

"I believe I could tell Mr. Berrington almost as much about himself as I was able to tell you, Preston; what do you think?"

"Baron Poppenheimer is an extraordinarily clever clairvoyant and palmist, Mr. Berrington," Preston said. "I place such implicit confidence in his forecasts that I persuade him, whenever I can, to help me in my work. Yesterday he took it into his head to read my palms, and he told me things about myself that staggered-me - I almost begin to believe in black magic!"

I became greatly interested.

"I wish I could some day persuade the Baron to read my palms," I exclaimed, "Palmistry has always rather appealed to me."

"So?" Baron Poppenheimer answered. "I will read your palms for you now, if you will, I am sure."

He took my right hand, flattened it, palm upward, on his knee, studied it closely for a moment or two, then, after a few moments' silence, began to talk fluently and rapidly. The things he told me about myself, things I had done, even things I had only thought, made me almost gape with amazement. Then he took my left hand, examined both sides of it closely through his monocle, and continued his disclosures. He told me to within a day or two how long I had been engaged to be married, and described Dulcie's appearance to the life; he even went so far as to tell me exactly how she talked. For some moments I wondered if Preston could have coached the Baron in my movements; then I remembered that the Baron had told me things about myself of which Preston knew nothing.

"And that is all I have to tell you, my dear Mike," the "Baron" suddenly exclaimed in quite a different voice. I sprang back in my chair as I looked up sharply. Jack Osborne had pulled off his black, curly wig, and sat laughing loudly. Preston too was considerably amused.

"Yes, George," Jack said at last, "that disguise will do; you certainly are a marvel in the art of 'make-up.' If I can deceive Mike Berrington, who is one of my oldest friends, I shall be able to hoodwink anybody. Now you had better try your hand on Mike. What sort of person do you propose to turn him into? I have told you that he is an excellent actor, and can mimic voices to perfection."

Osborne then explained why he had telegraphed to me. Preston had made a discovery - a rather important discovery. Exactly what it was they would not tell me then, but Preston had suggested that on that very night the three of us should visit Easterton's house in Cumberland Place, where Gastrell's reception had taken place, wearing effectual disguises which he would attend to, and see for ourselves what there was to be seen. It was Osborne, I now learned for the first time, who had effected the introduction between Hugesson Gastrell and "Lord Cranmere" - the actual Lord Cranmere had been consulted by Jack on the subject of his being impersonated, and when Jack had outlined to him his plan and told him why the detective, Preston, wished to impersonate him, Lord Cranmere had entered into the spirit of the thing and given his consent. He had, indeed, expressed no little alarm when Jack had told him how the mysterious, unseen individual at the house in Grafton Street had cross-questioned him with regard to Eldon Hall, Cranmere's place in Northumberland, the whereabout of the safe that Cranmere had bought ten months previously, the likelihood of there being a priests' hiding-hole at Eldon, and so on.

"The whole idea regarding to-night, and our plan of action, originates with Preston," Jack said to me. "He believes - in fact, he is almost sure - that Gastrell and his associates know nothing of him by repute as a detective, also that they don't know him by sight, or by name either. He says, however, that they believe they are now personally acquainted with Lord Cranmere, upon whose property we think they have evil designs. 'Lord Cranmere' is now, in turn, going to introduce to Gastrell and his associates two particular friends of his. Those friends will be 'Baron Poppenheimer' and - who is Cranmere's other friend to be, George?" he inquired, looking up at Preston.

"'Sir Aubrey Belston,'" Preston answered at once. "Mr. Berrington is not at all unlike Sir Aubrey, in build as well as in feature."

"'Baron Poppenheimer' and 'Sir Aubrey Belston,'" Jack said, "who in private life are Jack Osborne and Michael Berrington. And if George disguises you and coaches you as well as he did me, I undertake to say that nobody will suspect that you are not actually Sir Aubrey Belston."

CHAPTER XIV

IN THE MISTS

At a quarter to one in the morning Cranmere's big, grey, low-built car slid noiselessly along Wigmore Street and drew up at the entrance to one of the most imposing-looking houses in Cumberland Place.

The imposing footman got down and rang the bell - he pressed the button four times in succession, as "Lord Cranmere" had told him to do. Almost at once the door was opened, and from the car window we saw a tall man in knee-breeches silhouetted, while a little way behind him stood another man. "Lord Cranmere" stepped out of the car, and we followed him - "Baron Poppenheimer" and "Sir Aubrey Belston." In point of fact, the real Sir Aubrey Belston was at that moment somewhere in the Malay States, making a tour of the world.

"Lord Cranmere" had told the chauffeur that he would not require him again that night, and I had noticed the man touch his hat in the belief that this actually was his employer who addressed him, for the real Earl of Cranmere had lent us his car. I heard the car purr away in the darkness, and an instant later the door of number 300 Cumberland Place shut noiselessly behind us.

The footman in knee-breeches and powdered head, who had admitted us, led us without a word across the large hall, turned into a long corridor dimly-lit by tinted electric lamps, turned to the left, then to the right, then showed us into a small, comfortably-furnished room in which a fire burned cheerily, while in a corner a column printing machine ticked out its eternal news from the ends of the earth. We waited several minutes. Then the door opened and Hugesson Gastrell entered.

Like ourselves, he was in evening clothes. He advanced, shook hands cordially with "Lord Cranmere," saying that he had received his telephone message.

"These are my friends of whom I spoke," Cranmere said, "Baron Poppenheimer and Sir Aubrey Belston."

"Delighted to meet you," Gastrell exclaimed. "Any friend of Cranmere's is welcome here; one has, of course, to be careful whom one admits on these occasions - isn't that so, Cranmere? Come upstairs and have some supper."

We followed him, ascending to the first floor. In a large, high-ceilinged, well-lit room an elaborate supper was spread. There were seats for thirty or forty, but only ten or a dozen were occupied. A strange atmosphere pervaded the place, an atmosphere of secrecy, of mystery. As we entered, the people at supper, men and women, had glanced up at us furtively, then continued their conversation. They talked more or less under their breath.

Gastrell called for a bottle of "bubbly," and about half an hour later we rose. The room was by this time deserted. Following Gastrell along a narrow passage, we presently found ourselves in a room larger than the one we had just left. Here between forty and fifty men and women sat at several tables. At one *chemin-de-fer* was in progress; at another *petits chevaux*; at a third the game which of late years has become so popular in certain circles - "Sandown Park." On all the tables money was heaped up, and on all sides one heard the musical chink of gold and the crackle of bank-notes. Nobody spoke much. Apparently all present were too deeply engrossed to waste time in conversation.

As I glanced about me I noticed several people I knew intimately, and four or five I knew only by sight, people well known in Society. I was on the point of bowing to one woman I knew, who, looking up, had caught my eye; just in time I remembered that she would not recognize me in my disguise. Then a man nodded to me, and I nodded back. He looked rather surprised at seeing me, I thought, and at once it flashed across me that of course he was under the impression that I was Sir Aubrey Belston, and probably he had heard that Sir Aubrey was travelling round the world.

Gastrell, after a few minutes' conversation, found us places at a table where "Sandown Park" was being played. As I seated myself I found, facing me, Jasmine Gastrell, and for some moments I felt uncomfortable. I could feel her gaze upon my face as she scrutinized me closely, but even she did not penetrate my disguise.

"Lord Cranmere" sat upon the opposite side of the table, "Baron Poppenheimer" on my side, two seats from me. On my right was one of the unintelligent-looking women I had met at Connie Stapleton's dinner party at the Rook Hotel in Newbury; on my immediate left a man I did not know. Connie Stapleton I had looked about for, but she was nowhere visible.

So this was one of the ways Gastrell amassed money - he ran a gaming-house! I now began to see his object in cultivating the acquaintance of people of rank and wealth; for I had long ago noticed that Jasmine and Hugesson Gastrell never missed an opportunity of becoming acquainted with men and women of position. Also I began to grasp Preston's line of action. Disguised as the Earl of Cranmere, who was known to be extremely rich, he had cleverly ingratiated himself with the Gastrells and led them on to think him rather a fool who could easily be gulled. Jack had more than once told me how artfully Preston played his cards when on the track of people he suspected and wished to entrap, so that I could well imagine Preston's leading the Gastrells on to ensnare him - as they no doubt supposed they were doing. For that he would not have been admitted to this gambling den - it evidently became one at night - unless the Gastrells had believed they could trust him and his friends implicitly, I felt certain.

My friends tell me that I am a rather good actor, and Preston's coaching in Sir Aubrey Belston's mannerisms and ways of talking had given me a measure of self-confidence. When, therefore - I had played for a quarter of an hour and won a good deal - Jasmine Gastrell suddenly addressed me, I did not feel disconcerted.

"I mean to follow your lead," she said. "You are so extraordinarily lucky. How is it you manage to win every time?"

"Not every time," I corrected. "It's quite easy if you set about it in the right way."

"I wish I knew the right way," she answered, fixing her eyes on me in the way I knew so well. "Won't you tell me how you do it?"

"Different people must 'do it,' as you put it, in different ways," I said. "Forgive my asking, but are you superstitious?"

She broke into rippling laughter.

"Superstitious? I?" she exclaimed. "Oh, that's the last thing my enemies would accuse me of being!"

I paused, looking hard at her.

"And yet," I said seriously, "judging by your eyes, I should say that you are remarkably psychic, and most people who are psychic are superstitious up to a point."

I went on looking at her, staring right into her eyes, which she kept set on mine. She did not in the least suspect my identity -

I was now positive of that. I had spoken all the time in an assumed voice.

"Yes," I said at last, impressively.

"Yes what?" she asked quickly; she was not smiling now. "Why do you say 'yes' like that? What does it mean?"

Apparently our conversation disturbed some of the players, so I said to her seriously, indicating an alcove at the end of the room:

"Let us go over there. I should like to talk to you."

She made no demur, and presently we sat together in the alcove, partly concealed by palms and other plants, a small table between us.

"Now tell me how you win, and how I am to win," she exclaimed, as soon as we were seated. "I should dearly love to know."

I reflected, as I sat looking at her, that she was a consummate actress. I could not doubt that she ran this establishment in connection with Gastrell, yet here she was feigning deep anxiety to discover how she could win.

"I don't know your name," I said at last, ignoring her inquiry, "but you are one of the most amazing women, I would say one of the most amazing human beings, I have ever met."

"How do you know that - I mean what makes you say it?" she asked quickly, evidently disconcerted at my solemnity and at the impressive way I spoke.

"Your aura betrays it," I answered in the same tone. "Every man and woman is surrounded by an aura, but to less than one in ten thousand is the human aura visible. It is visible to me. The human aura betrays, in too many cases, what I would call its 'victim.' Your aura betrays you."

I leaned forward across the table until my face was close to hers. Then, still looking straight into her eyes, I said, almost in a whisper:

"Shall I tell you what I see? Shall I tell you what your life has been?"

She turned suddenly pale. Then, struggling to regain her composure, she said after a brief pause, but in a tone that lacked conviction:

"I don't believe a word you say. Who are you? Whom have I the pleasure of speaking to?"

"Sir Aubrey Belston," I answered at once. "You may have heard of me. Good God - the things I see!"

I pretended to give a little shudder. My acting must have been good, for on the instant she turned almost livid. Again she made a terrific effort to overcome the terror that I could see now possessed her.

"I *will* tell you what I see!" I exclaimed, suddenly snatching the wrist of her hand which lay upon the table, and holding it tightly. Though almost completely concealed by the palms and plants, she strove to shrink still further out of sight, as though the players, engrossed in their games, would have spared time to notice her.

My eyes met hers yet again, but the expression in her eyes had now completely changed. In place of the bold, impelling look I had always seen there, was a fearful, hunted expression, as though she dreaded what I was going to say.

"I see a room," I said in a low, intense tone, holding her wrist very tightly still. "It is not a large room. It is a first-floor room, for I see the exterior of the house and the two windows of the room. I see the interior again. Several people are there - I cannot see them all clearly, but two stand out distinctly. One is Gastrell, to whom I have this evening been introduced; the other is you; ah, yes, I see you now more clearly than before, and I see now another man - handsome, fair, about twenty-eight or thirty - I can see his aura too - his aura within your aura - he loves you desperately - and - ah, I see something lying on the floor - a woman - she is dead - you - "

Her thin wrist suddenly turned cold; her eyes were slowly closing. Just in time I sprang to my feet to save her from falling off her chair, for she had fainted.

None of the players were aware of what had happened; all were too deeply engrossed. Without attempting to restore my companion to consciousness - for, in the face of what I had now learned practically beyond doubt to be a fact, I had no wish to revive her - I left her lying in her chair, stepped noiselessly along behind the mass of plants which occupied one side of the room, emerged further away, and presently took a vacant seat at a *chemin-de-fer* table.

I glanced at my watch. It was nearly two o'clock. Thinking over what had just happened, and wondering what my next move had better be, and what Jack and Preston intended doing, I stared carelessly about the room.

At all the tables play was still in progress. At some complete silence prevailed. From others there arose at intervals a buzz of conversation. Behind some of the lucky players stood groups of interested watchers. About the sideboard were clustered men and women refreshing themselves, the majority smoking and laughing, though a few looked strangely solemn. Among the latter I suddenly noticed a face I had seen before. It was the demure, dark little woman who at Connie Stapleton's dinner party had all the evening seemed so subdued. She was dressed quietly now, just as she had been then, and she looked even more out of place in this crowd of men and women gamblers, all of whom were exceedingly well-dressed, than she had looked at that dinner party. "There is only one person I should be more surprised at seeing here," I said mentally, "and that is Dulcie."

The thought of her made me wonder what she would think if she could see me at this moment, when suddenly my heart seemed to stop beating.

Seated at the table nearest me but one, a table partly surrounded by a group of excited onlookers, was Connie Stapleton. And close beside her, engrossed in the game, Dulcie Challoner herself!

CHAPTER XV

THE MODERN VICE

So staggered was I that for the moment I almost forgot my disguise, and the *role* I was playing, and was on the point of hurrying over to Dulcie and asking her how she came to be there. That Mrs. Stapleton must have brought her, of course I guessed.

Fortunately I restrained myself just in time. Dulcie, I saw to my dismay, was not merely playing, but was deeply engrossed in the game. "Sandown Park" was the game in progress at that table, a game which to all intents is a series of horse-races, but whereas at a race-meeting only half a dozen or so races are run in an afternoon, the players at "Sandown Park" can back horses in half a dozen races in as many minutes. Judging by the interest she evidently took in the game, Dulcie must, I conjectured, have been playing for some time, for she appeared to be quite *au fait*. Never had she mentioned this game to me, and never had I known her to take interest in backing horses or in any form of reckless speculation. Consequently I had reason to suppose that this was the first time she had played, if not the first time she had seen or heard of the game.

Did I dare approach her? Would my feelings get the better of me and lead to my betraying who I was? Though I had not been identified by people who knew me, would Dulcie's perception be keener and lead to her seeing through my disguise? These and similar doubts and questions crowded my brain as I stood there watching her from a distance, but in the end indiscretion got the better of prudence, and I decided to join the men and women grouped about the table at which she and her friend sat.

For fully ten minutes I stood there, and during that time I saw her win seven times in succession. She seemed to play without judgment or calculation, in fact, with absolute recklessness, and after winning three "races" in succession she had increased her stake each time. In the fourth "race" she had backed a horse for ten pounds at four to one, and won. In the next race she had planked twenty sovereigns on an outsider, and raked in over a hundred pounds. The next two races had increased her pile by between three and four hundred pounds. I could see her panting with excitement. Her lips were slightly parted. Her eyes shone. Her whole soul seemed centred upon the game.

And then she began to lose.

At first slowly, then rapidly, her pile of gold and notes dwindled. Time after time she backed the wrong "animal." Now only a few five- and ten-pound notes and a little heap of sovereigns - twenty at most - remained. Her face had turned gradually pale. Connie Stapleton leant towards her and whispered in her ear. I saw Dulcie nod; then, taking up all the money in front of her, she handed it to the man who held the bank, and received a ticket in return.

The board with the graduated divisions and the names of the horses marked upon them spun round once more. Dulcie's brows were contracted, her face was drawn, her expression tense. Slowly the board now revolved, slower still. It stopped. I saw her give a little start, and distinctly heard the gasp which escaped her.

She had lost everything.

Connie Stapleton's hand closed over hers, as though to reassure her. Again the widow spoke into her ear. A moment later I saw a roll of notes pushed towards Dulcie. Eagerly she grabbed them.

This was terrible. I realized at once what was happening. The widow was lending her money. I wondered if the money she had already lost had been lent to her by her friend. Instantly it dawned upon me that it must have been, unless, indeed, Dulcie had, before I arrived, been extraordinarily lucky, for I knew that she had not money enough of her own to gamble with for such high stakes. She was playing again now - and losing. Once or twice she won, but after each winner came several losers. I was gradually getting fascinated. Again the widow lent her money, and again she lost it all.

At last they rose. Never, as long as I live, shall I forget the expression that was on my darling's face as, with the widow's arm linked within her own, she made her way towards the door.

I followed them to the supper room. They stopped, and, standing at one of the tables, Mrs. Stapleton filled two glasses with champagne. She gave Dulcie one, and herself emptied the other. She filled her own again and once more emptied it. Dulcie only half emptied her glass, then set it down.

Out of the room they went. While they put on their wraps I went in search of my hat. A few minutes later Mrs. Stapleton and Dulcie were entering a car which I at once recognized as Connie Stapleton's. As the car started I saw a taxi approaching, and hailed it.

"Follow that car," I said to the driver. "Keep it in sight, and, when you see it stop, stop forty or fifty yards behind it."

Right up into Hampstead the grey car sped. It slackened speed near Southend Road, eventually pulling up at a house in Willow Road. Leaning forward, I rubbed the frosted glass in the front of my taxi, and peered out. I saw Mrs. Stapleton alight first; then she turned and helped Dulcie to get out. Both entered the house. The door closed quietly, and the car rolled away.

For some minutes I waited. Then I told my driver to pass slowly by the house and make a note of the number. The number was "460."

That, at any rate, was satisfactory. I had discovered what was, presumably, Mrs. Stapleton's London address. Only then did I begin to wonder what Osborne and Preston would think when they found that I had gone. So engrossed had I become in Dulcie's movements that for the time all thought of my two companions had passed out of my mind. I thought of returning to the house in Cumberland Place; then, deciding that it was too late, I told the driver to go direct to my flat in South Molton Street.

A letter was lying on the table in my sitting-room. I seemed to recognize the writing, and yet -

I tore open the envelope and pulled out the letter. To my surprise it was from Dick, who was now back at Eton. "My dear Mike," it ran. "I have something very important to say to you, and I want to say it at once. But I don't want to write it. Can you come here to see me to-morrow as soon as possible, or can you get leave for me to come to London to see you? I don't want to go home, because if I did father and Aunt Hannah and Dulcie would ask questions, and what I want to say to you is *quite private.* Will you telegraph to me as soon as you get this to say what I can do and where I can see you at once?

"Your affectionate brother-in-law-to-be,

"DICK."

I read the letter through again; then refolded it and put it in a drawer. The letter, I saw by the postmark, had arrived by the last post.

What could the boy want to see me about? What could he have to say to me that he wished to keep secret from his family? I could not imagine. Anyway, I would, I decided, gratify him - I was very fond of Dick. Then and there I wrote out a telegram to be sent off early in the morning, telling him that I would come down in the afternoon; I had decided to try to see something of Dulcie during the morning, also to telephone to Holt to inquire for her, though without betraying to Sir Roland or Aunt Hannah that I knew anything of her movements during the previous night.

But Sir Roland forestalled me. Shortly after eight o'clock I was awakened by the telephone at my bedside ringing loudly. Still half asleep, I grabbed the receiver and glued it to my ear.

"Had I seen anything of Dulcie? Did I know where she was and why she had not returned?"

The speaker was Sir Roland, and he spoke from Holt Manor.

"Why, isn't she at home?" I asked, controlling my voice.

"If she were here I shouldn't ask where she is," Sir Roland answered quite sharply. "Mrs. Stapleton called yesterday afternoon to ask if Dulcie might dine with her in town and go to the theatre. Of course I raised no objection" - Sir Roland in no way shared my suspicion concerning Mrs. Stapleton; on the contrary, she attracted him and he liked her, though Aunt Hannah did not - "and Dulcie dressed and went off at about five o'clock. They were to go to 'The Rook,' Mrs. Stapleton said, where she would dress, and then they would motor to London. Mrs. Stapleton assured me that she would bring Dulcie back here by about midnight or one o'clock, and Dulcie took with her the key of the back door, so that nobody need wait up for her - she told her maid to go to bed. Her maid has just come to tell me that when she went to awaken Dulcie, she found that she had not returned. I have telephoned to 'The Rook,' and they tell me there that Mrs. Stapleton has not been back to the hotel since yesterday soon after lunch. So

I suppose that after leaving here she decided to motor straight to town, and dress there. I suppose she has some *pied-a-terre* in London, though she has never told me so."

"And you say that Dulcie has the door key with her," I said. "Do you think it was wise to give it to her?"

"Why in the world not? She has often taken it before. But tell me, have you seen anything of Dulcie?"

I didn't like telling an untruth, but, questioned in that point-blank way, I had to prevaricate; otherwise I should have been forced to say all I knew.

"She has not been to see me," I answered. "Perhaps Mrs. Stapleton's car broke down and they have been obliged to seek refuge at some wayside inn. I wouldn't be anxious, Sir Roland," I added, knowing how little it needed to make him anxious about Dulcie. "You will probably get a telegram from one of them presently."

We exchanged a few more remarks, and then Sir Roland exclaimed suddenly:

"Hold the line a moment. Hannah wants to speak to you."

Aunt Hannah, who, whatever faults she possessed, rarely lost her head, spoke sensibly and incisively. She didn't like this affair at all, she said, and intended to speak very seriously to Dulcie immediately upon her return. Also she was determined to put an end to this strong friendship between her niece and Mrs. Stapleton. On Dulcie's side, she said, it was nothing less than an absurd infatuation. She would not have minded her being infatuated about some women, but she had come thoroughly to mistrust Mrs. Stapleton.

I asked her to telephone or telegraph to me the moment Dulcie got home, and said that if I saw Dulcie in town or heard anything of her during the morning I would at once ring up Holt Manor. With that we rang off.

"Can I see Mrs. Stapleton?" I inquired, as the door of the house in Willow Road was opened by a maid with rather curious eyes; I had come there straight from my flat, no longer wearing my disguise, and it was nearly eleven o'clock. Just then I had an inspiration, and I added quickly, before she had time to answer, "or Mr. Hugesson Gastrell?"

An arrow shot at random, it proved a lucky shot, for the maid answered at once:

"Mrs. Stapleton isn't dressed yet, sir; but Mr. Gastrell can see you, I expect. What name shall I say?"

I was shown into a small morning room, and there I waited for, I suppose, five minutes. At last I heard footsteps approaching, and in a moment Gastrell entered.

"Dear me, this is a surprise," he exclaimed cordially, extending his hand. "I didn't know I had given you this address. Well, and what can I do for you?"

His tone, as he said this, was rather that of a patron addressing an inferior, but I pretended not to notice it, and, drawing upon my imagination, answered:

"I don't think you did give me this address; it was somebody else - I forget who - who mentioned it to me the other day in course of conversation. Really I have come to see Mrs. Stapleton and inquire for Miss Challoner."

"Miss Challoner? Do you mean Miss Dulcie Challoner, Sir Roland's daughter?"

"Yes."

An extremely puzzled look came into his eyes, though this he was probably not aware of.

"But what makes you think Miss Challoner is here?" he inquired quickly.

"She spent the night here with Mrs. Stapleton."

He looked still more puzzled.

"Did she really?" he answered in a tone of surprise which obviously was feigned.

"Yes. Didn't you know?"

"This is the first I have heard of it, but I dare say you are right. Mrs. Stapleton has rooms in this house - it's a little private establishment of mine - but beyond that I know little of her movements. I'll go and inquire if you'll wait a moment."

"Clever scoundrel!" I said aloud when he had left the room and shut the door. "Rooms here," "knows little of her movements," "first he has heard of it." But I am going to bowl you out in the end, my friend, I ended mentally as I seated myself and picked up one of the morning papers which lay upon the table. It was the *Morning Post.* I noticed that several little bits had been cut out of the front page - presumably advertisements.

I had scanned one or two pages and was reading a leading article when Gastrell returned.

"You are quite right," he said, offering me his cigarette case. "Miss Challoner is here. After supper last night at the Carlton with Mrs. Stapleton she didn't feel very well, so Mrs. Stapleton persuaded her to come back and sleep here instead of motoring back to Newbury. She told her maid to telegraph early this morning to Sir Roland Challoner, in case he should feel anxious at Miss Challoner's not returning last night, but the maid stupidly forgot to. She is sending a telegram now. Miss Challoner is quite all right this morning, and will be down presently, but I am afraid you won't be able to see Mrs.

Stapleton, as she isn't up yet."

I thanked him for finding out, thinking, as I did so, that certainly he was one of the most plausible liars I had ever come across; and then for a few minutes we conversed on general topics.

"You don't remember who it was told you my address?" he presently asked carelessly, flicking his cigarette ash into the grate.

"I am sorry, I don't," I answered, pretending to think. "It was some days ago that somebody or other told me you lived here, or rather that you had an address here."

"Oh, indeed. It's odd how people talk. By the way, how did you come to know that Mrs. Stapleton and Miss Challoner were here?"

His question was interrupted by Dulcie's entering, wrapped in a great fur coat. There were dark marks under her eyes that I had never seen there before, but she seemed in quite good spirits as she came across the room and greeted me.

"How in the world did you find out I was here!" she exclaimed. "It is most astonishing. Did you know that Connie had rooms here? I didn't, until last night. It was so good of her to put me up. I can't think what it was upset me so last night, but I am quite all right this morning. Connie has just telegraphed to father to explain my absence - you know how little it takes to worry him. I've got my evening dress on under this coat that Connie's lent me. She wanted to lend me one of her day dresses, but not one of them comes near fitting me."

I gasped. I couldn't answer. It was bad enough to find people like Gastrell and Jasmine Gastrell and Connie Stapleton perjuring themselves in the calmest way imaginable; but that Dulcie, whom I had until now implicitly believed to be everything that was good should thus look me in the eyes and lie to me - with as much self-assurance as though she had been accustomed to practising deception all her life.

A kind of haze seemed to rise before my eyes. My brain throbbed. All the blood seemed suddenly to be going out of my heart. Mechanically putting out an arm, I supported myself against the mantelpiece.

"Mike! Mike! What is the matter? Are you ill? do you feel faint?"

Her voice sounded a long, long way off. I heard her words as one hears words in a dream. My mouth had turned suddenly dry. I tried to speak, but could not.

"Here, Berrington, drink this and you'll feel better."

These were the next words I remember hearing. I was lying back on the settee, and Gastrell was holding a tumbler to my lips. It contained brandy slightly diluted. I drank a lot of it, and it revived me to some extent.

Still uncertain if I were sleeping or awake, I passed out through the hall, slightly supported by Dulcie, and clambered after her into the taxi which awaited us outside.

"Go to Paddington," I heard her say to the driver, as she pulled the door to. No servant had come out of the house, and Gastrell had disappeared while we were still inside the hall.

CHAPTER XVI

SECRETS OF DUSKY FOWL

To this day that drive to Paddington recalls to mind a nightmare. The entire confidence I had placed in Dulcie was shattered. Had anybody told me it was possible she could deceive me as she had done I should, I know, have insulted him - so infuriated should I have felt at the bare thought. And yet she clearly had deceived me, deceived me most horribly, inasmuch as she had done it in such cold blood and obviously with premeditation. Her eyes, which had always looked at me, as I thought, so truthfully, had gazed into mine that morning with the utmost coolness and self-possession while she deliberately lied to me. Dulcie a liar! The words kept stamping themselves into my brain until my head throbbed and seemed on the point of bursting. As the car sped along through the busy streets I saw nothing, heard nothing. The remarks she made to me seemed to reach my brain against my will. I answered them mechanically, in, for the most part, monosyllables.

What did it all mean? How could she continue to address me as though nothing in the least unusual had occurred? Did she notice nothing in my manner that appeared to be unusual? True, she addressed to me no term of endearment, which was singular; but so engrossed was I in my introspection and in my own misery that I scarcely noticed this. Indeed, had she spoken to me fondly, her doing so just then would but have increased the feeling of bitterness which obsessed me.

Several times during that drive I had been on the point of

telling her all I knew, all I had seen and heard: the suspicions I entertained regarding her friend Connie - her abominable friend as she now seemed to me to be; the grave suspicions I entertained also regarding Gastrell, with whom she seemed to be on good terms, to say the least - these, indeed, were more than suspicions. But at the crucial moment my courage had failed me. How could I say all this, or even hint at it, in the face of all I now knew concerning Dulcie herself, Dulcie who had been so much to me, who was so much to me still though I tried hard to persuade myself that everything between us must now be considered at an end?

I saw her off at Paddington. Mechanically I kissed her; why I did I cannot say, for I felt no desire to. It was, I suppose, that instinctively I realized that if I failed to greet her then in the way she would expect me to she would suspect that I knew something. She had asked me during our drive through the streets of London who had told me where to find her; but what I answered I cannot recollect. I made, I believe, some random reply which apparently satisfied her.

For two hours I lay upon my bed in my flat in South Molton Street, tossing restlessly, my mind distraught, my brain on fire. Never before had I been in love, and perhaps for that reason I felt this cruel blow - my disillusionment - the more severely. Once or twice my man, Simon, knocked, then tried the door and found it locked, then called out to ask if anything were amiss with me. I scarcely heard him, and did not answer. I wanted to be left alone, left in complete solitude to suffer my deep misery unseen and unheard.

I suppose I must have slept at last - in bed at three and up at eight, my night had been a short one - for when presently I opened my eyes I saw that the time was half-past two. Then the thought flashed in upon me that in my telegram I had promised to go to Eton to see Dick by the train leaving Paddington at three. I had barely time to catch it. A thorough wash restored me to some extent to my normal senses, and at Paddington I bought a sandwich which served that day instead of lunch.

Once or twice before I had been down to Eton to see Dick, though on those occasions I had been accompanied by Sir Roland. I had little difficulty now in obtaining leave to take him out to tea. He wanted to speak to me "quite privately," he said as we walked arm in arm up the main street, so I decided to take him to the "White Hart," and there I ordered tea in a private room.

"Now, Mike," he said in a confidential tone, when at last we were alone, "this is what I want to draw your attention to," and, as he spoke, he produced a rather dirty envelope from his trousers pocket, opened it and carefully shook out on to the table several newspaper cuttings, each three or four lines in length.

"What on earth are those about, old boy?" I asked, surprised. "Newspaper advertisements, aren't they?"

"Yes, out of the *Morning Post*, all on the front page. If you will wait a minute I will put them all in order - the date of each is written on the back - and then *you* will see if things strike *you* in the way they have struck me."

These were the cuttings:

"R.P, bjptnbblx. wamii. xvzzjv. okk.
zxxp. - DUSKY FOWL."

"Rlxt. ex. lnvrb. 4. zcokk. zbpl. qc.
Ptfrd. Avnsp. Hvfbl. Ucaqkoggwx. - DUSKY
FOWL."

"Plt. ecii. pv. oa. t1vp. uysaa. djt. xru.
przvf. 4. - DUSKY FOWL."

"Nvnntltmms. Pvvvdnzzpn. ycyswsa.
Bpix. uyyuqecgsqa. X. W. ljfh. sc.

jvtzfhdvb. - DUSKY FOWL."

"I can't make head or tail of them," I said when I had looked carefully at each, and endeavoured to unravel its secret, for obviously it must possess some secret meaning. "What do you make of them, Dick - anything?"

"Yes. Look, and I will show you," he answered, going to the writing-table and bringing over pen, ink and paper. "I have always been fond of discovering, or trying to discover, the meanings of these queer cypher messages you see sometimes in some newspapers, and I have become rather good at it - I have a book that explains the way cyphers are usually constructed. I have found out a good many at one time and another, but this one took me rather a long time to disentangle. I can tell you, Mike, that when I found it concerned you I felt frightfully excited."

"Concerned me!" I exclaimed. "Oh, nonsense. What is it all about?"

"Follow me carefully, and I'll show you. I guessed from the first that it must be one of those cyphers that start their alphabet with some letter other than A, but this one has turned out to be what my book calls a 'complex alphabet' cypher. I tried and tried, all sorts of ways - I began the alphabet by calling 'b' 'a'; then by calling 'c' 'a'; then by calling 'd' 'a,' and so on all the way through, but that was no good. Then I tried the alphabet backwards, calling 'z' 'a'; then 'y' 'a'; right back to 'a,' but that wasn't it either. Then I tried one or two other ways, and at last I started skipping the letters first backwards, and then forwards. Doing it forwards, when I got to 'l' I found I had got something. I called 'l' 'a'; 'n' 'b'; 'p' 'c'; and so on, and made out *bjptnbblx*, the first word in the first cypher, to be the word 'improving,' and the two letters before it in capitals 'R.P.' to be really 'D.C.' The next cypher word, *wamii*, stumped me, as the code didn't make it sense; then it occurred to me to start the alphabet with 'm' instead of 'l,' skipping every alternate letter as before, and I made out *wamii* to mean 'shall.' The next cypher word, *xvzzjv*, I couldn't get sense out of by starting the alphabet with either 'l' or 'm,' so I tried the next letter, 'n,' skipping alternate letters once more, and that gave me the word 'settle.' I knew then that I had got the key, and I soon had the whole sentence. It ran as follows:

"*D.C. improving shall settle all soon. - Dusky Fowl.*"

"Still, I wasn't much the wiser, and it never for a moment occurred to me that D.C. stood for Dulcie Challoner - "

"Good heavens, Dick!" I cried, "you don't mean to tell me that Dulcie - "

"Do be patient, brother-in-law, and let me go through the whole thing before you interrupt with your ejaculations," Dick said calmly. "Well, four days went by, and then in the *Morning Post* of February 7th the second advertisement appeared:

"Rlxt. ex. sroehnel. 28. Zcokk. zbpl. qc.
Ptfrd. Avnsp. Hvfbl. Ucaqkoggwx. - DUSKY
FOWL."

"The code was the same as the first, and I deciphered it quite easily. Here it is," and he read from a bit of paper he held in his hand:

"*Date is February 28. Shall stay at Mount Royal Hotel, Bedlington. - Dusky Fowl.*"

There was nothing more after that until February 12th, when the third advertisement appeared, same code, - here it is deciphered:

"*Car will be at Clun Cross two day February 28. - Dusky Fowl.*"

"That 'Dusky Fowl' bothered me a lot. I couldn't think what it meant. Several times I had gone through the names of all the 'dusky birds' I could think of - blackbird, rook, crow, raven, and so on, but nothing struck me, nothing seemed to make sense. Then the next day - yesterday - an advertisement in the same code appeared which startled me a lot because your name and Mr. Osborne's were in it, and it didn't take me long then to get at the meaning of 'Dusky Fowl.' Here is the advertisement from yesterday's *Morning Post*, and directly I had read it I wrote that letter asking you to come to see me at once, or to let me come to you."

He read out:

"*Osborne and Berrington suspect. Take precautions. D.C. with me Hampstead. - Dusky Fowl*"

"'Dusky Fowl' evidently stands for 'rook,' and 'rook' for 'Rook Hotel,' and 'Rook Hotel' for 'Mrs. Stapleton.' And that being the case, who else can 'D.C.' stand for but 'Dulcie Challoner'? It's as plain as a pike-staff."

"By Jove, Dick," I said after a few moments' pause, "I believe you are right!"

"I am sure I am," he answered with complete self-assurance.

This clearly was a most important discovery. I decided to take the cuttings and their solutions to Osborne the moment I got back to town, and I intended to go back directly after delivering Dick safely back at his school.

"Really," I exclaimed, feeling now almost as excited as the boy, "you are pretty clever, old chap, to have found out all that. I wonder, though, why Mrs. Stapleton doesn't telegraph or write to the man or people these messages are intended for. It would be much simpler."

"It wouldn't be safe, Mike. I read in a book once that people of that sort, the kind of people Mr. Osborne always speaks of as 'scoundrels,' nearly always communicate in some sort of cypher, and generally by advertising, because letters are so dangerous - they may miscarry, or be stopped, or traced, and then they might get used as evidence against the people who wrote them. By communicating in cypher and through a newspaper of course no risk of any sort is run."

"Except when the cyphers get deciphered," I said, "as you have deciphered these."

"Oh, but then people seldom waste time the way I do, trying to find these things out; when they do it's generally a fluke if they come across the key. It took me hours to disentangle the first of those advertisements - the rest came easy enough."

All this conversation had distracted my mind a good deal, and I began to feel better. For several minutes I was silent, wrapped in thought, and Dick had tact enough not to interrupt me. I was mentally debating if Dick might not, in more ways than one, prove a useful associate with Osborne, Preston and myself in our task of unveiling the gang of clever rogues and getting them convicted. One thing, which had struck me at once, but that I had not told Dick, for fear of exciting him too much, was that Bedlington was the large town nearest to Eldon Hall, the Earl of Cranmere's seat, the place the mysterious, unseen man in the house in Grafton Street had asked Jack Osborne about while he lay bound upon the bed; also that February 28th was the date when Cranmere's eldest son would come of age, on which day a week's festivities at Eldon would begin - and festivities at Eldon were events to be remembered, I had been told. What most occupied my thoughts, however, was the question I had asked myself - should I make a confidant of little Dick and tell him how things now stood between Dulcie and myself?

"Dick, old boy," I said, at last, "I wonder if I can treat you as I would a grown man - as I would treat some grown men, I should say."

"I dare say you could, brother-in-law," he answered. "Why don't you try?"

"Supposing that you were not to become my brother-in-law, as you seem so fond of calling me, would you be sorry?"

"I jolly well think I should!" he replied, looking up sharply. "But what makes you say a thing like that? It's all rot, isn't it?"

He seemed, as he looked at me with his big brown eyes which were so like Dulcie's, to be trying to discover if I spoke in jest or partly in earnest.

"You are going to marry Dulcie, aren't you? You're not going to break it off? You haven't had a row or anything of that kind"

"No, not exactly a row," I said, staring into his nice frank face.

"Then why do you talk about not becoming my brother-in-law? If you don't marry Dulcie you'll jolly nearly kill her. You don't know how fearfully fond of you she is. You can't know, or you wouldn't talk about not marrying her."

"I haven't talked about not marrying her," I answered hurriedly. "Tell me, Dick, is that true - what you say about her being so awfully fond of me?"

"I shouldn't say it if it wasn't true," he said with a touch of pride. "But what did you mean when you said you wondered if you could treat me as if I were a man?"

I put my arm round the lad, as he stood at the table, and drew him close to me.

"Dick, old boy," I said with a catch in my voice, "I am very unhappy, and I believe Dulcie is too, and I believe it is possible you may be able to put things right if you set about it in the right way. But first, tell me - you have talked to Mrs. Stapleton; do you like her?"

"I have never liked her from the first time she talked to me," he answered without an instant's hesitation. "And I don't like her any the better since I have heard you and Mr. Osborne talking about her, and since I spotted her in that advertisement yesterday."

"Well, Dick," I went on, "Mrs. Stapleton and Dulcie are now tremendous friends, and I believe that Mrs. Stapleton is trying to make Dulcie dislike me; I believe she says things about me to Dulcie that are untrue, and I think that Dulcie believes some of the things she is told."

"What a beastly shame! But, oh no, Mike, Dulcie wouldn't believe anything about you that was nasty - my word, I'd like to see anyone say nasty things to her about you!"

"I am glad you think that, but still - anyway, certain things have happened which I can't explain to you, and I am pretty sure Dulcie likes me less than she did. I want you to try to find that out, and to tell me. Will you try to if I can manage to get you a week-end at Holt?"

"Will I? You try me, Mike. And I won't only try to find out - I shall find out."

It was six o'clock when I arrived back at Eton with Dick. Word was sent to me that the headmaster would like to speak to me before I left. He came into the room a few minutes afterwards, told Dick to go away and return in ten minutes, then shut the door and came over to me. He looked extremely grave.

"Half an hour ago I received this telegram," he said, pulling one out of his pocket and handing it to me. "As I know you to be an intimate friend of Sir Roland's, you may like to read it before I say anything to Dick."

I unfolded the telegram. It had been handed in at Newbury at five o'clock, and ran:

"My daughter suddenly taken seriously ill. Dick must return at once. My butler will await him under the clock on Paddington departure platform at 7:15, and bring him down here. Please see that Dick is under clock at 7:15 this evening without fail. - CHALLONER."

I read the telegram twice, and even then I seemed unable to grasp its full significance. Dulcie seriously ill! Good God, what had happened to her - when we had parted on Paddington platform only a few hours before she had appeared to be in perfect health. Had this sudden attack, whatever it might be, any connection with Mrs. Stapleton, or with that hateful affair that I had witnessed the night before - my darling Dulcie gambling recklessly and losing, and then borrowing - from a woman I now fully believed to be an adventuress - money to go on gambling with? Was it even possible that, beside herself with dismay at the large amount of money she now owed Mrs. Stapleton, she had in a sudden moment of madness attempted to take -

I almost cried out as I banished from my brain the hideous thought. Oh, God, anything rather than that! I must get further news, and without a moment's loss of time. I must telegraph or telephone to Holt.

The headmaster's calm voice recalled me to my senses.

"It is indeed terrible news," he said sympathetically, struck, no doubt, at the grief which the news had stamped upon my face. "But it may, after all, be less serious than Sir Roland thinks. I was about to suggest, Mr. Berrington," he went on, pulling out his watch, "that as you are, I take it, returning to London by the 6:25, you might take Dick up with you and place him in charge of Sir Roland's butler who will be awaiting him at a quarter past seven under the clock on Paddington platform. If you can be so very kind as to do this it will obviate the necessity of my sending someone to London with him. I have given an order for such things as he way require to be packed, and they should be ready by now. We must break the news very gently to the boy, for I know that he is devoted to his sister, so for the boy's sake, Mr. Berrington, try to bear up. I know, of course, the reason of your deep grief, for Dick has told me that you are engaged to be married to his sister."

Hardly knowing what I said, I agreed to do as he suggested, and see Dick safely to Paddington. How we broke the news to him, and how he received it when we did break it, I hardly recollect. All I remember distinctly is standing in a telephone call office in Eton town, and endeavouring to get through to Holt Manor. Not until it was nearly time for the London train from Windsor to start, did the telephone exchange inform me they had just ascertained that the line to Holt Manor was out of order, and that they could not get through.

Anathematizing the telephone and all that had to do with it, I hurried out to the taxi in which Dick sat awaiting me.

All the way from Windsor to London we exchanged hardly a word. Dick, I knew, was terribly upset at the news, for his devotion to his sister was as well known to me as it was to his father and to Aunt Hannah. But he was a plucky little chap, and tried hard not to show how deeply the news had affected him. For my part my brain was in a tumult. To think that I should have parted from her that morning with feelings of resentment in my heart, and that now she lay possibly at death's door. Again and again I cursed myself for my irritability, my suspicions. Were they, after all, unjust suspicions? Might Dulcie not have excellent reasons to give for all that had occurred the night before? Might she not have been duped, and taken to that house under wholly false pretences? An uncle of hers believed to be dead, a brother of Sir Roland's, had, I knew, been a confirmed gambler. There was much in heredity, I reflected, in spite of modern theories to the contrary. Was it not within the bounds of possibility that Dulcie, taken to that gambling den by her infamous companion, and encouraged by her to play, might suddenly have felt within her the irresistible craving that no man or woman born a gambler has yet been able to overcome? And in any case, what right had I had metaphorically to sit in judgment upon her and jump to conclusions which might be wholly erroneous?

The train travelled at express speed through Slough, Didcot, and other small stations. It was within a mile of London, when my thoughts suddenly drifted. Why had Sir Roland not sent James direct to Windsor to meet Dick, instead of wasting time by sending him all the way to London? But perhaps James had been in town that day - he came up sometimes - and Sir Roland had wired to him there. Again, why had he not sent the car to Eton to fetch Dick away? That would have been the quicker plan; ah, of course he would have done that had it been possible, but probably the car had been sent into Newbury to fetch the doctor. That, indeed, was probably what had happened, for the telegram had been handed it at Newbury instead of at Holt Stacey. I knew that Sir Roland's chauffeur had a poor memory - it was well known to be his chief fault; probably he had shot through Holt Stacey, forgetting all about the telegram he had been told to send off there, and, upon his arrival in Newbury, remembered it and at once despatched it. Sir Roland had, I knew, a rooted dislike to telephoning telegraphic messages direct to the post office, and I had never yet known him dictate a telegram through his telephone. Oh, how provoking, I said again, mentally, as I thought of the telephone, that the instrument should have got out of order on this day of all days - the one day when I had wanted so urgently to use it!

Now the train was slowing down. It was rattling over the points as it passed into the station. Looking out of the window I could see the clock on the departure platform. A few people were strolling near it, but nobody was under it - at least no man. I could see a woman standing under it, apparently a young woman.

Dick's luggage consisted of a suit-case which we had taken into the carriage with us, and this I now carried for him as we descended into the sub-way. The clock on the departure platform is only a few yards from the exit of the sub-way, and, as we came out, the woman under the clock was not looking in our direction. Somehow her profile seemed familiar, and -

I stopped abruptly, and, catching Dick by the arm, pulled him quickly behind a pile of luggage on a truck. An amazing thought had flashed into my brain. As quickly as I could I gathered my scattered wits:

"Dick," I said after a few moments' reflection, trying to keep my brain cool, "I believe - I have an idea all isn't right. There is no sign of James, though our train was some minutes late and it is now twenty past seven - James was to be here at a quarter past, according to that telegram. But that woman waiting there - I know her by sight though I have never spoken to her. She might remember me by sight, so I don't want her to see me. Now look here, I want you to do this. Take hold of your suit-case, and, as soon as that woman's back is turned, walk up and stand under the clock, near her, as though you were awaiting someone. Don't look at her or speak to her. I believe this is some trick. I don't believe that telegram was sent by your father at all. I don't believe Dulcie is ill. I think that woman is waiting for you, and that when you have been there a few moments she will speak to you - probably ask you if you are Master Challoner, and then tell you that she has been sent instead of James to meet you, and ask you to go with her. If she does that, don't look in the least surprised, answer her quite naturally - you can inquire, if you like, how Dulcie is, though I shall not be a bit surprised if we find her at home perfectly well - and if she asks you to go with her, go. Don't be at all frightened, old chap; I shall follow, and be near you all the time, whatever happens. And look here, if I have guessed aright, and she does say that she has been asked to meet you and tells you to come along with her, just put your hand behind you for an instant, as you are walking away, and then I shall know."

"Oh, Mike, if Dulcie isn't ill, if after all nothing has happened to her - "

His feelings overcame him, and he could not say more.

I moved a little to one side of the pile of trunks, and peered out.

"Now, Dick - now!" I exclaimed, as I saw the woman turn her back to us.

Dick marched up to her, carrying his suit-case, and waited under the clock, just as I had told him to. He had not been there ten seconds when I saw the woman step up to him and speak to him.

They exchanged one or two remarks, then, turning, walked away together. And, as they walked, Dick's hand went up his back and he scratched an imaginary flea.

Instantly I began to walk slowly after them. Dick was being taken away by the dark, demure, quietly-dressed little woman I had seen at Connie Stapleton's dinner party, and, only the night before, standing among the onlookers in Gastrell's house in Cumberland Place.

CHAPTER XVII

IS SUSPICIOUS

They walked leisurely along the platform, Dick still carrying his suit-case, and at the end of it passed down the sloping subway which leads to the Metropolitan Railway. For a moment they were out of sight, but directly I turned the corner I saw them again; they walked slower now, Dick evidently finding his burden rather heavy. At the pigeon-hole of the booking-office a queue of a dozen or so were waiting to buy tickets. The woman and Dick did not stop, however. I saw them pass by the queue, and then I saw the woman hold out tickets to the collector to be clipped, and as I took my place at the back end of the queue she and Dick passed on to the Praed Street platform.

To what station should I book? I had no idea where they were going, so decided to go to High Street, Kensington, and pay the difference if I had to follow them further. There were still six people in front of me, when I heard the train coming in.

"Hurry up in front!" I called out in a fever of excitement, dreading that I might not get a ticket in time.

"All right, my man - don't shove!" the man immediately before me exclaimed angrily, pushing back against me. "This ain't the only train, you know; if you miss this you can catch the next!"

I believe he deliberately took a long time getting out his money.

Anyway, before I had bought my ticket the train had started. A moment later I stood upon the platform, watching, in a frenzy of despair, the red tail-light of the train containing Dick and the strange woman disappearing into the tunnel.

I felt literally beside myself. What in the world had I done! I had deliberately let the strange woman take Dick away with her, without having the remotest idea where she was going or why she had, to all intents, abducted the boy. It was awful to think of - and I alone was entirely to blame! Then the thought came back to me that I had told Dick to have no fear, assuring him that I would be near him all the time. What would the headmaster say who had confided him to my care? Worse, what would Sir Roland say when I confessed to him what I had done?

These and other maddening thoughts were crowding into my brain as I stood upon the platform, dazed, and completely at a loss what to do, when somebody nudged me. Turning, I recognized at once the man in the snuff-coloured suit who had told me so rudely "not to shove," and had then dawdled so while buying his railway ticket. I was about to say something not very complimentary to him, when he spoke.

"I trust you will forgive my apparent rudeness a moment ago at the booking-office," he said in a voice I knew quite well, "but there's a method in my madness. I am Preston - George Preston."

"Good heavens!" I exclaimed, the sudden revulsion of feeling almost overpowering me. "But do you know what has happened - do you know that Sir Roland Challoner's son I had charge of has - "

"Don't distress yourself, Mr. Berrington," he interrupted reassuringly, "I know everything, and more than you know, but I rather feared that you might see through this disguise. I have been loafing about Paddington station for nearly an hour. The lady I expected to see arrived just after seven, and took up her position under the clock. Then I saw you and the lad arrive; I saw you recognize the woman; I saw you put yourself out of sight behind the pile of trunks, and talk earnestly to the lad for a few moments, and I guessed what you were saying to him. I walked right past you in the sub-way, and intentionally made you miss this train, because it is inexpedient that you should follow those two. I know where they are going, and Mr. Osborne knows too; I needn't trouble to explain to you here how I come to know all this. The thing you have to do now is to come with me to my house off Regent Street, where Mr. Osborne awaits us."

Never in my life, I suppose, have I felt so relieved as I did then, for the mental pain I had endured during these few minutes had been torture. Indeed, I felt almost indignant with Preston for his having made me suffer so; but he explained that he had revealed himself to me the moment he felt justified in doing so. Suddenly a thought occurred to me.

"Do you know," I asked him quickly, "anything of a telegram sent to Eton this morning, apparently by Sir Roland, saying that Miss Challoner had been taken suddenly ill, and requesting that his son might be sent home to Holt at once?"

"Yes, I know, because - I sent it."

"*You* sent it!"

"Yes - though I didn't write it. Mrs. Stapleton wrote it. She gave it to her chauffeur, who was in the hall at the Rook Hotel, and when she was gone he asked me if I would mind handing it in, as I had intentionally told him I was going to the post office. I was a chauffeur, too, at the time, chauffeur to 'Baron Poppenheimer,' whom I drove down this morning in his car ostensibly to see the beautiful widow. 'Baron Poppenheimer' was, of course, Mr. Osborne. The widow was not at 'The Book' when we arrived - we knew she wouldn't be, and, of course, you know where she was, she was at the house in Hampstead where you found Miss Challoner when you called there this morning; she arrived home about two o'clock, however, and while 'Baron Poppenheimer' was making himself agreeable to her - your friend Mr. Osborne is a most splendid actor, and ought to have been in the detective force - I was making headway with her chauffeur out in the garage. Yes, Mr. Berrington, you can set your mind at rest - Miss Challoner is perfectly well. I wonder if by chance you telephoned to Holt this afternoon."

"I tried to."

"And you couldn't get through? The line was out of order?"

"Yes."

"Good!" Preston exclaimed, his small, intelligent eyes twinkling oddly. "That is as I thought. One of Gastrell's accomplices set the line out of order between three and five this afternoon. When the line comes to be examined the electrician will, unless I am greatly mistaken, find the flaw at some point between Holt Stacey and Holt Manor - if you should happen to hear, you might tell me the exact point where they find that the trouble exists. My theories and my chain of circumstances are working out splendidly - I haven't as yet made a single false conjecture. And now come along to my house, and I'll tell you more on the way."

Osborne sat in Preston's sitting-room, smoking a long cigar. He no longer wore the disguise of "Baron Poppenheimer," or any disguise, and upon our entry he uttered an exclamation.

"By Jove, Mike," he said, "you are the very man we've been wanting all day. Where did you disappear to last night?" And turning to Preston he added, "Were you right? Did he follow the widow and Miss Challoner home last night?"

"Yes," I answered for him, "I did. Did you see Dulcie at Gastrell's last night?"

"I should say so - and we saw you gazing at her. You nearly gave yourself away, Mike; you did, indeed. You ought to be more careful. When we saw you follow them out of the room, we knew, just as though you had told us, that you meant to follow them home. And what about the boy?" he said, addressing Preston. "Did he turn up? And was he met?"

"Yes, just as I expected; but he wasn't met by Sir Roland's butler, of course. He was met by Doris Lorrimer - you have probably noticed her, that dark, demure, quietly dressed girl who was at Connie Stapleton's dinner party at 'The Rook,' and at Gastrell's last night."

"You don't mean to say that she, too, is one of Gastrell's accomplices!" Jack exclaimed. "It seems impossible - looking like that!"

"I have suspected it for some time. Now I am sure. She has taken Dick Challoner to Connie Stapleton's house in Hampstead. It's one of the headquarters of the set, though, of course, the principal headquarters are at 300 Cumberland Place. How furious Lord Easterton would be if he knew! He suspects nothing as yet, I think."

"But how do you know that Doris Lorrimer has taken the boy to that Hampstead house?" Osborne asked quickly; "and why has she taken him?"

"The gang have kidnapped him - it was Connie Stapleton's idea - in order to get the reward they feel sure Sir Roland will offer for his recovery. How I know where Doris Lorrimer has taken him is that Connie Stapleton's chauffeur, with whom I fraternized this afternoon in Newbury, happened to mention that his mistress had told Miss Lorrimer to be under the clock at Paddington at seven-fifteen this evening to meet the man with the parcel,' as she said, and then to take the 'parcel' to her house in Hampstead! I won't tell you until later how I come to know the kidnapping was Mrs. Stapleton's idea; I have a reason for not telling you - yet."

"You certainly are a marvel, George," Jack said, as he blew a cloud towards the ceiling. "We seem to be well on the way now to running these scoundrels to ground. I shall be glad to see them convicted - right glad."

"We are 'on the way' - yes," Preston answered, "but you'll find it a longer 'way' than you expect, if you are already thinking of convictions. You don't know - you can't have any idea of - the slimness of these rogues if you suppose we are as yet anywhere near running them to ground. Just look how clever they have already been: first there is the fire in Maresfield Gardens and the discovery of the stabbed and charred body, for you may depend upon it that fire was meant to conceal some crime, probably murder, by destroying all traces, including that body which ought by rights to have been entirely consumed; then there is the robbery at Holt Manor; then the affair in Grafton Street, with yourself as the victim; then the murder of Sir Roland's gardener, Churchill - all these constitute mysteries, undiscovered crimes, and now comes this business of kidnapping Sir Roland's young son."

We talked at considerable length, discussing past and present happenings, and arranging our future line of action. Preston was immensely interested in the cypher messages unravelled by Dick - I had brought the cuttings with me to show to him and Jack. The reference to the date of the coming of age of Cranmere's son, considered in connection with the questions about Cranmere's seat, Eldon Hall, put to Osborne during his mysterious confinement in Grafton Street, made the detective almost excited. The unravelling of those cyphers was, he said, perhaps the most important discovery as yet made. Indeed, he believed that our knowledge of these messages might simplify matters Sufficiently to lead directly to the arrest of at any rate some members of the gang at a much earlier date than he had previously anticipated.

"It is clear," he said, as he put the cuttings into the envelope again and handed them back to me, "that Gastrell and company contemplate a coup of some sort either on the day

Lord Cranmere's son comes of age, or on one day during the week of festivities that will follow. 'Clun Cross.' We must find out where Clun Cross is; probably it's somewhere in Northumberland, and most likely it's near Eldon Hall. I suppose, Osborne, that you are invited to the coming of age, as you know Cranmere so well?"

"Yes, and I mean to go. But Berrington isn't invited; he doesn't know Cranmere."

"He probably knows what he looks like, though," Preston answered, laughing - he was thinking of his impersonation of the Earl, and his wonderful make-up. "I am not invited either, professionally or otherwise, so that Mr. Berrington and I had better go to Bedlington and put our heads together there, for something is going to happen at Eldon Hall, Osborne, you may take my word for that. We mustn't, however, forget that last cypher message: 'Osborne and Berrington suspect; take precautions.' 'Precautions' with such people may mean anything. I am firmly of opinion that poor Churchill's assassination was a 'precautionary' measure. It was on the afternoon before that murder, remember, that Churchill found the paste buckle at the spot where a grey car had been seen, left deserted, on the morning of the robbery at Holt. It was on the afternoon before that murder that he brought the buckle to Miss Challoner, told her about the grey car he had seen, which, he said, led him to suspect something, and asked to have the afternoon off. It was on that same afternoon that Mrs. Stapleton happened to motor over to Holt, and while there was told by Miss Challoner all about the finding of the buckle, also all about Churchill's secret suspicion about the car, and his asking to have the afternoon off, presumably to pursue his inquiries. And what happened after that? Don't you remember? Mrs. Stapleton telephoned from Holt to the Book Hotel in Newbury and talked to someone there - her maid, so she said - for five minutes or more, talked to her in Polish. Now, does anything suggest itself to either of you? Don't you think it quite likely that Mrs. Stapleton, hearing from Miss Challoner all about what had happened, telephoned in Polish certain instructions to somebody in Newbury, most likely one of her accomplices, and that those instructions led, directly or indirectly, to Churchill's being murdered the same night, lest he should discover anything and give information? One thing I am sure of, though - Mrs. Stapleton's chauffeur is an honest man who does not in the least suspect what is going on; who, on the contrary, believes his mistress to be a most estimable woman, kind, considerate, open-handed. I found that out while associating with him to-day as a fellow-chauffeur."

It was nearly nine o'clock before we went out into Soho to dine. Preston told us that he had arranged to call at Willow Road for Dick between ten and half-past. The three of us were to go to Hampstead and represent ourselves as being instructed by Sir Roland to take the boy away. Preston himself would, he said, represent himself as being an Eton master, and Doris Lorrimer was to be closely cross-questioned as to who had authorized her to meet the boy and take him to Hampstead and -

Well, Preston had thoroughly thought out his plan of action down to the smallest detail, and during dinner in the little restaurant in Gerrard Street, to which he had taken us, he explained it to us fully. Briefly, his intention was to frighten Doris Lorrimer half out of her senses by threatening instant prosecution if she did not, then and there, make certain disclosures which would help on our endeavour to bring to justice the whole gang with which she was evidently associated.

"But supposing," I hazarded, "we don't see Doris Lorrimer. Supposing we see only a servant, who assures us that we are mistaken, and that Dick isn't there. Supposing that Mrs. Stapleton, or even Gastrell, should confront us. What then?"

"I have carefully considered all those possibilities," Preston answered lightly as he refilled my glass, then Jack's, and then his own. "If anything of that kind should happen I shall simply - but there, leave it to me and I think you will be satisfied with the outcome. You must remember, Mr. Berrington, that I have been at this sort of thing over twenty years. Well, here's luck to our enterprise," and, raising his glass, he clinked it against our glasses in turn, then emptied it at a draught.

"And now," he said, preparing to rise, "we must be moving. We have rather a ticklish task before us, though I have no fear whatever as to its sequel, provided you leave most of the talking to me. In any case there must be no violence, remember. The only thing I regret is that the lad will most likely be asleep, so that we shall have to awaken him."

Punctually at half-past ten our taxi drew up outside the house numbered 460 Willow Road, Hampstead.

CHAPTER XVIII

CONTAINS ANOTHER SURPRISE

Lights were in most of the windows, as though a party were in progress.

Preston rang the bell. It was answered at once by a maid who had answered it in the morning, and before Preston had time to speak the maid asked us if we would come in. This time she showed us into a room a good deal larger than the one in which I had been interviewed by Gastrell in the morning. Very beautifully furnished, on all sides what is termed the "feminine touch" was noticeable, and among a number of framed photographs on one of the tables I recognized portraits of well-known Society people, several with autograph signatures, and one or two with affectionate inscriptions. I wondered to whom they had been presented, and to whom the affectionate inscriptions were addressed.

We waited a few minutes, wondering what would happen next, and who would come in to see us, for the maid had not even asked our names, though I saw that she had recognized me. For a moment it occurred to me that we ought to have changed into evening clothes, and I was about to tell Preston so when the door opened and Jasmine Gastrell entered, accompanied, to my amazement, by Dulcie Challoner.

I think even Preston was taken aback - and it took a great deal to astonish Preston. Osborne, I could see, was dumbfounded. Jasmine Gastrell was the first to speak, and she addressed me without looking either at Osborne or Preston.

"Good evening, Mr. Berrington," she said, with one of those wonderful smiles of hers which seemed entirely to transform her expression; "this is an unexpected pleasure."

How strangely different she now looked from the way she had looked at me in Cumberland Place when, disguised as Sir Aubrey Belston, I had pretended to read her past life! She turned to Jack, and, raising her eye-brows as though she had only that instant recognized him, "Why," she exclaimed, "it's Mr. Osborne! I had no idea we were to have the pleasure of seeing you here to-night - had you, Dulcie?"

Dulcie, who was standing by quite unconcernedly, turned at once to me without answering Mrs. Gastrell's question.

"Dear old Mike," she said, "how delightful of you to have come. I do hope you have entirely recovered. You looked so ill when you saw me off at Paddington this morning that I felt anxious about you all the way home. What was the matter with you? Have you any idea?"

I was so staggered, first at finding her at this house again, and then at her addressing me in the calm way she did, that for some moments I could not answer. Jack and Preston, now in conversation with Jasmine Gastrell, did not notice my hesitation. At last, collecting my scattered thoughts, I answered:

"I am quite well, Dulcie. There was nothing really much amiss with me this morning - I thought you knew that."

I stopped abruptly. What else could I say?

Under the circumstances I could not well speak about the telegram, and say why we had arrived in this way at such an unusual hour.

"I suppose you have come about Dick," she went on suddenly. "He is asleep now - he was so tired, poor little chap."

"Dulcie," I burst out impetuously under my breath, casting a hurried glance at the other three, who, still in conversation, did not appear to notice us. "Dulcie, what is the meaning of all this? Why are you here? Why is Dick here? I want to see you - I must see you alone as soon as possible - there is so much I want to say to you, want to ask you; such a lot has happened during the past day or two that I can't understand, and that I want to have explained. Tell me, my darling," I went on hurriedly, "when and where can we can meet - alone?"

She gave a delightful little laugh, and tapped me playfully with her fan - she and Jasmine were in evening dress. Then, looking roguishly up into my eyes, she went on:

"So far as Dick is concerned, everything is easily explained. When I got home this morning I felt very unwell. I found father terribly anxious at my absence, and Aunt Hannah in what I call one of her fits of tantrums. I went to lie down, and, while I was asleep, father came and looked at me. For some reason he got it into his head that I looked very ill, and just then Connie arrived in her car - she went to Holt direct from London, as she wanted to explain to father the reason she didn't take me home last night, and at the same time make her apologies for the anxiety she knew she must unintentionally have caused him; father, you know, likes Connie very much. After seeing me in bed he had jumped to the conclusion that I was really very ill and ought to see a doctor at once. Connie said that as she was going straight to Newbury she would, if he liked, send Doctor Claughton out to Holt. Then father said something about letting Dick know I was ill, and Connie volunteered to send a telegram to Eton, signed with father's name, and father said he wished she would. And that is the explanation of the whole affair."

"Explanation!" I exclaimed. "I don't call that half an explanation. What about James being told to meet Dick at Paddington and then not turning up?"

"Oh, that was a mistake of Connie's. James was in town

to-day, and Connie understood father to say that he would telegraph to James and tell him to meet Dick at Paddington. After telegraphing to Eton in father's name, from Newbury, she found she had made a mistake, so then she telegraphed to Doris Lorrimer to meet Dick. After the doctor had seen me, he told father there was nothing to be in the least alarmed about; in fact gave father to understand that his imagination had played pranks with him; so then father telephoned to Connie at the Book Hotel, and they decided there was no need for Dick to come home, and Connie suggested Dick's spending the night here and returning to Eton to-morrow."

I did not speak for some moments. At last I said:

"Dulcie, who told you all this?"

"Why, Connie, of course. Father had to attend an important magistrates' meeting in Newbury this afternoon, and, as I seemed quite well again, she got father's leave to bring me up to town again to meet some friends of hers who are here to-night. Now are you satisfied, Mike?"

"No, I am not," I answered bluntly. "Dulcie, have you seen Dick since he arrived here?"

"No, he had gone to bed before I arrived, and Connie said I had better not disturb him."

"My darling," I said a moment later, "I must see you alone. When can I?"

"Would to-morrow morning suit you, dear?" she asked, looking at me with her frank brown eyes. As I returned the gaze I found it impossible to believe that she had wittingly deceived me that morning, or indeed at any time, and yet -

"Yes. Shall we say at twelve o'clock?" I suggested. "And shall I call here for you?"

"That will do beautifully. Oh, Mike, my darling," she said quickly, under her breath, "I hope you still love me just as much as you did; I don't know why, but somehow I sometimes feel that you mistrust me - even that you suspect me of something or other, I don't know what."

"Dulcie!" I exclaimed impulsively, and I made as though to seize her hand, then remembered we were not alone, and refrained. "Dulcie, there are things I want you to explain to me, mysteries that only you can clear up. I don't really mistrust you, my own darling; indeed, indeed I don't; but I mistrust some of the people you mix with and have made friends of, more than that, I happen to know that some of them are no better than adventurers, and I want to get you away from them. What house is this we are in? I mean whose is it and who lives here?"

But at that instant our conversation was interrupted by Jasmine Gastrell.

"Oh, you lovers!" she exclaimed, laughing as she looked across at us. "What heaps and heaps lovers seem to have to tell each other after being parted for a few hours. It reminds me of my own young days," she added archly, for she looked barely seven-and-twenty. "Mr. Osborne has just told me, Dulcie, that he is asked to stay at Eldon Hall for Lord Cranmere's son's coming of age, on the twenty-eighth. I have been invited too; I do wish you were going to be there. Connie has accepted."

Ten minutes later, as the three of us sauntered slowly along Willow Road, we realized - at least I can answer for myself - that in spite of our careful scheming, and our complete confidence in the success of our plan, we had been cleverly outwitted. Not for a moment had Preston, or Jack Osborne, believed the long story that Jasmine Gastrell had related to them while Dulcie and I had been engrossed in conversation, a story it is unnecessary to repeat, though it had been told apparently with a view to leading them to think that Mrs. Gastrell was shortly to make a tour round the world. In the same way I had not been deceived by the ingenious tissue of implications and falsehoods that Connie Stapleton had poured into Dulcie's ear, and that Dulcie had innocently repeated to me. What most astonished me, however, was the rapidity with which Connie Stapleton and Jasmine Gastrell seemed able to concoct these ingenious and plausible narratives to account for anything and everything that happened on any occasion. A single discrepancy, for instance, in the story that Dulcie had just repeated to me would have brought the whole fabric of what appeared to be true statements - though I believed them to be false - crumbling to the ground. But there had been no such discrepancy. Everything that had occurred during the afternoon in relation to Dick, the telegram sent to Eton, Doris Lorrimer's meeting him in place of Sir Roland's butler, had been accounted for simply and quite rationally. And yet I felt firmly convinced the statements must in the main be a series of monstrous untruths, a belief in which Preston, with all his experience, concurred. Only two points puzzled me. Neither Jasmine Gastrell nor Connie Stapleton, nor, indeed, anybody else, could by any possibility have known that Preston, Jack, and I contemplated calling at the house in Willow Road that evening. How came it, then, that everything had been so skilfully arranged with a view to disarming our suspicions when we did call? That, I confess, was a problem so complicated that it formed the one and only argument in favour of the story that Dulcie had repeated to me being in part true. The other puzzling point was Dulcie's being at that house that night, and her knowing that Dick was there. Surely if Connie Stapleton and her accomplices had intended to kidnap Dick for the purpose of extorting money from Sir Roland, they would not intentionally have let Dulcie know what was happening. And, arguing thus with myself, I began at last to wonder if, after all, I had been mistaken; if, after all, Mrs. Stapleton had not invented that story, but had told Dulcie the truth. I confess that the more I thought it all over and the harder I tried to sift possible facts from probable fiction the more hopelessly entangled I became. Perhaps the strongest argument in favour of my theory that we were being cleverly and systematically hoaxed lay in Dick's discovery of the cypher messages in the *Morning Post.* There could, at any rate, be no getting away from the cypher message which had appeared on the previous day and that ran: "*Osborne and Berrington suspect. Take precautions*"

Then I thought again of Dulcie. It was appalling, almost incredible, that she should be allowed to associate with men and women whom we practically knew to be adventurers, and who might be not merely adventurers, but criminals masquerading as respectable members of Society. Yet I was impotent to prevent her; it was, of course, Sir Roland's duty to forbid her to mix with these people, but then Sir Roland, from being powerfully attracted by the young widow Connie Stapleton, was, as I had long ago guessed, becoming deeply enamoured of her; so that, far from preventing Dulcie from associating with her - Dulcie, with her strange infatuation for the woman - he deliberately encouraged the intimacy. Well, next morning, at any rate, I should see Dulcie alone, I reflected, with a feeling of satisfaction, and then I would have it out with her and go into the whole affair thoroughly, speaking to her with brutal frankness - even at the risk of hurting her feelings and incurring her displeasure I would tell her everything I knew and all that I suspected. Something must be done, and at once, to put an end to her absurd attachment to the widow - I had thought it all over quite long enough; it was now time to act. And Dick too; I must get hold of him and question him narrowly to find out if his story of what happened from the time he left me on Paddington platform and went and stood beside Doris Lorrimer under the clock, and his arrival at Willow Road, Hampstead, tallied with the story that Connie Stapleton had told Dulcie, and that Dulcie had related to me - for I somehow fancied that the two narratives might differ to some extent, if only in their minor details.

We were approaching Hampstead Tube station when Preston, turning to me from Jack Osborne, with whom he had been in close conversation, inquired:

"Has Sir Roland lately said anything to you, Mr. Berrington, that interested you particularly? Has he thrown out any hint of any sort?"

I reflected.

"Nothing that I can recollect," I said. "Have you reason to suppose that he has something of special interest that he wants to say to me?"

"I have, but until he speaks it is not for me to make any comment."

We had reached the Tube station. Jack booked to Russell Square; Preston to Piccadilly Circus; and I took a ticket to Bond Street, those being the stations nearest to our respective destinations.

"Are you aware," Preston said soon after the train had started, "that since we left my house and went to dine in Soho, we have been followed? I wanted to be perfectly certain before telling you, but I see now that I was right in my suspicion. Look to your left presently, one at a time, and at the end of the compartment you'll see quite an ordinary-looking man, apparently a foreigner, smoking a cheroot - the man seated alone, with a lot of hair on his face."

"You wouldn't notice him if he passed you in the street, would you?" he said after we had looked, "but I have noticed him all the evening. He was in Warwick Street when we all came out of my house; he followed us to Soho; he was in Gerrard Street, awaiting us, when we came out of the restaurant after dining; he came after us to Hampstead; he has followed us from Willow Road to the Tube station, and he is in this compartment now for the purpose of observing us. I want you each not to forget what he is like, and in a few minutes, when we all separate, I shall be curious to see which of us he follows - to know which of us he is really shadowing."

Jack was the first to alight. He bade us each a cheery good

night, after reminding us that we were all three to meet on the following afternoon, and hurried out. The hairy man with the cheroot remained motionless, reading his newspaper.

My turn came next - at Oxford Circus station. As I rose, I noticed the man carelessly fold up his newspaper, cram it into his coat pocket, and get up. Rather to my surprise I did not, after that, see him again. He was not with me in the carriage of the train I changed into, nor was he, apparently, on the platform at Bond Street station when I got out. As I pushed my latch-key into the outer door of South Molton Street Mansions, I glanced quickly up and down the street, but, so far as I could see, there was no sign of the man.

However, a surprise awaited me. Upon entering my flat I noticed a light in the sitting-room at the end of the little passage - the door stood ajar. Entering quickly, I uttered an exclamation of amazement. For in the big arm-chair in front of the fire - the fire burned as though it had lately been made up - Dick lay back fast asleep, his lips slightly parted, his chest rising and falling in a way that showed how heavily he slept.

Recovering from my amazement, I stood for a minute or two watching him. How delightful he looked when asleep like that, and what a strong resemblance he bore to Dulcie. But how came he to be here? And how came Dulcie to have told me, less than an hour before, that he was in the house at Hampstead, and asleep there? Gazing down upon him still, I wondered what really had happened since I had last seen him that evening, and what story he would have to tell me when he awoke.

My man had gone to bed, for it was now past midnight. Considering where I had better put Dick to sleep, my glance rested upon some letters lying on the table. Mechanically I picked them up and looked at the handwritings on the envelopes. Nothing of interest, I decided, and I was about to put them down again, unopened, when I noticed there was one from Holt that I had overlooked. The handwriting was Sir

Roland's. Hastily tearing open the envelope, I pulled out the letter. It was quite short, but its contents sent my heart jumping into my mouth, and had Dick not been asleep close by in the chair I believe I should have used some almost unprintable language.

"Oh, the fool - the silly, doddering, abject old fool!" I exclaimed aloud as I flung the open letter down on to the table and began to pace the room in a fury of indignation. "'No fool like an old fool' - oh, those words of wisdom - the man who first uttered them should have a monument erected to his memory," I continued aloud; then suddenly, as Dick stirred in his sleep, I checked myself abruptly.

The letter Sir Roland Challoner had written to me ran as follows:

"My dear Mike, - As you and Dulcie are engaged, I dare say you will be interested, and you may be surprised, to hear of another engagement. I have asked Dulcie's beautiful friend, Mrs. Stapleton, to become my wife, and she has done me the honour of accepting my proposal. Write to congratulate me, my dear Mike, and come down again soon to stay with us.

"Yours affectionately,

"ROLAND CHALLONER."

CHAPTER XIX

"IN THE PAPERS"

Dick was sleeping so heavily that he hardly stirred when I picked him up, carried him into my bedroom, laid him on my bed and loosened his clothes; I had decided to sleep on the settee in the room adjoining. Soon after seven next morning I was awakened by hearing him moving about. He had made himself quite at home, I found, for he had had a bath and used my towels and hair-brushes and found his way into a pair of my slippers.

"I hope you don't mind," he said apologetically, after telling me what he had done. "And now shall I tell you how I come to be here, Mike?" he added, clambering up on to my bed and lying down beside me.

I told him I wanted to know everything, and at once, and, speaking in his rapid, vivacious way, he went on to explain exactly what had occurred.

It seemed that when he went and stood by Doris Lorrimer under the clock at Paddington station, she had, as I had told him she probably would, asked him if he were Dick Challoner. Upon his telling her that he was, she said that she had been sent to meet him, and asked him to come with her. She had not told him where they were going, but when she got out at Baker Street station and he got out after her, a man had suddenly come up to her and said he wished to speak to her privately. She had told Dick to wait, and had then walked a little way away with the man, and for about ten minutes they had stood together, conversing in undertones.

"What was the man like?" I interrupted.

Dick described him rather minutely - he said he had taken special notice of his appearance "because he was such a hairy man" - and before he had done I felt practically certain the man who had met Doris Lorrimer was the foreign-looking man who had shadowed Preston, Jack, and myself the night before.

"I think," Dick went on, "the lady altered her plans after meeting that man; because for some moments after he had gone she seemed undecided what to do. Finally she went out of the station, hailed a taxi in Baker Street, told me to get into it, and then said something to the driver that I couldn't hear. We went straight down Baker Street, down Orchard Street - I noticed the names of both streets - then turned to the right and stopped at a house in Cumberland Place. As you had disappeared, I was beginning to feel a bit frightened, Mike, - I didn't much like the woman, who had spoken hardly a word to me all the time, - so just as she got out of the taxi on the left side, I quickly opened the door on the right side, popped out while her back was still turned, and ran away as hard as I could, leaving my suit-case in the taxi. It was very dark, and I believe that until after she had paid the driver she can't have missed me, as nobody came after me."

"Well, and what did you do then?"

"As soon as I had got well away, I went up to a policeman and asked him the way to South Molton Street. He explained clearly, and I came straight on here and asked for you. Your man, Simon, said you weren't in, and that he didn't know when you would be, so I asked if I might come in and wait, as I said I had something important to say to you. Of course he knew me by sight from seeing me with you sometimes, so he said 'Certainly,' and put me into your sitting-room. It was past eight when I got here. I was awfully hungry, so I ate all the cake and all the biscuits I found in the sideboard in your dining-room, and then I sat down in your big chair to wait for you - and I suppose I then fell asleep."

This report interested me a good deal, and I was still pondering it when my man came in with my letters and the newspaper, which he always brought to me before I got up. After reading my letters I picked up the newspaper, telling Dick to lie still and not disturb me until I had glanced through it. I had read the principal items of news, when suddenly my attention became centred upon an article which was headed:

AMAZING SERIES OF ROBBERIES
POLICE COMPLETELY BAFFLED

The article made up nearly a column of closely set type, and ran as follows:

Within a brief period of three months, that is to say since the beginning of December last, no less than eleven great robberies have been committed in various parts of Great Britain. Up to the present, however, no clue of any sort has been obtained that seems likely to lead to the discovery of the perpetrators of any one of these crimes. The victims of these robberies are the following:

Here followed a list of names of eleven well-known rich people; the names of the houses where the robberies had been committed; a brief description of the method employed by the thieves; and the value, approximately, of the property stolen in each case. The houses were for the most part large country mansions situated in counties far apart, and "Holt Manor, Sir Roland Challoner's seat in Berkshire," figured in the list. The article then continued:

When eleven such serious robberies, as we may rightly term them, are committed in comparatively rapid succession, and our police and detective force, in spite of their vaunted ability, prove themselves unable to effect a single arrest, what, we have a right to ask, is amiss with our police, or with their methods, or with both?

Questioned upon the subject, a well-known Scotland Yard Inspector yesterday informed our representative that official opinion inclines to the belief that the crimes mentioned have one and all been effected by a group of amazingly clever criminals working in combination. "How many members the gang consists of," he said, "how they obtained the special information they must have possessed to enable them to locate so accurately the exact whereabouts of the valuables they seized, and how they succeeded in securing those valuables in broad daylight, we have not the remotest notion. The theory held at present," he continued, "is that a number of expert thieves have by some means succeeded in becoming intimate with the owners of the houses that have been robbed. We repudiate entirely the theory that servants in the different houses must have been accomplices in the robberies either directly or indirectly."

The article then proceeded to advance a number of apparently plausible theories to account for the non-discovery of the thieves, and finally ended as follows:

If, then, our police and detectives would retain, or rather regain, their prestige, it is incumbent upon them at once to take steps to prevent any further outrages of this kind. Otherwise the police of Great Britain will run a grave risk of becoming the laughing-stock of Continental countries, where, we make bold to state, such a series of robberies, all more or less of the same nature, and involving a loss of, in the aggregate, approximately L50,000, would not thus have been committed with impunity.

I handed Dick the paper. When he had carefully read the article right through, he looked up abruptly.

"By Jove," he exclaimed, "I have an idea!"

I waited. For some moments he was silent. Then he continued:

"Do you remember the account of the robbery at Thatched Court, near Bridport? It's one of the robberies mentioned in this list."

"I can't say I do," I answered. "I don't read the newspapers very carefully. Why?"

"I happened to read that account, and remember it rather well. The robbery took place about five weeks ago - the house was entered while everybody, including some of the servants, was at a race-meeting. Among the things stolen was a pair of shot-guns made by Holland and Holland."

"But what on earth has that to do with anything? Where does the 'idea' come in?"

"It doesn't come in - there. It comes in later. You know that every shot-gun has a number on it, and so can be identified. Now, if these thieves are people who are pretending to be gentlemen - how do you put it? There's a word you use for that, but I've forgotten it."

"Do you mean masquerading as gentlemen?"

"Masquerading - that's the word I was thinking of; if they are masquerading as gentlemen they'll probably keep good guns like that to shoot with - they can do that, or think they can, without running much risk, whereas if they sold them they'd run rather a big risk of being caught, because I happen to remember that the numbers of the stolen guns were mentioned in the newspaper account of the robbery. They said the guns were in a case, and almost new. Now, this is where my idea 'comes in,' as you put it. I heard you tell Dulcie only the other day that you wanted a pair of guns by a tip-top maker. Just afterwards I happened to hear her talking to Mrs. Stapleton about her wedding - by the way, Mike, have you fixed the date yet?"

"Not yet. But what about Mrs. Stapleton?"

"Well, Dulcie spoke about wedding presents, just casually in course of conversation, and I heard her tell Mrs. Stapleton that you had said you hoped among your wedding presents there would be a good gun, 'or, better still, a pair,' I heard her say that you said. Mrs. Stapleton didn't answer at once, but I noticed a queer sort of expression come on to her face, as if she'd just thought of something, and presently she said: 'I have a good mind, darling, to give him a pair of guns that belonged to my poor husband. They are quite new - he can't have used them more than once or twice, if that. They were made by a Bond Street gun-maker he always went to, one of the best in London.' Mike, is Holland and Holland's shop in Bond Street?"

"Yes," I answered, "at the top of Bond Street. Oh, but there are several good gun-makers in Bond Street. Besides, why should Mrs. Stapleton give me such a present as that? I really hardly know her."

"Wait until I've finished, Mike, you always jump at conclusions so. Dulcie said almost at once: 'Oh, don't do that, Connie. Mike wouldn't expect such a present as that from you. He mightn't like to take it; you see, you hardly know him really' - just what you have this moment said. Then Dulcie said: 'I tell you what I wish you would do, Connie - let me buy them from you to give to him. What shall I give you for them?' I believe that was what Mrs. Stapleton had been driving at all the time - she wanted to sell the guns without running any risk, for of course you would never think of noticing the numbers on them, and nobody would ever suppose that guns given to you by Dulcie, apparently new guns, were guns that had been stolen. In the end Dulcie said she would give Mrs. Stapleton eighty pounds for the pair, and that was agreed upon, so that Dulcie has practically bought them for you, in fact she may have paid Mrs. Stapleton for them already. Now look here, I'll get hold of that newspaper that gave the numbers of the guns, and I bet you when Dulcie gives you those guns you'll find they're marked with the numbers of the stolen guns."

"Dick," I said thoughtfully, after a moment's pause, "were you eavesdropping when you heard all this?"

"Why, no, of course not!" he exclaimed indignantly. "I was in the room, reading a book, and I couldn't help hearing all they said, though they were talking in undertones."

I turned over in my bed, and looked into his eyes for an instant or two.

"Would you be surprised to hear, Dick," I said slowly, watching to see what effect my words would have upon him, "would you be surprised to hear that Dulcie gave me a pair of guns, as her wedding present, only last week?"

Dick sprang up in the bed.

"Did she?" he cried out, clapping his hands. "Oh - Mike, tell me, are they Holland guns?"

I nodded.

Dick jumped off the bed and began to caper about the room.

"Have you got them here?" he exclaimed at last, as his excitement began to subside.

"They are in the next room. You shall see them after breakfast."

I had difficulty in calming Dick's excitement and inducing him to eat his breakfast, and directly breakfast was over I took him into the next room, produced the gun-case, pulled out the two pairs of barrels, and together we examined the numbers stamped upon them. Dick wrote the numbers down in the little notebook he always carried in his trousers pocket, and a little later we drove down to Fleet Street to look up the file of the newspaper in which Dick had, he declared, read the report of the robbery at Thatched Court, near Bridport.

I confess that I had not placed much faith in Dick's theory about the numbers. I had taken him down to Fleet Street chiefly because he had so earnestly entreated me to. When, therefore, after turning up the report, Dick discovered, with a shout of triumph, that the numbers on my guns were actually identical with the numbers mentioned in the newspaper as those of the stolen guns, I was not merely greatly astonished, but also considerably perturbed.

"Dick," I said thoughtfully, when I had to some extent recovered from my surprise, "I really think we shall have to make a private detective of you. Would you like me to take you now to one of the most famous detectives in London - a man who was connected with Scotland Yard for twenty years, who is helping Mr. Osborne to try to discover who the thieves are who robbed Holt Manor, and who it was who killed poor Churchill?"

"Do you mean Mr. Preston?" the boy asked quickly, peering up at me out of his intelligent brown eyes.

"Yes. I suppose you have heard Mr. Osborne and me speak of him."

"Of course I have, and I should love to see him. Are you going to see him now?"

"I am going straight to him to tell him of your discovery of these numbers. He already knows all about your having deciphered the newspaper cyphers; in fact, he has the cuttings at this moment, and your translation of them. He told me the other day that he would like to meet you."

Preston was at home at his house in Warwick Street, off Recent Street.

In a few words I had explained everything to him, and at once he grew serious.

"The unfortunate part," he said at last, "is that in spite of this young man's sharpness in making this discovery, it really leaves us almost where we were, unless - "

"Unless what?" I asked, as he paused, considering.

"Well, Mr. Berrington, it's like this," he said bluntly. "You are engaged to be married to Miss Challoner, and she gives you a wedding present - a pair of new guns; at least they are to all intents new, and naturally she expects you to think they are, and might be vexed if she thought you had found out that she picked them up as a bargain. Now, it all turns on this: Have you the moral courage to tell your *fiancee* that you believe the wedding present she has given you is part of the plunder secured in a recent robbery, indeed that you know it is, and that therefore you and she are unwittingly receivers of stolen goods? I have never myself been in love, so far as I can recollect, but if I were placed as you are I think I should hardly have the courage to disillusion the young lady."

I am bound to admit that until he put this problem to me it had not occurred to me to look at the matter in that light, and now I felt much as Preston declared he would feel if he were in my place. Dulcie might not mind my having discovered that she had picked up the guns as a bargain - indeed, why should she? But when it came to hinting - as I should have to do if I broached the matter at all - that I believed that her great friend Connie Stapleton knew, when she sold the guns to her, that they had been stolen - Connie Stapleton, who was about to become her stepmother -

No, I shouldn't have the pluck to do it. I shouldn't have the pluck to face the storm of indignation that I knew my words would stir up in her - women are logical enough, in spite of all that the ignorant and unthinking urge to the contrary, but in this particular case Dulcie would, I felt perfectly certain, "round" upon me, and, in the face of evidence, no matter how damning, declare that I was, to say the least, mistaken. She would go at once to Connie Stapleton and tell her everything, and immediately Connie Stapleton would invent some plausible story which would entirely clear her of all responsibility, and from that moment onward I should probably be her bitterest enemy. No, I thought; better, far better, say nothing - perhaps some day circumstances might arise which would of themselves lead to Mrs. Stapleton's, so to speak, "giving herself away." Indeed, in face of the discovery, I now decided not to make certain statements to Sir Roland that I had fully intended to make. After all, he was old enough to be my father, and if a man old enough to be my father could be so foolish as to fall in love with an adventuress, let him take the consequences. I should not so much have minded incurring Sir Roland's wrath, but, knowing him as well as I did, I felt positive that anything I might say would only strengthen his trust in and attachment to this woman he had decided to wed. He might even turn upon me and tell me to my face that I was striving to oppose his marriage because his marrying must, of course, affect my pecuniary position - an old man who falls in love becomes for the time, I have always maintained, mentally deranged.

Preston conversed at considerable length with Dick Challoner, and, by the time I rose to leave - for I had to call at Willow Street for Dulcie at noon - the two appeared to have become great friends.

"I shall take you with me to call for Dulcie," I said to Dick as we went out. "Then we shall drive you to Paddington, put you in the train for Windsor, and leave you to your own devices."

"I wish I hadn't lost my suit-case," Dick observed ruefully. "I bet anything it's in that house in Cumberland Place where the taxi stopped - unless the woman who met me at Paddington intentionally left it in the taxi when she found I had jumped out and run away. We ought to inquire at Scotland Yard, oughtn't we?"

We arrived at Willow Road, Hampstead, at ten minutes to twelve. Telling Dick to remain in the taxi, I got out and rang the bell. The door was opened by a maid I had not seen before, and when I inquired for Miss Challoner she stared at me blankly - indeed, as I thought, suspiciously.

"Nobody of that name lives here," she said curtly. Quickly I glanced up at the number on the door. No, I had not mistaken the house.

"She is staying here," I said, "staying with Mrs. Stapleton."

"With Mrs. who?"

"Mrs. Stapleton."

"You have mistaken the house. There's nobody of that name here."

"Well, Mr. Gastrell, then," I said irritably. "Ask Mr. Gastrell if I can see him."

"I tell you, sir, you've come to the wrong house," the maid said sharply.

"Then who does live here?" I exclaimed, beginning to lose my temper.

The maid looked me up and down.

"I'm not going to tell you," she answered; and, before I could speak again, she had shut the door in my face.

CHAPTER XX

PRESTON AGAIN

I had seen Dick off at Paddington, after asking the guard to keep an eye on him as far as Windsor, and was walking thoughtfully through the park towards Albert Gate, when a man, meeting me where the paths cross, asked if he might speak to me. Almost instantly I recognized him. It was the man who had followed Preston, Jack, and myself on the previous night, and been pointed out to us by Preston.

"I trust," he said, when I had asked him rather abruptly what he wanted to speak to me about, "that you will pardon my addressing you, sir, but there is something rather important I should like to say to you if you have a few minutes to spare."

"Who are you?" I inquired. "What's your name?"

"I would rather not tell you my name," he answered, "and for the moment it is inadvisable that you should know it. Shall we sit here?" he added, as we came to a wooden bench.

I am rather inquisitive, otherwise I should not have consented to his proposal. It flashed across me, however, that whereas there could be no harm in my listening to what he wished to say, he might possibly have something really of interest to tell me.

"You are probably not aware," he said, when we were seated, "that I followed you last night from a house in Warwick Street, Regent Street, to a restaurant in Gerrard Street, Soho; thence to Willow Road, near Hampstead Station; and thence to South Molton Street Mansions. Two gentlemen were with you."

"And may I ask why you did that?" I said carelessly, as I lit a cigarette.

"That is my affair," he replied. "You have lately been associating with several men and women who, though you may not know it, belong to a gang of exceedingly clever criminals. These people, while mixing in Society, prey upon it. Until last night I was myself a member of this gang; for a reason that I need not at present mention I have now disassociated myself from it for ever. To-day my late accomplices will discover that I have turned traitor, as they will term it, and at once they will set to work to encompass my death," he added. "I want you, Mr. Berrington, to save me from them."

I stared at him in surprise.

"But how can I do that, and why should I do it?" I said shortly. "I don't know who you are, and if you choose to aid and abet criminals you have only yourself to thank when they turn upon you."

"Naturally," he answered, with what looked very like a sneer; "I don't ask you to do anything in return for nothing, Mr. Berrington. But if you will help in this crisis, I can, and will, help you. At this moment you are at a loss to know why, when you called at Willow Road an hour or so ago, the woman who opened the door assured you that you had come to the wrong house. You inquired first for Miss Challoner, then for Mrs. Stapleton, and then for Hugesson Gastrell - am I not right?"

"Well, you are," I said, astonished at his knowledge.

"I was in the hall when you called, and I heard you. Gastrell, Mrs. Stapleton, and Miss Challoner were also in the house. They are there now, but to-night they go to Paris - they will cross from Newhaven to Dieppe. It was to tell you they were going to Paris that I wished to speak to you now - at least that was one reason."

"And what are the other reasons?" I asked, with an affectation of indifference that I was far from feeling.

"I want money, Mr. Berrington, that is one other reason," the stranger said quickly. "You can afford to pay for information that is worth paying for. I know everything about you, perhaps more than you yourself know. If you pay me enough, I can probably protect myself against these people who until yesterday were my friends, but are now my enemies. And I can put you in possession of facts which will enable you, if you act circumspectly, presently to get the entire gang arrested."

"At what time do the three people you have just named leave for Paris?" I asked, for the news that Connie Stapleton and Dulcie were going to France together had given me a shock.

"To-night, at nine."

"Look here," I exclaimed, turning upon him sharply, "tell me everything you know, and if it is worth paying for I'll pay."

In a few minutes the stranger had put several startling facts into my possession. Of these the most important were that on at least four occasions Connie Stapleton had deliberately exercised a hypnotic control over Dulcie, and thus obtained even greater influence over her than she already possessed; that Jack Osborne, whom I had always believed to be wholly unsusceptible to female influence, was fast falling in love, or, if not falling in love, becoming infatuated with Jasmine Gastrell - the stranger declared that Mrs. Gastrell had fallen in love with him, but that I could not believe; that an important member of this notorious gang of criminals which mixed so freely in Society was Sir Roland's wastrel brother, Robert, of whom neither Sir Roland nor any member of his family had heard for years; and that Mrs. Stapleton intended to cause Dulcie to become seriously ill while abroad, then to induce Sir Roland to come to France to see her, and finally to marry him on the other side of the Channel in the small town where she intended that Dulcie should be taken ill. There were reasons, he said, though he would not reveal them then, why she wished to marry Sir Roland on the Continent instead of in England, and she knew of no other way of inducing him to cross the Channel but the means she intended to employ.

The man hardly stopped speaking when I sprang to my feet.

"How much do you want for the information you have given me?" I exclaimed, hardly able to conceal the intense excitement I felt.

He named a high figure, and so reckless did I feel at that instant that I told him I would pay the amount to him in gold - he had stipulated for gold - if he would call at my flat in South Molton Street at five o'clock on the following afternoon.

His expressions of gratitude appeared, I must say, to be most genuine.

"And may I ask," he said, "what you propose to do now?"

"Propose to do!" I cried. "Why, go direct to Willow Road, of course, force an entrance, and take Miss Challoner away - by force, if need be."

"You propose to go there alone?"

"Yes. For the past fortnight I have somehow suspected there might be some secret understanding between Mr. Osborne and Mrs. Gastrell - they have been so constantly together, though he has more than once assured me that his intimacy was only with a view to obtaining her confidence. I don't know why I should believe your word, the word of a stranger, in preference to his, but now you tell me what you have told me I remember many little things which all point to the likelihood of your statement that he is in love with Mrs. Gastrell being true."

"I wouldn't go alone, Mr. Berrington," the stranger said in a tone of warning. "You don't know the people you have to deal with as I know them. If you would like to come to Paris with me to-night I could show you something that would amaze you - and you would come face to face there with Connie Stapleton and Miss Challoner, and others. Be advised by me, and do that. I am telling you to do what I know will be best for you. I don't ask you to pay me until we return to England."

I paused, uncertain what to decide. Thoughts crowded my brain. Supposing, after all, that this were a ruse to entrap me. Supposing that Dulcie were not going to Paris. But no, the man's statements seemed somehow to carry conviction.

"If we cross by the same boat as they do," I said suddenly, "we shall be recognized."

He smiled grimly.

"Not if you disguise yourself as you did at Hugesson Gastrell's the other night," he said.

"Good heavens!" I exclaimed, "how do you know that?"

He looked to right and left, then behind him. Nobody was near. Then, raising his hat, like lightning he pulled off his wig, eyebrows and moustache, whiskers and beard, crammed them into his jacket pocket, and, with his hat on the back of his head, sat back looking at me with a quiet smile of amusement.

"Preston!" I gasped. "Good heavens, man, how do you do it?"

Producing his cigarette case, in silence he offered me a cigarette. Then he spoke - now in his natural voice.

"I always test my 'impersonations' when I get a chance of

doing so," he said, "upon people who know me well, because if one can completely deceive one's friends it gives much confidence when one comes to serious business. Mr. Berrington, all I have just told you is absolute truth. I have found it all out within the last eleven hours. More than that, I am myself now one of the gang, and if I 'turn traitor' I shall be done to death by them just as certainly as I am sitting here. I flatter myself that I have arranged it all rather cleverly - I have succeeded in placing in confinement that man who shadowed you last night, without any member of the gang's knowing anything about his arrest or in the least suspecting it, and I have literally stepped into his shoes, for these clothes and boots that I am wearing are his. I believe the end of this abominable conspiracy is now within sight. To-night you must come with me to Paris on the boat that Miss Challoner, the woman Stapleton, Gastrell, and one or two others will cross by. I shall assume the disguise I have just removed. You will become once more Sir Aubrey Belston, we shall travel from Victoria in separate compartments, and on board the boat I shall casually mention to my 'friends' that Sir Aubrey Belston is on board. In Paris we ought to find out a lot - I have a friend there named Victor Albeury, who already knows a lot about this affair - and we shall, unless I am greatly mistaken. Now I must go home and get some hours of sleep, for I have been busy since we parted in the 'Tube' at Oxford Circus at midnight last night."

"But tell me," I exclaimed, my brain a whirl, "is what you told me really true: that Osborne has become a victim to the wiles of Jasmine Gastrell?"

"Absolutely. I have suspected as much for several weeks, and last night I discovered it to be an absolute fact. Mr. Berrington, when Osborne left us last night at Russell Square station he didn't return to his hotel. Would you believe it, he had an assignation with the woman, and kept it? But what is more curious still is what you wouldn't believe when I told it to you some minutes ago - Jasmine Gastrell has fallen madly in love with Osborne! Isn't it astonishing? To think that an amazingly clever woman like that should let her heart get the better of her head. But it's not the first case of the sort that I have known. I could tell you of several similar instances of level-headed women of the criminal class letting their hearts run away with them, and some day I will. But now I really must leave you. Go back to your place, pack as much luggage as you will need for a week or ten days - for we may be away that long - write Sir Aubrey Belston's name on the luggage labels in a disguised handwriting; send it to Victoria by messenger - not by your own man, as we must take no risks whatever - and come to me not later than six, and I will then again disguise you as Sir Aubrey Belston. You won't be followed by any member of the gang, for the man I am impersonating is supposed to be shadowing you. Connie Stapleton expects Alphonse Furneaux - that's the man who followed you last night, and whom I am now impersonating - to meet her at Victoria at a quarter past eight to-night. You will get there a little later, and of course we must appear to be total strangers. Keep out of sight of the woman, and of Gastrell, and of anyone else you may see whom you remember seeing at Cumberland Place the other night. You can speak to anybody you like once we are on board the boat, but not before. The train leaves at nine. My! I am disappointed with Osborne, more disappointed and disgusted than I can tell you. And to think that if I had not made this discovery about him he might unwittingly have brought about some fearful tragedy so far as you and I are concerned! But I must really go," and, with a friendly nod, he rose and strolled away.

He had spoken rapidly, with hardly a pause, and as I watched him pass out of the park I wondered how he had managed to ingratiate himself with this gang of scoundrels. Only a day or two before we had discussed the advisability of informing Easterton of what was taking place nightly in the house in Cumberland Place which he had leased to Hugesson Gastrell, but we had come to the conclusion that no good end would be served by telling him, for were any complaint to be made to Gastrell he would of course declare that the people who gambled in the house were personal friends of his whom he had every right to invite there to play.

I returned to my flat, told my man what to pack, then went out again and walked aimlessly about the streets. A feeling of restlessness was upon me, which I could not overcome. Many strange things had happened since Christmas, but this, surely, was the strangest thing of all, that Jack Osborne, who had persuaded me to help him in his self-imposed task of tracking down these people, should actually have come under the spell of Jasmine Gastrell's beauty and undeniable fascination. I recollected now his saying, when, weeks before, he had spoken of Jasmine Gastrell for the first time, that everybody on board the ship had fallen in love with her, and that he himself had been desperately attracted by her. But I had thought that he spoke in jest; it had not occurred to me that he really thought seriously about the woman. Of late, however, his manner towards her had certainly been different, and I knew that night after night the two had spent the evening together, ending up with supper at one of the fashionable restaurants.

Then my thoughts drifted to Dulcie. What had come over her since she had formed this violent attachment for Connie Stapleton? In some ways she seemed unchanged, yet in other respects she was completely altered. For a brief ten days after we had become engaged I had seemed to be all in all to her. But from then onward she had appeared to come more and more under the influence of her friend, who seemed, in a sense, to be supplanting me in her affection. And now Preston had told me that several times Connie Stapleton had intentionally hypnotized Dulcie, no doubt for the purpose of obtaining greater control over her and still further bending her will to hers. I could not, under the circumstances, wholly blame Dulcie for what I had at first believed to be a change in her attitude towards me. Far more readily could I blame her father for his monstrous infatuation for the widow.

And what could be the meaning of this sudden flitting to Paris? Preston had given the reason, had explained it in detail, but his theory was so horrible that I refused to believe it. Connie Stapleton might be, and obviously was, an adventuress, but surely a woman of such beauty, with such charm of manner and personality, and apparently so refined, could not actually be the monster Preston would have had me believe. The view I held was that Connie Stapleton and some of her accomplices for some reason found it expedient to forsake England for a little while - Preston had assured me that they meant to remain upon the Continent for several weeks at least - and that the woman thought that by taking Dulcie with her she would be better able to persuade Sir Roland to cross the Channel, a thing he had done only once in his life, and that I had heard him declare he would never do again, so ill had he been on that occasion.

One of the first men I saw upon my arrival at Victoria in my disguise was Preston disguised as Alphonse Furneaux. With him were Connie Stapleton, Dulcie, Gastrell, and one or two men I did not remember having seen before. Doris Lorrimer was also there.

Obsequious officials were hurrying about doing their bidding, in anticipation of generous *largesse*. Here and there little groups of passengers stood staring at them, obviously under the impression that they must be people of some importance. Acting upon Preston's instructions I kept well out of sight until within a minute or two of nine o'clock, by which time the widow and her companions had entered their saloon carriage.

I had hardly stepped into my first-class compartment, which was some way behind the saloon, and settled myself comfortably for the journey to Newhaven, when a lady, the only other occupant, suddenly exclaimed:

"Aubrey, don't you recognize me, or are you intentionally cutting me?"

I glanced across at her. She was a woman of middle age, obviously a lady, well dressed, but not good-looking. Hastily recovering my presence of mind, I answered quickly:

"I beg your pardon. Please don't think me rude; I was worrying about a trunk of mine that I think has been left behind, and for the moment I didn't see you" - she was seated on the opposite side, in the corner farthest from me.

"Of course I don't think you rude, you foolish boy," she exclaimed gaily. "How could I? And how are you, dear? and where are you going? I had no idea you had already returned from your travels."

"I got back only last week," I said, feeling my way cautiously. "How well you are looking. Let me see, when was it we last met?"

She broke into a ripple of laughter.

"Oh, Aubrey," she exclaimed, "what a wag you are! When are you going to grow up, I wonder. Now, do be serious and answer that question I put to the last night we were together."

This was awful. The train had only just started, and here I was face to face with a woman evidently an intimate friend of Sir Aubrey Belston's, who for aught I knew might insist on talking to me and cross-questioning me all the way to Newhaven. I decided to take the bull by the horns.

"Look here," I exclaimed, becoming suddenly serious, "don't let us talk about that any more. The answer I gave you that night was final. I have thought the whole thing over carefully, and, much as I should like to, I can't change my mind."

She stared at me, evidently dumbfounded. I thought she looked rather frightened. Her lips parted as if she were going to speak again, then shut tightly. A minute or more passed, during which time she kept her head averted, gazing out into the darkness. And then all at once, to my horror, she burst into tears, and began sobbing hysterically.

The sight of a woman in tears always affects me strangely. I rose from my seat and went over to her, and, now seated facing her, endeavoured by every means I could think of to soothe her.

"Don't cry - oh, please don't," I said sympathetically. "It isn't my fault, you know; I would do anything I could for you, I am sure you know that, but what you ask is impossible."

"But *why* is it impossible?" she suddenly burst out impetuously, looking up into my face with tear-stained eyes. "Give me a good reason for your refusal and I won't say a word more."

Oh, if only I knew what it was she had asked Sir Aubrey that night - what it was she wanted him to do. Never in my life before had I been in such an awful predicament. And then suddenly it flashed upon me that some day she would for certain meet the real Sir Aubrey Belston again, and what would happen then when she referred to this meeting in the train and he stoutly denied - as of course he would - meeting her at all? What mischief might I not unwittingly be doing? What havoc might I not be creating? If only I could discover her name it might in some way help me to get out of this terrible tangle.

The train was slowing down now. Presently it stopped. We were at Croydon. The door opened and other travellers entered our compartment. Putting some of my belongings on to my seat, I passed into the corridor and entered a smoking compartment.

The man seated opposite me was buried in a newspaper. Some moments after the train had started again, he lowered it, and I saw his face. At once he raised his eyebrows in recognition; then, extending his hand, greeted me most cordially.

I was face to face again with Hugesson Gastrell!

CHAPTER XXI

A CHANNEL MYSTERY

Nobody could have seemed more friendly or more thoroughly pleased to see me again than Hugesson Gastrell as he grasped me heartily by the hand, expressing surprise at our meeting so unexpectedly.

On the night I had talked to him at Cumberland Place, when I was masquerading for the first time as Sir Aubrey Belston, I had experienced a growing feeling of revulsion against him, and now as he took my hand the same feeling returned and I could not dispel it, for the thought had flashed in upon me: could it be that I was shaking hands with a man whose hand was stained with blood? I had, of course, no proof that Gastrell had committed murder, but in face of what Harold Logan had told Sir Roland Challoner and myself upon his death bed, added to other things I knew, it seemed well within the bounds of possibility that -

"And are you crossing to France?" he inquired, cutting my train of thought.

"Yes," I answered mechanically.

"Going to Paris?"

"Yes."

"Why, how capital!" he exclaimed. "You must make one of our party on the boat, and when we land. Connie Stapleton will be delighted to meet you again, Sir Aubrey; she is on this train, and so are other mutual friends. Connie was speaking of you not half an hour ago."

"Indeed?" I said, feeling that I must say something.

"Why, yes. Try one of these cigars, Sir Aubrey," he added, producing a large gold case from his inside breast pocket.

I had to take one, though I hated doing it. I tried to look him in the face as I did so, but I couldn't. It was not that I feared he might recognize me, for I did not - experience had proved to me that my disguised appearance and voice were most effectual. But there was something about the man that repelled me, and I hated meeting his gaze.

The noise of the train caused us presently to relapse into silence, and, picking up my newspaper, I tried to read. My thoughts were too deeply engrossed, however, to allow me to focus my attention on the printed page. Could it really be possible, was what I kept wondering, that this smooth-spoken, pleasant-mannered man was actually a criminal? Again Harold Logan's dying eyes stared into mine; again I saw him struggling to speak; again I heard those ominous words, almost the last words he had spoken before his spirit had passed into Eternity:

"Hugesson Gastrell - don't forget that name, Sir Roland. You may some day be glad I told it to you."

I shuddered. Then I remembered Preston's warning and the part I had to play. Up to the present, Gastrell suspected nothing - of that I felt positive; but let the least suspicion creep into his brain that I was not the man he believed he had been speaking to -

Instantly I pulled myself together. For Dulcie's sake even more than for my own I must exercise the utmost care. Her life as well as mine might depend upon the skill and tact I must exercise during the next few hours, possibly during the next few days. I felt I would at that moment have given much to be able to look into the future and know for certain what was going to happen to me, and, most of all, to Dulcie, before I returned to England.

Well it was for my peace of mind that that wish could not be gratified.

On board the boat, rather to my surprise in view of what had happened and of what Gastrell had just said to me, I saw nothing of Gastrell or of any of his companions, including Preston. Apparently one and all must have gone to their cabins immediately upon coming on board.

It was a perfect night in the Channel. Stars and moon shone brightly, and a streak of light stretched away across the smooth water until it touched the sky Hue far out in the darkness. For a long time I stood on deck, abaft the funnel, smoking a cigar, and thinking deeply. I had turned for a moment, for no particular reason, when I thought I saw a shadow pass across the deck, then vanish. I saw it again; and then again. Stepping away from where I stood, hidden by a life-boat, I distinctly discerned three figures moving noiselessly along the deck, going from me. Curiosity prompted me to follow them, and to my surprise I saw them disappear one after another down the hatchway leading to the steerage. As they must, I felt certain, have come out through the saloon door, this rather puzzled me.

It was past midnight when, at last, I went below. The saloon, smoking-room and alleyways were deserted and almost in darkness. No sound of any sort was audible but the rhythmic throbbing of the engines. The boat still travelled without the slightest motion.

Hark!

I stopped abruptly, for I had heard a sound - it had sounded like a gasp. Hardly breathing, I listened intently. Again I heard it - this time more faintly. It had seemed to come from a cabin on my left, a little further forward.

I stood quite still in the alleyway for several minutes. Then, hearing nothing more, I went on to my own cabin.

But somehow, try as I would, I could not get to sleep. For hours I lay wide awake upon my bunk. What had caused that curious sound, I kept wondering, though I tried to put the thought from me. And who had those men been, those three silent figures passing like spectres along the deck, and what had they been doing, and why had they gone down into the steerage?

I suppose I must at last have fallen asleep, for when I opened my eyes the sea had risen a good deal, and the boat was rolling heavily. Pulling my watch from beneath my pillow, I saw that it was nearly four - we were due into port at Dieppe before four. The timbers of the ship creaked at intervals; the door of my cabin rattled; I could hear footsteps on deck and in the alleyway beside my door.

"Have you heard the dreadful news, sir?" a scared-looking steward said to me as I made my way towards the companion ladder half an hour later - I had taken care to adjust my disguise exactly in the way that Preston had taught me to.

"No - what?" I asked, stopping abruptly.

"A saloon passenger has hanged himself during the night."

"Good God!" I exclaimed. "Who is it?"

"I don't know his name. He was in number thirty-two - alone."

"Thirty-two! Surely that was a cabin in the alleyway where I had heard the gasp, not far from my own cabin."

"Are you certain it was suicide?" I asked.

"Oh, it was suicide right enough," the steward answered, "and he must have been hanging there some hours - by a rope. Seems he must have brought the rope with him, as it don't belong to the boat. He must have come aboard intending to do it. My mate - he found him not half an hour ago, and it so scared him that he fainted right off."

"Have you seen the poor fellow? What was he like?"

"Yes. Most amazing thing, sir," the steward continued volubly, "but it seems he'd disguised himself. He'd got on a wig and false moustache and whiskers."

All the blood seemed to rush away from my heart. Everything about me was going round. I have a slight recollection of reeling forward and being caught by the steward, but of what happened after that, until I found myself lying on a sofa in the saloon, with the ship's doctor and the stewardess standing looking down at me. I have not the remotest recollection.

The boat was rolling and pitching a good deal, and I remember hearing someone say that we were lying off Dieppe until the sea should to some extent subside. Then, all at once, a thought came to me which made me feel sick and faint. While I had been unconscious, had the fact been discovered that I too was disguised? I looked up with a feeling of terror, but the expression upon the faces of the ship's doctor and of the stewardess revealed nothing, and my mind grew more at ease when I noticed that the few people standing about were strangers to me.

I saw nothing of any member of the group of criminals I now felt literally afraid to meet until the Paris express was about to start. More than once I had felt tempted to alter my plans by not going to Paris, or by returning to England by the next boat. But then Dulcie had risen into the vision of my imagination and I had felt I could not leave her alone with such a gang of scoundrels - I might be leaving her to her fate were I to desert her now. No, I had started upon this dangerous adventure, and at all costs I must go through with it, even though I no longer had poor Preston to advise me.

"Ah, Sir Aubrey, we have been looking for you."

I turned sharply, to find at my elbow Connie Stapleton and Doris Lorrimer. The latter stood beside her friend, calm, subdued; Mrs. Stapleton was in her usual high spirits, and greeted me with an effusive hand-shake.

"Hughie told us you were on board," she said, "and he says you are going to stay at our hotel. I am so pleased. Now, you must dine with us to-night - no, I won't take a refusal," she added quickly, as I was about to make some excuse. "We shall be such a cheery party - just the kind of party I know you love."

There was no way of escape, at any rate for the moment. Later I must see what could be done. My desire now was to keep, so to speak, in touch with the gang, and to watch in particular Dulcie's movements, yet to associate on terms of intimacy with these people as little as possible. We had not been long in the train, on our way to Paris, when someone - it was Dulcie who first spoke of it, I think - broached the subject which had created so much excitement on board - the suicide of the disguised stranger.

"I wonder if his act had any bearing upon this robbery which is said to have been committed on board between Newhaven and Dieppe," a man whom I remembered meeting at Connie Stapleton's dinner party, presently observed - I suddenly remembered that his name was Wollaston.

"Robbery?" I exclaimed. "I have heard nothing about it. What was stolen? and who was it stolen from?"

"Well," he answered, " the stories I have heard don't all tally, and one or two may be exaggerated. But there is no doubt about the robbery of Lady Fitzgraham's famous diamonds, which I have always heard were worth anything between thirty and forty thousand pounds. She was coming over to stay at the Embassy, and had them with her, it seems, in quite a small dressing-bag. I am told she declares she is positive the stones were in the bag, which was locked, when she went on board at Newhaven; yet early this morning they were missing, though the bag was still locked. The theory is that during the night someone must by some means have forced an entrance to the cabin - they declare the cabin door was locked, but of course it can't have been - in which she and her maid slept, have unlocked the bag and extracted the jewels. Lady Fitzgraham was travelling alone with her maid, I am told," he ended, "but Sir Aubrey Belston travelled with her part way from London to Newhaven."

"You are talking to Sir Aubrey at this moment," Connie Stapleton said quickly. She turned to me: "Sir Aubrey, let me introduce Mr. Wollaston."

"I beg your pardon," Wollaston stammered, "I had no idea - I know you by name, of course, but I have not before, I believe, had the pleasure of meeting you. It was Hughie Gastrell, whom I expect you know, who told me he had seen you in Lady Fitzgraham's compartment on the way to Newhaven. I suppose Lady Fitzgraham didn't, by any chance, speak to you of her jewels - say she had them with her, or anything of that kind?"

"She didn't say a word about them," I answered. "Is she on this train?"

"Yes. Gastrell has gone to suggest to her that she should stay with us at the 'Continental,' and - "

"Sir Aubrey has just decided to stay there," Mrs. Stapleton interrupted, "and I have proposed that to-night we should all dine together."

Conversation then reverted to the suicide and the robbery, and as Connie Stapleton's friends who shared the private car entered it, she introduced them to me. They seemed pleasant people enough, and, as the subject of conversation did not change, one after another they propounded ingenious theories to account for the way the robbery might have been committed. I noticed that they spoke less about the alleged suicide, and that when the subject was broached they confined their remarks chiefly to the question of the dead man's disguise, suggesting reasons which they considered might have prompted him to disguise himself. They ended by deciding there was no reason to suppose that the suicide and the robbery had any bearing on each other.

The run from Dieppe to Paris by express takes about three hours, and we were about half-way through the journey when Wollaston, who had been absent at least half an hour, re-entered our compartment in conversation with my recent travelling companion, whom I now knew to be Lady Fitzgraham. She hardly acknowledged my look of recognition, and out of the tail of my eye I saw Connie Stapleton glance quickly at each of us in turn, as though Lady Fitzgraham's unmistakable stiffness surprised her.

Now the train was running at high speed across the flat, uninteresting stretch of country which lies about thirty miles south of Rouen. Presently the Seine came in sight again, and for some miles we ran parallel with it. We had just rushed through a little wayside station beyond Mantes, the train oscillating so severely as it rattled over the points that Dulcie, Connie Stapleton and Lady Fitzgraham became seriously alarmed, while other occupants of the car glanced apprehensively out of the windows.

"This car wants coupling up," Gastrell exclaimed suddenly. "At our next stopping place I'll complain, and get it done."

The words had scarcely passed his lips when the swaying increased considerably. All at once the brakes were applied with great force, the train began to slacken speed, and a moment later we knew that we had left the metals.

To this day it seems to me extraordinary that any of us should have escaped with our lives. We probably should not have done so had the land not been on a dead level with the rails at the point where the train jumped the track. As a result, the cars did not telescope, as is usual on such occasions, nor did they capsize. Instead, the locomotive dashed forward over the flat, hard-frozen meadow, dragging the cars behind it, then came gradually to a standstill owing to the steam having been shut off.

My first thought as soon as the train had stopped was for Dulcie. As I crawled along the car - for we had all been flung on to the ground - I came upon her suddenly. Pale as death, and trembling terribly, she stared at me with a scared expression, and so great was the wave of emotion which swept over me at that instant that I all but forgot my disguise in my wild longing to spring forward and take her in my arms and comfort her.

"Are you hurt?" I gasped, retaining only with the utmost difficulty the artificial tone I had adopted from the first, the tone poor Preston had coached me in until my accents, so he had assured me, exactly resembled those of Sir Aubrey Belston.

"No - no," came her answer, in a weak voice, "only shaken - but oh, the thirst this shock has given me is fearful. Is there anything I can drink?"

I looked about me. On all sides was a litter of hand-baggage that the accident had hurled pell-mell about the car. Beside me was a large dressing-bag lying on its side, partly open, the force of the blow as it was flung up against the woodwork having burst the lock. Thinking there might be something in it that I could give to Dulcie to relieve her burning thirst, I set the bag upright, and pulled it wide open.

As my gaze rested upon the contents of that bag, astonishment made me catch my breath. For the bag was half filled with jewellery of all descriptions jumbled up as if it had been tossed in anyhow - there had been no attempt at packing. During the brief moments which elapsed before I shut the bag, I noticed rings, brooches, bracelets, scarf pins, watches, hair combs and three large tiaras, all of them, apparently, set in precious stones - mostly emeralds, rubies and diamonds.

Hastily closing the bag, and fastening the clips to keep it shut, I left it where I had found it and was about to go in search of water, when the sight I saw made my heart nearly stop beating.

For at the end of the car, standing motionless, and looking straight at me, was Alphonse Furneaux! Almost as I returned his dull gaze the truth seemed to drift into my brain. Furneaux must have escaped from Preston's house, from the room where Preston had confined him. He must have discovered that Preston was impersonating him. He must have followed him from London, followed him on to the boat -

I dared not let my thoughts travel further. Horrible suspicions crowded in upon me. Could the man standing there staring at me be Preston's murderer? Was he aware of my identity too, and, if so, had he designs upon my life as well? Had he told the gang I was now mixed up with of my disguise, and had they entrapped me in order to wreak vengeance? And that hoard of jewellery I had so unwittingly discovered - had the man now standing there before me seen me looking at it?

CHAPTER XXII

THE THIN-FACED STRANGER

I pretended not to notice him as I pushed past him and presently returned with water. Lady Fitzgraham, Connie Stapleton, and several others also clamoured for water to moisten their parched lips, and when I had attended to Dulcie I gave them some. For the next two hours everything was confusion. All the passengers had been severely shaken, and some were seriously hurt, but fortunately not one had been killed. Our extraordinary escape I shall always attribute to the fact that we travelled in a Pullman, a car that has most wonderful stability.

A large crowd had assembled at Gare St. Lazare to witness the arrival of the special with the passengers who had travelled in our ill-fated train. Now that I had collected my scattered thoughts once more I was resolved at the earliest possible moment to inform Lady Fitzgraham of the discovery I had made, for I had come to the firm conclusion that some, at any rate, of the jewellery that bag contained must be hers, some of the jewellery which had been stolen on board the boat.

Upon our arrival at the "Continental" I discovered that Gastrell and Connie Stapleton's friends numbered no less than twelve, without counting Lady Fitzgraham or myself, so that in all we were sixteen. Of the people I had met before, whom I believed to be members of the gang, only Jasmine Gastrell was absent. What most puzzled me was what the reason could be they had all come to Paris. Did the London police suspect them, and were they fleeing from justice in consequence? That,

I decided, seemed hardly likely. Could they be contemplating some *coup* on the Continent, or had they come over to prepare with greater security some fresh gigantic robbery in England? That seemed far more probable, and just then I remembered that in less than a fortnight the coming-of-age festivities of Lord Cranmere's son would begin - February the 28th. What complicated matters to some extent was that I had no means of ascertaining beyond doubt which members of this large party were actually members of the gang I now knew to exist, and which, if any, besides Dulcie, Lady Fitzgraham, and myself, also, I fancied, the man named Wollaston, were honest folk, some of them possibly dupes. Lady Fitzgraham I knew well by name and repute, and there could be no possibility of her being mixed up in criminal or even shady transactions. That the robbery of her famous jewels, by whomsoever it had been committed, had been premeditated and carefully planned, there seemed hardly room to doubt.

Next day all the Paris newspapers contained reports of the suicide - as they evidently all believed it to have been - and of the robbery on board the boat. The usual theories, many of them so far-fetched as to be almost fantastic, were advanced, and all kinds of wild suggestions were made to account for the dead man's having been disguised. Not until three days later was the sensational announcement made in the newspapers that he had proved to be George Preston, the famous English detective, who had retired upon pension only the year before.

We had been four days in Paris, and nothing in the least suspicious had occurred. I had been unable to tell Lady Fitzgraham of my suspicions regarding the whereabouts of her stolen jewels, for she had not dined at the "Continental," nor had I seen her after our train had reached Paris, or even on the train after the accident. The hotel manager was under the impression, I had discovered while conversing with him, that we had all met by accident either in the train or on the boat, as the accommodation needed had been telegraphed for from Dieppe. He also was quite convinced - this I gathered at the same time - that our party consisted of people of considerable distinction, leaders of London Society, an impression no doubt strengthened by the almost reckless extravagance of every member of the party.

The robbery and the supposed suicide on board the boat were beginning to be less talked about. It was the evening of our fourth day in Paris, and I had just finished dressing for dinner, when somebody knocked. I called "Come in," and a man entered. Without speaking he shut the door behind him, turned the key in the lock, and came across to me.

He was tall and thin, a rather ascetic-looking individual of middle age, with small, intelligent eyes set far back in his head, bushy brows and a clean-shaven face - clearly an American. He stood looking at me for a moment or two, then said:

"Mr. Berrington, I think."

I started, for my make-up was perfect still, and I firmly believed that none had penetrated my disguise. Before I could answer, the stranger continued:

"You have no need to be alarmed, Mr. Berrington; I am connected with the Paris *Surete*, and George Preston was a colleague and an intimate friend of mine. We had been in communication for some time before his death, and I knew of his disguise; he had given me details of his line of action in connection with the people you are with; for he knew that in impersonating Alphonse Furneaux and associating himself so closely with this group of criminals he ran a grave risk. Still," he went on, speaking smoothly and very rapidly, "I believe this tragedy would not have occurred - for that he was murdered I feel certain, though I have no proof - had the real Furneaux not succeeded in making good his escape from the room where Preston had confined him in his own house, a room where he had more than once kept men under lock and key when he wanted them out of the way for a while."

As the stranger stopped speaking, he produced from his pocket a card with a portrait of himself upon it, and the autograph signature of the Prefect of Police.

"Well," I said, feeling considerably relieved, "what have you come to see me about?"

"Your life is in danger," he answered bluntly, "in great danger. Alphonse Furneaux has penetrated your disguise, and I have every reason to believe that he has betrayed your identity to the rest of the gang. If that is so, you can hardly escape their vengeance unless you leave here at once, under my protection, and return to London. Even there you will need to be extremely careful. Please prepare to come now. It may already be too late."

"I can't do that," I answered firmly, facing him. "Miss Challoner, the daughter of Sir Roland Challoner, has unwittingly become mixed up with these people; she suspects nothing, and as yet I have been unable to warn her of the grave risk she runs by remaining with them. It is solely on her account that I am here. I must remain by her at all costs to protect her - and to warn her as soon as possible."

"You can safely leave that to me, Mr. Berrington," the stranger answered, with a keen glance. "If you stay here another night I won't be responsible for your safety - indeed, I don't consider that I am responsible for it now. Quick, please, pack your things."

"Impossible," I replied doggedly. "You don't understand the situation, Mr. - "

"Albeury - Victor Albeury."

"You don't understand the situation, Mr. Albeury - I am engaged to be married to Miss Challoner, and I can't at any cost desert her at such a time. She has struck up an extraordinary friendship with Mrs. Stapleton, who is staying in this hotel and is mixed up with the gang, and I want to watch their movements while retaining my disguise."

"But of what use is your disguise," Albeury cut in quickly, "now that, as I told you, these scoundrels are aware of your identity, or will be very soon? You have no idea, Mr. Berrington, of the class of criminal you have to deal with. These men and women have so much money and are so presentable and plausible, also so extremely clever, that you would have the greatest difficulty in inducing any ordinary people to believe they are not rich folk of good social standing, let alone that they are criminals. If you insist upon remaining here it will be nothing less than madness."

"And yet I insist," I said.

The stranger shrugged his shoulders. Then he sat down, asked if he might light a cigarette, and for a minute or so remained wrapped in thought.

"Supposing that I could induce Miss Challoner to come away," he said suddenly, "would you come then?"

"Of course I should," I answered. "I have told you it is only because she is here that I remain here."

Albeury rose abruptly, and tossed his half-smoked cigarette into the grate.

"Wait here until I return," he said.

He unlocked the door, and went out of the room. I heard his footsteps grow fainter and fainter as he went along the corridor.

At the end of a quarter of an hour, as he did not return, I went out into the passage, locked the door of my room behind me, and walked slowly in the direction Albeury had gone. I knew the number of Dulcie's room to be eighty-seven - it adjoined the bedroom occupied by Connie Stapleton, which opened into a private sitting-room; this I had ascertained from one of the hotel porters. As I reached the door of the sitting-room I heard voices - a man's voice, and the voices of two women. The man was Albeury. The women, who both spoke at once, were certainly Connie Stapleton and Dulcie. They were in the room, and by their tones I judged them to be wrangling with Albeury. I knocked boldly.

Summoned to enter by Connie Stapleton, I walked straight in and faced them. At once the wrangling ceased.

There was a look in Connie Stapleton's eyes that I had never seen there before. Hitherto I had seen only her attractive side. When I had conversed with her she had always seemed most charming - intelligent, witty, amusing. Now her eyes had in them a cold, steely glitter.

"What do you want, Michael Berrington?" she asked icily. "Don't you think it's time you took off that disguise?"

The sound of a little gasp diverted my attention. I turned, and my gaze met Dulcie's. Her expression betrayed fear.

"Yes, I am Michael Berrington," I said quietly, speaking now in my natural voice, and looking Connie Stapleton full in the eyes. "As you have discovered my identity you probably know why I am disguised - just as you most likely know why George Preston was disguised when you, or some of your gang, strangled him on board the boat."

Connie Stapleton's eyes seemed gradually to resemble a snake's. Her lips were tightly closed. Her face was livid. For some moments she stood there, glaring at me. Then she spoke again:

"This man," she said, indicating Albeury, "has been speaking of you. He tells me that he has advised you to return to England, and I have told him it is now too late. You won't see England again, Mr. Berrington - I tell you that quite openly, before this police officer, whom I have known for many years. I do so with impunity because he knows that if he betrays me I can reveal something I know about him - and should do so at once."

I was about to speak, when my gaze again met Dulcie's. She had turned suddenly pale. Now she glanced apprehensively first at her friend, then at me, and then at the American detective Albeury. Deep perplexity as well as fear was in her eyes.

"Do tell me what it all means," she implored, looking up at me; for the first time for many days she seemed to need my help. "So many things have puzzled me during the past days - I have seen so much and heard so much that I can't understand." She turned to Mrs. Stapleton. "Connie," she cried out impetuously, "why have you suddenly changed? Why have you turned against me? What have I done or said that has given you offence?"

Before Mrs. Stapleton had time to answer, I spoke:

"Dulcie," I exclaimed, "I will say now what I have wanted for days to tell you, though I have not had a chance of doing so, and I knew that if I wrote a letter you would show it to this woman, who would invent some plausible story to make you disbelieve me. Now listen. This woman is not what you believe her to be. In her presence I tell you that she is an adventuress of an odious description, and that, in becoming friendly with you, also in becoming engaged to your father, she has acted from the basest motives. Dulcie, you must leave her at once, and come away with me."

I saw an extraordinary look of repugnance creep into Dulcie's eyes as she cast a half-frightened glance at Connie Stapleton, seated staring at her with an unconcealed sneer.

"Connie," she said bitterly, "oh, Connie, don't look at me like that!"

The woman laughed.

"Can't you see I have no further use for you, you little fool?" she retorted harshly. "Go with him - go with your lover, return to your doddering old father - if you can get to him - who had the amazing effrontery to ask me to become his wife - I, who am young enough to be his granddaughter!"

At that instant I caught the sound of a door being closed carefully. Something prompted me to step out into the passage, and I came face to face with Gastrell, who had evidently just left Connie Stapleton's other room and so must have overheard our conversation, also whatever conversation with Albeury she might have had before I entered. For some moments we stood looking at each other without speaking. He appeared to be calm and wholly unconcerned.

"Do you want me for anything?" he asked suddenly.

"No," I answered. "I have been to see Mrs. Stapleton."

"That's rather obvious, as you have this instant left her room. Is there anything she can do for you?"

"Do for me?"

"Yes."

He came slowly up to me; then, speaking into my face, he said in a hard undertone:

"You have tried to spy upon us - and failed. Your companion, George Preston, spied upon us - he is dead. By this time to-morrow - "

Without another word he went past me down the corridor. He turned the corner at the end, and a moment later I heard the iron gates of the lift shut with a clatter, and the lift descending.

Just then it was that Dulcie rushed out into the corridor. Catching sight of me, she sprang forward and clung to me, trembling.

"Oh, Mike! Mike!" she cried piteously, "I am so terrified. I have just heard such dreadful things - Mike, your life is in danger - you must get away from here at once!"

"That's what I am going to do," I said, with an assumption of calmness I was far from feeling. "And you must come with me, my darling. What about your clothes and things? Can you get them packed quickly?"

Still clinging to me, she hesitated.

"I - I am afraid to go back into that room," she exclaimed at last. "Connie has suddenly turned upon me - I believe she can't bear me any more."

"I'm glad to hear that," I answered, intensely relieved at last. Ah, if only the woman had "turned upon" her long before, I thought, how much better it would have been for Dulcie.

"But surely," I said, "you can go into your own room to pack your things."

This proposition evidently troubled her.

"No," she said after an instant's pause. "Doris Lorrimer is in my room."

"And what if she is? She can't prevent your packing your own things?"

"She can, and she will. Oh, Mike," she continued bitterly, "you don't know - you can't understand. Doris Lorrimer is under Connie's control, just as I have been. Connie seems to have some extraordinary power over her. She does everything Connie tells her to, and Connie has told her not to let me go -

to retain my belongings if I attempt to leave."

"But a moment ago Mrs. Stapleton told you to go - she said she had done with you; I heard her myself."

"She doesn't mean it. I am terrified of her now, Mike; I want to get away from her, but I daren't. If I go, something awful will happen to me - I know it will!"

Though I had long suspected it, only now did I realize the fearful hold that this woman had obtained over Dulcie, who seemed hardly able any longer to exercise her will. This, I knew, must in a measure be the result of the woman's having hypnotized her. My mind was made up in a moment.

"Dulcie," I exclaimed firmly, "you are coming with me to-night - you understand? To-night - whether you take your things or not is not of consequence. I'll see to everything. Don't return to your room. Don't see Mrs. Stapleton again. Come with me - now."

Albeury appeared in the passage. Seeing us, he approached.

"Go at once, Mr. Berrington," he said in a tone of authority. "It is even more serious than I thought. You haven't a moment to lose."

"I am taking Miss Challoner with me," I replied. "I refuse to leave her here."

He glanced at each of us in turn.

"Must you?" he said. "Why not leave Miss Challoner to me? I will answer for her safety. I am too well known in Paris even for reckless people such as we have to deal with now to attempt to oppose me or to do *me* an injury."

"Either Miss Challoner comes with me, or I remain," I replied stubbornly. Something seemed suddenly to have set me on my mettle. "But how is it, Mr. Albeury," I added quickly, "that if these people know you are connected with the police, and you know as much about them as you appear to do, you can't at once have them arrested?"

"We require circumstantial evidence," he answered, "definite evidence of some kind, which at present we haven't got. In cases such as this we can't arrest on suspicion. Much of my information about these people comes from George Preston. People of this description are extremely difficult to arrest, because, in spite of what is practically known about them, nothing against them can be proved. That is where their cleverness comes in - no matter what they do, they keep out of reach of the law. But come, Mr. Berrington, I must get you away at once - no, don't return to your room," as I was moving in that direction, "Come downstairs at once, and bring Miss Challoner with you - we won't go by the lift, if you don't mind."

Dulcie had an evening wrap over her arm. Taking it from her, I wrapped it about her shoulders, then slipped on the thin overcoat I had with me.

Quickly we followed Albeury to the end of the corridor. We were about to descend the stairs, when an unexpected sight arrested our attention.

CHAPTER XXIII

RELATES A QUEER ADVENTURE

Up the great stairway, slowly, very carefully, came four men carrying a stretcher. The form extended upon it was completely covered by a white sheet, all but the feet - a man's feet. Behind and on each side were men, apparently gentlemen, all strangers to me. So deeply occupied were their thoughts, seemingly, that they appeared not to notice Albeury, Dulcie and myself as we stepped aside to let them pass. For the moment my attention was distracted. What had happened? Had there been an accident? If so, who was the victim, and who were these men with him?

"Can you show me the way to room eight eight?" one of the leading bearers asked as he came up to me. He stopped, waiting for me to answer, and as he did so the men beside the stretcher gathered about me, so that for the instant I lost sight of Dulcie, who had instinctively stepped back a pace or two.

I indicated the whereabouts of the room.

"And can you tell me which is Mr. Berrington's room?" he then asked.

"Yes. But I am Mr. Berrington. What is it you want?"

"You are? Are you Mr. Michael Berrington?"

"Yes."

"Oh, then you had better come with us now."

"Whom are you carrying? What has happened?"

Without answering he moved onward down the corridor, with the stretcher.

I walked a little way ahead, and at the room numbered eighty-eight, Mrs. Stapleton's room, I knocked.

Again I was face to face with the woman. Seated in an arm-chair, a cigarette between her lips, she appeared to be reading a newspaper. Upon seeing me she rose abruptly; then, as the covered stretcher was borne slowly in, I saw the cigarette fall from her lips on to the floor, and with surprised, frightened eyes, she gazed inquiringly at the bearers, then down at the outline of the figure beneath the sheet.

"Who is it?" she gasped. "Tell me who it is, and why he has been brought here!"

Nobody answered, though now the bearers, also the men who accompanied them, had all crowded into the room.

Suddenly I noticed that the door of the room had been shut, and instantly the thought came to me -

Where was Dulcie? What had become of her? Also where had Albeury gone?

Hardly had the thought flashed into my mind when I was pounced upon from behind, a hand covered my mouth, my wrists were tied tightly behind me, and my feet bound with a cord. Now I saw the figure that had lain beneath the sheet upon the stretcher rise up of its own accord. The covering fell away, and Gastrell stood before me. I saw him make a sign. At once a gag was crammed into my mouth with great force, so that I could neither cry out nor speak. In a few moments I had been lifted by two men, extended on my back upon the stretcher, and the white cloth had been thrown over me, covering me completely.

Now, the stretcher being raised, I knew that I was being conveyed along the corridor. I was being carried down the stairs, slowly, carefully. In the hall I heard a confused murmur of voices; somebody was telling someone that "the poor fellow" was more seriously hurt than had at first been supposed, and that they were taking him to the hospital. Suddenly I recognized a voice. It was Albeury's, and he spoke in French. Presently I knew that I was being carried out of the hotel, and down the hotel steps. I was being lifted into a car. The ends of the stretcher rested upon the seats. There were expressions of sympathy; questions were being asked and answered in French; the door of the car was shut quietly, and the car swept away.

For twenty minutes or more we passed through the streets of Paris, slowing down at frequent intervals, turning often to right or left. Gradually the sound of the traffic passing grew less, our speed increased, and I judged that we must be out in the environs. Now we were going slowly up a steep hill. We reached the top of it, and our speed increased considerably.

On and on we sped. We must, I gathered, have travelled well over an hour, and now be far out in the country. There was no light inside the car, and though still covered by the sheet, I somehow seemed to feel that the night was very dark. In what direction had we come? Whereabouts, outside Paris, was that long hill up which we had travelled so slowly?

Suddenly someone inside the car moved. An instant later the sheet over my face was pulled back. In the darkness I could still see nothing, but I felt that someone was staring down at me. How many occupants the car contained, of course I could not tell. Still no one spoke, and for five minutes or more the car tore faster and faster along the straight country road.

Then, all at once, a light flashed in my eyes - the light of an electric torch.

"You have but a few minutes to live," a man's voice exclaimed in a low tone. "If you want to say your prayers, you had better do so now."

The voice was clearly Gastrell's. Now I realized that two men besides myself were in the closed car. The light from the electric torch still shone down upon my face. My eyes grew gradually accustomed to the bright light, which had at first dazzled them.

"This is to be your fate," Gastrell continued a minute later. "At a spot that we shall presently come to, far out in the country, fifty miles from Paris, you will be taken out, bound as you are, and shot through the head. The revolver has your initials on it - look."

He held something before my eyes, in such a way that I could see it clearly in the disc of light. It was a pistol's grip. On it shone a little metal plate on which I could distinctly see the engraved initials - "M.B."

"When you are dead, your wrists and legs will be released, and you will be left by the roadside in the forest we are now in, the revolver, with its one discharged chamber, on the ground beside you. Look, whose handwriting is this?"

A letter was passed into the ring of light. I started, for the writing was apparently my own, though certainly I had not written the letter. It was written on notepaper with the Continental Hotel heading, and my handwriting and signature had been forged - a wonderful facsimile of both. On the envelope, which was stamped, were written, also apparently by me, the name and address:

"Miss DULCIE CHALLONER,
Holt Manor,
Holt Stacey,
Berkshire, England."

"My dear Dulcie," the letter ran, "I hope you will forgive the dreadful act I am about to commit, and forget me as quickly as possible. I am not insane, though at the inquest the coroner will probably return a verdict of 'Suicide during temporary insanity.' But my life for years past has been one continuous lie, and from the first I have deceived you most shamefully. I asked you to become my wife, yet I am already married, and have been for some years. Though I am very fond of you, I do not love you, nor have I ever loved you. The things I have said and hinted about your friend Mrs. Stapleton were all utterly false; they emanated entirely from my imagination and were wholly without foundation. This is all I have to say, except again - forgive me.

"Your sincere and miserable friend,

MICHAEL BERRINGTON."

The letter was undated.

What my feelings were when I had read that letter, I find it impossible to describe. The fury of indignation that surged up within me as the car continued to glide smoothly along with unabated speed seemed to drive from my thoughts the sensation of terror which had at first possessed me. Death would be awful enough, especially such a death, but that Dulcie should think I had intentionally and consistently deceived her; that she should be made to believe I had never loved her and that I had wantonly taken my life like a common coward, were too fearful to think about. In an access of mad passion I wildly jerked my wrists again and again in vain attempts to get free. My mouth was still gagged, or I should have called loudly in the desperate hope that even in the deserted spot we were in the cry might be heard and bring assistance. Oh, those moments of frantic mental torture! To this day I can hardly bear to think of them.

Gradually I grew calmer. The electric torch had been extinguished and we still swept on through the darkness. If only the engine would give out, I kept thinking; if only the car would for some reason break down; if only an accident of any sort would happen, I might yet escape the terrible fate awaiting me. To think that a crime such as this could be committed with impunity; worse still, that my name should be handed down to posterity dishonoured and disgraced. To be shot like a dog, with arms and legs bound like a felon's! The more I strove to distract my thoughts the more my mind dwelt upon the immediate future. What would Sir Roland think, and Jack Osborne, and all my friends - even old Aunt Hannah? While pretending to feel pity, how they would inwardly despise me for my apparent cowardice - that cruel letter, too, it would be printed in the newspapers. Yet even that I could have borne with fortitude, I thought, if by some means Dulcie could be made to know that the letter which in a day or two would be found upon my dead body had not been written by me, and that I had not taken my life.

The car was slowing down. Presently it stopped. Once more the disc of light shone down upon my face. Quickly my disguise as Sir Aubrey Belston, which I still wore - wig, moustache and eyebrows, whiskers and beard - was removed. Hurriedly my face and neck were rubbed all over with a sponge soaked in some greasy liquid smelling strongly of turpentine, then rapidly dried with a cloth. Next, two men raised me off the stretcher, lifted me out of the car and set me on my feet, propping me against the car to prevent my falling over, for my legs were still tightly bound.

Instinctively I glanced about me. We seemed to be in the depths of some forest. The road we were on was rather narrow. On both sides of it dark pine trees towered into the sky, which itself was inky, neither moon nor stars being visible.

A light breeze moaned mournfully up the forest. As I stood there, unconsciously listening, the sound seemed to chill me. In vain I strained my ears again in the mad hope that even at this last moment help of some sort might arrive. To right and left I looked along the road, but the blackness was as dense as the blackness of the sky above.

The lamps of the car had been extinguished. Now the only light visible was the glow of the electric torch. For a moment it flashed upon a face, and on the instant I recognized Gastrell, also a man I knew by sight though not by name.

So these were my persecutors, two men moving in the best society, and wholly unsuspected of anything approaching crime. They were to be my murderers! Even in that moment of crisis I found myself unconsciously wondering who the driver of the car could be, for obviously he too must be implicated in this plot, and a member of the gang. Another thought flashed through my mind. Which of all these criminals had done poor Churchill to death? Which had assassinated Preston on board the boat, leaving the impression that he had intentionally hanged himself? Was Gastrell the assassin? Was -

"Here is a place - beside this tree."

The remark, uttered by the stranger, cut my train of thought. Now Gastrell stood beside me. In one hand he held the torch. The fingers of his other hand were unfastening my coat. Soon I felt him push his hand, with a letter in it, into my inside pocket.

The letter intended for Dulcie! The letter which would besmirch my name, dishonour and disgrace it for ever!

In a fit of mad frenzy I tugged wildly at my bonds again in frantic attempts to free myself. As well might I have tried to free myself from handcuffs. Calmly Gastrell rebuttoned my coat, heedless of my struggles.

"And when you are dead," he said quietly, "Holt Manor and estates, and the Challoner fortune, will come eventually to my companions and myself, for Connie, in spite of what she said, is going to marry Roland Challoner, and I intend to marry Dulcie - if she likes it or if she doesn't. So now you realize, I hope, when it is too late, how ill-advised you and your folk were to attempt to overthrow our plans. Several before you have tried, and all have failed; the majority are dead. Very likely more will try, and they too will fail. You know the fate of Churchill and of Preston. You know your own fate. Osborne has saved himself by becoming one of us, for when he marries Jasmine he will join us or else - "

He stopped abruptly. A moment later he added:

"Two of your friends we still have to reckon with, though neither counts for much: Challoner's sister, and his son."

A cold sweat broke out upon me as the ruffian mentioned Dick. God! Was it possible these fiends would wreak their vengeance on a mere boy? And yet if they meant to, how could he escape them? How simple for such men to get him in their power. Ah, if only I could have spoken I should, I truly believe, have humiliated myself by beseeching the monsters to spare poor little Dick.

"Come, hurry along," the stranger, who was standing by, exclaimed impatiently.

"Bob," Gastrell called, without heeding the interruption.

At once the driver of the car approached. He spoke no word. The disc of light shone upon his face and - "Pull your cap off," Gastrell said sharply.

The fellow did so. As I stared hard at him, something in his face seemed familiar to me. Fat and bloated though the face was, and though the eyes sagged, in the man's expression there was something -

Gastrell turned to me.

"Don't you see the likeness?" he asked quickly.

Gagged as I was, of course I couldn't speak.

"Bob is Sir Roland's brother - Robert Challoner," he said. "At Holt his name is never spoken, but you have heard of him. Bob Challoner was kicked out of his home, first by his father, Sir Nelson Challoner, and afterwards by his own brother, Sir Roland. I will now tell you it was Bob who suggested the robbery at Holt, and who, with Connie, helped us through with it. He is going now to see to it that Dulcie becomes my wife."

"Stop your talk, for God's sake!" the stranger interrupted again, his patience at an end. "Time is slipping by. Bring him here and finish him."

They carried me a little way into the forest, then set me on my feet again, propped against a tree. That I did not feel utterly terrified at the thought of my approaching death astonished me. After the mental torture I had endured, however, I felt comparatively calm.

Gastrell approached to within about a yard. Again the wind moaned up through the forest. No other sound whatever broke the night's stillness. Once more a disc of light shone straight into my eyes, though now from a distance of a few inches only. I saw the muzzle of a pistol glitter above the light - I knew now that the electric torch was connected with the weapon.

There came a sharp, metallic "click," as Gastrell cocked the hammer.

CHAPTER XXIV

IN STRANGE COMPANY

A load report rang out just behind me. The light before my eyes vanished. Something lurched up against my chest, knocking the breath out of me, then collapsed in a heap on to the ground at my feet.

There was an instant's stillness. Now footsteps could be heard crackling forward through the undergrowth. There came the sound of a heavy blow, a stifled cry, a dull thud as though a body had fallen heavily. What had happened? And what was happening? Helplessly I stared about me, striving in vain to pierce the blackness of the forest. I heard people moving close beside me, but no word was spoken.

Then suddenly someone touched me. The ropes which bound my wrists were being severed with a blunt instrument. Now my legs were being released. Some fragments of rope dropped to the ground. *I was free!*

Nowhere was there any light, and still nobody spoke. Taking me by the arm, the man who had set me free led me forward through the darkness. Now we were close to the car. Men were beside it, apparently very busy, though what they were engaged in doing I could not ascertain. And then, all at once, the road became flooded with light - the headlights of the car had been switched on simultaneously.

Almost immediately I saw what was happening. Several large bags had been placed inside the car, and others were being pushed in after them. What did they contain? For the moment I was puzzled. Then suddenly the obvious truth flashed across me. The group of men - I could see them indistinctly in the darkness - must be poachers, and poaching out of season I knew to be an offence punishable in France with a very heavy sentence. There seemed to be five men engaged in handling the sacks, while a sixth stood looking on.

"*Entrez*" a voice beside me said suddenly. At the same instant I was gripped by the arm and pushed forward towards the car.

"Who fired that shot?" I exclaimed quickly, in French.

"I did - and saved your life," the man who held me answered. "Why?"

"And you killed him?"

"Yes."

"The report sounded like a rifle shot."

"It was a pistol shot. But what matters, so long as he is dead?"

"Have you his revolver? Did you pick it up?" I asked anxiously.

"Yes."

"Show me both pistols."

My thoughts were travelling with extraordinary rapidity. Rather to my surprise he handed the pistols to me without a word. Quickly I held them in the light cast by the car's lamps and hurriedly examined them. Yes, both were weapons of the same calibre, both took the same cartridges. Below the barrel of Gastrell's revolver was the small electric lamp from which the light had shone on to my face. I gripped the pistol tightly and the light shone out again.

"I will return here in a moment," I said in French, as I moved away, for the man had released my arm.

With the help of the pistol glow-light I made my way back to the tree where a few minutes before I had been propped up, helpless. On the ground, close to the trunk, Gastrell's body lay huddled in a heap, a red spot in the middle of his forehead showing that death must indeed have been instantaneous. I had, however, no time for reflection. Quickly I thrust my hand into the dead man's pockets, one after another. All were empty - someone must already have gone through them. Glancing about me to make sure I was not observed, I hastily transferred to the dead man's pocket, from the inside pocket of my own coat, the letter which he himself had placed there not ten minutes before. Then I rebuttoned his coat, picked up the bits of severed rope lying about - the ropes that previously had bound me - threw the pistol on to the ground close to the dead man's hand, and turned to retrace my steps. Suddenly I stopped. I had forgotten something. Picking up the pistol again I fired a shot into the air, then once more threw it down. My ruse would have proved truly futile had Gastrell's body been discovered, shot through the head, a letter in his pocket pointing directly to suicide, and a revolver on the ground - still loaded in every chamber!

A minute later I was hustled into the car, squeezed tightly between several men. On the floor of the car were a number of large sacks, exhaling an odour none too savoury. The door was slammed, I saw a figure step on to the driving seat, and once more the powerful car shot out into the night, its search-lamps lighting up the road as far as we could see.

For a while nobody spoke.

"I don't know who you are," I said at last in French, breaking the silence, "but I am most grateful to you for saving my life."

Still nobody uttered.

"On my return to England," I continued, "I shall prove my gratitude in a way you may not expect. Meanwhile, I should like to know if you heard what happened, what was said, after the car pulled up and I was lifted out of it."

"We heard everything," one of the men answered in English, out of the darkness. "The man who shot your enemy is driving this car now."

"And may I ask where we are going?" I said, as the car still tore along the white, undulating road, scattering the darkness on either side and far ahead, for we were still deep in the forest.

"Yes. We shall stop first at Chalons-sur-Marne, to deposit these," and he indicated the sacks, which I had by now discovered contained dead pheasants, tightly packed.

"And then?"

"You will see."

Later I gathered from them that the police, as well as gamekeepers, were their deadliest enemies. That night, it seemed, they had been almost captured by some of the forest keepers, who had succeeded in securing their car. The car we were in, they told me quite frankly, they intended to get rid of at once, in a far distant town. That town we were now on our way to - after leaving Chalons we should not stop until we got there. The car, they added, had happened to pull up close to where they lay hidden. Upon discovering that it contained only four men, including the driver, they had intended to overpower all of us and seize the car. Then, overhearing some of the conversation, they had decided to pause and await developments. Owing to that decision it was that my life had so fortunately been saved.

"And how do you poach the birds?" I asked a little later; as they became gradually more talkative we began to grow quite friendly.

They laughed.

"It is easily done," one of them answered, and went on to explain that the method they adopted consisted in burning brimstone under the trees where the pheasants roosted, the fumes causing the birds to tumble off their perches and down to the ground.

They further told me that different parts of the forest teemed with different kinds of game, and that most of it was preserved. In the section we had just been in, pheasants were most abundant. Poached out of season they were additionally valuable, being placed in cold storage directly they were sold, and eventually exported. Equally ingenious were the methods they employed for poaching other sorts of game - some of these methods they described to me in detail - and certain dealers in the town of Chalons, they ended, were always ready to receive it.

At last we passed out of the forest, which I felt glad to leave behind. Now the road twisted a good deal, also it grew more hilly. The darkness, however, became gradually less intense. In Chalons we pulled up in a curious little street. The driver, having clambered down, knocked three times at a small door. Instantly it was opened; the sacks, one after another, were handed in, the door shut noiselessly, and once more we started off.

"Have you any idea," I asked suddenly, "what became of the companions of the man who meant to kill me?"

"Yes," came the immediate reply. "One of them attacked us, and was knocked senseless."

"And the other?"

"I can't say. He suddenly disappeared. We emptied the dead man's pockets to prevent, if possible, his identity being established. You might tell us who he was, and all about him."

I had already told them a good deal, but now I told them more, explaining, eventually, how I had come to be with Hugesson Gastrell and his companion, and the wastrel, Robert Challoner; why they had wished to murder me; how they had already murdered Churchill and George Preston, and the reason they had done so. Miscreants of sorts themselves, as I now knew, they became immensely interested. As we proceeded I told them of the letter that Gastrell had pushed into my pocket, and how, on the following day, it would be found in his own pocket.

"So that until I reveal myself," I added, "I shall, after the discovery of that letter, be dead to my friends and relatives. That, according to a plan I have now thought out, should facilitate my getting the gang arrested, if not in France, at any rate in England."

On and on the car sped at the same regular speed. Village after village was left behind. Now and again we skirted large towns, keeping, however, well without their boundaries. What departments we travelled through I had not the least idea. The driver's knowledge of the country was remarkable. Upon my expressing surprise at the geographical knowledge he possessed, they told me that at one time he had been chauffeur to a nobleman who moved about a great deal.

When I pulled out my watch I found it was half-past two.

"I wish you would tell me how much further you are going," I said at last, yawning. "How many more hours are we going on like this?"

"We are now on our way to Lyons," the man who had last spoken answered quickly - the cigar that he was lighting cast a red glow in his face. "To sell the car nearer Paris wouldn't be safe; besides, in Lyons we have a purchaser awaiting it. We have passed Troyes, Chatillon, and Dijon. We are now in the Department of Saone-et-Loire."

Again we sank into silence. The soft purring of the car seemed to increase our drowsiness. Colder and colder the night air grew - in my evening clothes and thin overcoat I felt it very keenly.

I suppose I must have dozed, for when, presently, I opened my eyes, the streaks of dawn were visible. My neck and limbs were stiff, and, as I looked about me dully, I saw that my companions one and all were fast asleep.

I turned, rubbed the frosted glass in front of me, and peered out at the driver. There he sat, motionless, almost rigid, his hands still gripping the wheel, his gaze set straight ahead. That the cold outside must be intense, I knew, yet he seemed not to notice it.

At a village beyond Louhans we stopped for breakfast, and to cool the engine; but in less than half an hour we were on the road again. As the car swiftly passed over one of the bridges in Lyons a church clock was striking eight. Gradually slackening speed, we turned abruptly to the right, then began a maze of narrow streets. At last, at a quiet-looking hotel out on the road to Vienne, we stopped, and I knew that our journey of three hundred miles or so was at last at an end.

Cafe-au-lait was served for us in a private room on the first floor, and I was able, for the first time, to scrutinize my companions closely. Six in all, they certainly looked a dare-devil, reckless lot. To guess from their appearance what their trade or calling had originally been seemed impossible. Two of them might certainly have belonged to the farmer class had the expression in their eyes been less cunning, less intelligent. The man who had saved my life, and whom I judged to be their leader, was tall, dark, thick-set, with a heavy beard and moustache, and dark, deep-set eyes. His voice, full and resonant, was not unpleasant. Seldom have I seen a man who looked so absolutely fearless.

It was, I suppose, the confidence they felt that I should not betray them after what had happened that made them speak so freely before me. That very morning, I gathered, they would rid themselves of the car to a big receiver of stolen goods, whose headquarters were in Lyons, the largest receiver of stolen goods in the whole of Europe, so they said. With the money thus obtained they would buy a car to replace the one seized on the previous night; it was interesting to find that these lordly thieves and poachers found a car essential to enable them to carry on their business.

The time for parting soon arrived, and once more I thanked my rescuer and his accomplices for the great service they had rendered me. That a human life should have been sacrificed was terrible to think of, and yet -

The reflection that, but for the sacrifice of Gastrell's life, I should myself have been lying dead, set my mind at ease; and after all, I said mentally, the death of a man like Gastrell must do more good than harm.

The first thing I did after leaving them was to buy some clothes and other necessaries, and a valise to pack them in. After that I set out for a quiet stroll through the quaint old town, which I had never before visited. Reviewing the situation, as I walked slowly along, and debating in my mind whether to return to Paris or go straight back to England by the next boat, various possibilities presented themselves in turn. Virtually I was dead to all my friends in England, or I should be in a day or two, when the letter which would be found in Gastrell's pocket had been printed in the newspapers. That belief, I felt, would help me to carry out the plan I had formed for discovering at first hand the actual movements of the gang, some members of which would, I felt sure, be present at Eldon Hall for the coming-of-age festivities of Lord Cranmere's eldest son.

Yet what about Dulcie? I felt that I must see her, and see her as soon as possible. That thought it was which now entirely obsessed me. To see her meant, of course, that I must at once return to Paris, for almost for certain she would still be there. True, her last words, uttered in the corridor of the "Continental," had convinced me that she now strongly suspected Connie, that she wished to get away from her. But would she succeed in getting away? Already I had proofs of the woman's extraordinary will power, and Dulcie, I knew, had been hypnotized by her more than once. I had doubts of Dulcie's ability to resist the woman's spell. Obviously, then, my duty lay before me. I must at once return to Paris. I must see Dulcie again - if possible, see her in private. I must get her away from that woman and take her back to England, no matter how great the risk I might have to run. And what, I wondered suddenly, was Albeury doing all this time?

Still pondering all this, I sauntered into a restaurant I happened to be passing, ordered a bottle of wine, and asked for a copy of the latest railway time-table.

The *rapide* for Paris was due, I saw, to leave Lyons Perrache at eight that night. That would suit me well, and I at once decided to go by it. Then, having nothing to do until the time of starting, I once more strolled out into the town.

A newsboy was shouting the news, and I bought a paper from him. Almost the first headline upon which my glance rested stirred a recollection in my mind. Where, before, had I heard that name - "the Duchesse de Montparnasse"? Ah, now I remembered. When Jack Osborne, confined so mysteriously in the house in Grafton Street, in London, had been cross-questioned in the dark, he had been asked various questions concerning the Duchesse de Montparnasse. And now, right before me, was an account of a strange robbery, a robbery committed the day before at the Duchesse's great chateau on the Meuse!

At once I guessed that this robbery must be yet another of the gang's outrages. My suspicion became conviction when, on reading further, I learned that it had taken place on the occasion of a great reception, when the servants at the chateau had been busily engaged. The goods stolen, the report ended, were valued at many thousands of pounds.

Finding little else of interest in the paper, I continued my ramble. Glancing at my watch I found it was past six. At that moment it was that, turning aimlessly into a side street, I came suddenly face to face with Francois, my rescuer.

"We seem fated to meet!" he exclaimed in his patois French, and he laughed.

He looked hard at me for some moments; then, as though his mind were suddenly made up, he said abruptly:

"I wonder, Mr. Berrington - I fancy that by nature you are inquisitive - if you would like to see something you have never seen before. I don't believe you fully realize how implicitly I now trust you. I should like to prove it to you."

"I should like to see it, immensely," I answered, wondering what on earth, in the nature of a novelty, such a man could have to show me.

"Come," he said in the same tone, linking his arm in mine. "I will show it to you now. As I say, I have no fear at all that you will betray me, yet there isn't another living person, excepting my own accomplices, I would take where I am going to take you now."

Down the side street he had just come up I followed him. We turned to the right again, then to the left. A little further on he stopped at a greengrocer's shop, a small, insignificant shop with one window only.

"Wait here," he said as he entered.

A minute later he reappeared and beckoned to me.

"My friend," he said, presenting me to a cadaverous man of

middle age, with a thin, prominent, rather hooked nose, high cheek-bones, and curious eyes of a steely grey, which bushy eye-brows partly concealed.

The man looked at me keenly, but he neither smiled nor spoke, nor did he offer to shake hands.

We were now inside the shop. Quickly we passed into an inner room, and thence to a room beyond it. This room was lined apparently with bookshelves. Advancing to a corner of it, after carefully locking the door, the cadaverous man, standing on tiptoe, pressed what appeared to be a book in the topmost shelf. At once a door in the bookshelves opened. In silence we followed him through it, and the door shut noiselessly behind us.

I suppose we had walked ten or twelve yards along the narrow, low-ceilinged, uncarpeted passage, lit only by the candle lantern that our guide had unhooked from a nail in the wall, when he suddenly stopped and bent down. Now I saw that he was lifting the boards, one after another. A few moments later the upper rungs of a ladder became visible. Francois descended, I followed carefully - I counted fifteen rungs before I reached the ground - and the gaunt man came after me, shifting the boards back into position above his head when he was half-way down the ladder.

The darkness here was denser than it had been in the passage above, but the lantern served its purpose. We were in a much narrower passage now, so low that we had to stoop to make our way along it. The ceiling was roughly hewn, so was the ground we walked upon. Half a dozen steps along the rough ground and we stopped again. Facing us was a low, extremely narrow door, apparently an iron door - it resembled the door of a safe. Fitting a key into it, the gaunt man pushed it open, and one by one we entered.

At once I became aware of a singular change in the atmosphere. In the narrow, cavernous, obviously subterraneous little passage we had just left the air had been humid, chill, and dank, with an unpleasant earthy odour. Here it was dry and stuffy, as if heated artificially. So intense was the blackness that I seemed almost to feel it. There was a dull thump. Turning, I saw that the cadaverous man had shut this door too. Just as I was wondering why he took such precautions something clicked beside me, and the chamber was flooded with light.

For an instant the glare blinded me. Then, as I looked about me, the sight that met my gaze made me catch my breath. Was this an Aladdin's Palace I had suddenly entered? Had my brain become deranged, causing a strange, an amazing hallucination? Or was I asleep and dreaming?

CHAPTER XXV

THE GLITTERING UNDERWORLD

Never shall I forget that astounding spectacle. Even as I think of it now, it rises once more before me.

The room, though low, was very long and very broad; I guessed at once that originally it must have been a cellar, or possibly a series of cellars. Now as the brilliant electric rays from a dozen powerful ceiling lamps shone down through their tinted shades, they lit up a collection of treasure such as few indeed can have gazed upon.

Heaped upon trays on tables all about the room were unset precious stones of every conceivable description, which glittered and scintillated in the most wonderful way imaginable. Upon the floor, in rough, uncovered boxes, heaps of gold bracelets and brooches, gold rings and gold chains, gold ornaments and trinkets, and bits of miscellaneous jewellery were piled high in inextricable confusion, as though they had been tossed there to be thrown on to a waste heap. Upon the ground were bars of gold, the thickness of a brick, ranged carefully in rows. At one end of the room was a small smelting furnace, not now alight, and above it an iron brazier. Upon the walls hung sets of furs, many seal-skin and ermine, while at one side of the room, upon the ground, lay piled up some thousands of silver spoons and forks, also silver drinking cups and candlesticks, many silver salvers, and an endless assortment of silver articles of every kind.

When at last I had recovered from my astonishment, I turned

abruptly to Francois, who stood at my elbow.

"This, I suppose," I said, speaking in a whisper, "is a sort of clearing-house for stolen property."

He nodded.

"The largest in the whole of France" - he added a moment later, "the largest, possibly, anywhere in Europe. Stolen goods come here from all the Continental centres; also from Great Britain, the United States, and even from Australia."

"But surely," I said, "the police know of this place?"

"They know that it exists, but they don't know where it is. You see how implicitly I trust you, what faith I place in the honour of - a gentleman."

"I think not," I corrected. "You know that my tongue is tied - because you saved my life. That is why you trust me."

He smiled grimly.

"But why have you brought me here?" I asked, after a pause.

"For the reason I have named - to show how implicitly I trust you."

It was only then that a thought flashed in upon me.

"You say," I exclaimed sharply, "that jewellery stolen in Great Britain sometimes finds its way here?"

"Most of the English stuff is got rid of in this room."

"And are you - do your - your 'clients' tell you where the 'stuff' comes from?"

"Always," the gaunt man answered. "That is a condition of my taking it off their hands. You will understand that large rewards are sometimes offered for the return of property intact and uninjured."

I paused to collect my thoughts before speaking again, anxious not to make a false step.

"Can you recollect," I said at last, "if jewellery taken from a country house in Berkshire, England - the house is called Holt Manor - just after Christmas, ever found its way here?"

The gaunt man reflected for a moment. Then, without speaking, he walked across the room, unlocked the door of a little safe which was let into the wall, took from the safe a fat, leather-bound ledger, opened it, and ran his finger down a page.

"Yes," he said in his deep voice. "The property was valued at about twelve or fourteen thousand pounds. I have here a list of the articles."

Turning, he peered oddly at me out of his strange eyes.

"May I see the list?" I asked quickly.

"Have you a reason for wanting to see it?"

"Yes. Some of the jewellery taken had been generations in the family. If it is intact still, I may be able to get a fancy price offered for it, or for some of it."

"*Bien*" he said. "Much of the stuff has been melted down, but not all."

I read carefully down the list, which, arranged neatly and systematically, showed at once what had been melted down, and how it had been disposed of, while a complete list was given of articles kept intact. Among the latter I recognized several bits of jewellery which Dulcie had greatly valued, and quickly I arranged with the gaunt man to buy them from him then and there. After that the three of us sat talking for a considerable time, and before the time arrived for me to leave I knew beyond doubt that the jewellery I had caught sight of when Connie Stapleton's bag had burst open in the train had been the jewellery, or some of it, stolen on board the boat.

"Some day we may meet again," I said as I parted from Francois and his companion, in the little greengrocer's shop.

"Some day we shall," the cadaverous man answered in a strange voice. He extended his hand, and I shook it. A minute later I was in a taxi, hurrying through the streets of Lyons towards the Perrache station.

As the express sped rapidly towards Paris, endless strange reflections and conjectures crowded my brain. Was I acting wisely in thus returning to the French capital, where I might so easily be recognized, seeing how anxious I was that my friends in England should think me dead? I was - I knew - though I did not admit it even to myself - returning to Paris mainly in the hope that I might catch a glimpse of Dulcie. And yet if I did see her, of what use would it be? Also, what should I do? Let her recognize me, and the plan I had formed to get the scoundrels arrested would most likely be spoiled at once - and more than ever I was now determined to bring them to justice in the end.

I fell into a deep sleep, for I was tired out; I had slept little enough during that night-long journey in the stolen car. When I awoke, the train was steaming into Paris; an official, who had aroused me by rubbing his hand upon my cheek, stood awaiting a *pourboire.*

"Go to the Hotel Continental," I said in French to the driver of the taxi into which I had just stepped with my newly-bought valise. "Get there as quickly as you can."

That I was doing a mad thing in thus returning to the hotel, where in all probability the members of the gang were still staying, I knew. But a man in love hardly reckons with risks, and as I lay back in the taxi, my brain awhirl, I knew that I was as desperately in love as it is possible for man to be.

Paris - gay Paris - looked gloomy enough in the dull blue haze which hung over and partly enveloped its deserted, dreary streets. Happening to glance up at the windows of a house with green sun-shutters half open, my eyes met those of a faded girl with touzled hair, peering down into the street, and mechanically she ogled me. In disgust I averted my gaze, hating, for the moment, my own sex, which made such women possible. On and on the car rolled. Some revellers in dishevelled evening clothes, their eyes round and staring, their faces ghastly in the morning light, stumbled out beneath an archway above which a lamp burned dully with an orange glow.

Everything and everyone seemed only half awake. The reception clerk at the hotel was sulky and inclined to be argumentative. Yes, he was positive, he said in reply to my inquiry, that nobody of the name of Challoner was staying at the hotel, - no, nor yet of the name of Stapleton. They had slept there the night before? Yes, that was quite possible, but he was not concerned with people who had stayed there, only with the people who were there then. He had no idea, he added, at what time they had left, nor yet where they had gone - and did I need a room, or didn't I? Because if I didn't I had better go away.

His impertinence annoyed me, but I had too much to think about to have time to lose my temper. I told him I needed a room, and I sent up my valise. A bath, a shave and a change of clothes braced me considerably, and by the time I reached the coffee-room I felt thoroughly refreshed.

What adventures had befallen me since I had breakfasted in that room, only forty-eight hours before, I reflected, as the waiter approached with the *Figaro*. Breakfast was laid for a hundred or more, but barely a dozen people were in the room. All were strangers to me, so I soon became engrossed in the newspaper.

My attention was distracted by the waiter, who, again approaching, turned up two chairs at my table.

"With all those tables empty," I said to him with a wave of the hand, "you can surely put people elsewhere. I don't want strangers here."

He smiled pleasantly, showing extraordinarily white teeth.

"A gentleman and lady wish to sit at monsieur's table," he said, bowing politely, and still smiling.

"Monsieur will not object?"

He seemed so amiable that I felt I couldn't be rude to him.

"But who are the lady and gentleman? And why did they specify this table?" I asked, puzzled.

The waiter gave a little shrug, raising his eyebrows as he did so.

"How can I tell?" he answered. "They come to the door a moment ago, while monsieur is reading his newspaper; they see monsieur; they speak *ensemble* in whispers for some moments, it would seem about monsieur; and then they call me and tell me to serve their *dejeuner* at monsieur's table."

Hardly had he stopped speaking, when my gaze rested upon two people who had just entered and were approaching.

One was the police official, Victor Albeury. The other was Dulcie Challoner!

They greeted me with, I thought, rather exaggerated non-chalance as they came up, then seated themselves, one on either side of me, Albeury telling the waiter to "hurry up with the breakfast that he had ordered five minutes ago."

I was puzzled, rather than surprised, at the matter-of-fact way that Albeury and Dulcie conversed with me - few things astonished me now. Had we all been on the best of terms, and met after being separated for half an hour or so, they could hardly have been more composed. For five minutes we discussed commonplace topics, when suddenly I noticed that Albeury was looking at me very hard. Dulcie, too, seemed to have grown curiously uneasy.

"Whereabouts is he?" Albeury said quickly in a low tone, glancing sharply at Dulcie. The door was at the back.

"Gone," she whispered. She seemed greatly agitated.

"Mr. Berrington," Albeury said hurriedly, his eyes set on mine, "I suspect that man. They all left last night. He arrived just before they left. I happened to see Doris Lorrimer engaged in earnest conversation with him."

"Of whom are you speaking?" I asked, not understanding.

"Of the waiter at this table - that polite, unctuous man I saw talking to you. Listen. I have rescued Miss Challoner from Stapleton and her accomplices. We are going to leave Paris for London in less than half an hour; it's not safe for Miss Challoner to stay here longer. And you must travel with us. It is imperative that you should. I can't say more to you now, while that man is hanging about. Tell me quickly, before he returns: what happened to you yesterday? Where were you last night?"

"Oh, Mike!" Dulcie interrupted, "if you only knew the mental agony I have suffered, all that I endured last night - Mike, I dreamed that you were dead, I dreamed that they had killed you!"

I stared at her, startled.

"They tried to," I almost whispered. "But they failed, and now I - "

"Mr. Berrington," Albeury cut in, "you must forgive my brusqueness - your breakfast will be brought to you in a moment; when it is, don't eat it. Make any excuse you like, but don't eat it."

"Good God!" I exclaimed, instantly guessing his thought, "surely you can't suppose - "

"I can, and do suppose. More than that, I am practically certain that - "

He cut his sentence short, for Dulcie had signalled with her eyes. The waiter had re-entered the room.

I breathed more freely when at last the three of us were on our way to the railway station. Strange as it may seem, I had experienced some difficulty in ridding myself of the officious attentions of the smiling, smooth-tongued, extremely plausible waiter.

On board the steamer, in a corner of the saloon where none could eavesdrop, I related to Dulcie how I had been bound, gagged, borne out of the hotel upon the stretcher concealed beneath a sheet, and all that had subsequently occurred that I felt justified in telling her. Of the thieves' clearing-house in Lyons and my rescuer's connection with it, also of the discovery of the whereabouts of her stolen property, I could of course say nothing, my lips being in honour sealed.

A little later, as beneath the stars we slowly paced the deck - the sea was wonderfully smooth for the end of February - Dulcie opened her heart to me, as I had so long hoped she some day would.

"Oh, if only you knew," she suddenly exclaimed in an access of emotion, after I had, for a little while, tried to draw her on to talk about herself, "if only you knew all that I have been through, Mike, you would be sorry for me!"

"Why don't you tell me everything, my darling?" I answered gently, and, almost without my knowing it, I drew her closer to me. "You know - you must know, that I won't repeat to a living soul anything you may say."

"Oh, yes, Mike, of course I know," she said, pressing my hands in hers, as though she sought protection, "but there is - "

"There is what?"

She glanced to right and left, up the dark deck, and down it, then gave a little shudder. But for ourselves, the deck was quite deserted.

"I hardly know," she almost whispered, and I felt her trembling strangely. "Somehow I feel nervous, frightened. I feel as if some danger were approaching - approaching both of us."

Again she looked about her. Then, as I spoke soothingly, she gradually grew calmer.

"I was very, very fond of Connie Stapleton, you know," she said presently, "and I thought that she liked me. That time, at Holt, when you warned me to beware of her, I felt as if I hated you. She influenced me so strangely, Mike, - I cannot explain how. Mike, my darling, I tell you this now because somehow I feel you will forgive me, as at last it's all over. It seems so odd now to think of it, but as I grew to love her my love for you seemed to grow less - I knew from the first that she detested my loving you so, and if I spoke much about you to her it annoyed her. She wanted to destroy my love for you, Mike, but never, all the time I have been with her, did I say a word against you. Do you believe me when I tell you that?"

Later she told me that the woman had quite recently hinted at her doing certain things she hardly dared to think about, and that, the very day before, she had disclosed a horrible plan which she had formulated, in which Dulcie was to play a very important part - a plan to do with a robbery on a very extensive scale.

"Oh, Mike, Mike," she went on, "I must have been mad during these past weeks to have listened to what she hinted at - I was mad, or else she had completely hypnotized me. You remember Mr. Osborne's being taken to that house in Grafton Street, and kept there in confinement, and the telegram I received that was supposed to come from you? Well, I know now who it was who kept him there a prisoner, and came to him in the dark, and questioned him, and tried to get him to reveal information which he alone could give. The man who did all that was - "

A footstep just behind us made us both turn quickly. A faint light still shone along the almost dark deck. Before I could recognize the figure, before I had time to speak, Dulcie had sprung suddenly forward and gripped the muffled man by the arm.

"Father!" she exclaimed under her breath, with difficulty controlling her emotion, "father, what are you doing here?"

CHAPTER XXVI

"THAT WOMAN!"

Sir Roland, whose appearance the cap pulled over his eyes had partly disguised, made a motion with his hand, enjoining silence. Then, linking Dulcie's arm in his, he walked slowly towards the saloon entrance. I walked beside them, but for the moment nobody spoke.

We presently found ourselves in a small, deserted room, apparently a card room. Here, after carefully shutting the door, Sir Roland seated himself. Then he indicated the seats that he wished us each to occupy, for he was rather deaf.

"It is unwise," he said, as he offered me a cigar, "ever to converse privately on the deck of a steamer. Though I have travelled little by sea, I know that on board ship, especially on a small boat like this, voices carry in an extraordinary manner. Standing down wind of you, on deck, some moments ago, I heard your remarks quite distinctly, in spite of my deafness. I even recognized your voices - until then I did not know you were on board."

"But why are you here, father?" Dulcie exclaimed. "When did you leave England?"

"I crossed the night before last. Connie wired to me to come at once - she said in her telegram 'most urgent,' though she gave no reason for the urgency."

"And have you seen her? Where is she now?"

"I was to meet her in the lounge of the Hotel Bristol in Paris last night. Punctually at nine o'clock, the time arranged, I arrived there. I waited until nearly ten, and then a messenger arrived with a note. It was from her. She said in it that she had been telegraphed for to return to England, that she was leaving by the night boat. She expressed deep regret, and said she hoped that I would come back to London as soon as possible - and so here I am."

Again, for some moments, nobody spoke. Dulcie was the first to break the silence.

"Father," she exclaimed impetuously, "are you really going to - are you still determined to marry that woman?"

Sir Roland stared at her.

"'That woman'?" he said in surprised indignation. "Whom do you mean by 'that woman'?"

"Connie Stapleton, father," she answered, looking him full in the eyes. "Have you the least idea who and what she is?"

Sir Roland gazed at her aghast. Then, obviously controlling himself:

"I know that she has done me the honour of accepting my offer of marriage," he replied, with cold dignity. "More than that, I don't ask to know; her circumstances don't interest me; my fortune is ample for both."

Dulcie made a gesture of impatience.

"For goodness' sake, father," she exclaimed, "how can you talk like that? Connie Stapleton is - "

She turned to me abruptly.

"Oh, Mike," she said in a tone of great vexation, "tell him

everything - I can't."

I cleared my throat to gain time to collect my thoughts. Sir Roland's rather dull stare was set upon my face inquiringly, though his expression betrayed astonishment and keen annoyance.

"It's just this, Sir Roland," I said at last, bracing myself to face an unpleasant task. "You, Dulcie, and I too, have been completely taken in by Mrs. Stapleton. We believed her to be as charming as she certainly is beautiful, we thought she was a lady, we - "

"'Thought'!" Sir Roland interrupted, cold with anger. "I still consider her to be - "

"Will you let me finish? I say we all thought that, I say we supposed that Mrs. Stapleton was just one of ourselves, a lady, an ordinary member of society. Then circumstances arose, events occurred which aroused my suspicions. At first I tried to dispel those suspicions, not only because I liked the woman personally, but because it seemed almost incredible that such a woman, mixing with the right people, received everywhere, could actually be what the circumstances and events I have hinted at pointed to her being. But at last proof came along that Mrs. Stapleton was - as she is still - a common adventuress, or rather an uncommon adventuress, a prominent member of a gang of clever thieves, of a clique of criminals - "

"Criminals!" Sir Roland stormed, bursting suddenly into passion. Often I had seen him annoyed, but never until now had I seen him actually in an ungovernable fury. "How dare you say the lady I am about to marry is - is - "

"I have proofs, Sir Roland," I cut in as calmly as I could. "You may doubt my word, you can hardly doubt the word of a famous Continental detective. He is on board. I will bring him here now."

As I quietly rose to leave the room, I saw Sir Roland staring, half stupidly, half in a passion still, from Dulcie to me, then back again at Dulcie. Before he could speak, however, I had left the little room and gone in search of Victor Albeury. He was not in his cabin, nor was he in the smoking-room, where men still sat playing cards, nor was he in the big saloon. On the forward deck I found him at last, a solitary figure leaning against the stanchion rail, smoking his pipe, and gazing abstractedly out across the smooth sea, his eyes apparently focussed upon the black, far-distant horizon.

Gently I tapped him on the arm, as he seemed unaware of my approach.

"Well, Mr. Berrington," he said calmly, without looking round or moving, "what can I do for you?"

"Please come at once," I exclaimed. "Sir Roland and Miss Challoner are in the small saloon; we have been trying to explain to Sir Roland that the woman Stapleton is an adventuress. Probably you don't know that she is engaged to be married to Sir Roland. He won't believe a word we say. We want you to come to him - to speak to him and open his eyes."

It was no easy matter, however, to get the old man to believe even Albeury's calm and convincing assurance that Connie Stapleton belonged to a gang of infamous people, some of whom we knew beyond question to be cold-blooded assassins. It was due, indeed, largely to Albeury's remarkable personality that in the end he succeeded in altering the opinion Sir Roland had held concerning this woman of whom he was evidently even more deeply enamoured than we already knew him to be.

"But she has been such a close friend of yours, Dulcie," he said at last, in an altered tone. "If she is all that you now say she is, how came you to remain so intimate with her all this time?"

"She has tricked me, father, just as she has hoodwinked you," she answered, with self-assurance that astonished me. "And then she seemed somehow to mesmerize me, to cast a sort of spell over me, so that I came almost to love her, and to do almost everything she suggested. By degrees she got me in her power, and then she began to make proposals that alarmed me - and yet I was drawn to her still. Once or twice Mike had warned me against her, but I had refused to believe his warnings. It was only two days ago that the crisis came. She didn't ask me to do what she wanted; she told me I *must* do it - and then, all at once, the scales seemed to fall from my eyes. At last her true nature was revealed to me. It was an awful moment, father - awful!"

Far into the night the three of us remained talking. At last, when we rose to separate, Albeury turned to me.

"I sleep with you in your cabin to-night, Mr. Berrington," he said quietly. "And I have arranged that one of the stewardesses shall share Miss Challoner's cabin. Nobody can tell what secret plans the members of this gang may have made, and it's not safe, believe me it isn't, for either of you to spend the night unprotected. Locks, sometimes even bolts, form no barrier against these people, some of whom are almost sure to be on board, though I haven't as yet identified any among the passengers. You will remember that Lady Fitzgraham's cabin was ransacked last week, though she was in it, and the door locked on the inside. And poor Preston - we can't risk your sharing his fate."

These ominous warnings would assuredly have filled me with alarm, had not Albeury's calmness and complete self-possession inspired me with a strange confidence. Somehow it seemed to me that so long as he was near no harm could befall either Dulcie or myself. Even Preston's presence had never inspired such confidence as this clever and far-seeing detective's presence had done ever since I had come to know him.

But nothing happened. When I woke next morning, after a night of sound rest, the boat was steaming slowly into port.

Together the four of us journeyed back to town, and for the first time for many weeks I had an opportunity of a lengthy talk with Dulcie. Somehow her association with the woman Stapleton seemed to have broadened her views of life, though in all other respects she was absolutely unchanged. To me she seemed, if possible, more intensely attractive and lovable than during the period of our temporary estrangement - I realized now that we had during those past weeks been to all intents estranged. Perhaps, after all, the singular adventures she had experienced - some which she related to me were strange indeed - had served some good purpose I did not know of. What most astonished me was that, during those weeks which she had spent in close companionship with Stapleton, Gastrell, Lorrimer, and other members of the criminal organization, nothing had, until quite recently, been said that by any possibility could have led her to suppose that these friends of hers, as she had deemed them to be, were other than respectable members of society. Certainly, I reflected as she talked away now with the utmost candour and unconcern, these people must constitute one of the cleverest gangs of criminals there had ever been; the bare fact that its members were able to mix with such impunity in exclusive social circles proved that.

Before the train left Newhaven I had bought a number of newspapers, but not until we were half-way to London did it occur to me to look at any of them. It was not long, then, before I came across an announcement which, though I had half expected to see it, startled me a little. The report of my supposed suicide was brief enough, and then came quite a long account of my uneventful career - uneventful until recently. Turning to Dulcie, who, seated beside me, was staring out at the flying scenery, I handed her one of the papers, indicating the paragraph.

"Good heavens, Mike!" she exclaimed when she had read it. "How awful! Supposing I had read that without knowing it to be untrue!"

She held out the paper to Sir Roland.

"Father, just read that," she said.

He had heard me relate to Dulcie the story of my narrow escape in the forest near Martin d'Ablois, and I was pleased to see a smile at last come into his eyes, for since his cruel disillusionment he had looked terribly depressed.

"After all," I said as he put the paper down, "I am glad I returned to Paris, if only because my doing so has saved you from this shock."

"If I had read that, believing it to be true," he answered quietly, "the shock would probably have killed me."

"Killed you!" I exclaimed. "Oh, no, Sir Roland, a little thing like that would not have killed you; a family like yours takes a lot of killing - the records in history prove that."

He gazed at me with a strange seriousness for some moments. At last he spoke.

"Michael," he said, and there was an odd catch in his voice, "I wonder if you have the remotest conception of the strength of my attachment to you. I don't believe you have. And yet I could hardly be more attached to you than I am if you were my own son."

When, after parting from Sir Roland and Dulcie in London - they were to return to Holt direct - I arrived with Albeury at my flat in South Molton Street, I found a stack of letters awaiting me, also several telegrams. Simon, my man, was expecting me - I had telegraphed from Newhaven - but almost directly he opened the door I noticed a change in his expression, and to some extent in his manner. Deferential, also curiously reserved, he had always been, but now there was a "something" in his eyes, a look which made me think he had something on his mind - something he wished to say to me but dared not say.

I had sent Albeury into my study to smoke a cigar and drink a glass of wine while I went up to my room to have a bath. Simon was still busy with my things when I came out of the bathroom, and, while I dressed, I took the opportunity of questioning him.

"What's amiss, Simon?" I asked lightly.

He looked up with a start.

"Amiss, sir?" he repeated, with obvious embarrassment.

"I said 'amiss.' Out with it."

He seemed, for some moments, unable to meet my glance. Then suddenly he faced me unflinchingly.

"Yes?" I said encouragingly, as he did not speak.

"I'll tell you what's amiss, sir," he answered abruptly, forcing himself to speak. "The day after you'd left, a peculiar-looking man called here, and asked to see you. When I told him you were not at home, he asked if you were out of town. I didn't answer that, sir, but I asked him quite politely if I couldn't give you any message. He answered No, that he must see you himself. Then he started to question me, in a kind of roundabout way, about you and your movements, sir."

"I hope you kept your counsel," I exclaimed quickly, for, excellent servant though Simon, was, he occasionally lacked discretion.

"Indeed I did, sir. Though I was quite courteous, I was a bit short with him. The next day he come again, about the same time - it was close on dinner time - and with him this time was another man - a rather younger man. They questioned me again, sir, quite friendly-like, but they didn't get much change out of me. Yesterday they tried it on a third time - both of them come again - and, well, sir, happing to put my hand into my jacket pocket soon after they were gone, I found these in it."

As he spoke he dived into his jacket, and pulled out an envelope. Opening the envelope, he withdrew from it what I saw at a glance were bank-notes. Unfolding them with trembling hands, which made the notes crackle noisily, he showed me that he had there ten five-pound notes.

"And they gave you those for nothing?" I asked, meaning to be ironical.

"Well, sir, they didn't get anything in return, though they expect something in return - that's only natural. They said they'd come back to see me."

"Did they say when they'd come back?"

"To-day, sir, about the same time as they come yesterday and the day before." He pulled out his watch. "It's close on seven now. Perhaps you will like to see them if they come presently, sir."

"On the other hand, perhaps I shall not," I said, and I lit a cigarette. "At the same time, if they call, you can tell me."

"Certainly, sir - if anybody rings, I'll come at once and tell you."

He shuffled for a moment, then added:

"And these notes, sir; am I entitled to keep them?"

"Of course you are. Anybody has a right to accept and keep a gift. At the same time, I would warn you not to be disappointed if, when you try to cash them, you find the numbers have been stopped."

Downstairs, with Albeury, I began to look through my correspondence. The third telegram I opened puzzled me.

"Is it all right? - Dick."

It had been awaiting me two days. Guessing that there must be a letter from Dick which would throw light on this telegram, I glanced quickly through the pile. I soon came to one addressed in his handwriting.

I had to read it through twice before I fully realized what it all meant. Then I turned quickly to Albeury.

"Read that," I said, pushing the letter to him across the table.

He picked it up and adjusted his glasses. A few moments later he sprang suddenly to his feet.

"My God! Mr. Berrington!" he exclaimed, "this is most serious! And it was written " - he glanced at the date - "eight days ago - the very day you left London."

"What is to be done?" I said quickly.

"You may well ask," he answered. He looked up at the clock. "The police must be shown this at once, and, under the circumstances, told everything that happened in France. I had hoped to be able to entrap the gang without dealing with Scotland Yard direct."

For some moments he paced the room. Never since I had met him had I seen him so perturbed - he was at all times singularly calm. I was not, however, surprised at his anxiety, for it seemed more than likely that quite unwittingly, and with the best intentions, Dick Challoner had not merely landed us in a terrible mess, but that he had certainly turned the tables upon us, leaving Dulcie and myself at the mercy of this desperate gang. On board the boat I had mentioned Dick to the detective, and told him about the cypher, and the part that

Dick had played. He had not seemed impressed, as I had expected him to be, and without a doubt he had not been pleased. All he had said was, I now remembered: "It's a bad thing to let a boy get meddling with a matter of this kind, Mr. Berrington" - he had said it in a tone of some annoyance. And now, it would seem, his view had been the right one. What Dick had done, according to this letter just received from him, had been to start advertising in the *Morning Post* on his own account - in the cypher code which he had discovered - serious messages intended for the gang and that must assuredly have been read by them. With his letter two cuttings were enclosed - his two messages already published. As I looked at them again a thought flashed across me. Now I knew how it came about that my impenetrable disguise had been discovered. Now I knew how it came about that Alphonse Furneaux had been released from the room where Preston had locked him in his flat. And now I knew why the members of the gang had left the "Continental" so suddenly, scattering themselves probably in all directions, and why the woman Stapleton had dashed back to London.

I caught my breath as my train of thought hurried on. Another thought had struck me. I held my breath! Yes, it must be so. Try as I would I could not possibly deceive myself.

Dick had unwittingly been responsible for the murder of George Preston!

This was the most awful blow of all. Unconsciously I looked up at the detective, who still paced the room. Instantly my eyes met his. He may have read in my eyes the horror that I felt, or the strength of my feeling may have communicated my thought to him, for at once he stood still, and, staring straight at me, said in a tone of considerable emotion:

"That boy has done a fearful thing, Mr. Berrington. He has - "

"Stop! Stop!" I cried, raising my head. "I know what you are going to say! But you mustn't blame him, Albeury - he did it without knowing - absolutely without knowing! And only you and I know that he is to blame. Dick must never know - never. Nobody else must ever know. If his father ever finds it out, it will kill him."

For some moments Albeury remained quite still. His lip twitched - I had seen it twitch like that before, when he was deeply moved. At last he spoke.

"Nobody shall ever know," he said in the same strained tone. He paused, then:

"I must talk on your telephone," he exclaimed suddenly, turning to leave the room.

As he did so, Simon entered.

"The two men are here, sir," he said. "I have told them you are quite alone. Shall I show them in?"

CHAPTER XXVII

THE FOUR FACES

They were quietly dressed, inoffensive-looking men, one a good deal younger than the other. Judged by their clothes and general appearance they might have been gentlemen's servants or superior shop-assistants. Directly they saw that I was not alone, the elder, whose age was fifty or so, said, in a tense voice:

"We wish to see you alone, Mr. Berrington. Our business is quite private."

"You can talk openly before this gentleman," I answered, for, at a glance from me, Albeury had remained in the room. "What do you want to see me about?"

"In private, please, Mr. Berrington," he repeated doggedly, not heeding my question.

"Either you speak to me in this gentleman's presence," I answered, controlling my irritation, "or not at all. What do you want?"

They hesitated for barely an instant, and I thought my firmness had disconcerted them, when suddenly I saw them exchange a swift glance. The younger man stepped quickly back to the door, which was close behind him, and, without turning, locked it. As he did so his companion sprang to one side with a sharp cry. Albeury had him covered with a revolver. The younger man had already slipped his hand into his pocket, when I sprang upon him.

Though some years have passed since I practised ju-jitsu, I have not forgotten the different holds. In a moment I had his arms locked behind him - had he attempted to struggle then he must have broken his wrists. Turning, I saw that Albeury had the other man still at his mercy with the revolver - not for an instant did he look away from him.

I was about to call loudly to Simon to call the police, when the elder man spoke.

"Stop!" he gasped, just above a whisper. "You have done us. Give us a chance to escape and well help you."

"Help me! How?" I said, still gripping my man tightly. "What have you come for? What did you want?"

"We're under orders - so help me, we are!" he exclaimed huskily. "We had at any cost to see you."

"And for that you bribed my man, or tried to?"

"Yes - to let us see you alone."

Albeury's arm, extended with the cocked revolver, was as rigid as a rock. The muzzle covered the man's chest. Again the man glanced swiftly at the detective, then went on, speaking quickly:

"If you'll let us go, we'll tell everything - anything you want to know!"

I glanced an inquiry at Albeury. Though his gaze was still set upon his man, he caught my look.

"Right - we'll let you go," he said, without moving, "if you'll tell us everything. Now speak. Why are you here?"

"We're under orders," the man repeated. "We were not to leave this flat with him alive in it," he jerked his chin at me. "If we do we shall be killed ourselves when The Four Faces know. But you've done us. We've got to escape now somehow, if you'll let us, and our only way is to give you information that'll help you to get the whole gang arrested. You've discovered a code we use, and you've tampered with it, and that's what's done it."

"Done what?"

"Got The Four Faces down on you, and made them set on killing you."

"Whom do you mean by 'The Four Faces'?"

"Why, the men and women - you know them; Gastrell, Stapleton, and the rest - the gang known as The Four Faces."

"Why are they known as 'The Four Faces'?"

"Because there are four heads, each being known as 'The Fat Face,' 'The Long Face,' 'The Thin Face,' and 'The Square Face.' And each head has four others of the gang directly under his or her orders."

"And Gastrell and Stapleton are 'faces'?"

"Yes."

"But Gastrell is dead."

"Dead? Gastrell? Impossible!"

"Yes. Go on."

For some moments astonishment held him dumb.

"Gastrell and the rest of them will be at Eldon Hall, in

Northumberland, the day after to-morrow," he said at last, "for the coming of age of Cranmere's son. The house is to be looted - cleaned out. Everything is arranged - the plan is perfect - as all the arrangements of The Four Faces always are - it can't fail unless - "

"Yes?"

"Now that you know, you can warn Cranmere. You must warn him to be very careful, for if they get wind there's suspicion about they'll drop it and you won't catch them. You know the robberies and other things there've been, and nobody's been caught - they've not even been suspected. Now's your chance to get them all - the first real chance there's ever been. But you mustn't show up, mind that. This house is watched - to see when we come out. Nor you nor your man must go out of this flat till the gang's been caught, every one of them - it's the day after to-morrow they'll be at Eldon Hall. They're expecting a gigantic haul there, including all the Cranmere diamonds - they're worth thousands on thousands. You're both known by sight, and if you're seen about we're just as bad as dead."

He stopped abruptly, then went on:

"And you mustn't answer if anybody rings or knocks. And you mustn't answer the telephone. You understand? Nobody must answer it. It's got to be supposed you're both in here, dead - you and your man. They've got to think we done it. There's no one else living in this flat, we know that."

"I can't warn Lord Cranmere if I don't go out of here."

"He can" - he indicated the detective. "He can go out at any time. They don't know he's in here. If we'd known you'd anybody with you we'd have come another time. Your man said you were alone - quite alone, he said - and, well, we thought the fifty quid had squared him."

Still holding my man tightly in the ju-jitsu grip, I again spoke quickly to the detective.

"Isn't he lying?" I asked. "Is it safe to let them go?"

"Quite safe," he answered, without an instant's hesitation. "I know them both. This fellow has been four times in jail - the first time was seventeen years ago - he got fourteen months for burglary; the second time was thirteen years ago, for attempted murder, when he got five years; the third was eleven years ago; the fourth was nine years back. He's got half a dozen aliases or more, and your man - let me see, yes, he's been once in jail: ten years for forgery, went in when he was eighteen and not been out above three years. It's safe to let them go - quite safe - they've spoken straight this time, couldn't help themselves."

While Albeury was speaking I had seen the men gasp. They were staring at him now with a look of abject terror. But still I held my man.

"I don't like to risk it," I expostulated. "The whole tale may be a plant."

"It's not, Mr. Berrington. I tell you they're straight this time, they've got to be to save their skins. I could put the 'Yard' on to them right away - but it wouldn't serve our purpose, the gang would then escape."

His revolver still covered the elder man's chest.

"Hand out your gun," he said sharply, "and empty out your pockets - both of you."

Soon everything the men's pockets had contained lay upon the floor. Among the things were three pistols, two "jemmies," some curious little bottles, and some queer-looking implements I couldn't guess the use of. Just then a thought occurred to me.

"But they'd have robbed this flat," I said, "if what they say is true."

"You are mistaken," Albeury answered. "They didn't come for robbery, but on a more serious errand - to put an end to you. I know the methods of this gang pretty well, I can assure you. You would have been found dead, and your man dead too most likely, and the circumstances attending your death would all have pointed to suicide, or perhaps to accidental death. But we've not much time to spare. Come."

He turned to the men.

"Come over here, both of you," he said sharply, and signalled to me to release my man. I did so. To my surprise, both men seemed cowed. In silence, and without attempt at violence, they followed Albeury across to the escritoire. At that moment it was that the bell of the flat rang loudly. Without stirring, we stood expectantly waiting. I had unlocked the door of the room, and presently Simon entered.

"Mr. Osborne would like to see you, sir," he said in his usual tone of deference. "When I told him you had visitors he said he wouldn't come in. He's waiting at the door, sir."

"Jack! Splendid!" I exclaimed. "The very man we want to see - you have heard me speak of Mr. Osborne, Albeury, and you know plenty about him." I turned to Simon. "Show him in here at once," I said. "If he still hesitates, say I want particularly to see him."

It seemed quite a long time since last I had met Osborne - on the night we had gone together, with poor Preston, to Willow Road, and had afterwards been followed by Alphonse Furneaux. I had felt so annoyed with Jack for becoming enamoured of Jasmine Gastrell after all we had come to know about her that I had felt in no hurry to renew my friendship with him. But now circumstances had arisen, and things had changed. If he were still infatuated with the woman, we should, between the lot of us, I thought, quickly be able to disillusion him.

He looked rather serious as he entered, and glanced from one to another of us inquiringly. I introduced Albeury to him; as I mentioned Albeury's name I saw the two scoundrels start. Evidently he was well known to them by name, and probably by repute.

"As I was passing, I looked in," Osborne said, "as we haven't run across each other for such a long time, but I don't know that I've got anything in particular to say to you, and you seem to be engaged."

"But I have something particular to say to you," I answered quickly, coming at once to the point, as Simon left the room and shut the door behind him. "You've made pretty much of a fool of yourself with that Gastrell woman, Jack," I went on, with difficulty restraining the indignation I felt. "You are largely responsible for terrible things that have happened during the past few days - including the murder of George Preston."

"Murder? The newspapers said it was suicide."

"Of course they did - it was arranged that they should. Now listen, Jack," I continued seriously. "We are on the eve of what may prove to be a tremendous tragedy, of an event that in any case is going to make an enormous sensation - nothing less than the capture, or attempted capture, of the whole of the notorious and dangerous gang that a short time ago you appeared to be so desperately anxious to bring to justice. These two men," I indicated them, "belong to the gang in the sense that they are employed by it; but they have now turned King's evidence."

In a few words I outlined to him exactly what had happened. As I stopped speaking, Albeury interrupted.

"And if you will now listen, Mr. Osborne," he said, "you will hear a complete statement of facts which should interest you."

With that he pulled a notebook out of his pocket, opened it, laid it flat on the escritoire and seated himself, producing his fountain pen. Both men stood beside him.

Rapidly he cross-questioned them, writing quickly down in shorthand every word they spoke. Almost endless were the questions he put concerning the whole gang. One by one the name of each member of it was entered in the notebook, followed by an address which, the men declared, would find him - or her. The number of members, we thus discovered, amounted to over twenty, of whom no less than eight were women. Jasmine Gastrell's career was described in detail, also Connie Stapleton's, Doris Lorrimer's, Bob Challoner's, Hugesson Gastrell's, and the careers of all the rest in addition. The names of some of these were known to us, but the majority were not. Incidentally we now found out that Hugesson Gastrell had never been in Australia, nor yet in Tasmania, and that the story of his having been left a fortune by an uncle was wholly without foundation. The natural son of well-to-do people in Yorkshire, he had been launched penniless on the world to make his way as best he could, and the rapidity with which he had increased his circle of acquaintance among rich and useful people from the time he had become a member of the gang had been not the least remarkable feature in his extraordinary career.

I shall never forget that cross-examination, or the rapidity with which it was conducted. In the course of a quarter of an hour many mysteries which had long puzzled us were revealed, many problems solved. The woman whose stabbed and charred body had been found among the *debris* of the house in Maresfield Gardens burnt down on Christmas Eve was, it seemed, another of Gastrell's victims; he had stabbed her to death, and the house had been fired with a view to destroying all traces of the crime. Questioned further, the elder of the two scoundrels went on to state that he had been in the house in

Maresfield Gardens on the night that Osborne and I had called there, just before Christmas, the night we had driven up there from Brooks's Club on the pretext of Osborne's having found at the club a purse which he believed - so he had told the woman Gastrell - to have been dropped by Hugesson Gastrell. Other members of the gang had been in the house at the time, the man said, - just before we entered they had been in the very room into which Jasmine Gastrell had shown us when she had at last admitted us, which of course accounted for the dirty tumblers I had noticed on the table, and the chair that had felt hot when I sat in it. She had first opened the door to us, the man continued, under the impression that we were additional members of the gang whom she expected - our rings at the door had accidentally coincided with the rings these men would have given. Then, at once discovering her mistake, and recognizing Osborne's voice, she had deemed it prudent to admit us, thinking thus to allay any suspicion her unusual reception might otherwise arouse in us.

He told us, too, that the great cobra kept by Gastrell - he had owned it from the time it was a tiny thing a foot long - had once or twice been used by him in connection with murders for which he had been responsible - it was far from being harmless, though Gastrell had declared to us that night that it couldn't harm anybody if it tried. Indeed, it seemed that his first intention had been to let it attack us, for he feared that our having recognized him might arouse our suspicion and indirectly lead to his arrest, and for that reason he had, while we were left in darkness in the hall, opened the aperture in the wall through which it was allowed to pass into the room into which Jasmine Gastrell had then admitted us. But a little later, deeming that the crime might be discovered in spite of all the precautions that he would have taken to conceal it, he had suddenly changed his mind, unlocked the door, and come to our rescue at the last moment.

The mysterious affair in Grafton Street had been arranged - they went on to say when threatened by Albeury with arrest if they refused to tell everything - by Hugesson Gastrell and two accomplices, the two men with whom Osborne had entered into conversation on the night of Gastrell's reception in Cumberland Place, and it was a member of the gang, whose name I had not heard before - the sole occupant of the house at the time - who had questioned Osborne in the dark. Upon the unexpected arrival of the police at Grafton Street this man had clambered through a skylight in the roof, crawled along the roofs of several houses, and there remained hidden until nightfall, when he had escaped down a "thieves' ladder," which is made of silk rope and so contrived that upon the thief's reaching the ground he can detach it from the chimney-stack to which it has been fastened. Jasmine Gastrell herself it was who had sent Dulcie the telegram signed with my name, her intention being to decoy me into the Grafton Street house, where I should have shared Osborne's unpleasant experience. It was Gastrell who had murdered Churchill. Who had murdered Preston on board the boat, they declared they didn't know, nor could they say for certain who had inserted in the newspaper the cypher messages disentangled by Dick, for Gastrell, Stapleton, Jasmine Gastrell, and other leaders of the gang were in the habit of communicating with their crowd of confederates by means of secret codes. Incidentally they mentioned that Connie Stapleton was in reality Gastrell's wife, and that Jasmine was his mistress, though Harold Logan, found in the hiding-hole at Holt, had been madly in love with her.

"There," I said, turning to Jack Osborne as Albeury ended his cross-examination, "now you've got it all in black and white. And that's the woman you've been fooling with and say you're going to marry - not merely an adventuress, but a criminal who has herself instigated common burglaries and has connived at and been an accessory to murders! You must be mad, Jack - stark, staring. For Heaven's sake get over your absurd infatuation."

"It's not 'infatuation' on my side only, Mike," he answered, with a curious look that came near to being pathetic. "Jasmine is in love with me - she really is. It sounds absurd, I know, under the circumstances, but you know what women are and the extraordinary attachments they sometimes form - yes, even the worst of them. She's promised to start afresh, lead a straight life, if only I'll marry her; she has indeed, and, what's more, she'll do it."

I heard Albeury snort, and even the scoundrels, who had stood by looking on and listening, grinned.

"In forty-eight hours she'll be arrested and sent to jail," I said calmly. "Don't be such an utter idiot, Jack!"

He sprang to his feet.

"Jasmine arrested!" he cried. "My God, she shan't be! I'll go to her now! I'll warn her! I'll - "

"You'll do nothing of the sort," Albeury interrupted. "We've a trap set for the whole crew, more than twenty of them in all, and if you warn that woman she'll tell the rest and then - "

"Well, what?"

"Our plan will be defeated - more than that, the whole lot of us in this room will be murdered as sure as I'm sitting here. You've heard the truth about this gang from these two men. You know what a desperate crowd they are; what they'd be like if they get their backs against the wall you ought to be able to guess. Mr. Osborne, unless you pledge your solemn word that you'll not warn Jasmine Gastrell, I shall be forced to retain you here. Mr. Berrington has told you that I am an international police detective. I have, under the circumstances, the power to arrest you."

Osborne was evidently terribly upset. For a minute he sat, thinking deeply. A glance showed how madly in love he obviously was with the woman. Looking at him, I wondered whether what he had said could by any possibility be true – that Jasmine Gastrell had really lost her heart to him. The idea, at first thought, seemed absurd, even grotesque, and yet -

Suddenly Jack looked up.

"Supposing," he said, speaking with great deliberation, "I pledge my solemn word that I won't warn her of what you intend to do, or give her any reason to suspect that such a plot exists, and that I undertake to take her abroad with me and keep her there for one year from now - I shall marry her at once - will you undertake that she shall leave the country unmolested, and be left unmolested?"

I looked inquiringly at Albeury.

"Yes," he said at once. "I agree to that - we both agree to it; that's so, Mr. Berrington?"

I nodded. A thing I liked about Albeury was that he made up his mind almost instantly - that he never hesitated a moment.

"All the same, Mr. Osborne," he added quickly, "you must pardon my saying that I consider you barely sane. It's no business of mine, I know, but do for God's sake think what you are doing before you bind yourself for life to such a woman - think of it, *for life!*"

"That's all right," Jack answered quietly. "Don't distress yourself. I know exactly what I am doing, and - "

He paused, looking hard at Albeury.

"From now onward," he said slowly, "Jasmine Gastrell will be a wholly different woman. I am going away with her at once, Albeury; to-morrow, at latest - we may even leave to-night. We shall not return to England for a year - that I promise you. For a year I shall see neither Berrington nor you nor any of my friends. But in a year's time you and Berrington and I, and Jasmine too, will meet again, and then - "

The telephone in the flat rang loudly. Albeury sprang up. An instant later he was in the hall, preventing Simon from answering the call. Quickly he returned, while the bell continued ringing.

"What's your code - Morse?" he said sharply to the men.

"No - secret," the elder man answered.

"Quick, then - go; if it's not for you, say so."

Carefully the man Albeury had cross-questioned unhooked the receiver. He held it to his ear, and an instant later nodded. Then, with the pencil which hung down by a string, he tapped the transmitter five times, with measured beat.

Still holding the receiver to his ear, he conversed rapidly, by means of taps, with his confederates at the other end. From where we stood, close by, the taps at the other end were faintly audible. For nearly five minutes this conversation by code continued. Then the man hung up the receiver and faced us.

"I done it," he said. "Now me and my pal can get away from here at once - and both of you," indicating Albeury and Osborne. "We shall meet our pals who've watched this house - we shall meet them in Tottenham Court Road in half an hour. I've told them we've done out Mr. Berrington and his man. They think you both dead. It's a deal, then?"

"What's 'a deal'?" I asked.

"That you and your man stick in here until after the gang has been taken."

"Yes, that's understood."

"And that you won't answer any bell, or knock, nor any telephone, nor show any sign of life till after they've been took?"

"Of course. That's all arranged."

"Then we'll go, and - and good luck to you."

A few moments later we heard them going down the stairs. At once Albeury called Osborne and myself into the room we had just left. Then he rang for Simon.

Everything was quickly settled. Albeury was to go at once to Scotland Yard and make arrangements for the arrest of the gang at Eldon Hall on the following day but one; the arrival of the large body of detectives that would be needed would have, as he explained, to be planned with the greatest secrecy. After that he would catch the night express to the north, and, on the following morning, himself call at Eldon Hall to see Lord Cranmere. He would not alarm him in the least, he said. He would tell him merely that there were suspicions of a proposed attempted robbery, and ask leave to station detectives.

"And I'm to stay here with Simon, I suppose," I said despondently, "until everything is finished."

"Not a bit of it," he answered. "Simon will stay here, and with him a detective who will arrive to-night at midnight. We may need you at Eldon Hall, and you must be there."

"Meet you there? But I have promised those men that - besides, supposing that I am seen."

"As far as those scoundrels are concerned," he answered, "all they care about is to save their wretched skins. You won't be seen, that I'll guarantee, but none the less you must be there - it's absolutely necessary. A closed car will await you at the Bond Street Tube station at three o'clock to-morrow morning. Ask the driver no questions - he will have his orders."

Some minutes later Albeury left us. Osborne had already gone. I told Simon, who had been taken into our confidence, to pack a few necessaries in a small bag for me, and then, seated alone, smoking a cigar for the first time since my return, I allowed my thoughts to wander.

CHAPTER XXVIII

THE FACES UNMASKED

Eldon Hall is one of those fine old country mansions so much admired, and not infrequently coveted by, rich Americans who come over to "do England."

It was the late Colonel North, of nitrate fame, who, upon visiting Killeen Castle, in County Meath, with a view to buying the place for his son, laconically observed: "Yes, it's not a bad old pile, but much too ramshackle for my son. I could manage to live in it, I dare say, but if my son buys it he'll pull it down and rebuild it," a remark which tickled its owner a good deal.

Eldon Hall, in Northumberland, is fully as old and in some respects as venerable a "pile" as Killeen Castle, though its architecture is wholly different. Many attempts have been made to fix the date of Eldon - the property has been in Lord Cranmere's family "from a period," as the lawyers say, "so far back that the memory of man runneth not to the contrary" - but experts differ considerably in their opinions.

This is due to the fact that though a portion of the old place is undoubtedly Elizabethan, there yet are portions obviously of a much earlier date. According to several authorities the earlier building must at some period have been in part destroyed, most probably, they say, by fire, the portion left intact being then deserted for generations, and, towards the end of the sixteenth century, inhabited again, when, it is further conjectured, the latter part must have been built. The effect produced by this architectural medley is bizarre in the extreme, and many and strange are the local legends and traditions connected with Eldon Hall.

Situated on the slope of a gigantic ravine, twelve miles from the nearest town, and eight from the nearest railway station, and the roads in that part of Northumberland being far from good, until the advent of the automobile Eldon Hall was looked upon by many as, in a sense, inaccessible.

The house being far from the beaten track, few excursionists or trippers came near the place in those days, and, indeed, even to-day the sightseers who find their way there are for the most part Americans. From the ridge of hills which shuts in and practically surrounds the estate - hills all densely wooded - a panoramic and truly glorious view can be obtained of the wonderfully picturesque scenery that unfolds itself on all sides. Here, then, it was that, on the 28th day of February, 1912, many hundreds of people from all parts of the country, exclusive of local residents and of Lord Cranmere's own tenantry, were to assemble for a week of festivity and rejoicing which, so rumour said, would eclipse anything of the kind ever before seen at Eldon, which long had been famous for its "outbursts" of entertainment.

Lord Cranmere's elder son, who was about to come of age, was like the typical athletic young Briton. Tall, well-built, handsome, with plenty of self-assurance and a wholly unaffected manner, he was worthy of his father's pride. It was no exaggeration to say that everybody, rich and poor alike, who came into contact with him, at once fell under the spell of his attractive personality. A popular man himself Lord Cranmere had always been, but his outlook upon life was somewhat narrow - in spite of his opportunities he had seen little of life and had few interests beyond fox-hunting, game-shooting and salmon-fishing. His eldest son, on the contrary, had, from the age of eighteen, travelled constantly. Twice already he had been round the world, and so quick was his power of observation that at twenty-one he knew more of life and of things that matter than many a man of his class and twice his age.

It was a glorious morning, the sun shining brightly, and strangely warm for February, as the car in which I had travelled from London with three companions, all of them Scotland Yard men, pulled up at a farmhouse within two miles of Eldon. The journey from London, begun at three in the morning on the previous day, had been broken at Skipton, near Harrogate, where we had spent the night. Now, as the five of us - for our driver was also, I discovered, a member of the force - walked briskly along the narrow, winding lane in the direction of the park which surrounds Eldon Hall, the morning air was refreshing, also intensely invigorating.

We looked little enough like London men, and I doubt whether anybody meeting us would for an instant have supposed that we were not what we intended that we should look like, namely well-to-do tenantry of Lord Cranmere's bound for the scene of the coming-of-age festivities. It was barely nine o'clock, and at eleven the morning's sports were to begin. Several carts overtook us, loaded with cheery fellows; some of whom shouted rustic jests as they passed us by, which my companions were quick to acknowledge. We had walked, I suppose, rather less than a mile, when we suddenly came to a stile.

"Here's our short cut," the man who walked beside me said, as he stopped abruptly. "Many's the time I've climbed over this stile more years ago than I like to think, sir," he remarked lightly. "My father was under-keeper to his lordship's father, and I've not been back since twenty years. It's not a bit changed, though, the old place, not a bit, I'm going, when I retire on my pension, to live down here again. I want to leave my bones where I was born, and where my father's and mother's are. It's a fine country, this sir, not a county like it in the whole of England," he added with enthusiasm. "And you see yonder cross-roads?

That's Clun Cross - there's said to be a highwayman buried at that cross-roads with a stake pushed through his body."

"Clun Cross." I remembered the name at once. It was the name that had appeared in one of the advertisements deciphered by Dick.

We made our way up the steep footpath which led across a cramped field. Now we were on the boundary of a thickly underwooded cover.

"There's not a tree in this wood I don't remember," he said, looking about him as we scrambled up the bridle path. Bracken up to our waists was on both sides, and it grew and hung over so thickly that the path was barely visible. As we reached the top of the track he gave a low whistle. Instantly the whistle was answered. A moment later half a dozen men rose up out of the undergrowth.

At the foot of a clump of pine trees in the middle of the wood, we lay down to confer. Then it was I learned, for the first time, something of the line of action the police had decided to adopt.

Forty police officers in various disguises, the majority dressed to look like the tenantry in their holiday clothes, were, it seemed, concealed in the various covers, in addition to a dozen disguised as labourers, stationed in fields beside the roads leading to Eldon Hall.

Besides these were fifteen officers, guests to all appearance, who would arrive with the other guests and mingle with them freely. There were also eight men disguised as hired waiters, who would help the servants below stairs in the Hall, and five female detectives assisting the maids in their work.

"You've got the revolver I gave you?" the gamekeeper's son said, turning to me suddenly. His name, he had told me, was Ross.

"Yes, though I all but forgot it."

"Let me see it," he said.

I produced it from my pocket, and handed it over.

"I thought so!" he exclaimed. "Not loaded." He loaded it with the cartridges I gave him, then gave it back to me.

Half an hour passed. One by one the men had risen and wandered away. Now only three remained. Ten minutes later two more rose and went, leaving me alone with Ross. His reminiscences of game-keeping - a calling he seemed still to love - and of the former Lord Cranmere and his relations and his friends, also his experiences during the eighteen years he had been in the police force, were interesting to listen to. Brighter and brighter the sun shone. The weather was almost spring-like and no breath of wind stirred. Half a mile or so away, in the valley far beneath us, well-dressed men and women sauntered in the gardens and out upon the lawns. Larger and larger grew the number of these guests. From varying distances came the sound of cars rapidly approaching. In the broad, flat meadow, far down to our right, sports of different sorts were in progress. Beyond them were swings and similar attractions where children in their hundreds thronged and clustered. In all directions flew flags and bunting, while the sharp reports of the shooting-gallery rifles were audible above the blare of the roundabouts' steam organs.

Ross pulled out his field glass, and, kneeling up in the deep bracken, focussed the crowds in turn. It was now past noon. From the lawn facing the house the strains of a Strauss valse, played by an excellent band, floated up to where we knelt, though the racket of the steam organs clashed with it to some extent.

Slowly the time crept on. Longer and longer grew the approaching queue of cars. In one field alone, set aside as a garage, I counted over a hundred. Others were left out in the stable yards. Others could be seen, deserted by the roadsides. Beyond the band upon the lawn mammoth marquees had been erected, in which lunch for the vast concourse would presently be served. Already servants in their dozens hurried in and out as they made ready for the feast.

"About the queerest job I've ever had a hand in, this is," Ross observed presently, lowering his glass. "What do you make of it, Mr. Berrington?"

"Nothing as yet," I answered. "What puzzles me is - why did they want to bring me here?"

Ross chuckled.

"He's most likely got some reason," he presently murmured. "I don't suppose Albeury'd fetch you here for your health."

Again he focussed his glass. Now the people were gradually drifting. Slowly the crowds began to surge in the direction where the tents stood. Now the tents were filling fast. Once more the band was playing. Everyone seemed happy. Joy and laughter were in the air. Engrossed in the panorama which interested me considerably, all thought of my reasons for being there had for the moment faded from my mind, and - "

"Hark!" Ross exclaimed.

He remained silent, listening.

"What did you hear?" I asked, when half a minute had passed.

"Didn't you hear it?"

"No. What?"

"That buzzing sound. It wasn't a car, I'm certain. I believe it was a - there, listen!"

I heard it now, distinctly. Away to our right it sounded, high in the air, apparently; a strange, humming noise.

"An aeroplane?"

He nodded.

Quickly the sound increased in volume. Now we saw that the crowds down in the valley had heard it. They were gazing up in the sky, away to our right. Now they were getting excited. Like ants they hurried about. Out of the tents they swarmed, like bees out of a hive that has been stirred up with a stick. And now out of the house, too, they came hurrying - guests, men and maidservants, hired helpers, everybody.

The humming grew louder and louder.

"'Scot! What an idea!"

"Idea?" I exclaimed. "What do you mean?"

"We'd a rumour before leaving town that something unexpected and startling might occur in connection with this affair. This is it, you may depend."

Still I was perplexed.

"I don't follow your line of thought," I said. "What can an aeroplane have to do with the gang, or they with it? They wouldn't come down in an aeroplane to commit a robbery, surely?"

He looked at me, as I thought, pityingly, as though sorry for my lack of imagination, or intelligence, or both.

Now everybody was rushing about; all were hurrying in one direction; a few later stragglers still came stumbling out of the house, running as fast as their legs would carry them. The humming sounded just above our heads. Looking up, we suddenly saw the aeroplane.

A large biplane, containing two passengers, it passed not thirty feet above us, flying horizontally in a straight line. Now it descended a little way, then slowly began to circle. At that moment we heard a shot, fired somewhere in the woods.

"Our signal," Ross murmured. "Are you ready to go?"

"Go where?"

"You'll see."

The aeroplane was descending rapidly. Almost immediately beneath it was gathered a dense crowd. Looking through Ross's glass, I saw one of the passengers waving to the crowd to clear out of the way. A moment later, and the biplane was dashing straight at the people beneath.

"Quick! My glass."

I handed it to him. Instantly he levelled it in the direction of the house.

"See those men?" he said, pointing.

I turned in the direction he was looking. In the main road, just beyond the house, two men seemed to be busy with a large car. As I looked, a third man appeared in the roadway, walking quickly towards them. He stepped into the car behind the one where the two men already were, and, crouching, was at once lost to sight.

"Come - quickly!" Ross exclaimed. "You see the idea now? That aeroplane arrival is a ruse to distract everybody's attention. There's never been an aeroplane up here before. This is the first time most of that crowd, except the guests, have ever seen one. When we get into the house you'll find it completely deserted - or apparently so. But some of the gang will be busy there, that you may depend upon - our men are already there."

With all speed we scrambled through the bracken and down the steep slope towards the house. In five minutes or less we were within fifty yards of Eldon Hall.

The back door stood wide open. Entering cautiously, we found ourselves in the kitchen premises. Kitchen, pantry, every room and the stone-flagged passages were deserted. A moment or two later we pushed open a spring door, to find ourselves in the hall. Nobody was there either, and the front door stood ajar.

"Off with your boots - quick!"

A glance into the various downstair rooms, all of which were deserted, then up the front stairs we crept in our stockinged feet. On the landing two men stepped noiselessly out of a doorway. Both, I saw, were detectives in rubber shoes.

"You know the men of the gang by sight?" one of them whispered, as he stood beside me.

"Some of them," I answered.

"And they know who you are, we understand."

"Yes."

"Then if you meet one - shoot! He'll shoot you if you don't shoot first."

My hand trembled with excitement as I clutched the pistol in my pocket. My mouth was dry. I could hear my heart thumping. Cautiously I followed Ross along the corridor.

Suddenly a loud report almost deafened me. At the same instant Ross fell forward on to his face, with a hideous crash - I can hear it now as I think of it. A moment later a man dashed past me, and tore furiously down the stairs. Springing after him I fired wildly as he ran - once - twice. I had missed him and he was gone. In one of the rooms I could distinctly hear sounds of a scuffle. There were blows, some oaths and a muffled groan. Now the house was suddenly in uproar. The deafening sound of several shots echoed along the corridors. Two men were running towards me. Wildly I flung out my arm, the revolver in my hand aimed point blank at one of them, and then -

Something struck me from behind, a fearful blow, and, stumbling, I lost consciousness.

* * * * *

I was in a room, almost in darkness. Like shadows two figures moved noiselessly about. They were figures I didn't recognize. My head ached fearfully. Where was I? What had happened? I remember groaning feebly, and seeing the two figures quickly turn towards me.

Again all was blank.

CONCLUSION

It was broad daylight now, but the blinds were all pulled down. I was in the same room; my head felt on fire. Never had I suffered so terribly. Never, I hope and trust, shall I suffer so again. A woman beside the bed gently held my wrist - a nurse.

Something soothing was passed between my lips. It relieved me. I felt better.

Many days passed before I became convalescent - dark days of nightmare, hideous days of pain. A month elapsed before I was allowed to ask questions concerning that awful day and all that had taken place.

Three of the detectives had been shot dead - poor Ross had been the first victim. Five had been seriously wounded. Several others had been injured. But the entire gang of The Four Faces had finally been captured. Some had been arrested in the house, red-handed; among these were Connie Stapleton and Doris Lorrimer - guests at Eldon for the week, they had been discovered in Mrs. Stapleton's bedroom in the act of packing into a bag jewellery belonging to Lord and Lady Cranmere. Others had been run down in the woods. Several had been arrested on suspicion at Clun Cross, and upon them had been found evidence proving their identity. Six cars had been held up and their occupants taken into custody.

What upset me most, when all this was told to me, was the news of poor Ross's death. During the short time I had known him I had taken a strong liking to him. He had seemed such a thoroughly honest fellow, so straightforward in every way. He had a wife and several children, he had told me - several times he had spoken of his wife, to whom he had evidently been devoted. And he had so looked forward to the time, now only two years off, when he would have retired on his pension and returned to his native county - returned to settle down, if possible, on the Eldon Hall estate. Yet in an instant he had been shot down like a dog by one of those scoundrels he was helping to arrest. It all seemed too terrible, too sad. Well, as soon as I was sufficiently recovered to get about again I would, I decided, visit his widow in London, and see if I could help her in any way.

* * * * *

Six weeks had passed, and I was almost well again. Once more I was staying at Holt Manor. Already the breath of spring was in the air. Sir Roland, recovered at last from the mental shock he had sustained, was there. Aunt Hannah was away, making her annual round of visits. Dulcie and I were wholly undisturbed, except by little Dick, who was at home for his Easter holidays.

As we sauntered in the beautiful woods on a sunny afternoon towards the end of April, discussing our plans for the honeymoon - for we were to be married in a week's time - Dulcie suddenly asked, apropos of nothing:

"Mike, why did that detective, Albeury, make you go to Eldon Hall? You were not to take part in the capture. You could quite well have stayed in London."

"In a way that was a mistake," I answered. "He never intended that I should go further than the farm two miles from the Hall, where we had pulled up. He thought he would need me to identify some of the men about to be arrested, and so he wanted me on the spot. But he had not told me why he wanted me there, so when the police officers prepared to start out for Eldon from the farm, naturally I insisted upon going with them - I wanted to see some of the fun, or what I thought was going to be an extremely exciting event."

"Which it proved to be," she said seriously.

Just then I remembered something.

"Look, my darling," I said, "what I received this morning."

I drew out of my pocket a letter, and handed it to her. It bore a German postmark. It had been posted in Alsace-Lorraine.

She unfolded the letter, and slowly read it through.

"How dreadful," she said. "Poor Jack!"

I paused.

"It may not be," I said at last. "All his life he has done odd and unexpected things, and they have generally turned out well. He has written to me twice since he left England, and I am convinced, now, that he and Jasmine Gastrell - or rather Jasmine Osborne - are tremendously in love with each other. I told you of his idea that she would, when he had married her, entirely change her life. Perhaps that idea is not as quixotic as we first thought."

"Perhaps, if they really love each other - " she began, then stopped abruptly.

"My darling," I murmured, "is there any miracle that love isn't able to accomplish? Look what you have faced, what I have faced, during these dreadful months of anxiety and peril. It was love alone that strengthened us - love alone that held us together in those moments of terrible crises. Come."

So we turned slowly homeward in the golden light of the spring afternoon, secure in our love for one another and in the knowledge that the black shadows which had darkened our lives during the past months had at last vanished for ever.

Choose from Thousands of 1stWorldLibrary Classics By

Adolphus WilliamWard
Aesop
Agatha Christie
Alexander Aaronsohn
Alexander Kielland
Alexandre Dumas
Alfred Gatty
Alfred Ollivant
Alice Duer Miller
Alice Turner Curtis
Alice Dunbar
Ambrose Bierce
Amelia E. Barr
Andrew Lang
Andrew McFarland Davis
Anna Sewell
Annie Besant
Annie Hamilton Donnell
Annie Payson Call
Anton Chekhov
Arnold Bennett
Arthur Conan Doyle
Arthur Ransome
Atticus
B. M. Bower
Basil King
Bayard Taylor
Ben Macomber
Booth Tarkington
Bram Stoker
C. Collodi
C. E. Orr
C. M. Ingleby
Carolyn Wells
Catherine Parr Traill
Charles A. Eastman
Charles Dickens
Charles Dudley Warner
Charles Farrar Browne
Charles Ives
Charles Kingsley
Charles Lathrop Pack
Charles Whibley
Charles Willing Beale
Charlotte M. Braeme
Charlotte M.Yonge
Clair W. Hayes
Clarence Day Jr.
Clarence E. Mulford
Clemence Housman
Confucius
Cornelis DeWitt Wilcox
Cyril Burleigh
D. H. Lawrence
Daniel Defoe
David Garnett
Don Carlos Janes
Donald Keyhole
Dorothy Kilner
Dougan Clark
E. Nesbit
E.P.Roe
E. Phillips Oppenheim
Edgar Allan Poe
Edgar Rice Burroughs
Edith Wharton
Edward J. O'Biren
John Cournos
Edwin L. Arnold
Eleanor Atkins
Elizabeth Cleghorn
Gaskell
Elizabeth Von Arnim
Ellem Key
Emily Dickinson
Erasmus W. Jones
Ernie Howard Pie
Ethel Turner
Ethel Watts Mumford
Eugenie Foa
Eugene Wood
Evelyn Everett-Green
Everard Cotes
F. J. Cross
Federick Austin Ogg
Ferdinand Ossendowski
Francis Bacon
Francis Darwin
Frances Hodgson Burnett
Frank Gee Patchin
Frank Harris
Frank Jewett Mather
Frank L. Packard
Frederick Trevor Hill
Frederick Winslow Taylor
Friedrich Kerst
Friedrich Nietzsche
Fyodor Dostoyevsky
Gabrielle E. Jackson
Garrett P. Serviss
Gaston Leroux
George Ade
Geroge Bernard Shaw
George Ebers
George Eliot
George MacDonald
George Orwell
George Tucker
George W. Cable
George Wharton James
Gertrude Atherton
Grace E. King
Grant Allen
Guillermo A. Sherwell
Gulielma Zollinger
Gustav Flaubert
H. A. Cody
H. B. Irving
H. G. Wells
H. H. Munro
H. Irving Hancock
H. Rider Haggard
H. W. C. Davis
Hamilton Wright Mabie
Hans Christian Andersen
Harold Avery
Harold McGrath
Harriet Beecher Stowe
Harry Houidini
Helent Hunt Jackson
Helen Nicolay
Hendy David Thoreau
Henrik Ibsen
Henry Adams
Henry Ford
Henry Frost
Henry James
Henry Jones Ford
Henry Seton Merriman
Henry Wadsworth
Longfellow
Henry W Longfellow
Herbert A. Giles
Herbert N. Casson
Herman Hesse
Homer
Honore De Balzac

Horace Walpole
Horatio Alger, Jr.
Howard Pyle
Howard R. Garis
Hugh Lofting
Hugh Walpole
Humphry Ward
Ian Maclaren
Israel Abrahams
J.G.Austin
J. Henri Fabre
J. M. Barrie
J. Macdonald Oxley
J. S. Knowles
J. Storer Clouston
Jack London
Jacob Abbott
James Allen
James Lane Allen
James Andrews
James Baldwin
James DeMille
James Joyce
James Oliver Curwood
James Oppenheim
James Otis
Jane Austen
Jens Peter Jacobsen
Jerome K. Jerome
John Burroughs
John F. Kennedy
John Gay
John Glasworthy
John Habberton
John Joy Bell
John Milton
John Philip Sousa
Jonathan Swift
Joseph Carey
Joseph Conrad
Joseph Jacobs
Julian Hawthrone
Julies Vernes
Justin Huntly McCarthy
Kakuzo Okakura
Kenneth Grahame
Kate Langley Bosher
L. A. Abbot
L. T. Meade
L. Frank Baum
Laura Lee Hope
Laurence Housman
Leo Tolstoy
Leonid Andreyev
Lewis Carroll
Lilian Bell
Lloyd Osbourne
Louis Tracy
Louisa May Alcott
Lucy Fitch Perkins
Lucy Maud Montgomery
Lydia Miller Middleton
Lyndon Orr
M. H. Adams
Margaret E. Sangster
Margaret Vandercook
Maria Edgeworth
Maria Thompson Daviess
Mariano Azuela
Marion Polk Angellotti
Mark Overton
Mark Twain
Mary Austin
Mary Cole
Mary Rowlandson
Mary Wollstonecraft Shelley
Max Beerbohm
Myra Kelly
Nathaniel Hawthrone
O. F. Walton
Oscar Wilde
Owen Johnson
P.G.Wodehouse
Paul and Mable Thorn
Paul G. Tomlinson
Paul Severing
Peter B. Kyne
Plato
R. Derby Holmes
R. L. Stevenson
Rabindranath Tagore
Rahul Alvares
Ralph Waldo Emmerson
Rene Descartes
Rex E. Beach
Richard Harding Davis
Richard Jefferies
Robert Barr
Robert Frost
Robert Gordon Anderson
Robert L. Drake
Robert Lansing
Robert Michael Ballantyne
Robert W. Chambers
Rosa Nouchette Carey
Ross Kay
Rudyard Kipling
Samuel B. Allison
Samuel Hopkins Adams
Sarah Bernhardt
Selma Lagerlof
Sherwood Anderson
Sigmund Freud
Standish O'Grady
Stanley Weyman
Stella Benson
Stephen Crane
Stewart Edward White
Stijn Streuvels
Swami Abhedananda
Swami Parmananda
T. S. Ackland
The Princess Der Ling
Thomas A. Janvier
Thomas A Kempis
Thomas Anderton
Thomas Bailey Aldrich
Thomas Bulfinch
Thomas De Quincey
Thomas H. Huxley
Thomas Hardy
Thomas More
Thornton W. Burgess
U. S. Grant
Valentine Williams
Victor Appleton
Virginia Woolf
Walter Scott
Washington Irving
Wilbur Lawton
Wilkie Collins
Willa Cather
Willard F. Baker
William Makepeace Thackeray
William W. Walter
Winston Churchill
Yei Theodora Ozaki
Young E. Allison
Zane Grey

www.ingramcontent.com/pod-product-compliance
Lightning Source LLC
LaVergne TN
LVHW091639100826
845152LV00006B/98/J
* 9 7 8 1 4 2 1 8 1 0 9 7 3 *